DOOMSDAY

By Gordon Anthony

ISBN-13: 978-1080978977

Part 1: The Rebels

Chapter 1

The fields were golden seas of ripe corn under a blazing summer sun, yet nobody was harvesting the crop because war was coming. The peasants, having seen the mounted scouting parties, had all run off to barricade themselves into their homes or to hide in the woods, for they knew what those few riders signified. If any of them had been brave or foolish enough to stay and watch, they would soon have witnessed the sight of a long column of soldiers moving steadily along the rutted path which served as the main road.

There were mounted knights at the head of the column, each man wearing chainmail and armed with shield, sword and lance. They wore iron-banded helmets on their heads, with heavy guards to protect their noses. Their boots were thick and heavy, some banded by yet more iron to ward off any blows their enemies might aim at their lower legs and feet. They were dressed for war, and they sweated under the weight of their heavy gear, but their mood was cheerful because this promised to be the last action of a long campaigning season.

Next in the long, winding train came the foot soldiers, trudging stoically behind the more exalted cavalrymen. Some were armed with spears and swords, others carried bows and arrows, while some bore the heavier and more modern crossbows which, although they had a slower rate of fire than the bowmen could achieve, had greater range and power.

Behind the armed men came the siege weapons and the baggage wagons which contained all the supplies the army required, from food and tents to iron-working tools, horseshoes and spare arrows.

All of them marched in good spirits, because only one rebel castle now held out against their lord. In the entire troublesome province of Maine, these men had brought every rebel Baron back under the control of William, Duke of Normandy and King of England.

William himself rode in the midst of his cavalry. He was a big man, his reddish hair betraying his Viking ancestry, and he was dressed in armour just as his mounted knights, except that his helmet was ringed by a crown of gold.

He turned to the man who rode beside him, a dark-haired, lithe but powerful figure who had removed his helmet to wipe sweat from his brow as they plodded on under the hot sun of a late summer's day.

"Well, Malet," the King said, "we will soon be there. I want this siege ended quickly."

William Malet, who was reputed to be the finest swordsman and the finest horseman in Europe, gave his monarch a reassuring smile.

"It will not take long, Your Majesty. Baron Reynard has few fighting men. He will probably surrender as soon as we invest his castle."

"I hope so. I have more than enough to do."

The King's tone betrayed his irritation. He had conquered England only to find that the English were not disposed to have a Norman king, and he had spent four years putting down rebellion after rebellion only to discover that the nobles of Maine, the province which lay to the south of Normandy and which he had brought under control only a few years earlier, had risen in revolt while he was away in England. Acting decisively, he had spent the summer dealing with that revolt in the only way he knew; by extracting violent retribution. Any Baron who had not immediately bent the knee to him and paid homage had been killed or exiled. The castles of the rebel nobles had either been garrisoned by loyal Normans or burned to the ground to prevent anyone setting up a stronghold to defy their rightful lord. This was Duke William's way. Ever since he had become Duke of Normandy as a teenage boy, he had been compelled to fight for everything he had. Being an illegitimate son of the former Duke had made life doubly difficult for him, but he had succeeded by sheer strength of will. He understood the primal motives of fear and greed which drove most men, and he employed both incentives liberally. The revolt in Maine could not be subdued by offering inducements, so he had launched a massive campaign to bring the Barons to heel. Still, it irritated him that such a campaign had been necessary at all.

Fortunately, it was almost at an end. Now there was only one Baron who had not paid him the fealty he demanded.

The castle of Baron Reynard was a small affair, yet well situated on the top of a low hill. A double ditch, backed by a tall palisade, surrounded the buildings which housed Reynard's household, and there was a large, imposing keep on the summit of the hill.

William's forces began to spread out as soon as they sighted the enemy fort. In well practised manoeuvres, the mounted men rode to left and right, circling around the hill to ensure that nobody could enter or leave without being seen. The footmen gathered in strength out of bowshot of the castle's wooden wall, the bowmen and crossbowmen lining up in positions from where they could fire on the defenders.

The heavy catapults were then dragged into position. They would be used to bombard the fort, aiming heavy boulders at the main gate. Once that was breached, the footmen would storm the castle.

It was a process William's army had become accustomed to over the past few months. Many of these men were veterans from the battle at Hastings which had won the crown of England for William. That had been a brutal, terrifying and bloody day, but the experienced soldiers knew that such set piece battles were uncommon. Most warfare comprised skirmishes, ambushes and, as would happen again this day, sieges.

William sat on his horse, watching the preparations with an eagle eye. None of his men would dare shirk their duty while he was nearby, but even a severe taskmaster like William was pleased with the efficiency his army displayed as it took up position around the hilltop castle. Unit commanders pointed and shouted, but the reality was that the soldiers needed few instructions because, under William's leadership, besieging a castle had become a routine task.

Malet observed, "This won't take long, Your Majesty. There is no water supply on the hilltop."

He waved a gauntleted hand towards the narrow stream which ran past the foot of the hill on the far side, its course marked by stands of bushes and reeds.

"Our cavalry will prevent them collecting water," he went on. "They'll be desperate in a few days."

"I'd rather have their surrender in a few hours," William muttered. "From all accounts, Reynard is no fool. He'll have stored water inside as soon as he heard we were coming."

"He should have surrendered along with the other Barons," Malet said. "Whether he has stored reserves of water or not, he cannot withstand a direct attack."

The King turned in his saddle. Behind him, as always, were two squires who sat on ponies, and four of his most experienced knights who served him as bodyguards. One of the squires held a long pole atop which hung a red banner emblazoned with two yellow leopards. Those ferocious beasts were invisible now, for the banner hung limply in the still air.

The squires, sons of men who had aided William gain the throne of England and who had been admitted to the King's retinue as a reward for their fathers' loyalty, also displayed the King's symbol. Each boy wore a red tabard over his chainmail, with the two yellow leopards bright on their chests.

The King signalled to the boy who held the banner.

"Go and demand their surrender," he told the lad.

"Do you wish to offer terms, Your Majesty?" the boy asked.

Malet growled, "We should kill them all. That will teach them a lesson."

The King gave a harsh smile. William Malet was half-English and half-Norman, but he had long ago pledged his loyalty to Duke William of Normandy. After Hastings, Malet had been given a position in York, but the locals had rebelled, forcing him to take shelter inside the city's castle. The siege had been lifted by the arrival of the King, and Malet had taken part in the ensuing retribution, burning the city to the ground in the process. Yet the experience had left him with an undying hatred of all rebels.

The King told the squire, "Tell them they can all live if they open the gates and surrender. I want Reynard's homage, and I will demand hostages."

The squire nodded his understanding.

"And if they refuse, Your Majesty?"

"Then I will follow Malet's advice."

"Yes, Your Majesty," the boy said, his serious young face shining with pride at the honour he had been given. Kicking his heels to his pony, he set off towards the castle's gate, holding the flag high to show the defenders that he would speak for the King.

William watched, his eyes scanning the palisade and taking in the sight of men standing behind the wooden wall.

"I count twenty-six," he remarked scornfully.

"That is my count, too, Your Majesty," Malet agreed.

"He cannot hope to hold us off with such a meagre force," the king frowned. "It makes no sense for him to defy me."

Malet said, "If he had any sense, Majesty, he'd have run off to join Fulk of Anjou."

The mention of his old adversary brought a scowl to the King's features. He and Count Fulk of Anjou had both wanted to add Maine to their dominions, but it had been William who had seized control and brought the province under Norman domination. Fulk, though, had never abandoned his desire to take over, and William was certain this rebellion by the nobles of Maine had been stirred up by the Angevin Count. Naturally, the wily Fulk had not been prepared to pit his own armed forces against the army of William. The Normans were famous for their fighting prowess, and few would dare oppose them in open battle. Instead, Fulk had spread rumours and gold, encouraging the Barons to declare themselves free of Norman rule. No doubt he had promised them his protection if they had paid him homage, but those who had listened to the whispers had preferred to proclaim their independence. They had paid a heavy price for that folly when William brought his army into Maine.

Which made Reynard's continued resistance puzzling.

"He'll bring down his own flag as soon as he hears your terms," Malet opined.

William eyed the banner which hung limply above the fort's gates. He could make out nothing of its design, only its dark green colouring.

The squire had stopped only a few yards from the castle's entrance. William could see him calling up to the men who looked down at him from behind the thick, heavy timbers of the palisade.

Restless and eager for this to be over, he twisted in his saddle, checking the disposition of his troops. All was in order. The archers and crossbows stood ready, the phalanx of infantry were standing poised, and his cavalry continued to patrol all around the perimeter of the low hill.

Except one group of seven riders who were trotting slowly back towards the spot where he and his small retinue had taken up position out on the left flank of the assembled army. They were

5

circling around behind the ranks of foot soldiers and moving purposefully towards him.

"Who are they?" he asked.

Malet, the second squire and the four guards turned to look at the approaching band of riders. Like all the other mounted warriors, the seven knights wore chainmail and helmets, with large, kite-shaped shields held on their left arms and long, iron-tipped lances in their right hands.

"I don't recognise them," Malet frowned.

Even as he uttered the words, the riders clapped their mounts into a canter as they headed straight towards the King and his entourage.

"Treachery!" screamed Malet as he drew his sword, simultaneously jabbing his spurred heels into his horse's sides and yanking the reins to face the charge.

The four men of William's personal guard were slower to react, but they, too, turned to meet the seven riders who had now pushed their horses into a gallop as they thundered across the turf, lances poised and glittering in the afternoon sun.

William felt a surge of anger as understanding came to him. Reynard had known he could not withstand a siege, so he had staked everything on striking a direct blow and killing William himself. William realised the Baron must have hidden out of sight until the Normans had spread out, and now he was gambling everything on this bold ambush.

Even as he cursed the man, William could not help admiring his cunning and bravery, but he soon forgot all thoughts of anything except preserving his life.

Malet was already trying to thwart Reynard's attack. He spurred his own horse into a charge, holding his sword ready as he galloped directly towards the seven attackers. The leading rider swerved slightly as if to avoid him, while two others aimed directly to meet Malet's seemingly reckless charge.

Malet was too quick for them. His horse reacted to the commands he relayed with his thighs, knees and heels so that his hands were free. His shield arm knocked a lance thrust aside, while his sword flashed to right and left. Both of his opponents fell, one with blood gushing from an awful wound to his jaw, the other crashing to the ground with a bone-breaking thump. The horses

6

screamed and veered aside, but Malet was already turning to pursue the five remaining riders who were closing on William.

The four guards had managed to draw their own swords and had formed a line to protect their King. Behind the attack, footmen were running in pursuit, but they were too far away to have any chance of intercepting Reynard's' charge, so the four mounted men and a young squire were all that stood between William of Normandy and the men who were intent on killing him.

The charge struck with horrifying power, weapons thudding home against shields and armour, horses whinnying in terror, and men yelling their own, personal war cries. Two of William's men were sent thudding to the ground, the survivors wheeling to block their own opponents as they slashed and hacked with their swords.

The young squire bravely dashed his pony in front of another charging knight only to have the point of a lance drive through his tabard and the links of his chainmail armour. Impelled by the weight of the galloping horse, the razor-sharp blade plunged deep into his body. His assailant released the lance as the squire fell, then the man was twisting to draw his sword while he urged his horse to continue its gallop.

William was ready. He knew his only chance was to meet the attack head on, and his horse was moving now, gaining speed as he yelled his fury at the man who had dared to attack him.

They met in a tangle, swords clashing so loudly that the echo rang across the field. Then they had passed one another and were wheeling around to face each other again.

William was vaguely aware of the battle behind him as his two surviving guards struggled to hold off four knights. He was trapped between them and the man he presumed was Reynard who was now urging his horse into another furious gallop. William knew he must face him, but to do so would leave him exposed to the other riders behind him.

Yet he had no choice. It was galling to realise that he might die here beside this miserable castle, but he had been raised as a warrior, and he would not flee from Reynard's challenge.

Even as he readied himself, he heard more loud clashes and shouts from behind him, followed by the pounding of hoof beats as another rider thundered past him and raced towards Reynard.

Malet!

William frantically twisted around to survey the scene of carnage behind him. All four of his guards had been hurled to the ground. Two were moving feebly, while the other two lay very still. But around them were the bodies of three other armoured men, while a sixth, still on horseback but obviously injured, was already being surrounded by a horde of William's vengeful foot soldiers.

William turned his attention back to Malet and Reynard. The two riders hurtled towards one another, swords raised. They struck home, blocking each other's attack, then wheeled and whirled, knee to knee as they attempted to use brute strength and the power of their horses to knock the other man down. The horses wheeled in a tight circle while their riders slashed and cut at each other with furious strength. Reynard, the King recognised, was skilful and strong, but he had never encountered anyone with the talent of the man he faced now.

Malet's sword was a blur as he slashed at Reynard. Then he gave a final heave, knocking the Baron sideways in his saddle, and his sword lashed out, drawing blood from Reynard's unprotected neck.

Reynard toppled from the saddle, crashing limply to the grass. His horse ran off, leaving him to Malet's mercy.

Malet, though, had no intention of showing clemency. He edged his horse forwards, encouraging it to trample the fallen man, its hooves smashing down on his body until Malet was satisfied his opponent could offer no resistance. Reynard, William thought, was probably dead before Malet dismounted and finished him off.

William eased his mount towards the victor.

"I thank you," he said.

It was less than Malet deserved, but the dark-eyed knight simply said, "It was a pleasure, Your Majesty. I think they will surrender now."

"They will," the King agreed. "But I think my terms may have changed."

"You will kill them all?" Malet asked eagerly.

"No, I will be merciful. I shall only have a foot or a hand removed from every man and boy inside the castle. And the buildings must burn."

"I shall see to it," Malet said with a fierce grin.

8

William smiled, sheathing his unbloodied sword. He took a deep breath, composing himself. He had come close to death, and the men who protected him had paid a heavy price for their loyalty, but Malet had saved him. The man's skill was uncanny, and William knew he must provide him with a suitable reward. That should not be too difficult since there was plenty of land in England which he could allot to those who did him service.

Malet, though, seemed unconcerned by such things. Where other noblemen sought land to enrich themselves, Malet wanted only to fight. His reputation was everything to him, and William could see in the man's eyes that his hunger for combat was undiminished.

Still, there was work to be done which might sate that hunger. Under Malet's supervision, the occupants of the castle were led outside as soon as they had opened the gates. The Normans plundered the fort for any food and valuables, then set the wooden buildings alight. Finally, the men and boys were separated from the women and children, and each had a foot or a hand chopped from their bodies. That, the King knew, would prevent them ever daring to rebel against him again.

"What happens next, Your Majesty?" Malet asked once he had completed the King's instructions. "Do we march against Fulk of Anjou?"

William scowled at the mention of his nemesis. Angrily, he shook his head.

"It is too late in the season to begin a lengthy campaign," he conceded. "No, I must now rely on diplomacy. Fulk is not the only one who has been plotting behind my back while I have been in England. Philip of France wants to regain Normandy for the French crown, and Robert of Flanders has declared himself my enemy."

With a sigh, he continued, "And do not forget King Sweyn of Denmark has already tried to take England from me once. I bought him off, but everyone knows that paying gold to a Dane only encourages him to return. When you add in the Scots and the Welsh, I have too many enemies to fight them all at once."

"So we return to Rouen?" Malet enquired, doing his best to conceal his disappointment.

"Yes. There is much to do, and Normandy needs my attention for the moment."

"So we will not be returning to England, Majesty?"

"Not for a while yet. But that should not be a problem. Almost all resistance has been crushed. There is only one band of outlaws who still cause trouble, and they should have been dealt with by now."

"Hereward's gang, you mean?" Malet asked, his eyes sparking. "I have heard he is a formidable warrior. I would be happy to bring you his head."

"There should be no need for you to do anything," the King informed him. "The man they call Hereward has only a few hundred peasants behind him. I left Ivo de Taillebois and Abbot Turold more than enough men to overcome that rabble. Even hiding away in the fenlands will do them no good."

"I am sure you are correct, Your Majesty," Malet said, his tone implying that he held a low opinion of the two local nobles the king had put in charge of quelling the fenland uprising.

"I am correct," William stated. "This fellow Hereward may have gained a reputation of sorts, but he leads a party of vagabonds. He cannot hope to hold out against the army I sent against him. That would require a miracle."

Chapter 2

Edric could scarcely believe their miraculous survival. The Normans had been routed, and he was still alive.

He leaned on his axe, taking deep breaths and trying to calm himself after the fury of the battle. His entire body ached with the effort it had endured during the desperate fight. His left arm throbbed from bearing the brunt of the attacks on his shield which now lay, dented and almost split in two, at his feet, while his right arm felt as if all the strength had drained from it now that he had stopped wielding his long-handled axe. Worse than these pains, though, was the cold sweat that had broken out all over his body at the realisation of just how close to death he and his companions had come.

He took another long, slow breath, telling himself not to allow the horror of those moments to linger in his memory. He was a warrior now, no longer a mere apprentice to a blacksmith. He was fighting to protect his friends and to free England from Norman rule, and he was now part of a rebel band which, against all the odds, had won a great victory in that struggle.

Yet it was hard to forget because the reminders lay all around him. The narrow space between the river and the defenders' earth rampart was choked with the debris and gruesome aftermath of the struggle, and everywhere he looked revealed just how brutal the combat had been. Discarded swords, shields and helmets were strewn amongst the grotesque bodies and dismembered limbs, while English warriors were clambering down from the ramparts to begin the grisly task of stripping the dead and dumping the bodies into the river.

Winter strolled over to join him, his long moustache plastered with sweat, his chainmail tunic spattered with blood and gore. Yet the big axeman appeared almost relaxed as he slapped Edric on the back.

"Well, lad, we did it!" Winter beamed. "We are heroes now, and the rebellion has well and truly begun. Everything Hereward said would happen has come to pass."

Edric responded with a weak smile and a weary nod of his head.

"Yes," he said. "We have won."

"And not a single man lost," Winter continued happily.

That, Edric reflected, was partly due to good fortune. He had been dreading the confrontation as the Norman army which had been besieging Ely had built its bridge across the deep, dark river, the construction inching closer day by day. Then, when the Normans gathered for the final attack, Hereward had leaped over the rampart and slid down to stand at the end of the bridge, daring the enemy to come to him. Edric had followed without hesitation because he was Hereward's man and must stand beside his Lord, and Winter, Ordgar and Auti had come with him. Together, the five of them had taunted the Normans and urged them to hurry across the wooden bridge.

It had been madness, of course, and Edric had been convinced they were doomed, because there were hundreds of Normans on the far side of the river, but he had not known about Hereward's secret plan.

To build their crossing, the Normans had recruited dozens of local men who could fashion wood, so Hereward had made sure that some men loyal to the rebellion had been among those workers. Joints had been weakened, timbers half sawn through, and nails had been cut so that only the heads were hammered into the structure. With the weight of scores of men pounding across it, the bridge had collapsed, sending the Normans into the deep water where, weighed down by their armour, every one of them had drowned.

"He's a cunning bastard, is Hereward," Winter chuckled. "Damn me, but I had no idea he knew the bridge was weak."

Edric nodded again, glancing out at the surface of the water where only a few shattered stumps poked above the subsiding ripples to show where the bridge had stood. He had not believed they could withstand an assault unless Saint Etheldreda, patron of Ely, granted them a miracle. That miracle had occurred, yet it was, he knew, a result of Hereward's ingenuity.

The few Norman survivors who had crossed the bridge before it vanished beneath the water now stood morosely while Hereward gave orders to the men who were coming down from the defensive wall in answer to his summons.

Edric saw Hereward's two cousins among them. He had known those men when they had been mere outlaws who scraped a precarious living in the forests. Both had been minor noblemen who had been forced into lives of banditry when their lands were seized by the Norman invaders, and both bore the name of their grandfather Siward. Fortunately, although they both had the same name, telling them apart was easy thanks to the colour of their hair.

Edric heard Hereward tell the ginger-haired Siward Red, "Have the prisoners stripped of their armour. Distribute it among our men who have none."

"That one, too?" Red asked, pointing to a broad-shouldered, plump man who wore a heavy chainmail tunic and had a silver crucifix dangling in front of his chest. The surly man had already relinquished the huge mace he had carried into battle, and now removed his iron helmet to wipe sweat from his brow, revealing a face that was pale with helpless fury. With gritted teeth, he stood glowering at the Englishmen who were now crowding into the narrow space between the rampart and the river.

"No," Hereward replied. "Let him keep his armour. That's Abbot Turold. He's my prisoner. Make sure he is guarded, but I want him treated well."

"What about the others?" Red asked gruffly, eyeing the huddle of surviving Normans with a sour expression.

"I said they could go free," Hereward told him.

That reply surprised everyone who overheard it. Hereward was normally ruthless when it came to dealing with Normans. He held the view that the only way to rid England of the invaders was to kill every last one of them.

With an expansive smile, he explained, "I want them to help spread the word of what happened here. Let every Norman fear us now."

Then he glanced across the river and added, "But best wait until this evening before you let them go, otherwise they might be caught up in the pursuit."

His words drew Edric's eyes to the far side of the broad river where the Norman encampment had stood. That was the second part of the miracle, and it had nothing to do with Hereward's cunning even though he had assured them it would happen. Because the beleaguered rebels, who had been so seriously outnumbered by their enemies, had sparked a genuine rebellion. Against all expectation and hope, the armies of Mercia and Northumbria had come to the Isle of Ely to join them. They had appeared just as the bridge collapsed, striking at the Normans from

13

the rear and creating panic in Abbot Turold's army. Now, the men of the North were hunting down their fleeing enemy who were streaming away through the narrow, winding marsh paths in their attempt to escape.

"And make sure all the bodies are dumped in the river," Hereward concluded.

As Red began organising the work, Hereward turned to his other cousin, the fair-haired Siward White.

He ordered, "Send a messenger to Ely to tell them what has happened. And get as many boats here as you can. We're going to need to ferry all the Mercians and Northumbrians across to the island."

White observed, "That could take a while. There must be a couple of thousand of them."

"I told you they would come," Hereward grinned. "I suppose you'd better warn Abbot Thurstan that his abbey is going to need to host a couple of Earls. They'll want the best rooms he has."

"They'll want more than that," White remarked.

Hereward shrugged, "We shall see. I'd better go across and speak to them."

"Do you want me to come with you?" White offered.

"No need. You take charge here. I don't want our lads getting too drunk just because we've won today. And I don't want any trouble between them and the northerners. So keep a close eye on things."

White nodded his understanding, then went to climb one of the wooden ladders which had been propped against the ramparts to allow men to move up and down to the river bank.

Hereward turned to Edric and Winter.

"You two come with me. And where are Auti and Ordgar?"

"Helping strip the corpses," Edric told him.

"Looting the bodies, you mean?" Hereward replied with a sardonic smile. He glanced at Winter as he added, "I thought you'd be helping them with that."

The huge warrior grinned, "Ordgar and Auti will make sure we get our share."

Even as he spoke, the two other members of Hereward's personal guard came to join them, pushing through the growing

14

throng of men who now crowded the site of the brief but bloody fight which had taken place only moments before.

"There's not much to share," Ordgar grumbled.

He was another big man, shorter than Winter, but equally broad in the shoulders and equally tough and experienced. Like Winter, he showed no fear in battle and fought with a deadly fury that Edric could only hope to emulate.

Yet Hereward had appointed Edric as the leader of this small band of companions even though he was the youngest by far and had only joined the rebellion a few months earlier when he had helped the rebels break into a Norman castle in his home village of Bourne.

Mindful of his position, he said to Ordgar, "Make sure you divide it into five parts. Wulfric is due a share."

Ordgar nodded. Wulfric, the fifth member of their gang, had been left behind at Ely to act as a personal guard to Hereward's wife, Torfrida. He had not been happy about that, but someone had to stay behind, and Edric knew that, in a fight, Winter and Ordgar were indispensable. It had been a choice between Wulfric and Auti, and Auti had been desperate to join the fight because he had hoped it would allow him to die.

Everyone knew that the tall rebel yearned to join his twin brother who had been killed during a raid on Peterborough. Ever since that day, Auti had been grim and silent, searching for a way to avenge his twin's death that would also bring him peace. If Edric had told him to stay behind, Auti would probably have refused.

Now, Edric thought he could see a wistful look of regret in Auti's eyes. The rangy outlaw had been hoping to die, but he had survived what should have been an impossible fight with only minor cuts and bruises.

As for the others, Ordgar had a shallow cut on his leg, Winter's chainmail byrnie was hacked and had lost several iron rings, while Edric's shield was broken beyond repair, but they had escaped without any serious injury thanks to Hereward's carefully laid trap and a healthy dose of good fortune. Edric had no doubt that Auti would continue to search for a glorious ending in battle, but he was glad that the day of that event had been postponed for the time being.

"All right," Hereward said, "let's get over there and meet our new allies. There are boats on the way."

Edric felt his spirits lift when he heard the confidence in Hereward's voice. The fair-haired nobleman was not overly tall, but he was powerfully built and had the lithe step of a seasoned warrior. He was still only in his late twenties, but his competence, confidence and air of command meant that men twice his age would follow him unquestioningly. Edric had been captivated at their first meeting and had sworn to help Hereward defeat the Norman invaders. Now, after months of struggle, it seemed, at last, the rebellion had a chance of success. Looking across the river, he felt a growing confidence that the arrival of the armies of Mercia and Northumbria signalled a new beginning.

The first of the fen boats were now edging around a bend in the river, coming towards the narrow shelf of grass where the fight had taken place. Designed for navigating the waterways of the marshes, the boats were broad, with a shallow draught, and were propelled either by oars or long poles. The leading boat now bumped against the bank, the boatman giving Hereward a look of enquiry.

"You want to cross the river, Lord?"

"I certainly do. And I expect you and your fellows will be kept busy all day, because those men over there will need to come to the island."

The boatman looked at the hordes of Mercians and Northumbrians who were now busy plundering the Norman camp. He gave a shrug, accepting the task without demur.

Hereward looked at his four bodyguards and suddenly laughed.

"By God! You lot should terrify the Earls. Just remember to keep your mouths shut and look fierce."

"Are we trying to terrify the Earls?" Edric asked with a puzzled frown.

"We are trying to impress them with how tough we are," Hereward explained. "So I want to see a bit of swagger when we get across there. But keep in mind, these are powerful lords, so we need to treat them with respect."

"Respect should be earned," Winter growled. "From what I've heard of Edwin and Morcar, they don't inspire much respect."

16

"They have come to help us," Hereward pointed out, "so that deserves our thanks. It takes a lot to join a rebellion when you've already been beaten twice."

Edric nodded his agreement. In the past months he had encountered more noblemen than he had ever dreamed of, and had come to realise that, despite their exalted status, most of them had faults just like ordinary men. Yet the tales of Edwin and Morcar, the brothers who ruled Mercia and Northumbria, suggested they had more flaws than most. They had been defeated by King Hardrada of Norway when he had made his attempt to seize the throne of England, then they had been cowed into submission after twice attempting to rebel against King William, the bastard Duke of Normandy who had eventually seized power after all his rivals had been killed in battle. Surprisingly for such a vindictive man, William had not only allowed the Earls to keep their heads, he had left them in charge of their earldoms. Edric had heard some of the monks of Ely say this was because The Bastard had more than enough problems of his own quelling trouble in Normandy and did not want to give any of his followers title to the great northern earldoms for fear they would set themselves up as rivals to his authority. Edwin and Morcar might be English, but they were capable of being controlled.

Until now, it seemed, because the banners which waved above the host of armed men who were thronging the far bank proclaimed that the men of Mercia and Northumbria had again risen in revolt.

Edric reached back over his shoulder and pulled the leather sling he carried, lifting his axe to fit the long shaft into the loops. His fingers fumbled awkwardly as he tried to place the weapon into the holder, and he hoped none of the others had noticed. Silently, he swore at himself, annoyed that his body was reacting to the slaughter all around him. He had fought before, and had seen mutilated corpses more than once, yet this time seemed to be affecting him more deeply.

"Are you all right, lad?" Winter asked in a concerned whisper.

"I'm fine," Edric replied. "Just a bit tired."

He finally secured the axe and swung it onto his back. When he looked up, Winter was holding out a small skin of ale.

"Take a swig," the big man offered.

17

Edric removed the horn stopper and drank. He had felt bile rising in his throat at the sight of the gory bodies which were now being stripped, and the dark ale, bitter though it was, tasted good.

He handed the skin back to Winter with a word of thanks.

"You'll be fine," Winter said with surprising empathy.

"I need a new shield," Edric sighed, nudging the toe of his boot against the ruin of his shattered round shield.

"No problem," Winter grinned.

The big man scurried away, returning moments later bearing one of the large, kite-shaped Norman shields.

"This ought to do," he declared. "It's big enough to protect you even though you are almost as big as me."

Edric accepted the shield with a smile, running his hand through the grips and testing its weight. The shield was bulky, providing protection for his body, while the tapering lower end was long enough to guard his left leg as far as his knee. It curved slightly, moulding to his body shape.

"I think I prefer our round ones," he observed. "but it will do."

Briefly, he wondered who the man was who had carried this shield across the bridge. Was he one of the prisoners, or was his body one of those being carried to the bank of the river and thrown into the water?

Hereward broke his reverie by calling them to join him. Edric was grateful for the interruption because he knew it did not do to think of your enemies as human beings. They were foreign invaders who needed to be killed. He dismissed all thoughts of the shield's former owner and, hefting his new possession, he walked the few steps to the river bank.

Hereward had settled himself into the boat, so the four men followed, Edric clumsily holding his new shield as he sat on one of the low bench seats. As soon as they were seated, the boatman shoved his long pole into the water and began to slowly propel them across the river.

Edric could not help but peer down into the murky depths even though he dreaded seeing what now lay beneath the surface. Hundreds of men, men who would have killed him without a moment's thought, now lay drowned beneath him. It was a sobering thought.

Then he recalled something Siward White had said, and he turned to Hereward to ask, "What did White mean when he said the Earls would want more than the best rooms?"

Hereward's brow wrinkled in a slight frown and he paused before replying, "He meant that they will want to take command. They are Earls. I am nothing."

"You are a Thane!" Edric protested.

"My father was a Thane," Hereward corrected. "He died at Hastings, and my younger brother, who replaced him, was murdered. I have no title and no lands, only my sword."

"You have us," Edric said loyally.

Hereward smiled, "And I am grateful for that. I thank you all for standing beside me at the bridge."

"You are our Lord," Edric replied. "What else should we have done?"

Hereward said, "I keep telling you I am not a Lord, Edric."

"Yes, Lord," Edric grinned. "But whatever you call yourself, everyone knows you lead the resistance. It is your fame and your exploits that have brought so many men to join us."

Hereward smiled again, but there was a rueful tinge to his voice as he told them, "Nevertheless, I fear the Earls may not take kindly to accepting orders from a mere rebel war leader."

"So what are you going to do?"

"I am going to impress the hell out of them," Hereward told him with a laugh.

Privately, Edric could not see how the Earls could fail to be impressed by Hereward. The young nobleman had been exiled from England a few years before the Normans arrived, and he had earned a famous reputation in Flanders where he had won countless victories for the Count of that beleaguered state. Dismayed by the stories coming out of England, he had returned to seek out news of his family, only to learn that his father had been one of the victims at the bloody battle of Hastings, while his younger brother, Toki, had been executed by a Norman sheriff named Ivo de Taillebois who had seized the Thane's manor house and built a castle around it. Hereward had vowed revenge and, with Edric's help, had gained access to the castle, destroying it and slaughtering the garrison. Only de Taillebois had escaped, thus avoiding Hereward's vengeance. Despite his main aim having been thwarted, Hereward had struck a blow which the Normans were bound to answer, so his gang had fled into the fastness of the fenlands where they had joined other rebels on the island of Ely.

Now, just as Hereward had promised, the rebellion was spreading, and the men who lined the river bank to greet them were the evidence of that.

Edric saw a group of mounted men approach the river, the warriors standing aside to let them pass. Two of the men dismounted and stood waiting for the small boat to arrive. Both were dressed in fine mail, the shoulders and hems lined with silver. Their helmets were crested, and large, ornate rings adorned their gauntleted fingers. Compared to the lean, hard men who surrounded them, both looked plump and well fed.

"It's just a guess," Winter whispered, "but I reckon those are our men."

"Quiet!" hissed Hereward. "Keep your mouths shut and let me do the talking."

Then the boat bumped against the river bank and they stepped out to meet the smiling Earls.

Edric slung his newly acquired shield onto his back and did his best to look grim as he followed Hereward ashore.

With his four men standing respectfully in a row behind him, Hereward bowed low to the two noblemen.

"My Lords," he greeted. "Welcome to Ely, home of the free English. I thank you for your aid, and am very pleased to meet you."

The taller of the two men replied, "I am Edwin, Earl of Mercia. This is my brother, Morcar, Earl of Northumbria. I know you are not Siward Barn, who is reputed to be here, so I presume you must be the man called Hereward?"

"I am, Lord," Hereward confirmed. "My father was Asketil, a King's Thane."

"I hear great things of your exploits," Edwin said, his tone polite.

In contrast, Edric noticed that Morcar's face betrayed a hint of scorn that the man leading the rebellion was only a minor noble.

The younger Earl asked sharply, "And where is King Sweyn of Denmark? We had heard he was here. We have come to pledge our allegiance to him."

20

Edric held his breath as Hereward answered calmly, "The King has returned to Denmark, my Lord."

The expressions on the faces of the two Earls changed from happy friendliness to alarmed confusion.

"Gone back to Denmark?" Morcar blurted. "But we heard he had come to take the crown of England! Has he left an army here? When will he return?"

"He took all his men with him," Hereward replied flatly. "And I fear he does not intend to return."

Edric knew the departure of the Danish king and his army had been a bitter blow for Hereward, yet the young nobleman betrayed no hint of the anger and despair he had felt when the Danes had sailed away, taking with them most of the plunder from a raid on Peterborough which Hereward had planned and led.

The news was obviously a shock to the two Earls. Morcar's face had turned deathly pale beneath his silver helmet, beads of sweat running into his long, elegant moustache.

His older brother, Edwin, recovered his poise more quickly, but his voice was less certain as he asked, "So King Sweyn has abandoned us?"

"I fear so, my Lords. But now that you are here, we have a chance to reclaim England so that the Witan may elect a new, English king."

He stressed the word, "English", no doubt hoping to plant a seed in the minds of the two nobles that, as the senior surviving English Earls, one of them might be elected to rule the land once the Normans had been beaten. But if that had been his intention, it failed.

"We cannot defeat the Bastard without King Sweyn!" Morcar hissed, his eyes wide with barely suppressed panic and his hands flapping in agitation.

Edwin laid a gloved hand on his brother's shoulder and said softly, "Enough, Morcar. I think we need to continue this discussion in more comfortable surroundings."

What he meant, Edric realised, was that he did not want a crowd of warriors listening in. Already, news that the Danes were no longer on the island would be spreading through the northern army like wildfire and would inevitably lead to many of the men having second thoughts about the wisdom of joining the revolt.

Dismissing their obvious concerns, Hereward told the Earls, "Boats are being sent. Your horses will need to swim across behind the boats, but we will begin ferrying your men over as soon as we can. Then we shall go to the town of Ely where you will meet Abbot Thurstan and Thane Siward Barn."

Hereward made it sound as if all their problems would be resolved once they reached the great abbey in the town of Ely, but Edric knew that Abbot Thurstan, while he supported the rebellion and allowed the English warriors to live among his monks, was an old man who had no skill in politics or war, while Siward Barn, who had been on the isle of Ely longer than any of the rebels, was also aging and was not inclined to fight unless he had no choice. He and Hereward had often clashed over the best course of action, with Hereward favouring taking the war to the Normans, while Barn preferred to sit quietly in the marshland where he believed they would be left in peace if they did not cause too much trouble.

But trouble had arrived, because there was no way the Earls could conceal their latest rebellion, and William the Bastard would surely not allow them to defy him again.

Edwin, seeking to regain some authority after his brother's dismayed outburst, cast his eye over the river.

"What happened here?" he asked, his eyes scanning the water. "We saw men advancing across a bridge to attack you, but it vanished in an instant."

"The Lord God and his servant, Saint Etheldreda, saw fit to grant us a miracle, Lord," Hereward replied solemnly. "I and my companions prayed and our prayers were answered. The Lord and his saint destroyed a bridge the Normans had constructed. Their army was taken by the waters just as Pharaoh's host was drowned by the Red Sea."

When he said this, another murmur ran through the army of warriors who surrounded the group, and Edwin raised his eyebrows in surprise.

"A miracle indeed. If God and his saints are on our side, then we can surely reclaim England without the aid of the Danish King."

His words were obviously intended for the ears of the warriors who were clustered around him. Edric could see some of them nodding or making the sign of the cross. The news of the Danish king's departure was a major setback, but the miracle of the bridge proved that God was on their side. Even Edric, who knew the truth of how the bridge had been destroyed, felt a surge of confidence when he saw Earl Edwin's smile.

Then, as Hereward was inviting the Earls to board the first boat, Edric caught sight of another face in the crowd, a youthful, smiling face he had not seen for many weeks.

"Hello, Edric Strong," said Brother John. "What do you think of my army?"

The young monk stepped from between two burly housecarls and hurried to grasp Edric's hand.

"Well met!" Brother John said. "I should have known you would be in the thick of the fighting. I trust you are well?"

Edric nodded, dumbfounded by the sight of Brother John. The monk spent his life wandering the countryside, moving from place to place, offering spiritual succour to those in need, but never remaining in one place for more than a few days. He had been a regular visitor to the smithy in Bourne where Edric had been apprentice to his uncle, and he had been on Ely for a short time after the destruction of the Norman castle. He had left with the intention of heading northwards, perhaps as far as Scotland, but now he was back, smiling as usual, and firing a barrage of questions at a bemused Edric.

"How is Aelswith? And her baby? Are they still in the abbey? And the Lady Torfrida? How is she?"

Edric tried to gather his thoughts and stuttered a reply.

"Aelswith is tired and fed up of being confined to Ely, but her daughter, young Torfrida, is growing strong. And the Lady is well."

Torfrida was Hereward's wife, a dark-haired beauty who had once been a lady in waiting to the Countess of Flanders. Edric knew her relationship with Hereward had been strained by her husband's decision to remain in England, but he decided that was none of Brother John's business.

As for Aelswith, she had been a servant in the manor house at Bourne, a girl whose good looks had attracted the attention of Hereward's younger brother, Toki. She was pregnant with Toki's child when the young Thane had been executed by Ivo de Taillebois, and had come to Ely with Hereward's gang, claiming kinship even though she and Toki had never married. She had named her baby daughter in honour of

Hereward's wife, another cause of friction between Hereward and the elder Torfrida. Hereward was not pleased at having a bastard niece, and he put up with Aelswith only because Torfrida insisted that the girl and her baby should stay with them.

Edric's own relationship with Aelswith was one which caused him frequent anxiety, so he was pleased when Brother John's questions continued unabated.

"Is it true King Sweyn has gone?" the monk asked, his thirst for news and gossip as great as ever.

"It is true," Edric replied.

Brother John frowned, an unfamiliar expression of concern showing on his normally cheerful face. He seemed on the verge of asking another question, but Hereward was signalling to Edric to join them on the boat for the return crossing, so Edric tugged at the monk's sleeve.

"Come, we can talk on the way back to Ely."

The Earls were each stepping into a boat with several of their guards, leaving their servants to bring their horses across the river and giving instructions that all of their men should follow as quickly as the limited number of boats would allow. Hereward and his gang were already sitting in the same vessel which had brought them on the first crossing, so Edric hurried Brother John to join them.

The monk greeted the other warriors with a friendly wave.

"It is good to see you all again," he told them amiably. "I am glad God has seen fit to protect you. The miracle of the bridge will not be forgotten."

Hereward regarded the young monk with a blank expression, but Winter snorted, "We have Hereward to thank for that miracle."

Brother John raised a quizzical eyebrow when the other men joined in the laughter.

"I'll tell you about the miracle later," Edric told him. "But I want to know what you meant when you said this was your army."

Brother John regaled him with a broad smile, giving a casual flutter of one hand as if to suggest that accomplishing great feats was an everyday occurrence.

"Who do you think persuaded the Earls to come here?" he asked.

Hereward twisted around to see Brother John, his gaze taking on a sudden alertness.

"You convinced them to join us?" he demanded.

Brother John nodded, "I was heading northwards, seeking shelter for the night, and happened upon one of Earl Edwin's estates. It turned out that he was staying there and that his brother, Morcar, had joined him. When I arrived, they were eager for news of events, so I told them about you and the arrival of King Sweyn. After some discussion, they decided to pledge their allegiance to him."

"And now they have learned he is no longer here," Hereward murmured. "Well, Brother, I thank you for your efforts. The Danes may have gone, but we have a proper army now. How many men did they bring?"

Brother John replied, "I believe Edwin has around two thousand men, all of them well trained, while Morcar had a few hundred housecarls in his retinue. He has sent for more men to come from Northumbria, but that region suffered greatly when King William devastated the land after the last revolt, so I do not expect you will see many more arrive."

Hereward nodded, "Two thousand is a good start. More will come, especially now we have shown that the Normans can be beaten."

"Praise the Lord!" Brother John said enthusiastically, beaming in delight at the admiring looks Winter and the others were giving him.

They were nearing the island now, the boat pushing downstream, passing the earthworks and rounding a bend to a landing place where they would not need to clamber over the high ramparts. Here, the defensive wall was lower because the only way to reach this section was by boat, and the Normans had few boats. The wall was made from blocks of peat and tree trunks, two of which had been hauled aside to create an opening.

Hereward handed the boatman a silver penny as they disembarked to join the Earls on the island. The man bobbed his head in thanks, then turned to drive his boat back to collect more passengers.

Turning to the Earls, Hereward told them, "The town of Ely lies a few miles to the north. We shall set off as soon as your horses arrive. Your men can camp here, near the village of

Aldreth. This is the easiest part of the island to reach, so this is where any attack will come."

"I doubt they will attack again in a hurry," Edwin declared. "We have struck them a serious blow today."

"That is true, my Lord," Hereward agreed. "So we have time to make plans. But first, we should go to Ely and celebrate our victory."

The Earls were gazing around, studying their new surroundings. The isle of Ely was a haven within the almost inaccessible fens. Around seven miles in length, and three wide at its broadest point, it took its name from the town of Ely which housed the great abbey founded by Saint Etheldreda. There was ample grazing, and the rivers provided fish and the plentiful eels which gave the town its name. Here at the southern end, though, the island had become a fortified camp. The village of Aldreth, a tiny collection of low cottages with reed-thatched roofs, would soon be surrounded by even more warriors as the Mercians and Northumbrians completed the river crossing.

"This is the only part of the island where the Normans can bring any sizable force," Hereward explained. "In every other direction, the marshes prevent them reaching us. This island is the safest place in England."

He spoke as if to reassure the northern Earls who were still shaken by the news that the Danish king had returned home, but Edric could tell that his words had little effect. Morcar, in particular, had the air of a man who knew he had made a dreadful error of judgement.

"Too late now," Edric murmured to himself as he watched the Earls' horses being readied.

Siward White had found a horse for Hereward who now joined the Earls at the head of what soon became a small column marching towards the town of Ely.

Brother John strode alongside Edric and the other men of the gang, enquiring after their health and expressing sympathy for Auti when he heard of Duti's death.

"News of your attack on Peterborough has travelled," he told them. "It helped persuade the Earls to come and join you."

"What are they like?" Edric asked. "They don't seem very pleased to be here."

Brother John shrugged, "They are noblemen. They are rich, and they enjoy such pursuits as hunting."

"But can they fight?" Edric wanted to know. "I've not heard good things about them."

Brother John replied, "They command great earldoms, so many men follow them. But, as I am sure you know only too well, that does not mean they are great leaders. Edwin is clever and thoughtful, although I think he fears losing the wealth and status his position gives him. As for his brother …"

His voice trailed off. After a short pause, he went on, "Well, let us say that Morcar's main interest is Morcar and what is good for him."

"You do not sound as if you like them very much," Edric observed.

"I like all men," Brother John replied. "But I am able to recognise their faults as well as their good points. And the Earls certainly have good points. For one thing, they desire an England free of Norman rule, and that is something you should remember. What they need is some good advice when it comes to fighting a war."

"Hereward will give them that," Edric stated confidently.

"Then with God on your side and Hereward to lead the fight, England will surely be free before too long," Brother John said.

Winter, who had been listening to the conversation as he marched behind them, put in, "It sounds like you hate the Normans as much as we do."

Brother John laughed, "I try not to hate anyone."

Edric explained, "Brother John is originally from Anjou. His people have been at war with the Normans for years."

"Where's Anjou?" Ordgar asked.

"In France," Edric explained.

He glanced at Brother John who gave him a friendly wink. Until earlier that year, Edric had never heard of Anjou, but Brother John had revealed something of his past in an earlier conversation. The monk spoke fluent French and was welcomed wherever he went, but he had a habit of speaking about his social superiors in mocking terms which used to scandalise Edric's uncle.

"Have you been back to Bourne?" Brother John asked Edric, clearly recalling the day when they had first discussed his dislike of the Normans.

"No."

"So you have no news of your aunt and uncle?"

Edric shook his head.

"I expect Uncle Ethelred is still making horseshoes for the Normans," he muttered darkly.

"He was always a man who respected authority," Brother John said, his eye twinkling. "Not like you, Edric Strong."

"Respect must be earned," Edric replied, echoing the words he had learned from Winter.

Brother John chuckled, "And I am sure you will be respected when we march into the town of Ely. You are heroes, after all. You are the men whose prayers brought down God's wrath on the Normans and destroyed their bridge."

"It wasn't like that," Edric told him.

Brother John merely laughed, "But it is a good story, my young friend, and people will believe it. Why not revel in the glory?"

"Because it is not true!" Edric retorted.

"Perhaps not. You can tell me the truth of it later, but you should also remember this truth. People will join you more readily if they have some evidence that God is on your side. Mark my words, the people in the town will treat you as heroes."

Winter grinned, "I'm hoping some of the women will be grateful. I don't mind revelling in that sort of glory."

Ordgar uttered a throaty chuckle of agreement, and even Brother John did not take offence at the big man's crude remark.

"I am sure you will find everyone is grateful for your heroic deeds," he said mischievously.

His words appeared to be true. Warned by the messenger Siward White had sent to the town, the people of Ely had come out in numbers to greet the Earls and their entourage. Men and women cheered and waved. Some threw flowers, and children ran and danced alongside the warriors who grinned at the joyous mood their arrival had sparked.

"They are safe because of you," Brother John told Edric with a happy smile. "Enjoy the moment."

Edric found that he could not ignore the atmosphere of happiness and relief, and he began to relax as they marched along the narrow streets towards the abbey to the loud acclamation of the crowd.

Before long, they reached the abbey where a host of monks had clustered at the gates to greet them, the stooped figure of old Abbot Thurstan at their head. Peering past the mounted men who led the column, Edric could also see Siward Barn, the stern and elderly Thane who had fled to Ely when his own lands had been seized. Even the old Thane seemed to have been gripped by a sense of relief and joy that the Earls had come to join them, for he was smiling as much as anyone in the crowd.

Edric could not prevent his own broad smile when he saw the reception awaiting their return. Aelswith was there, dark-haired, slim and beautiful, holding her baby daughter in her arms, and so was Ranald Sigtrygsson, the Danish warrior who had been wounded during their raid on Peterborough and who was still recovering his health. Edric liked and admired the tall Dane, and was pleased to see him on his feet once again.

Then Edric caught sight of another figure standing near the abbey's gates, and his heart sank.

"Who is that?" Brother John enquired, nodding towards the woman who had caught Edric's attention.

"That," Edric replied grimly, "is the Lady Altruda."

"She is very beautiful," Brother John remarked admiringly as his eyes took in the voluptuous figure of the woman who wore a long dress of pale blue and whose brown hair fell unbound to her shoulders to signify that she was unmarried.

"Stay away from her," Edric warned.

Brother John shot him a questioning look.

"Oh? Why? I am a monk, my friend. I have sworn a vow of celibacy, so do not fear that I will succumb to her charms."

Edric repeated, "It would be best to have nothing to do with her, Brother. She may have the body and face of an angel, but she has the heart and mind of a devil."

Chapter 3

Altruda slipped away from the cheering crowd and stamped her way back to her room, unable to conceal her frustration. Fortunately, there was nobody around to see her mood since everyone had gone to greet the returning victors and their new allies.

"Fools!" she muttered to herself, although even she could not say precisely who the comment was aimed at. Perhaps, she admitted ruefully, she was the fool for trusting Abbot Turold and Ivo de Taillebois to overwhelm Hereward's pitifully small band of rebels. She had supplied them with all the information they needed and had even suggested how they should launch their attack across the river.

Yet they had failed, and now the pathetic people of Ely, buoyed by the arrival of the Mercian and Northumbrian Earls, were celebrating a victory when they should have been grovelling on their knees before their Norman overlords.

Frowning deeply, Altruda crossed the courtyard to the guest chambers, entering the long, stone-lined corridor and moving to the first room on the left, unlocking the door with the iron key which hung at her waist.

Behind her, she could sense the burly figure of Kenton, her personal guard. Wearing his chainmail and with his axe slung over one shoulder, he had maintained a discreet distance as he walked a few paces behind her, although she knew his demeanour would have been anything but subservient.

Kenton had been one of Siward Barn's housecarls, but Altruda had asked that he be transferred to her service. Old Barn had been puzzled by her choice but had agreed, perhaps because he was glad to be rid of the sly and brutish Kenton.

Altruda, as always, had reasons for her choice. Kenton may have been a housecarl, but his first loyalty was to himself rather than the lord to whom he had sworn an oath. Altruda had recognised Kenton as a man whose service could be bought if sufficient silver was paid, and she paid him well.

But the deciding factor which had persuaded her to choose Kenton as her guard was that he detested Edric Strong. That made him a natural ally.

"Come in and close the door," she ordered.

There was nobody else in the building, the man who always stood guard at Torfrida's door having gone with Hereward's wife to greet the returning heroes. Even the village wench, Aelswith, had taken her squalling brat to see the triumphant rebels. Still, Altruda knew the value of caution and would not say anything incriminating until the heavy oak door was firmly closed and bolted.

She eyed the small chamber with distaste. The bed was comfortable enough, the furnishings sparse but of good quality. Compared to the spartan cells the monks were determined to live in, this room was luxurious, yet Altruda had been expecting to move to accommodation which better suited her tastes. Now, thanks to Abbot Turold's failure, she would be compelled to remain here a while longer.

"I will need to hire some maids," she observed to herself.

"A Lady should have servants," Kenton agreed.

Altruda shot him a sharp look, wondering whether he was mocking her, but he, too, was clearly put out by the recent turn of events.

He propped his axe against the corner of the wall, then stood with his arms folded across his chest, bull-like and clearly angry, while Altruda seated herself in a comfortable chair, smoothing down her dress as she tried to compose herself.

"How is this possible?" Kenton asked her. "How can they have defeated Abbot Turold's army? You said the Normans would sweep them aside."

She sighed, "The Mercians and Northumbrians came to their aid. Nobody expected that."

Kenton persisted, "But the bridge? They are saying Saint Etheldreda appeared and smote the bridge with a holy sword."

"Do you really believe that?" she shot back.

"I've never seen anything like it," Kenton admitted. "But the monks keep telling us miracles can happen."

"Not miracles like that," Altruda scoffed. "The bridge may have collapsed, but I doubt Saint Etheldreda had much to do with it."

Then she relaxed, shaking her head.

"It does not matter how it happened," she sighed. "We must deal with the consequences."

"They will march against London," Kenton stated. "With the King gone to Normandy, they have a chance to seize power. Where does that leave you?"

"It leaves *us* with things to do," she replied, stressing the plural pronoun to make sure he understood that he was tied to her fate. "Do not underestimate the King."

"And you should not underestimate Hereward," he warned. "He may be an upstart, but he knows how to fight. I've seen him in action, my Lady."

Altruda returned a soft smile as she said, "I know all about Hereward's abilities, Kenton. I, too, have seen him fight. But even with the help of the northern Earls he will struggle to defeat King William."

"But if he does?"

Again Altruda smiled, this time more broadly as she spread her hands in a gesture of acceptance.

"Then there will be a new King, and he will need loyal servants who understand the realities of life in England."

Kenton's brow creased, then he gave a slow nod.

"All right," he grunted. "I trust your judgement, my Lady. So what do we do in the meantime?"

"We find out what their plans are," she told him. "They may march on London, but I think it will depend on how many men they have. That is what I want you to find out. Go to Aldreth if necessary. Bring me details of how many men they have and what sort. Are they housecarls or fyrdmen? Foot soldiers or cavalry? How well equipped are they? You know the sort of things I will need to report."

Kenton nodded but his face betrayed a hint of mockery as he sneered, "You will be writing another letter?"

"Indeed," Altruda admitted.

He argued, "But Abbot Turold is a prisoner. I saw him in the procession. Who will you write to?"

"Someone else will take charge," she replied evenly.

"And your tame monk will take your letters to whoever you tell him to?"

Altruda nodded again, although her mind was already occupied by other concerns because the failure of the Norman assault had left her in a difficult position.

32

Reflecting on the few positive aspects to come out of the fiasco, she at least knew that she could still send out secret communications. Brother Richard, the monk who ran the abbey's infirmary, had been taking messages and bringing back supplies of gold and silver for her for some months. Brother Richard was of Norman descent and detested the rabble of English rebels who wandered freely in the abbey, and his role as an apothecary meant he had an excuse to leave the island frequently in order to obtain supplies of medicinal herbs. As a bonus, Brother Richard was besotted with Altruda and would do whatever she wished.

After some thought, Altruda decided that her own position was still safe enough. Only Brother Richard and Kenton knew she had been aiding the Normans. Everyone else believed she was a refugee, fleeing the threat of a forced marriage to a Norman lord who wanted to inherit her lands. That tale was a fabrication to explain why she had been in Peterborough when Hereward and King Sweyn had sacked the abbey there, but nobody had challenged her claims.

Unfortunately, Abbot Turold also knew the truth, and he was now a prisoner. She hoped the boorish man would have the sense to keep his mouth shut if they met. She would do her best to avoid him, but the abbey was not a large place, so she would need to be prepared for any chance encounter with the captured Abbot.

Altruda sighed again. Everything had been going so well. She had persuaded King Sweyn to abandon his hopes of seizing the throne and return to his home in Denmark. She knew Hereward suspected her of complicity in that deed, but he had no proof, and she was a good enough actor to persuade the likes of Abbot Thurstan and Siward Barn that she was merely an unfortunate woman who had been captured, used and then cast off by the Danish king.

She looked up at Kenton once again.

"You had best set off first thing tomorrow," she told him. "Things will have settled down by then, but be quick about your task. I must have information."

"I want some information too," he growled, his hands clenching into fists. "I still haven't found my daughter."

Altruda cautioned herself to appear interested. She had told Kenton that she had a plan for finding his missing daughter, Ylva, but it was hardly her main priority.

33

She said, "Tell your son to keep following Edric Strong. He knows the truth of her whereabouts. Sooner or later, we will find her. If she is still on the island, that is."

"She must be," he rasped. "I've asked every boatman I can find, and none of them admits to taking anyone matching her description off the island."

His scarred face tinged with anger as he snarled, "Halfdan has been following Edric for weeks but has still learned nothing. I wish you'd just let me beat the truth out of him."

"No!" she snapped, holding up a hand to still his anger. "I want no trouble with Hereward. Not yet, at any rate. Leave Edric alone. Just tell your boy to keep trailing him."

Kenton grunted what passed for acceptance.

Altruda sighed again. She pitied the poor girl if Kenton ever did find her because the big housecarl was unlikely to be forgiving. Ylva had run away from him, seeking refuge with Hereward's gang, then she had simply vanished. Edric, who had been her principal protector, insisted she had left Ely altogether, but Kenton refused to accept that explanation. Altruda's solution was for Kenton's halfwit son, Halfdan, to follow Edric whenever he left the abbey in the hope that he might lead them to Ylva.

Privately, Altruda had no real desire to locate the girl. If Ylva was dragged back to the abbey it would only create more friction between Kenton and Hereward's gang. That, in turn, would make people pay more attention to Altruda, and that was something she had no wish for at all. Still, it was useful to let Kenton believe she was trying to help him, even if she did secretly believe the girl was probably long gone.

"If she is here, we will find her eventually," she promised. "Now, get me the information I need."

"And what will you be doing, my Lady?" he asked, his tone verging on a sneer.

"That is my business, Kenton. But be assured that this is a setback, nothing more. When King William returns, he will squash these rebels. Then you and I shall have our rewards."

He stared at her for a moment, his brooding eyes glinting malevolently, then he picked up his axe, slung it over his shoulder and left, slamming the door behind him.

Altruda let out another soft sigh. The man was a brute. She detested the way he looked at her, and she knew what he was thinking when he did, but as long as she paid him, and as long as he truly believed he would be rewarded when the inevitable Norman victory arrived, he would be her brute to command. For her part, she had already decided to dispose of the man once King William had crushed the rebellion.

But the rebellion, far from being crushed, was spreading. Edwin and Morcar, the two great northern Earls, had joined what had been a tiny rebel force. Altruda knew that, somehow, she needed to find out what they planned to do. And then she needed to ensure those plans failed.

Chapter 4

Abbot Thurstan announced that a banquet would be held in the refectory to mark Hereward's victory and to welcome the two great Earls who had brought their armies to the relief of Ely. Edwin and Morcar seemed less than enthusiastic about this but graciously acknowledged the honour the abbot was doing them.

Hereward wanted to hold a meeting to plan their next move, but the Earls seemed content to delay any discussions, and spent the day fussing over the details of their accommodation, visiting the tomb of Saint Etheldreda and touring the rest of the abbey.

"They're probably trying to think of a way to get out of the mess they've found themselves in," was Winter's cynical opinion.

"It's not a mess," Edric protested. "Now we have a proper army we can take the war to the Normans."

"It's not our army," Winter grunted. "The Mercians and Northumbrians are sworn to follow their Earls. If they decide to run away and skulk in the hope of escaping the Bastard's vengeance, their men won't argue. They'll just pick up their arms and march north again."

"I'm afraid that's probably true," Brother John agreed. "But it would be a foolish thing to do. The King is not renowned for his mercy. Their best chance lies in sticking together."

Edric said, "Then I hope Hereward can persuade them to stay and fight."

Hereward clearly shared Winter's concern, but Abbot Thurstan insisted that any discussion of military matters should wait until the following day.

"Today we must host our new guests," he stated.

The fare was, as usual, excellent, with the refectory serving up a variety of dishes. Edric, sitting with the other members of Hereward's gang, kept shooting glances at their leader who sat at the top table, his face stern while the Earls discussed anything except the question of what should happen next.

It was only at the end of the long meal when Earl Edwin announced, "We shall hold a council of war tomorrow, Father Abbot. My brother and our senior Thanes will discuss what must be done."

Glancing at Siward Barn, he added, "Thane Barn should also attend."

He gave no indication that anyone else was to be invited, and Edric thought Hereward's famous temper was about to explode, but Abbot Thurstan, to his credit, told the Earl, "Hereward must also be present, my Lord. He is the man who has led our warriors in battle."

Edwin clearly wanted to argue, but Hereward quickly put in, "My Lord, I may not be a Thane, but I led the war host of the Count of Flanders. My rank in his household was equivalent to that of any Thane here. And the reason I have no lands in England is because they were taken from my family."

Abbot Thurstan added, "Hereward is the man our warriors look to, my Lord. It would be foolish not to take his advice in military matters."

To Edric's surprise, old Siward Barn agreed, "Hereward should certainly be included, my Lord."

Faced with this support for Hereward, Edwin backed down.

"Very well. Then we shall meet tomorrow."

Thurstan said, "We can use the library. It has sufficient space, I think."

"Until tomorrow, then," Edwin said with as much grace as he could muster. He and his brother, together with their retainers, filed out of the refectory, giving the clear impression that, while they might be sharing Ely with the men who had begun the revolt, they were not yet a part of it.

"Snooty bastards!" Winter muttered darkly.

Brother John smiled, "I would not have put it so bluntly, my large friend, but I do believe your assessment is correct. Nevertheless, Hereward is going to have to deal with those great lords and their egos. I pray he will be able to persuade them."

The library was a large room where monks were usually able to read in contemplative silence. Now it was filled by men of war who strode into the home of learning with swords at their waists and gold rings on their arms and fingers.

There were several desks and lecterns arranged around the sides of the main space, but the room was dominated by the enormous reading table at its centre. This was where the senior men and their advisers met for their council of war.

Edric felt out of place among the glittering nobles and their Thanes, but Hereward had insisted he accompany him to the meeting.

"White and Red are still at Aldreth," he explained. "And every other man will have someone with them. I am not going to let them think I am without followers."

"But I can't advise you on how to fight," Edric objected.

"You don't need to advise me," Hereward told him. "Just stand behind me and nod your head when I say anything."

So Edric stood behind Hereward's chair, trying not to betray his nervousness as the other men took their seats or crowded around the table.

To distract himself, Edric took a long look around the library, staring in some amazement at the long shelves which were stacked with heavy books. He had only ever seen one book before; the Bible which had been owned by their village priest, but this room held hundreds, each with vellum pages bound in thick leather covers, some of which were encrusted with jewels. Edric dearly wanted to take one of the books down to look at the decorated pages, but he knew this was neither the time nor the place to indulge his curiosity. He knew the monks produced their own vellum and ink, and that many of the books were copied by scribes who sat in the scriptorium, laboriously scratching out the tiny scribbles which other monks could read. One day, he decided, he would need to ask permission to visit the scriptorium.

For the moment, he gazed around the wonders of the library, noting that the windows were tall and wide, admitting bright sunlight to aid the readers who normally used the room. This morning's light was sending motes of dust dancing in the air and reflecting off the polished surface of the table around which sat the men who wanted to depose the Bastard from the throne of England. It did not escape Edric that there was some irony in a place of learning and knowledge being used to discuss war, but England under the Normans had become a land of sharp contrasts. Here he was, a young man of barely twenty years of age, who could not read or write and had only joined the rebels a few months earlier, now attending a meeting where he could listen to Earls and Thanes discuss the future of the entire country.

Abbot Thurstan, flanked by two of his senior monks, began the meeting by welcoming everyone but, aside from those few opening remarks, the old abbot had little to add to the discussion and sat in virtual silence while the men of war spoke.

Earl Edwin and his brother, Morcar, were seated with their backs to the windows, while Hereward and Siward Barn sat opposite them. The earls were accompanied by senior Thanes, Barn had a couple of his veteran commanders, and Hereward had Edric who felt uncomfortably out of place in this exalted company.

Before long, though, he was growing frustrated as the four men squabbled for the better part of the morning.

The main problem, as Brother John had warned and Winter had feared, was that the two Earls were nervous, clearly believing they had made an error of judgement in joining the revolt.

"We thought King Sweyn was here," Morcar said on more than one occasion.

Both Earls gave every impression of having wished they had stayed at home instead of marching south and joining battle with the Normans. Edric thought many of their Thanes looked as if they wanted to protest at the brothers' stance, but none dared speak up.

Eventually, it was old Siward Barn who declared, "It is too late now for you to back out, my Lords. For better or worse, you are here, and the Normans are aware of it. You have thrown in your hand with us, so all that remains now is to surrender or to fight."

That sobering thought silenced the two noblemen for a moment, so Hereward seized the opportunity to move the discussion to practical matters, hoping to draw the Earls into accepting their situation.

"I have received a message," he told them. "It seems the Normans who fled have rallied on Belsar's Hill, where they are making a stand."

"Belsar's Hill?" Earl Edwin asked.

"It is an old Roman fort," Hereward explained. "It overlooks the approaches to the fens. The Normans took it over some time ago."

"Should we attempt to drive them out?" Edwin wanted to know, although he seemed less than enthusiastic about the prospect.

Hereward told him, "It will be difficult to dislodge them without suffering a great many casualties."

Edwin relaxed slightly when he heard that response.

"So we should simply leave them in peace?" he asked. "Or are you suggesting we should put them under siege?"

"There's no point in a blockade," Hereward replied. "It would need hundreds of men to surround the place, and the Normans can't hurt us if they stay there. It would be best to leave them for the time being, I think."

Siward Barn nodded, "I agree."

"So what should our men do?" Earl Morcar asked petulantly.

Hereward replied, "The first thing they need to do is build shelters for themselves. The weather is fine just now, but winter will soon be upon us."

"But after that?" Earl Edwin persisted. "You say we must either fight or surrender. Quite frankly, I do not like either of those choices. King William will not be easily defeated."

"He might still accept our submission," Morcar suggested tentatively, voicing the thought that had clearly been in his mind all morning.

Hereward gave a derisory snort, but Barn spoke quietly yet firmly, telling the Earl, "William is unlikely to accept your submission a third time, my Lord. You know only too well what he did in the north of your own lands when the people rose against him. There was mass slaughter, and his troops destroyed every farm and village in their path. That is why I came here."

Diplomatically, Barn did not mention that the brothers were fortunate the King had accepted their submission while he and others had been forced to flee William's vengeance. Still, the unspoken words hung over the table like an accusation.

Morcar clearly felt some embarrassment, for he reacted with indignant anger, saying, "I know what happened. I was there, but we did not have the strength to oppose the King."

"That may be so, Lord," Barn agreed. "But surrendering to William again would not be wise. You would be lucky if you only lose your lands. More likely, you will lose your heads."

Morcar paled as he spluttered, "But how can we defeat his army? We still do not have the strength."

"Strength is important," Hereward put in, attempting to defuse the growing tension, "but it is not all that matters in a war."

"So you are saying we must fight even though we cannot match the King's numbers," Edwin stated, managing to retain more composure than his younger brother. "How?"

"That is what we are here to decide," Barn nodded, his eyes scanning each man in turn as if he were endeavouring to instil confidence in them. "I have disagreed with Hereward on how we should wage our war, but there is no option now. We must take the war to the Normans."

Edwin looked appalled as he asked, "Are you saying we should march on London?"

Hereward quickly put in, "No, my Lord. We would need to leave a garrison here, so we could only take around two thousand men in all. More men might join us on the way, but not enough to make a huge difference. We would stand no chance against the main Norman army. William can easily gather five thousand to face us. And, as we know only too well, in open battle, defeating their cavalry is very difficult."

"Then what can we do?" Edwin sighed. "Thane Barn says take the war to the Normans, but you agree with me that we do not have the strength for that."

"You are both correct," Hereward said with a grim smile. "But there is another way to achieve our aim. We must spread our raids further, make attacks on any Normans in the areas around the fens, and provoke the Bastard into coming here in person."

"He is in Normandy," Earl Morcar reminded them.

"Then we have more time to prepare ourselves," Hereward told him.

"So what is it you are proposing?" Edwin asked with more than a degree of trepidation.

"We have more than three thousand men now," Hereward explained. "It has always been my plan to lure the Bastard into bringing his army here so that we can destroy it piecemeal. Once he is weakened, we can strike directly at him and kill him."

"Kill him?" Earl Morcar gasped, as if the thought horrified him.

"It is the only way to deal with him," Hereward insisted.

41

"But can we succeed?" Edwin frowned.

"That is not the right question, my Lord," Hereward replied. "The question is whether we can afford not to succeed. But now, with the help of your men, we can strengthen our defences while also carrying the war to the Normans. My men and I are well used to carrying out raids. If you lend me a few score of your best warriors, I can stir up enough trouble that the Bastard will have no choice but to come here in person. When he does, we will let him squander his energy attacking our fortress island while we pick his men off. We will wear him down, destroy his morale, then strike directly at him."

"I agree," put in Siward Barn. "I see no other course of action. But there is something else we can do."

"What is that?" Edwin asked weakly, clearly feeling overwhelmed by the scale of the task facing them.

"We can send word to Edgar the Atheling. He is in Scotland. He might be able to persuade King Malcolm to send an army to aid us."

Finding some determination, Edwin shook his head vehemently.

"No," he stated firmly. "I do not trust the Scots. Malcolm is a cunning devil. He would extract a high price for any help he might give. He only shelters the Atheling because he is married to Edgar's sister. She might wish to help us, but Malcolm is as likely to claim the throne of England for himself as allow Edgar to rule. At the very least, he will seize parts of Cumbria and Northumbria."

"The more men we have, the easier our task becomes," Barn said. "If not the Scots, then who will aid us?"

The Earls looked uncomfortable because they had no real answer to the question.

Tentatively, Morcar suggested, "I suppose we could call out the *fyrd*."

"Farmers will not leave their fields at harvest time," Siward Barn objected. "And even if they boost our numbers, they will need to face trained soldiers."

"The *fyrd* might prove useful next summer, though," Hereward remarked. "But it depends on how much time the Bastard allows us."

Morcar had no response, while his brother seemed distracted, paying little attention to the discussion. Tapping a finger to his cheek, he gave a pensive frown.

Then he smiled and said, "Speaking of Edgar the Atheling has given me another idea as to how we might resolve this situation to everyone's benefit."

"That seems unlikely," Hereward muttered grimly.

Edwin gave a forced smile as he explained, "Not at all. We could copy the treaty between the Great Cnut of Denmark and Edmund Ironside."

Barn frowned, "Divide the country in two, you mean?"

Edwin continued to smile, and Edric noticed Morcar sitting alertly and nodding agreement, as were some of their Thanes.

Edwin said, "When Cnut invaded England, neither he nor Edmund Ironside, son of King Ethelred, could gain the upper hand. Rather than fight to a standstill, they agreed to divide the kingdom in two, with each appointed as successor to the other."

Barn growled, "And Edmund conveniently died soon afterwards, leaving Cnut to rule the whole of England."

"Indeed," agreed Edwin. "But the principle is sound. The land was also divided back in the days of King Alfred and the Danelaw. Why can it not be so again?"

"You want to leave the Bastard in control of the South?" Hereward rasped.

"Why not?" Edwin responded. "As I say, it has been done before. It is a sensible solution because, despite your confidence, I do not believe we can defeat him with only three thousand men at our disposal."

"We can if he comes here to fight us," Hereward argued. "We know the fens and can travel through them easily. The Norman cavalry is useless in such terrain, and their horsemen are their greatest strength. If we nullify that threat, we can beat them."

"But why fight him at all?" Edwin countered. "We could anoint Edgar the Atheling as King in the North."

Hereward frowned, "The Atheling might go along with that, I suppose, since he is little more than a boy. But the Bastard will never agree to it."

"We cannot know that until we ask," Edwin insisted.

"And who will go to ask him?" Hereward demanded. "If any of us go anywhere near him, we are likely to end up with our heads cleaved from our shoulders."

At this, Edwin gave a faint smile.

"You have a prisoner," he said. "Abbot Turold could take the message."

"I don't want to simply release him," Hereward objected.

"Why not? He cannot be used as a hostage. Would you kill a man of God if William attacks us?"

"Turold is no man of God," Hereward argued. "He was wearing armour and carrying a bloody great mace when we caught him."

Abbot Thurstan cleared his throat and ventured softly, "Nevertheless, my son, Turold has been appointed Abbot of Peterborough. It would be a sin to harm him. As a hostage, he has no value."

Morcar muttered, "No man of honour would dare harm an abbot."

Hereward ignored the barely concealed insult. Instead, he glanced at Barn, who gave a slight nod, confirming his agreement with the Abbot.

Sighing, Hereward said, "Very well, I will send him to convey your message to the Bastard. But don't expect anything to come of it."

"That is all I ask," Earl Edwin smiled.

"And in the meantime," Hereward stated, "I shall show the local Normans that we mean business."

Chapter 5

To Edric's surprise, Hereward seemed quite pleased at the prospect of getting rid of Abbot Turold.

"In truth, the man's a bloody nuisance," the rebel chief said cheerfully. "Sending him off with the Earls' message means he can be of some use, I suppose."

"But you said you didn't think the Bastard will accept the offer," Edric reminded him.

"He won't," Hereward agreed. "But this solution gets the Abbot out of our way and also keeps the Earls happy. That leaves me free to get on with causing problems for the Normans."

Winter pointed out, "If we let that fat cleric go, he'll cause us more trouble."

"Probably," Hereward conceded. "But they have plenty of others who can cause us trouble. If we keep him as our prisoner, they'll just send someone else to take his place. No, we're as well getting rid of him this way."

He grinned as he added, "But first, I'm going to take him on a tour of the island."

Edric gaped in astonishment.

"You are? Why?"

"Because I want him to see how strong this place is. Either that will scare the Bastard off or, more likely, it will mean he will bring his whole army against us."

"The more, the merrier," Winter chortled, rubbing his hands together in apparent anticipation of a fight.

Edric was not so sure.

"Why do you want him to bring his entire army? Surely we'd have a better chance of beating him if he brings fewer men."

There was a glint of steel in Hereward's eyes as he replied, "Because I want to destroy the lot of them, not just some of them. We can't afford to leave this task half done. So I want the Abbot to help us achieve that."

Having made his decision, Hereward sent a message to Siward White to bring their own men back from Aldreth and make a new camp near the centre of the island. Then he set off on a tour of the defences with Abbot Turold and the two Siwards. Winter and

Ordgar, who were accustomed to riding horses, went with them as part of the escort, leaving Edric and Wulfric to help organise the new camp.

There was a lot of grumbling from the men and women who trudged north from Aldreth. They were unhappy at being turned out of their shelters to make way for the Mercians and Northumbrians, but Edric realised the wisdom of Hereward's decision. Most of these men were not trained warriors or housecarls; they were farmers or tradesmen who had lost their homes and livelihoods or who had joined the rebellion out of simple hatred of the Norman invaders. Their commitment to the rebellion could not be questioned, but the more experienced fighting men of Mercia and Northumbria had already made some disparaging remarks about what they viewed as this barely trained rabble. By removing the volunteers from Aldreth, Hereward had managed to defuse the situation, although the extra work required by the men was not welcomed.

Edric barely knew most of these men. Their training had been left to the two Siwards, White and Red, who had not mentioned that there were a few women and even a handful of children among the volunteers. He supposed they had accompanied their husbands and fathers because they had nowhere else to go.

The volunteers themselves were a mixed bag, with ages ranging from teenage boys to middle-aged men. They carried their possessions on their backs, and were armed with an assortment of weapons ranging from swords taken from the Normans to long scythes or home-made spears. A column of wagons rumbled after them, carrying more of their belongings and a couple of injured men who had trouble walking.

"I wouldn't fancy going into battle with this lot behind us," Wulfric whispered to Edric.

"They manned the walls behind us when we were facing the Normans across the bridge," Edric reminded him. "And White says they are good enough to stand in a battle line."

"Aye, well, they probably won't need to do that if Hereward gets his way," Wulfric said. "It will be hit and run raids, ambushes and skirmishes rather than a pitched battle."

"That's for the future," Edric told him. "Right now, we need to build homes for them."

So saying, he removed his helmet, discarded his byrnie of chainmail, laid down his axe and shield, and began helping build the volunteers' new homes.

First, they marked out where the new shelters would be built. There were more than a hundred men, so they would need at least two dozen small homes.

Wulfric went with one group of men to a nearby wood where they used saws and axes to cut and trim as many stout branches as they could, while most of the women set off for the town of Ely in the wagons with the aim of bringing back bundles of dried reeds. This left Edric to help those who would do the laborious work of digging.

The men divided into small teams, most of them sticking with the comrades who had shared their bivouacs at Aldreth. Edric helped lift clods of turf from one marked area, then grabbed a wooden shovel while two of his team mates attacked the earth with picks. Then he and a third man began scooping up the broken earth and piling it around the edges of the pit they were digging.

It was hard work, but Edric's arms were accustomed to being exercised. Years of growing up in a smithy had developed his muscles, and practising his axe work with Winter had added even more strength. Still, he soon found his arms and back aching as the rectangular hole deepened, requiring ever more effort to lift the earth.

They could not dig too far into the ground because the water table was fairly high, but they had soon carved out a wide rectangular hole, with its walls standing at head height because of the piled earth from the excavation.

"Now we need to beat the earth," one of the men, a tall, fair-haired young man named Thorkel, told Edric.

Edric looked puzzled until they demonstrated what they needed to do. All of them now had shovels which they used to flatten and compress the floor and walls of the pit as well as the piled earth around it. All of them were sweating now, their faces smeared with mud and dirt, but they worked quickly and efficiently, slapping the flats of the shovels against the earth to provide a semblance of smooth firmness.

When Thorkel was satisfied, he said to Edric, "Now you and I will dig an entrance while Wulfstan and Cedric begin the roof."

So Edric helped hack out a narrow stairway of ledges in one end of the pit while Wulfstan, a squat, middle-aged and rather ugly fellow, helped the younger Cedric prepare the roof.

To do this, they used some long boughs which had been cut down by Wulfric's team of woodsmen. These poles were rammed into the earth which had been piled around the pit. They were planted at an angle, then lashed together with matching poles from the opposite side of the pit to create a series of low arches over the rectangular hole.

Once Edric and Thorkel had finished digging the entrance, their next task was to reinforce the steps with short sections of wood. This did not take long, but Edric's tasks were not finished.

"Now we need to pile the turf back against the outer walls," Thorkel informed him with a grin. "That will help hold the roof in place and prevent rain washing the earth away."

Pausing only to wipe sweat from his brow, Edric helped place the blocks of turf against the outer edge of the walls, stamping them into place with his boots. When this job was done, he took a step back and regarded their work with a sense of achievement. The bulk of the shelter was below ground level, with low walls and the frame of a roof standing at waist height above ground.

The next task was to complete the roof. The wagons had returned from town piled high with bundles of reeds. In Ely, there was no shortage of reeds which were used to roof most buildings.

"Straw is easier to use," Cedric said knowledgeably, "but reeds will do the job."

He showed his expertise in thatching as he began lashing bundles of reeds together to cover the frame. Wulfstan helped him with this, while Thorkel and Edric walked to the trees where men were still working with saws and axes.

Wulfric grinned at Edric as he reached the copse.

"You look as if you're having fun," the tall warrior smiled.

"It's a new experience," Edric admitted.

"So what do you need?"

Edric deferred to Thorkel who explained, "We need a flooring of some sort. Sometimes these huts can flood, then the floor can turn very muddy."

Wulfric gestured to the trampled earth beneath the trees.

"There are plenty of twigs and small branches which have been trimmed from the larger boughs."

"That will do," Thorkel agreed.

So he and Edric carried armfuls of wood back to the hut where they spread it on the floor of the pit. They needed to make several trips to the woodland before Thorkel was satisfied they had enough depth to the covering. But he insisted on leaving a bare patch of earth in the centre of the floor.

"We need a hearth," he told Edric.

Which meant another trip back to the woodland, but this time to find rocks and stones. Even Edric's prodigious strength was failing by the time they had completed this task.

"We must be nearly finished now," he said wearily as Thorkel arranged the stones in a circle around one large, flat stone which would form the base of the hearth.

"Nearly," Thorkel agreed. "All we need to do now is lay some animal hides down. We brought them from our last hut."

By the time they had finished this task, the afternoon was waning, but the tiny home was almost ready. Cedric and Wulfstan had completed the roof covering, weaving the reeds together to provide protection from the elements.

Thorkel said, "Later, if we can find enough wood, we might cover the walls to save them crumbling in. Sometimes we use animal hides for that, but wood is better, especially if we are to be here for some time."

He shot Edric a questioning look, but Edric could only shrug in response.

"We'll be on Ely until the Normans have been beaten," he told the young man.

"Then I suppose we'll spend a lot of time making the hut more comfortable," Thorkel commented with a shrug of his own.

Wulfstan came to join them, wiping his hands on his trousers as he said wearily, "It will do for just now. We'll sleep dry tonight. We can finish things off tomorrow."

Edric nodded, feeling a deep sense of satisfaction at what they had achieved. It had taken most of the day, but there was a small hut here where there had been none before, and similar shelters had been erected all around it, creating a small village in what had been an open meadow only a few hours earlier.

Hot and sweating, they took welcome gulps of ale from a skin Thorkel produced.

Edric, his thirst slaked, said, "I'm starving."

"Horgar will have something cooking," Wulfstan told him.

They moved to the edge of the new camp where a large, beefy man stood over a huge cauldron which was propped over a blazing fire. He was stirring the contents of the enormous pot with a long, wooden spoon and gruffly snarling at the growing crowd of men who were gathering around him, most of them having produced wooden bowls from their packs.

"I have no bowl," Edric said.

"Horgar will have a few spare," Thorkel told him.

They joined a line of hungry men and women who waited until Horgar, the cook, lifted his spoon to his lips and tasted the concoction. Then he smacked his lips, looked thoughtful for a moment, and declared, "It's ready!"

Wulfric joined Edric in the queue. They exchanged stories of their work and Edric introduced the tall warrior to his new comrades.

"This is Wulfric," he told the three volunteers. "We call him The Heron because of his long legs."

They all laughed at that, and even Wulfric smiled. He had grown up in the fens and knew the paths as well as any man. He was also well known for using a long pole to vault across smaller streams, a feat Edric had never dared attempt.

They slowly moved to the cooking fire. When it was their turn, Edric sniffed appreciatively.

"It smells good," he told the cook. "What's in it?"

"Meat," the bulky man replied.

"What kind of meat?"

"If you need to ask, you're not hungry enough," the cook told him as he sloshed a thick broth into a wooden bowl which he handed to Edric.

"It'll be good," Thorkel assured him. "Horgar knows how to cook."

"I ought to," Horgar grunted. "I was cook to Thane Bjarni for many years. Until he went off with King Harold to Hastings and the Normans came and took over his lands."

The men murmured their sympathy. Each of them had a similar tale. Thorkel, Edric had learned, was the son of a farmer.

He had been called up to the fyrd when King Harold had marched north to confront the Norwegian king, Harald Hardrada at Stamford Bridge.

"I was at that battle," Edric told him. It's where I got my leg cut by an axe for my troubles."

Thorkel nodded, "It was a good day, though. We slaughtered them, didn't we?"

"Aye, we did," Edric agreed, although the truth was that he had seen very little of the battle after being wounded. He had been fortunate to survive the day, and it had left him with a thigh which was scarred and which ached whenever he was tired. It was aching now, but he did his best to ignore the throbbing as he listened to the men's tales. They sat or stood, bowls of broth in hand, exchanging their stories.

Thorkel went on, "We were left behind when the king marched south again. He knew we wouldn't be able to keep up with his mounted housecarls. Then we heard what happened at Hastings, and I decided I would join anyone who would stand up to the Normans. That's why I'm here."

Wulfstan said, "I had a plot of land near Lincoln. My oldest boy was at Stamford Bridge. He died there. Then my youngest boy went south to Hastings. My wife died of a broken heart when he did not come back."

He gave a helpless shrug as he sighed, "I'm here because I have nowhere else to go."

Others had similar tales. Cedric had been apprenticed to a thatcher, Athelwulf had been a weaver, while Stufi and his wife Ealdgifu had been forced to leave their village when the Normans had destroyed every house, leaving them and their baby daughter homeless.

Most of the volunteers, Edric soon learned, had been farmers whose livelihoods had been taken from them as a result of the invaders' policy of inflicting total devastation in any area where anyone dared display even the slightest signs of resistance. It was that brutal reaction which had driven most of the refugees to join the rebellion.

Edric could not remember the names of all the people who spoke, but he knew he would never forget their faces nor their stories.

And each man admitted that it was Hereward's fame which had brought them here.

"Were you with him when he stormed the castle at Bourne?" Thorkel asked.

"We both were," Edric said, indicating Wulfric. "That was when I joined Hereward's gang."

"That was when I decided to come here," Thorkel told him. "When I heard someone had done something at last, I knew I had to help."

Wulfstan grumbled, "But all we've done is dig ditches, build earthworks and shout at the Normans."

"That will change soon enough," Edric said. "Now that the Earls have brought their armies, we will take the war to the enemy."

That promise raised the spirits of the weary men. Edric wondered whether he should tell them more, but was interrupted when Wulfric nudged him.

The tall warrior nodded towards someone behind Edric and said, "I wonder what he's doing here?"

Edric turned in time to see a teenage boy trying to hide himself behind a cluster of volunteers, a guilty expression clearly visible on his young face.

"It's all right, lad!" he called. "Come and have some broth."

"That's Kenton's son, isn't it?" Wulfric asked in a low voice.

"Yes. His name is Halfdan."

Everyone had turned to look at the scrawny, dark-haired boy who seemed on the verge of running away, but one of the women gently touched his arm and encouraged him towards the cooking fire.

Edric moved to intercept him and said, "Come on. Have something to eat."

Halfdan clearly felt uncomfortable, but the smell of the food was too tempting. Still, he kept his head down and his eyes lowered as he shuffled slowly over to Horgar's cauldron.

Edric said to the ruddy-faced cook, "You can spare some for the lad, can't you?"

"Of course," Horgar agreed, picking up his own wooden bowl and spooning broth into it. "Here, lad, help yourself. It's good broth. Plenty of meat."

Halfdan took the bowl and the spoon which Horgar presented to him. Then, after shooting a nervous glance at Edric, he slinked away to the edge of the crowd without a word.

"Is he some sort of half-wit?" the cook asked Edric. "He never said a word of thanks."

"I hardly know him," Edric shrugged. "He's been in the monastery for months, but he's never spoken a word to me. I'd guess his father has beaten all the gratitude out of him."

Edric had often seen Halfdan hanging around the abbey in Ely. The boy never seemed to have very much to do and wandered at will. Ylva had told him that Halfdan received frequent beatings from his father because, being skinny and lanky, he seemed to have no aptitude for the life of a warrior. Kenton, whose first son had run away years earlier, seemed to resent his younger son's apparent unwillingness to train as a warrior. He despised the boy, yet kept trying to beat him into a copy of himself. Instead, Halfdan had become withdrawn and taciturn, uncomfortable around people, and kept very much to himself. And yet, to Ylva's great disappointment, her brother remained loyal to their vicious father. Or perhaps, Edric guessed, he was too afraid to run away as Ylva had done.

He began thinking of Ylva, and Wulfric obviously had the same thought.

"What did happen to that girl we rescued?" he asked.

Edric stuck to the lie he had told so often.

"I sneaked her out of the abbey and she took a boat off the island. I have no idea where she is."

Wulfric gave him a speculative look but did not challenge him.

"That's probably just as well," he sighed. "She would have caused trouble. With Kenton and with your other girl."

"What other girl?" Edric responded with surprise.

"Don't pretend, lad!" Wulfric grinned. "That Aelswith you brought away from Bourne after we burned the castle. You go all soppy every time you see her."

Edric did not want to talk about Aelswith. Dark haired and beautiful, she had been the unattainable object of his boyhood dreams, but he knew his chances of winning her heart were remote.

He told Wulfric, "She has barely spoken to me since that day Kenton broke into her room looking for his daughter. She was terrified, and she blames me for it."

"Aye, well, she may have a point there," Wulfric told him. "But she might come round if you tried talking to her."

Edric was desperate to change the subject. He had never been good around girls, and Aelswith in particular had always made him feel clumsy and awkward whenever they had spoken. In fact, the only girl he had ever been able to talk to without feeling tongue-tied was Ylva. But, although he knew precisely where to find her, he dared not go anywhere near her for fear her father would discover her whereabouts. He had promised to keep her safe, and that promise meant she was beyond his reach.

There was, he told himself, no point in fretting about the two unattainable women in his life. It only left him feeling confused.

Fortunately, everyone was distracted by the sight of Hereward leading his small group of horsemen back to the newly-constructed camp.

"You've been busy, lads!" Hereward called to the men as he rode among them. "It looks very comfortable here. I might move in with you."

There were smiles and laughter at this, the volunteers all standing and moving closer. For each of them, Hereward was the reason they had come to Ely. His was the name the Normans feared, his was the fame which attracted those who sought a leader who could win battles.

The riders dismounted, Abbot Turold looking even more miserable than before. He stood, arms folded across his chest, glowering at the men who watched him with amused eyes.

"These are not warriors," he snorted derisively.

"No," Hereward agreed. "They are ordinary men who have decided they would rather live freely than under the yoke of Norman rule. And we are training them, Lord Abbot. They can fight as well as any of the other men you have seen today."

The abbot blew breath from his nose in another snort but made no other reply.

Hereward smiled, "Well, my Lord, it is time for us to say farewell. You have seen how well defended and provisioned we are. This island is a fortress, and I hope you will tell your king that."

"He is your king too!" Turold rasped.

Hereward shook his head.

"No, he is not."

Before Turold could argue, Hereward turned to Ordgar.

"Go and find a boatman, would you?"

As Ordgar plodded off, Hereward looked up at the sky, judging the time.

"There are still a couple of hours of daylight," he declared. "Time enough to take you out of the marshes, Lord Abbot."

Turold, whose fleshy face was flushed, shot him an angry look.

"You will abandon me in the middle of nowhere at night?"

"I'm sure God will provide for you," Hereward told him airily. "As long as you don't run into any bandits or rebels."

Everyone laughed. Everyone except Turold.

Hereward went on, "I have been told I must let you go. I was going to keep you as a hostage, but the Earls have decided you would make a better messenger than a prisoner. Still, it irks me that you will be released without ransom."

"Ransom?" the Abbot scowled.

"I am sure you are familiar with the concept," Hereward said. "It is quite common in many parts of Europe."

Turold gaped at him.

"You expect King William to pay for my release?" he spluttered.

"No," Hereward grinned. "I expect you to pay your own ransom."

"I thought Earl Edwin said I could go free," Turold argued.

"He did. But he did not say you must be whole. I think you ought to be willing to pay your ransom if you wished to leave without leaving behind a few fingers or toes."

Turold was outraged, his face turning crimson as he shouted, "I am a man of God! You would not dare!"

"Would I not?" Hereward growled menacingly, his mood suddenly aggressive. "You came here wearing armour and carrying

55

a mace, intent on killing us. For a man of God, you seem happy to commit violence. If you wish to act like a warrior, then you should suffer the same fate as a captured warrior, and the loss of a few fingers is nothing compared to what your king does to our people if he catches them."

This brought an angry murmur of agreement from the watching crowd, and Edric heard more than one person urge Hereward to cut off various parts of the Abbot's anatomy.

For a long, tense moment, the two men stared at one another, then Hereward waved his hands in a gesture of conciliation.

"But I would be happy to let you go free unharmed if you would pay your own ransom."

Surrounded by a crowd of his enemies, Turold had no option. He clearly believed Hereward's threat, and the harsh looks of the crowd told him that most of them would be happy to help carry out the maiming.

"How much?" he asked reluctantly. "I am not a wealthy man. Most of what little gold I had was stolen when you and the Danes sacked Peterborough."

Hereward nodded to acknowledge the Abbot's complaint, but he did not respond to the accusation. Instead, he tugged at the end of his long moustache while he looked the portly Abbot up and down.

After some contemplation, he said, "I was tempted to suggest that you pay your weight in silver, but I doubt there is that much coin in England."

The crowd laughed, while Turold's fleshy jowls grew red with anger once again, but Hereward held up a hand to stifle his protest at the insult.

"I think we must be sensible about this," he stated. "Swapping insults solves nothing, and I gave a promise that I would release you in exchange for a fair ransom. So, how much do you have in your purse?"

Turold shook his head in bemusement, then reluctantly tugged open his purse and tipped the contents into his palm.

"Three silver pennies," he sneered, confident that he had confirmed his claim to relative poverty.

Hereward held out his own hand as he smiled, "Then I set your ransom at three silver pennies. It is an insultingly low amount for a man of your status, but perhaps that will teach you some humility."

Turold was furious. He shoved the coins into Hereward's hand with the snarling rejoinder, "I will take that back a thousandfold, you insolent whelp. As God is my witness, I will see you hang!"

He turned his head, scanning the men and women around him as he shouted, "I will see you all hang!"

This brought another angry reaction from the crowd, but Hereward shouted at them to hold their ground.

Glaring at the abbot, he said, "Perhaps you will. But not today. Today I will see you safely escorted off the island. You might remember our clemency the next time you have one of our people in your hands. And remember also to give your king a full account of how strong we are. Give him the Earls' message, but do not forget to tell him that there are many of us who look forward to him coming here in anger. We are ready for him."

Chapter 6

By mid-December, Edric had been on so many raids he could not easily remember them all. The two Earls, reluctant to commit any further acts of overt rebellion until they had heard the King's response to their proposal to split England into two separate states, had refused to allow any of their men to join the missions. So, while the Mercians and Northumbrians remained on the isle of Ely, digging deeper ditches and reinforcing the many defensive walls, it fell to Hereward's gang, backed by a dozen of Siward Barn's veteran housecarls, to form the backbone of the raiding parties. Supported by the men of the volunteer force, they had ambushed patrols and supply columns, attacked isolated outposts and burned several farms where the owner was known to be a Norman sympathiser. They had even disembarked from their fen boats in front of the Norman stronghold on Belsar's Hill. Hereward knew they could not storm the place, but he and his men selected a spot just beyond range of the Norman bows where they sat on the grass and broke out a lunch of cold meats, cheese and bread. There, in full view of the Norman garrison, they enjoyed a leisurely feast before mockingly returning to Ely.

"They were too afraid to come out and face us," Winter had chortled.

"Then our raids are working," Hereward grinned. "If they are afraid of half a dozen of us, imagine how they will feel when they face thousands of us. A frightened army is a beaten army."

And now they were preparing another audacious attack. It would, Hereward had told them, be the final one before Christmas.

Lying huddled beneath his cloak, with fallen leaves spread across his back to conceal him, Edric was glad they would soon have some respite. The weather had already turned very cold, a few flurries of snow having briefly turned the world white before melting and transforming the paths into muddy trackways. He could feel how cold the earth beneath him was, and that icy chill was gradually seeping into his bones.

He risked turning his head to glance to left and right. The grim, set expressions on the faces of his companions told him that he was not the only one who was dreaming of sitting in front of a blazing fire and drinking a mug of ale.

"It won't be long now," Hereward said encouragingly.

They were watching the path which wound its way along the firm ground towards Belsar's Hill. This was the only route the Norman supply wagons could take if they were to keep the old Roman watchtower supplied. They had struck at this route once before, but had deliberately left it alone for several weeks. Now they intended to make the Norman garrison on the hill suffer a miserable Christmas.

The path often ran close to the fringes of the marshes and was bordered by reeds for long sections of its route. There were also patches of woodland like the one where Edric and nearly three score other rebels now huddled. The trees were bare of leaves now, offering little cover, but Hereward had hidden his men in folds in the ground further back in the copse, while those who waited near the fringes of the woodland were concealed under piles of fallen leaves.

"Keep your heads down," Hereward reminded them.

The muddy path, rutted from the passing of countless wagons over the preceding months, and dotted with icy puddles, lay barely twenty yards away, but Hereward had walked along the route and was satisfied that his men were next to invisible.

Now, at last, they heard the sound of men and horses coming from their left.

"Quiet, now!" hissed Hereward. "Lie still!"

Edric could feel his heart begin to beat more quickly. He gripped the haft of his axe in one gloved hand, and he waited for the signal.

In a low whisper, Hereward passed the word of what they faced.

"Four horsemen in front," he reported. "Then six on foot. Six wagons, each with a driver and an armed soldier, then ten more foot soldiers. Four of these are archers."

Still they waited, and now Edric could clearly hear the soft thuds of hooves as the leading horses passed by, and he was certain they would be seen. Yet the column continued its slow course, the rumble and creak of the wagons clearly audible.

He held his breath, terrified that the Normans would see the wisps of steam if he exhaled, but the convoy seemed to take forever to pass. Eventually, he was forced to let out a long, slow breath, and still the Normans continued on their way.

The shout came from Edric's right, some hundred yards distant where the road crested a low hummock.

"Loose!"

It was Siward Red and half a dozen bowmen. They had been lying behind the rise, but now they stood, arrows already nocked, and they released a volley of shafts at the leading riders. One of the horses stumbled to its knees, then collapsed on the ground, two arrows protruding from its chest. The rider leaped clear, yelling in alarm. The other arrows had either missed their targets or bounced harmlessly from the mounted men's armour, but the fallen horse had blocked the path, causing the men and wagons to come to an abrupt halt.

"Now!" Hereward roared, and Edric joined his companions as they surged to their feet, leaves cascading from their backs as they leaped up.

This was no set piece battle where the two sides would line up in their shield walls, but a furious and deadly hand to hand scrap where numbers and ferocity counted for more than discipline.

Edric had left his shield on his back, and he gripped his axe in both hands as he charged wildly at the Normans. He and the rest of Hereward's gang were at the extreme left of the English attack, their immediate opponents being the ten infantrymen who brought up the rear of the column. Four of these Normans had bows, but they had barely enough time to draw one arrow from their quivers before the rebels were on them.

Edric pounded across the wet, slippery turf, axe raised as he joined in the screaming war cry.

"Saint Etheldreda!"

They struck home at full pace, axes and swords swinging. Edric found himself facing one of the archers who dropped his bow and began to scrabble for the long knife at his hip. Edric did not give him the chance to draw the weapon. His axe crashed down with such power that it clove through the man's leather jerkin, smashed his shoulder and collar bones, and ploughed deep into his chest.

The English battleaxe was a terrible weapon to face. The Housecarls practised for hours on end, weaving their blades in constant motion, creating a barrier of death no opponent faced without trepidation. The axe blade was narrow where it joined the four foot long haft, but it flared out to sharp points, its outer edge being curved so that all the weight of a blow was concentrated on the killing end of the weapon. The curve also meant that any strike would cause huge damage if the wielder slashed it across his target. Edric did just that, but he still had to exert his full strength to yank the blade free of the dying archer's mangled body.

Whirling, he saw Hereward and Ordgar facing two of the Norman swordsmen. He rushed to help, yelling ferociously to distract the nearest Norman, then swung his axe to take the man in the back. The blow shattered links of chainmail and dug into the protective padding beneath. It may not have drawn blood, but the shock of the impact was more than enough to make the Norman stagger wildly. Hereward instantly seized the opportunity, stabbing with the tip of his sword to take the man in the throat. Blood fountained, and the Norman fell.

His companion did not outlive him very long. Edric looked up in time to see Horgar, the cook, wielding a Norman sword in one hand and an enormous cleaver in the other, overwhelm the last Norman with a series of pounding, savage blows.

It had been over in seconds, the outnumbered Normans having had very little chance to fight back, but Hereward urged his men to keep moving.

"Get the men on the wagons!" he shouted.

But English rebels were already swarming over the wagons, dragging the drivers from their seats and stabbing up at the soldiers who were supposed to be protecting them.

Edric followed Hereward as the Thane sprinted along the column and reached the fight at the head of the line.

But that fight, too, was over.

Siward White was there, grinning hugely. He and Siward Barn's housecarls had made short work of the foot soldiers who had been trudging at the head of the Norman column.

"Three of the horsemen tried to get away," White informed Hereward. "Red and his archers got one of them, but the other two escaped."

"It won't take them long to reach Belsar's Hill," Hereward frowned. "So let's get these wagons unloaded and carry as much as we can back to our boats."

The rebels needed no encouragement to plunder the carts. They gleefully carried away sacks of grain, joints of smoked meat, cheeses and vegetables.

"Merry Christmas!" Winter shouted cheerfully as he lifted a keg of wine.

All of them were in good spirits. They had lost only one man killed and, while several others had been wounded, none of the injuries were serious. Only two of the Normans had escaped, and the six wagon drivers, Englishmen who had been forced into service, were released unharmed. The raid had been as successful as it had been brief. In little more than three minutes, the defenders had been completely overwhelmed, and now the produce they had been taking to the Norman garrison would instead help swell the already well-provisioned larders on the Isle of Ely.

"Time to go, lads!" Hereward shouted.

And with that, the rebels vanished back into the fens.

Once back in their dormitory within the abbey precinct, the gang were able to relax. They stripped out of their armour and spent some time mending broken links or sharpening their axes, while they waited for a large pot of water to warm on the small hearth fire. Mugs of ale were passed around, and they began to laugh and joke as they looked forward to the quieter months of winter.

"The Bastard won't come now," Ordgar grinned as he slurped at his ale. "He'll wait until springtime."

"He campaigned during the winter when he was harrying the North," Wulfric pointed out.

"Then we'd better enjoy our Christmas feast," Winter declared happily.

Edric changed into fresh trousers and tunic, throwing his sweat and battle-stained clothing into a bucket which the washerwomen would collect. He had washed himself in the warm water and felt cleaner than he had done for weeks.

As he made for the door, Winter called, "Going anywhere special, lad?"

"Just out," Edric mumbled in reply.

"He's going to see his girl," Ordgar suggested.

Edric hurried out of the room, slamming the door behind him to drown out their laughter. Winter and Ordgar, he knew, would soon be visiting the taverns in the town to find some whores, but that was a risk he had still not plucked up the courage to face. As a boy, he had heard too many sermons on the evils of sin, together with warnings of the effects such sin could have on his body.

He went out into the chill of the courtyard and headed across to the guest buildings where the nobler visitors to the abbey were given lodgings. He had barely walked half way when he stopped as someone emerged from the door of the long building.

"Edric!"

It was Torfrida, Hereward's wife. Her smile lit up her perfect features when she saw him.

She was wearing a thick, long cloak against the cold, and her lustrous, raven-dark hair was partially covered by a small cloth cap in deference to the customs of the abbey. Behind her, always a step or two back, was her maid, Alice.

"Good day, Lady," Edric said, his own smile matching hers. "Good day, Alice."

Alice flashed the briefest of smiles and bobbed her head, but she did not return his greeting. She was a quiet young girl who had followed Torfrida to England when Hereward had decided he must leave Flanders and return to his homeland. The maid seemed permanently nervous and shy, and she spoke little English despite having been in the country for several months.

Torfrida, on the other hand, spoke perfect English with an accent which Edric found tantalisingly attractive. Like all the members of the gang, he was devoted to her. She may have been born a noblewoman, but she had a heart full of compassion for others no matter their status.

"I'm glad I met you," she said, moving close to clasp his hands in welcome.

Leaning towards him and lowering her voice, she added, "I was at the market yesterday."

Her words filled Edric with anticipation, and he looked at her expectantly.

"I saw your old friend, Seaver," she went on.

"Is he well?" Edric asked, knowing there was more to come, but doing his best not to appear too eager.

Seaver had lived his whole life in Bourne, but he had joined the exodus after the sacking of the castle. No lover of the Normans, he was too old to fight, but he had insisted he would prefer to live freely among his native English rather than submit to the Normans. Several other villagers had followed his example, and Torfrida had made a point of helping them find lodgings in Ely. Seaver now lived with a potter named Cecil who had a large house to accommodate his young family.

"Seaver is very well," Torfrida confirmed. "And so is his granddaughter."

Edric could not help turning his head to check to see whether anyone was close enough to overhear them, but the courtyard was deserted.

"Jetta?" he asked.

"She has been asking for you," Torfrida confided. "I think she would like to see you."

"It is too dangerous," he replied.

"That is what I told Seaver. But she wanted you to know she is happy living with Cecil and Garyn."

Garyn, Edric knew, was Cecil the potter's wife. The couple had several young children, so Jetta would be kept very busy helping care for them.

Thinking of her roused an odd reaction in Edric, a yearning he had always tried to ignore. He barely knew Jetta, yet their brief time together had been strangely different to his few other encounters with young women. Jetta, he had discovered, was very easy to talk to.

But he could not see her again. It would be too dangerous for her.

Because Jetta's real name was Ylva, and she was the daughter Kenton was searching for. Edric had spirited her away one night because he had known he could not protect her from her abusive father if she remained in the abbey. He had told everyone Ylva had left the island; everyone except Torfrida. She had been the one person he could trust to convey messages because she often visited the town and made a point of checking on the villagers from Bourne. Meeting Seaver was therefore perfectly normal for her, and those meetings allowed her to pass messages between Edric and Ylva.

This arrangement had been going on for several months now, but still Edric feared revealing the secret to anyone else.

"I'll let you know the next time I am going to market," Torfrida told him. "If you have any messages for Seaver, let me know."

"I will, Lady," Edric promised.

"And now," she said with a bright smile, "I think you should speak to Aelswith. She has some good news."

"I was on my way to see her," Edric replied, feeling suddenly guilty that he had been thinking of Ylva when Aelswith was so close at hand.

Morosely, he added, "If she will speak to me at all."

"I am sure she will," Torfrida told him. "Now, I have an urgent errand of my own, so I will see you later."

So saying, she hurried off towards the abbey's main cluster of buildings with her maid, Alice, trailing dutifully behind her.

Edric turned back towards the guest lodgings only to find another person coming out of the door.

He froze, unable to move as the bulky figure of Kenton stepped out into the daylight. The housecarl was dressed, as usual, in his chainmail armour, although his only weapon was a long knife sheathed at his waist. He, too, stopped, his hard eyes staring at Edric.

Kenton's mouth twitched, making the scar on his cheek move in a fascinatingly hypnotic way.

"Out of my way, boy," he growled menacingly.

Edric stepped aside. There was plenty of room for Kenton to have walked past him, but Hereward had repeatedly told him not to give Kenton any excuse to cause trouble. Kenton might have been assigned to be Lady Altruda's bodyguard, but he was nominally one of Siward Barn's men, and Hereward wanted no fighting between the various groups who defended the island.

So Edric meekly stepped aside, allowing Kenton to swagger past him.

But the big housecarl stopped directly in front of Edric, turning to shove his face forwards until their noses were almost touching.

"Where's my daughter?" Kenton hissed.

"Gone," Edric replied, forcing himself to meet the man's belligerent stare. "She asked me to help her leave the island, so I did. I have no idea where she is now."

Kenton's breath stank, but Edric refused to back away from the man.

They stood face to face for a long, silent moment, then Kenton snarled, "One day, boy, I will rip your guts out. I don't know why the Lady wants you unharmed, but my patience is running short. We will have a reckoning. Do you understand?"

Edric's only response was to give a very slight and slow nod.

Kenton hawked, twisted his head, then spat on the ground. Then, without another word, he stalked off, leaving Edric to let out a long breath of relief.

It took him several moments to gather his composure. He was an experienced warrior now, but men like Kenton were utter brutes in a fight, and Edric had few illusions about who would win if they ever did face one another.

He watched the lumbering figure of Kenton disappear behind the abbey building, then he pulled open the door and stepped into the long corridor of the guest lodgings.

Auti was there, standing guard outside Hereward's room. There were eight rooms in total, four on either side. Edric knew that the two Earls, Edwin and Morcar, each had a room, as did the Lady Altruda. Hereward and Torfrida had the second room on the right, but the first door was where Aelswith had been permitted to stay.

Aelswith.

Even the thought of her set his heart racing. She was as beautiful as Torfrida, sharing the Lady's dark looks, but had a slimmer figure and was slightly taller. If she had not been born a peasant, she could have been a Lady herself. Indeed, she might have reached that exalted status if the Normans had not arrived, because Thane Toki had taken her to his bed and it was his daughter she had borne after she had fled to Ely.

Edric had always been too tongue-tied to have a proper conversation with Aelswith until they had both ended up in the abbey. Then, at last, she had seemed friendly towards him, and his hopes had begun to rise again. Until he had tried to help Ylva escape from Kenton's clutches. The housecarl had forced his way into Aelswith's room in search of his daughter, and Aelswith had still not forgiven Edric for that.

But Torfrida had said she had good news, so he knocked on the door and waited, uncertain of what welcome he would receive.

Aelswith opened the door herself, regarding him with large, expressive eyes which told him that, although she seemed rather stiff and formal, she was at least not going to send him away.

"Come in, Edric," she invited.

Edric stepped into the small chamber and was surprised to discover Aelswith already had a visitor. Brother John sat on a chair, holding baby Torfrida on his knees while he bounced her up and down, much to the child's delight.

"Hello, Edric," the monk smiled. "I'm glad you are here. We have some good news."

"Yes," Edric replied uncertainly. "I met Lady Torfrida. She told me you had something to celebrate."

If Brother John detected Edric's wariness, he gave no indication. He continued to pull faces for the baby's amusement, setting the child giggling happily.

Aelswith, who had retreated to the far side of the room, turned to face him. Folding her arms across her chest, she said, "The Abbot has agreed Torfrida may be baptised."

It took Edric a moment to realise she was speaking of her baby daughter rather than Lady Torfrida, but he managed a genuine smile as he said, "That certainly is good news. What changed his mind?"

"Brother John and the Lady Torfrida," Aelswith informed him.

Brother John gave Edric a bashful look.

"It was mostly the Lady's doing," he admitted.

Aelswith scolded, "Do not diminish your own role, John. I think you could persuade anyone to do whatever you want."

"Aye, that's true enough," Edric murmured. "But I'm surprised the Abbot agreed to baptise her when Hereward ..."

His voice trailed off. He could not find the right words to say without offending Aelswith. Hereward had never been convinced that Aelswith's child had been Toki's, and the fact the couple had not married had provided him with an excuse to deny Aelswith's claims of kinship.

Brother John filled the awkward silence by explaining, "Ah, to tell the truth, the agreement was on the condition Hereward would not object. But the Lady Torfrida tells us she has persuaded him to give his blessing."

Edric said nothing, but he tried to imagine how that conversation had turned out. He supposed Hereward had given in because Torfrida had gone along with his own plans for so long. She had given up her entire life to supporting Hereward's decisions, so perhaps she had claimed some concession from him.

Brother John went on, "And I will be the one who carries out the ceremony."

"It does not matter who performs the baptism," Aelswith put in a little too hurriedly.

Edric could see there were still some tensions over the baptism. If Hereward had formally acknowledged baby Torfrida as his niece, it would have been normal for the baptismal ceremony to be performed by a leading man of the Church such as Abbot Thurstan. So Hereward had perhaps imposed a condition of his own. Not that it mattered, really. What was important was that the child would be welcomed into the Church and so would be able to gain the Kingdom of Heaven in the afterlife instead of being condemned to eternal Purgatory if she remained unbaptised.

Edric had often had misgivings about this particular aspect of Church doctrine. A newborn child could, he had once argued with Brother John, not have committed any sins and so was being punished for the sins of her parents if she was not baptised. It seemed to Edric that a caring God would not punish an innocent for other people's immoralities, but Brother John had assured him that it was a far more complicated matter than that due to something called Original Sin. Edric did not begin to claim he understood this, but he was nevertheless pleased that baby Torfrida's future was secured.

"The baptism will take place on Sunday," Aelswith informed him. "I do hope you will come."

"Of course I will," Edric promised.

As it turned out, the whole of Hereward's gang came to the brief ceremony. In between sessions of formal prayers by the monks, Brother John conducted the baptism in the presence of Hereward, Torfrida and a small group of their closest companions.

Torfrida's maid, Alice, was there of course, as was Hereward's manservant Martin Lightfoot, and so was the Dane, Ranald Sigtrygsson, who appeared almost fully recovered from the wound that had almost ended his life. Edric stood with Winter, Ordgar, Auti and Wulfric who all wore clean shirts and had their moustaches neatly trimmed and the tangles combed out of their long hair. Together, they witnessed the young child being admitted to the Holy Church. Brother John sprinkled holy water on her head, resulting in the baby wailing in protest, but Brother John concluded the proceedings quickly so that he could pass the baby back to Aelswith for comforting.

Edric and the gang had each contributed some pennies which Edric handed to Aelswith once the formal ceremony was over.

"A small gift for her," he explained.

Aelswith, dressed in a fine robe of dark blue, and with her hair neatly pinned up on her head, thanked him, and he wondered whether he should pluck up the courage to kiss her on the cheek, but the moment passed as Aelswith moved on to let others congratulate her.

Hereward, meanwhile, stood aside with Martin at his shoulder, saying not a word to anyone.

Torfrida, resplendent in a long dress of red satin with frills of white at collar and wrists, pretended not to notice her husband's disapproval. Instead, she gushed over the baby, then gave the men some coins and ordered them to go and celebrate.

The gang were only too pleased to oblige, retiring to one of the town's less reputable taverns where they consumed far too much ale, and where Winter disappeared into the back room with one of the tavern's serving girls.

He returned with a satisfied smile on his craggy face.

"You ought to try it," he told Edric.

"Maybe later," Edric mumbled in response, much to the amusement of his comrades.

"He's saving himself for Aelswith," Ordgar chuckled.

"Aye, well, he could do a lot worse," Winter agreed with a smile. "She's a fine looking woman."

"Maybe you should get her drunk," Wulfric suggested to Edric.

"Christmas is the time for that," Winter nodded. "There's always plenty babies born nine months after the Christmas feast."

"Is that how you always get your women?" Edric shot back. "Get them drunk or pay for them?"

"It works for me," Winter grinned.

"Not for me," Edric insisted.

"You, lad," Winter told him, "are too saintly for your own good. As for me, I'm looking forward to Christmas. Plenty of ale, too much food and a plump young woman to entertain me. That's all I need."

Ordgar laughed, "Simple needs for a simple man!"

Which resulted in the two big men exchanging playful punches, and the tavern keeper yelling at them to behave unless they wanted him to set his dogs on them.

Christmas arrived with cold rain and strong winds, but the monks did not allow the weather to disrupt their celebrations. They paraded through the town, a large, golden cross being carried at the head of the procession while the monks distributed alms and food to the citizens before returning to the abbey for long sessions of prayer and song.

The warriors kept out of the way of these formal celebrations, although many of them did attend Church services on a daily basis to listen to the Abbot or some other senior monk preach a sermon.

Then, on Twelfth Night, a great feast was held in the refectory. Preparations had been going on for several days, and the cooks had done the monks and warriors proud. The benches were crammed, men of the Church mingled with men of the axe and sword, everyone determined to enjoy the fruits of the year's harvest. Platters were piled high with roast goose, baked eels, assorted fish and fowl, eggs, cheeses and a host of herbs and vegetables. All of this was accompanied by great quantities of ale, and followed by honeyed pastries and flour dumplings.

Edric found himself sitting beside Brother John who had, as usual, attached himself to Hereward's gang. The monk was in fine form, laughing and joking, happy to tell tales of his peripatetic adventures around England in the days before the Normans had come.

Unusually, because Christmas was a special celebration, the women had been allowed to sit in the refectory during the meal, although they would not remain throughout the evening in case things became too wild. But Torfrida sat beside Hereward, looking as radiant as ever, and Aelswith, holding baby Torfrida, was a few seats away at the end of the top table. Edric tried to catch her eye on more than one occasion, but she always seemed preoccupied.

Altruda was also there, sitting beside Earl Morcar and looking as gorgeous as an angel.

"I notice the Abbot has kept her away from Hereward," Edric mentioned.

Brother John laughed, "Haven't you heard?"

"Heard what?"

Brother John, who had perhaps drunk rather more than he was normally accustomed to, said, "The Lady ... and I use the term loosely, you understand, is sitting beside Earl Morcar because she is sharing his bed these days."

Edric gaped at the monk.

"She is?"

"She has been for the past few weeks, my friend. Of course, you have been out and about, terrifying Normans with your axe, but the Lady has clearly seen where her best opportunity to gain riches lies."

Edric scowled, "She slept with King Sweyn too, and he abandoned us. Hereward believes she is the one who persuaded him to go back to Denmark."

Brother John blinked owlishly at him.

"So you think she might be planning something similar?" he frowned.

Then he shook his head.

"No, that can't be it. If she wanted the Earls to leave, she'd have chosen Edwin. He has far more warriors here, and he is the older brother. He's the one who makes the decisions. No, I think she is seeking an influential marriage."

Edric was not convinced, but he had no argument against Brother John's assertion. Yet Altruda worried him. He had been a witness when she had attempted to persuade Hereward to surrender to King William, and Hereward had warned him often enough that the woman had a devious nature.

Brother John had already dismissed Altruda from his thoughts. Instead, he began asking questions on a subject Edric would have preferred to avoid.

"Aelswith tells me you rescued a damsel in distress," the monk probed. "It all sounds very mysterious. What happened to her?"

"She left Ely," Edric replied, maintaining his usual response.

"And her father? Has he caused any more trouble for you?"

"Not really," Edric shrugged, desperate to change the subject.

"From what Aelswith tells me, the girl is something of a sharp-tongued termagant," the monk revealed. "Perhaps it is as well she has departed."

Edric felt a surge of anger. He had hoped everyone would have forgotten about Ylva, yet not only was Kenton still brooding over her disappearance, now Aelswith had been talking about her to Brother John. Not only that, the way Aelswith had described Ylva did not match Edric's experience.

He snapped, "She was a young girl in danger. She was frightened and needed to escape from her father. I helped her. That's all there was to it."

Brother John gave him a keen look. He seemed on the point of saying more, but Edric interrupted, "Why don't you tell us all about the wonderful things you've seen in London? That's a more pleasant subject."

Brother John obliged, but Edric was still angry by the time he helped Winter carry Wulfric back to their dormitory, the three of them stumbling and staggering across the darkened courtyard.

"Merry Christmas!" Edric thought sourly when he eventually lay down on his own cot and tried to get to sleep. His discussions with Torfrida and Brother John had awakened desires he had been trying to suppress, and memories of Ylva haunted his dreams and his thoughts for the next few days. Eventually, he decided there was only one way to lance the simmering obsession. He would take a risk and visit the market. He might even return to Cecil's home when the day was done. After all, Seaver was a friend, and what harm could come of visiting an old friend?

He remained cautious, taking time to ascertain Kenton's whereabouts before he left for town. The scar-faced housecarl was, he discovered, with the Lady Altruda. Taking his chance, Edric hurriedly left the abbey precinct and walked into town.

It was another cold, blustery day, the road dotted with puddles and patches of mud, but Edric still felt conflicted as he strode to the marketplace at the centre of the town. He had sworn not to endanger Ylva, but how dangerous could it be to visit Seaver? Surely nobody would pay any attention to that?

He pulled his cloak tighter as he walked, the biting wind a chill reminder that it was barely past midwinter. Yet the market, the first after the Christmas holidays, was its usual thriving bustle of activity as the people of town and country brought their goods to barter.

Easing his way through the throng, he stopped at the tiny stall where Cecil was haranguing passers-by to purchase some of his fine pots.

As usual, Seaver was there as well. The old man welcomed Edric with a broad smile.

"It's good to see you, lad. How are you?"

"I am well, thank you," Edric assured him. "What about you? How are you faring?"

"Very well," Seaver smiled. "My arm is quite healed."

He pulled up one sleeve to show the clear, fresh skin of an arm which had once been thrust into a cauldron of boiling water in a trial by ordeal. Seaver had been accused of stealing joints of meat from his neighbour, an elderly, vindictive woman named Gytha. Edric was certain the accusation had been false, but Norman law required a judgement from God when there were no actual witnesses to the crime, so Seaver had undergone the cruel test under which his guilt would have been determined by how well the dreadful injuries healed. It seemed a bizarre belief, because Edric had heard priests and monks declare often enough that God's actions could never be predicted, but the Normans were fond of such trials. Fortunately for Seaver, Hereward had arrived in Bourne shortly before his bandages had been due to be unwrapped and his guilt or innocence determined. Seaver had been only too pleased to join the exodus to Ely, and Brother John had spun the abbey's physician a fanciful tale about how the wound had occurred, so healing salves had helped repair the damage to the old man's hand and arm.

"And Cecil is teaching me how to make pots," the old man went on, his delight evident.

"That is a useful skill to have," Edric nodded.

"So what brings you here?" Seaver asked knowingly. "Jetta has been asking for you, you know."

"Actually, I was thinking I might come back with you and see her for a while," Edric mumbled, his cheeks flushing as he made the admission.

Seaver gave him a wink as he laughed, "If you like. We'll be here a while yet, mind. But I'm sure the lass will be glad to see you."

Edric glanced up at the azure sky. The market would continue until dusk drew near, so he would either need to wait for a few more hours or make his own way to Cecil's home. After some thought, he decided he would prefer to speak to Ylva without Seaver looking over his shoulder, but caution reminded him to make a show of wandering around the marketplace and pretending to be interested in other stalls. Simply striding away and heading for Cecil's house might be noticed. Ely was a much larger place than his home village of Bourne, but tongues could still wag.

He wandered away from the potter's stand and spent some time idling his way between other stalls, surveying the various goods on sale but making no purchases. Slowly, he eased his way to the far side of the market square. As he drew near to the narrow road which would lead to the southern part of the town, he stopped and took another cautious look around.

To his horror, he caught sight of a young face peering at him from between two market stalls. For an instant, their eyes met, and Edric knew he had made a mistake by coming here. Before he could react, the boy slipped away, vanishing into the crowded market.

But that short glimpse had been enough to send a chill down Edric's spine. He immediately abandoned all thought of visiting Ylva because he had recognised the boy's face. He had seen him hanging around the abbey on so many occasions, and he had even turned up on the day they had built the new huts for the volunteers.

It was Kenton's son, Halfdan, and now Edric understood why the boy had been at their camp that day. He had been following Edric in the hope that he would lead him to Ylva.

Chapter 7

"He went to the market, you say?" Altruda asked.

Halfdan gave a curt nod.

"Yes, my Lady. He wandered around a bit. He stopped at a cobbler's stall to look at some boots, and at a potter's table, and then spent a long time rummaging through a tinker's goods."

The boy gave his report in a dull monotone, his eyes lowered and his face never showing any emotion. He was, Altruda thought, an odd child. He was clearly afraid of her, and terrified of his father, yet he attempted to conceal those raw emotions beneath a mask of blankness which made him appear remarkably slow and dull-witted.

Altruda disliked children of any sort, and she especially disliked Halfdan, but the boy was at least following her orders. Edric had been away from the monastery a great deal, but whenever he returned to the town, Halfdan would follow him. He had tracked the young warrior for months, dogging his footsteps and watching him wherever he went. Yet his reports were always the same, never providing any insight into a hidden secret she might exploit to allow her to turn Edric away from his devotion to Hereward. Even his latest foray into the marketplace, while it had been unusual, had yielded nothing of interest.

That was frustrating, and she had toyed with the idea of allowing Kenton to use his own methods on Edric, but she was not yet ready to initiate a direct confrontation with Hereward. She much preferred more subtle methods of attaining her goals.

Besides, she told herself, Edric Strong was the least of her problems.

"You may go," she told Halfdan, waving a delicate hand to usher the boy from the room.

Kenton closed the door behind his son, then turned to regard Altruda with flinty eyes.

"That's a waste of time," he growled. "Edric Strong isn't stupid enough to lead us to my girl."

"Be patient," Altruda told him. "We have more important things to discuss."

"Like what?" the housecarl snorted. "Have the Earls received an answer from the King, then?"

"The King will never agree to divide the kingdom," Altruda said dismissively.

"Why not?" the housecarl challenged. "It's been done before. The north is almost a different country from the south."

"You underestimate King William's passion for control," she told him.

"Edgar the Atheling has a better claim to the kingship," Kenton argued belligerently.

"Edgar the Atheling is a boy," she snapped. "He may have a claim through blood, but he has spent most of his life in Hungary. He knows very little about England or its people."

Kenton clearly had only the vaguest idea where Hungary was, but his own upbringing compelled him to mutter, "He's still of the English royal line."

"Power is more important than blood," Altruda stated firmly. "Would you prefer to back a teenage youth who has only those two earls as his major supporters, or a man who can command the finest army in Europe? William has drive, determination, and the wealth of England behind him."

Kenton gave a grudging nod.

"So you still think the Bastard will come here?"

Altruda frowned at the coarse nickname, but confirmed, "He will come. It is only a matter of time. So we must use that time wisely."

"What are you planning?" Kenton asked. "Are you going to shag Earl Morcar until he agrees to surrender to William?"

"Don't be so crude!" she ordered with a sharp rebuke.

Kenton shrugged her anger aside as he went on, "If you ask me, I think you are sleeping with the wrong Earl. Morcar only ever does as Edwin tells him."

Altruda shot him a cold look as she replied sharply, "Then I am glad I did not ask for your opinion. I know Edwin, and I also know he once harboured hopes of marrying one of King William's daughters. If I judge him correctly, he retains that ambition. He probably thinks it would help seal this ridiculous deal he has suggested, so I doubt he will risk an affair."

She paused, allowing the moment to stretch, before adding with a sly smile, "His brother, on the other hand, is a weak-minded dupe."

"So you'll keep …" Kenton leered as he made a coarse gesture with his fingers.

Altruda scowled at him, but gave a brief nod as she confirmed, "I do whatever I must in order to influence him. I am sure I can use him to get to Edwin."

Kenton smirked, clearly imagining how she was going about the task, but Altruda told him, "I have another job for you, though."

"What is it?" he grunted.

"It requires discretion and secrecy," she explained. "I need you to identify two or three men within Earl Edwin's guard who can be bought. Men like yourself, Kenton, whose loyalty is to their own skins and who will be happy to betray their Lord for the right price."

As she had expected, the thinly veiled insult made no impression on the scar-faced housecarl.

"What price?" he asked.

"Gold, of course. And exemption from whatever punishment King William metes out to the rest of the traitors here. But be subtle, Kenton. This plan will take weeks, perhaps months, to come to fruition. Do not charge in and offer bribes immediately. Ingratiate yourself with the men of Earl Edwin's guard. Buy them ale, play dice with them. Tell jokes of the crude and disgusting sort you prefer. Gain their confidence and get to know them until you are able to pick out one or two who might be willing to consider taking payment for turning against their Lord."

"I can do that," Kenton agreed. "If you have the gold to pay for it."

"Leave that to me," she said dismissively.

Kenton gave a surly nod, but she guessed from the look in his eyes that he might be having second thoughts about whether he had chosen the right side. Was he considering denouncing her to Hereward? She would not put it past him, especially if he discovered where she kept her secret hoard of gold and silver.

Understanding how Kenton's mind worked, she reminded him of where his best chances for survival lay.

"Remember, Kenton, King William will come here sooner or later. When he does, he will bring an army which will be large enough to crush this rebellion. He will take his revenge, and only those who have served him will remain unpunished. So, when that day comes, I will want to put my plan into action to ensure he knows we have been loyal to him."

The greed faded from Kenton's expression as he grumbled, "Aren't you going to tell me what you intend to do?"

"Certainly not!" she snapped. "You have your instructions. Carry them out. I will tell you more once the King makes his move. But we are playing a long game now, so be sure to take your time. We must be discreet. But we must also prepare. Then, when the time comes, we will help ensure the King's victory."

Altruda was correct in her assessment regarding the time she had, because the long, dark months of winter were fading by the time King William eventually returned to England.

As was his habit, William spent Easter at Winchester, the ancient capital of Wessex, where he paraded in full royal regalia in front of his nobles and courtiers, impressing upon them the majesty of his rank and the authority of his position over them.

Ivo de Taillebois stood among the spectators, bowing his head at the appropriate times, and falling to one knee when the King deigned to address him.

"Come forward, de Taillebois," William ordered. "You, too, Abbot Turold."

The two men edged out of the crowd to stand before their King, bowing their heads in fearful respect. They had already experienced his wrathful tongue when he had first returned from Normandy and demanded to see them in private in order to hear their excuses for the failure of their attempt to put down the rebellion in Ely.

The King had been furious, raging at them several times, both individually and together, and he had seen through their attempts to pin the blame on each other.

"Abbot Turold led the attack," de Taillebois had wheedled. "He was too impetuous."

Turold had countered, "De Taillebois was supposed to be supervising the bridge construction. He allowed saboteurs to weaken it. Then he ordered too many men onto the bridge at one time."

"Only because you commanded it!" de Taillebois had protested.

79

William had cut short the argument with a savage chopping motion of his hand, had blistered them with his harsh words, then demanded to know why Abbot Turold had been let free. When he heard the message the Abbot had brought from Earl Edwin, he had barked a humourless laugh.

"The man must be mad," he snorted. "Speak no more of that, Lord Abbot. I will not hear it."

After that bruising meeting, the king had spent several days ignoring the two men while he settled other affairs. Now, having summoned all the principal nobles of England to join him at Winchester, he had hauled them out in front of their peers, and both men feared the worst.

William's rage, however, had now transformed from red fury to an icy chill.

"I had hoped to return to England to find the country pacified," he announced in a coldly deliberate manner. "But it seems my trust in you was misplaced."

Turold and de Taillebois had enough sense to make no response. Attempting to defend themselves now would only increase William's ire.

The King went on, "It seems I must attend to this revolt in person. Has the Lady Altruda been in contact with you recently?"

Turold cleared his throat and reported, "Yes, Your Majesty. She assures us that she is ready to assist you in any way she can. She is hopeful of dealing with the Earls Edwin and Morcar."

"Those two!" William spat. "I was too lenient with them last time they caused trouble. This time, I will make them wish they had never dared oppose me."

"Of course, Your Majesty," de Taillebois murmured obsequiously. "They are traitors who deserve death."

"And what of this other man?" the King demanded. "The one called Hereward?"

"He is a landless nonentity," Abbot Turold spat. "The Lady Altruda told me he is the son of a former Thane and once held lands around Peterborough, but he was exiled by your esteemed predecessor, King Edward. Now he is nothing more than a rebellious peasant."

"Then he will hang when we catch him," William said absently.

De Taillebois plucked up the courage to say, "He may be a man of little status, Your Majesty, but he is a fearsome warrior. The rebels look to him for leadership."

He lowered his voice as he added warily, "And some say he is protected by magic. It is said his wife is a witch."

William glared at De Taillebois for a moment, then made the sign of the cross as he stated, "Dark magic will not protect him from my justice. I am protected by God. He granted me this land, and I will not have any of it taken from me!"

"Of course, Your Majesty," De Taillebois grovelled.

William, clearly irritated by the interruption, took a moment to regain his composure before returning his attention to Turold.

"Send word to Lady Altruda that I wish her to do everything in her power to weaken the rebels. I want them divided and arguing amongst one another. Tell her also, that I will be bringing the full power of my force to bear on Ely. I want no mistakes this time. By summer's end, this rebellion must be utterly quashed."

"As you command, your Majesty," Turold nodded.

"As for you two," William went on, "I will give you a chance to redeem yourselves."

Both men stood more upright when they heard this. William was not overly given to allowing second chances.

De Taillebois said, "Thank you, Your Majesty. We ask nothing more."

William's mouth twitched in a faint smile as he told them, "I want you to take what is left of the army I gave you. Return to the same point opposite the island. I want you to build boats, siege engines and high watchtowers."

Turold asked, "You wish us to cross the river in boats this time, your Majesty?"

"No," William stated with a bark of cruel laughter. "I want you to give the rebels the impression that you are going to cross the river in boats. Keep busy, and keep them watching you. Bombard them with rocks and send archers up a watchtower to rain arrows on them. Make them think you are going to attack them."

"We will be a diversion, Majesty?"

81

William smiled a thin smile as he nodded, "That is correct. I am also going to send a fleet to watch the seaward approaches and prevent any vessels entering or leaving. We shall slowly squeeze the life out of them."

Turold ventured to ask, "You expect a long siege, Your Majesty?"

"It may take a few weeks," William admitted. "But I will succeed. I will lead the main force myself, and I will seize the island while they are busy watching you."

Turold was about to protest the difficulty of the task, but a dark scowl from the king silenced his words.

With a satisfied nod, William gestured to another of the watching nobles.

"Malet," he commanded, "you will assist me."

"It will be an honour to serve you in this, Your Majesty," the dark-haired swordmaster said as he bowed his head to his monarch.

"Then we shall make for Ely as soon as the Easter celebrations are over," the king declared. "This rebellion will be crushed once and for all."

Unable to hold his tongue, Turold asked, "But, Your Majesty, how can you take an army through the Fens? Aldreth is the only place where the island can be approached by a force of any size, and even that is a difficult march. It is impossible to reach the island from any other direction."

"Impossible?" William said in mock astonishment. "Nothing is impossible, Lord Abbot. I have been anointed King with God's blessing. The land of England belongs to me, and I will not tolerate any dissension. I will capture Ely and deal with the rebels in such a way that none will dare rise up ever again!"

The hall fell silent apart from the fading echoes of the King's raised voice, which had been so savage that it cowed the assembled nobles with the power of its assertion. Even Malet, who was said to fear no man, appeared stunned by the ferocity in William's words.

The King turned his baleful stare on Abbot Turold once again, his voice subsiding to an icy calm as he explained, "There is only one way to ensure our army reaches Ely. If there is no road, we shall build one."

"A road?" Turold gasped.

"A causeway," the king confirmed. "We will tame these marshes and we will march our men directly to the isle. This time, they will not stop us."

Word of William's plans reached Altruda by way of a letter from Abbot Turold. Brother Richard delivered the sealed message to her with great solemnity when he returned from another of his journeys to Peterborough. She accepted it with a feeling of anticipation, for the Abbot had never formally replied to any of her previous messages. Cautiously, she examined the seal, checking that it was unbroken. She doubted whether Brother Richard had the nerve to read any of her letters, but it was nonetheless satisfying to see that he had left the Abbot's missive unread.

"Do you know its content?" she asked the serious young monk.

He shook his head.

"No, my Lady. But the Abbot impressed upon me that its content was important and of the utmost secrecy."

Altruda nodded. Brother Richard must be a complete fool if he had not yet realised the true purpose of the letters he had been carrying to Peterborough for her. The excuse that she was merely petitioning the King to free her from his injunction that she should marry some old goat of a Norman Baron could no longer be maintained. Brother Richard must know she was passing information to the Abbot, yet he continued to undertake the long journey to Peterborough every few weeks and had never questioned her about the content of her letters.

Still, she had taken the precaution of writing in Greek in case the letter should fall into the wrong hands, and Turold had replied in the same archaic language. She guessed Brother Richard, being a studious man of learning, could probably read Greek, but she did not feel overly concerned. If curiosity had overcome him and he had read any of her letters, he could hardly denounce her since he had been complicit in her espionage for over a year.

She took her time as she read the letter, then read it again, committing its short message to memory. Then she looked up at Brother Richard and smiled.

"It contains good news, my Lady?" he enquired, masking the curiosity she knew he must feel.

"Oh, yes, Brother Richard. Good news indeed. For those of us who wish to see an end to the conflict, at least, although perhaps not so good for those who might cling to their stubborn opposition to the King."

Brother Richard's eyes widened slightly as he guessed, "The King is coming?"

"Soon," she nodded.

Gripping the parchment by one corner, she held it to a candle until the flame caught hold. The letter flared as the fire consumed it, the flames writhing up towards her fingers as the parchment turned to heat and ash. She waited until all but a fragment remained, then dropped it on the floor and stamped out the small fire.

"Tell no-one," she told the monk.

"I swear," he promised before bowing and leaving her to her thoughts.

Once alone, Altruda sat in silent contemplation, considering her options and wondering how best to divide the rebels.

She dared not strike directly at Hereward because she would be the principal suspect should anything untoward happen to him. Besides, she knew well enough that he was still having his food tasted by his manservant, Martin Lightfoot.

As for Siward Barn, the old Thane had rebuffed her once, and she had no intention of making a second attempt to suborn him. Besides, he was less important now that the two Earls were in command, and she had been working her own special brand of magic on Earl Morcar for weeks. He was ready to do her bidding, she knew. And now it was time to put her plan into action.

First, though, she summoned Kenton.

He came with his usual surly indifference, as if he resented being ordered around by a woman, but she had grown accustomed to his sour moods by now.

"It is time, Kenton," she told him. "Have you found men who will do what I want?"

He nodded, "Aye, there are three of them I'd count on. But they won't do anything unless they are well rewarded."

She picked up a small leather pouch she had looked out earlier. It jingled and clinked with the promise of wealth.

"These coins came from the treasure looted at Peterborough," she informed him. "King Sweyn must have forgotten to take them with him when he returned to Denmark."

Kenton grinned, reaching out to take the pouch from her.

As she placed it in his calloused hand, she said, "Do not be tempted to keep any of it for yourself. You will receive your own reward once King William is in control here."

His brow furrowed as if the idea of helping himself to a portion of the gold had never occurred to him.

"What is it you want these men to do?" he asked her.

"It is very simple," she explained. "I am fairly certain that Earl Edwin will soon be going on a journey. He will travel with only a few companions. Three guards would be ideal, I think. The men you have selected must make sure they are the ones chosen."

"I suppose they could probably arrange that," Kenton nodded.

"Probably is not good enough, Kenton," she said coolly. "You will not pay them until they have ensured that they will accompany him."

Kenton shrugged, "All right. But what then?"

"I will tell you before they leave."

"I reckon I can guess," he grinned, drawing a finger across his throat in the universal gesture of death.

Altruda's face remained stonily blank as she looked at him.

"I will pass on my instructions once I know the Earl is leaving and that your men are to accompany him. Do not overstep the mark, Kenton. Now go. Find these men and tell them what is required."

Kenton was unabashed at her reprimand. He merely smirked and bobbed his head in a parody of a bow.

"As you wish, my Lady."

He departed, tucking the pouch into a pocket inside his cloak, and whistling jauntily as he went in search of his targets.

Altruda then spent some time arranging her hair in a severe bun, changed into a modest dress, and removed most of her jewellery before pulling her own cloak around her shoulders. Her only concession to vanity was a small crucifix which she hung prominently around her neck on a silver chain which ensured that the cross itself lay against her bosom.

She checked the effect in a mirror then, satisfied that she looked suitably demure, yet with the crucifix drawing attention to her breasts, went in search of Abbot Thurstan.

The old Abbot was in his study where he had been poring over some enormous ledgers. He was only too happy to push them aside, and he welcomed Altruda effusively when she requested a moment of his time.

"What can I do for you, my child?" he asked solicitously as she sat facing him across his wide desk.

She smiled, "I think, Lord Abbot, it is more a question of what I can do for you."

"I do not understand," the old man replied, still maintaining his avuncular attitude, although she noticed that his eyes kept straying towards her chest.

Altruda almost felt sorry for him. He was too old and dried up for her to have any real interest in him, but it was reassuring to know that she could turn the head of even an old man like Thurstan. Today, though, she had come with the intention of using a more subtle way to manipulate him.

"I have a confession to make," she told him.

"A confession? I fear this is not the right place for that, my child."

Altruda detested that the old fool addressed her as a child, but she restrained the mocking retort she wanted to spit at him, and merely smiled again as she explained, "Not that sort of confession, Lord Abbot. No, what I mean is that I have been in the habit of exchanging correspondence with Abbot Turold."

"Turold? Of Peterborough?"

Altruda wondered which other Abbot Turold he thought she was talking about.

"The very same," she confirmed. "I was, as you may know, his guest before that brute, Ivo de Taillebois, attempted to force himself on me."

Thurstan's eyebrows shot up in alarm.

"I had not heard that the Sheriff had attempted anything like that!" he exclaimed.

Altruda waved a dismissive hand. The truth was that she had ordered de Taillebois to strike her in order to convince King Sweyn that her claims to be a refugee from Norman brutality were true.

Concealing her real motives, she explained, "It is in the past now, Lord Abbot. But I wanted to remain on good terms with Abbot Turold, so I have sent him the occasional letter explaining that my presence here in Ely is solely because I felt in danger and wanted to escape both de Taillebois and the fate King William had set for me."

The lies came easily to her, and she could tell the old Abbot was convinced by her story. Even old men would readily believe a pretty face and a buxom figure, she thought wryly.

Maintaining a sombre expression, she went on, "I recently received a letter from Abbot Turold which contained very grave news indeed."

"Oh?" Thurstan responded, his mind clearly reeling from her earlier revelation.

"Very grave news," she repeated. "The Abbot tells me King William is coming here. He intends to stamp out all traces of the rebellion."

Thurstan relaxed slightly, for this was a possibility he had often discussed with Hereward and Siward Barn, so he had an answer for her.

As if explaining a new concept to a small child, he said, "Hereward assures us that we are safe enough here. Saint Etheldreda will protect us. The Normans cannot bring an entire army here."

It was almost a shame to puncture his confidence, but Altruda enjoyed seeing him wince as she replied, "I'm afraid Hereward is a conceited man, Lord Abbot. I have tried to warn others against believing him. King William, according to the letter I received, plans to attack the island from several different directions. He will come by land and sea, building roads through the Fens to allow his soldiers to storm our defences."

Her words had clearly dismayed the old Abbot, but he rallied himself sufficiently to tell her, "Nevertheless, I have faith that we will remain safe. The Earls have joined us, and our defences are strong."

"Strong enough to withstand attack from ten thousand Normans?" Altruda challenged.

The Abbot's face grew tense, but he waved off her question.

"I think we should trust the military men in such matters, my child. You and I are hardly competent to question them. I think you should inform Hereward of this news you have from Abbot Turold, don't you?"

Altruda gave him a thin smile as she responded, "No, Lord Abbot, I do not think that would be wise."

"Oh? Why not?"

"Because he will discover it for himself before too long," she replied smoothly. "And because Abbot Turold also revealed the King's intentions regarding your own fate, Lord Abbot. That is why I came to you and not to Hereward."

Thurstan's face paled slightly, and he leaned forwards, clasping his hands together on his desk as if to prevent them from trembling.

Altruda found his attempts to conceal his concern amusing. She knew that, as an English Abbot, Thurstan had no love for a Norman King, and he had vainly believed that the isolation of his abbey would keep him safe. He had welcomed the rebels because he saw them as a way to keep William from interfering in his marshy domain, and he still fondly believed in the impregnability of his island home.

Altruda had shaken that belief, and now it was time for her to deliver her masterstroke.

"My fate?" he asked in a voice which now contained a definite quaver.

"Yes, Lord Abbot. King William has apparently announced that you will be dismissed, and that your abbey will have most of its lands confiscated. He intends to see Ely impoverished."

That, she knew, would alarm him more than the threat of war. One thing all senior churchmen feared was losing the lands they had so assiduously acquired. They might be men of God who professed a love for a simple way of life, yet they controlled immense riches, living in relative comfort thanks to the rents their tenants paid. Losing that income would leave them destitute, and Thurstan understood this only too well.

"He intends to confiscate our lands?" he gaped, appalled.

"So I am told," she nodded. "And I believe the threat to be real. The King cannot abide what he regards as treason. As soon as his army arrives and drives Hereward's men back into the fens, he will seize control of all your tenants' lands. Even without attacking us in Ely itself, he will be able to distribute the abbey's property among his Barons, leaving the abbey with nothing. As for yourself, he will not dare harm you physically, but I imagine the least punishment you can expect will be banishment to a distant monastery."

"Hereward is confident we can defeat the King," Thurstan argued weakly as he struggled to fend off her warnings of doom.

"Hereward is wrong, Lord Abbot. You will see soon enough. When the ships arrive off the coast, and the roads are built through the fens, you will see that William, who has overcome more difficult opponents than Hereward, will stop at nothing. And when he does reach us …"

She left the sentence hanging, fixing the Abbot with a firm gaze.

"I cannot alter things now," he said with an air of defeat.

"Perhaps you can," she replied.

"I do not see how."

In spite of his words, she saw a glimmer of hope flare in his eyes at the prospect of avoiding the fate she had outlined.

Smiling, she said, "Then let me help you, Lord Abbot. Turold has told me that anyone who aids the King will be rewarded. For my part, I hope to escape the dreadful marriage the king had planned for me. That will be all the reward I require. For yourself, you could save your abbey from ruin. If you help me, the King might be prepared to allow you to keep all the land you presently hold."

"You are suggesting I betray the men who have defended us so bravely?" he asked, a spark of guilt rallying his spirit.

"I am suggesting you save them from a worse fate," she asserted. "If King William is forced to fight his way here, he will surely hang everyone who opposes him. If we can persuade enough of the defenders to lay down their arms, we will prevent a great slaughter."

She leaned towards him, holding his frightened gaze as she added, "And you will also save your abbey from destitution."

Thurstan was wavering, she could tell. He was torn between his desire to support the rebellion and his fear of the retribution William might exact. Men who took holy orders had a privileged position in society, and the prospect of losing his standing and his wealth had clearly shaken him, just as she had intended. The suggestion of guilt for not saving lives was an added weight on his elderly shoulders.

"Hereward will never agree," he murmured softly as if thinking aloud.

"Hereward is only a Thane's son," she reminded him. "There are two Earls here now. They command the bulk of the warriors."

"You think we should try to persuade them not to fight?" Thurstan frowned. "I do not think that is possible. They have rebelled too often."

"Let me speak privately to Earl Morcar," Altruda told him. "And perhaps I can write again to Abbot Turold. He might be prepared to seek clemency for our noble Earls."

Thurstan regarded her with tired, frightened eyes as he gave an indecisive shrug.

"I must think on this," he told her weakly. "I am not sure what to do for the best."

Adopting a sympathetic tone, Altruda said, "There is no need to make a hasty decision, Lord Abbot. Let us wait and see what happens. I only wanted to warn you. Perhaps Hereward is right, and the King will be unable to bring his army here. But if he does, we must speak again about what we are to do if we wish to prevent a disaster."

Thurstan attempted a smile which became more of a grimace. He nodded feebly, fluttering his hands in a gesture of helpless bewilderment.

Knowing she had achieved what she had set out to accomplish, Altruda slowly rose to her feet, giving him a gentle smile as she did so.

"We should keep this between ourselves, Lord Abbot. But I am sure we will speak again."

She left the old fool to his fears, permitting herself a satisfied smile as she returned to her chamber. Things were, she reflected, falling into place at last. There would be no mistakes this time. It may take a few months, but Ely would fall to King William. She would make sure of that.

"You should have listened to me, Hereward," she said to herself. "By summer's end, you will wish you had."

Chapter 8

Once again, Edric found himself attending a council of war in the abbey's great library. Standing behind Hereward's chair, he could feel the tension in the room. Shafts of bright sunlight streamed in through the large windows, attempting to banish the evening shadows, yet there was an invisible gloom hanging over the small assembly of warriors who had gathered to discuss the ever-growing problems they were facing.

"The fishermen say there are boats patrolling the sea lanes just offshore," Earl Morcar reported glumly. "They are driving back any boat which attempts to leave. They've even sunk a couple of fishing vessels."

His brother, Earl Edwin, nodded as he nervously fingered his neatly trimmed moustache.

"It's not just a naval blockade. The King is bringing a huge army here. He is building causeways from island to island as he crosses the Fens."

"And the Normans have returned in force opposite Aldreth," Morcar added despondently. "They are building boats, siege engines and catapults."

He hesitated, as if unsure whether to admit to his next concern, but eventually added, "And there is a rumour they have hired a witch woman to summon a great storm which will flood the island and destroy all the homes."

Edric noticed most of the other men making the sign of the Cross and nodding gravely. He, too, had heard that rumour. Two monks had been discussing it in quiet, nervous voices at breakfast the previous morning, and he had overheard others talking about it since then. It seemed to be causing greater concern than the combined military efforts of the besieging Normans, and Edric could understand that. Fear of dark magic was ingrained to such an extent that people were only too willing to believe the threat.

Now, all eyes turned to Hereward, who had sat very calmly while the Earls recounted the mounting difficulties facing them.

At length, he said, "Saint Etheldreda will protect us from any witch woman. Storms have battered us before and will no doubt do so again. But any storm violent enough to ravage the Isle

91

of Ely will also cause devastation among the Normans. They cannot build a causeway if the rain washes everything away."

It was a good answer, and Edric saw men nodding as they accepted the argument, but Hereward quickly moved on, dismissing the issue of the witch's alleged power.

"As for the rest," he said, "we knew this would happen. It is what we expected. And it will provide us with the chance to destroy the Bastard once and for all."

"How?" Earl Edwin demanded. "We are outnumbered four or five to one, and they are coming at us from several directions. We do not have enough men to guard all the approaches."

"We do not need to defend the entire perimeter of the island," Hereward replied. "And we can deal with their attacks independently. It will take a while for them to complete the road they are building. Even once it is complete, it will be easy to defend against. They can only come along the road a few at a time."

"That does not help us tackle their fleet," Morcar objected. "If the fishing boats cannot sail, we will soon starve."

"I don't think so, my Lord," Hereward argued. "We have plenty of food stored, and even though the weather has been poor so far this year, the harvest should be fair. There are eels and fish in the fen streams, there are sheep and cattle in the fields. We will not go hungry."

"We still need more men," Edwin insisted sullenly.

"We must make do with the men we have," Hereward told him. "It will be enough."

Edwin shook his head, and Morcar put in, "Perhaps we should send for help after all."

"What do you mean?" Hereward demanded as the two brothers exchanged a meaningful look.

Edwin cleared his throat, then said, "Perhaps it is now time to send word to King Malcolm of the Scots. If he sends an army to relieve us, or even simply launches a raid into northern England, William will be forced to break off his attack."

"I do not want him to break off his attack," Hereward responded. "We need him to come deeper into the fens so we can defeat him."

"But surely aid from Malcolm would make our victory more certain," Edwin persisted.

"I thought you distrusted him?" Hereward challenged, recalling the Earl's earlier objection to requesting help from the King of Scots.

Edwin waved a dismissive hand as he explained, "I had hoped King William would accept our proposal to divide the land. It is now clear he will not agree to that, so we must devise another plan. I did not wish to call on the Scots, but I fear we have no other choice now."

Hereward stared hard at the Earl for a long moment, resisting the temptation to remind everyone that he had predicted the failure of Edwin's initial plan. Then he turned to Siward Barn, raising an eyebrow in question. In response, the old Thane gave a shrug.

Hereward told the Earls, "I am glad you have had a change of heart, but I'm afraid it is too late now."

"Not necessarily," Edwin insisted. "If one of us can reach Scotland by boat, Malcolm could send his own fleet back in a matter of weeks."

"Except that we can't get any boats out to sea," Barn muttered.

"But we can find boats if we go further north," Morcar argued.

"You have clearly planned this already," Hereward accused. "Why don't you tell us what you have in mind?"

Earl Edwin grew enthusiastic as he sat erect in his chair and explained, "We need to send a messenger Malcolm will heed. My brother and I have agreed that I am best suited to this task. So I intend heading north through the Fens until I reach somewhere beyond the Norman blockade. Then I will find a boat, sail north and bring back help. At the very least, I am sure I can persuade Malcolm to raid Northumbria and Cumbria. He is always greedy for plunder. If he does that, William will be forced to send men to drive him off. That will mean we will face fewer Normans here."

"And if the Bastard goes north?" Hereward challenged? How do we kill him then?"

Edwin gave a smooth smile as he replied, "If he takes some of his army north, all we need do is defeat those he leaves here. Then, either Malcolm will kill him for us, or he will be forced to return here with a much smaller army."

Morcar enthusiastically added, "Or we could march to join Malcom and catch William between our two armies."

Siward Barn put in, "The plan has some merit. At the very least it would delay William's assault on us, and it gives us a chance to weaken him."

Hereward looked at each man in turn while he considered the Earls' proposal. After some thought, he said, "Have you forgotten that the Bastard can always call for more men from the continent? There are always mercenaries eager to plunder a rich land."

"He has enemies in Europe as well as here," Barn pointed out.

Hereward nodded, "I suppose we can only benefit if he can be forced to split his army in two."

"Exactly!" beamed Earl Edwin, obviously delighted that Hereward was coming round to his point of view.

Hereward said, "But it all depends on getting a message to the Scots. How many men do you propose taking with you?"

"Don't worry," Edwin smiled. "I will not reduce the garrison. I need to move quickly, and a single boat will serve better than a fleet. I thought to take only two or three of my housecarls."

Edric could tell that Hereward still had some reservations, but the young Thane conceded, "I suppose it can do no harm to try."

"Then I shall make the arrangements in the morning and set out tomorrow night," Edwin declared. "There is nothing to be gained by delaying."

The two Earls exchanged smiles and nods, clearly pleased with themselves, but Barn had another question.

"What do we do in the meantime?" the old Thane asked.

Hereward told him, "I'd like you to take charge of attacking the road they are building. Send out small groups in fen boats and try to disrupt the construction work. Take no risks, because we don't want to discourage them, but make life difficult for them."

"I can do that," Barn nodded. "If you can give me enough men."

In response, Hereward looked at Earl Edwin and raised an eyebrow.

"My Lord? Your men could help with this task."

"I shall give the necessary orders," Edwin agreed amiably, his mood lightened now that his proposal had been agreed.

"And what of the siege engines and boats they are building at Aldreth?" Barn asked pointedly.

"I shall deal with them," Hereward assured him.

"How?" Barn wanted to know.

"Wait and see," grinned Hereward.

"You think we cannot be trusted to hear your plan?" Barn scowled.

"I think the fewer people who know what I intend, the better," Hereward replied. "But I promise I will inform you nearer the time."

Barn was unhappy, but subsided into a brooding silence, and Hereward moved the discussion on to other aspects of the defence. He spent several minutes going over routine issues such as arranging patrols, confirming supply levels and the training of the handful of new recruits who had managed to circumvent the Norman patrols and reach the island. It was in these details that Hereward shone. Where the Earls and even Siward Barn were only vaguely interested in such matters, Hereward displayed a grasp of the details which astonished everyone.

"So you see," Hereward assured them once he had outlined how the defences were arranged, "we have nothing to fear. Thane Barn's men can harass the building of the causeway, while I will deal with the boats and siege engines opposite Aldreth. Once they have been destroyed, we will turn our full attention to the advance along the road. Using boats, we can attack all along their line of approach. We can divide and separate them, because their greater numbers are useless if they are confined to a narrow roadway. The further they come, the more targets they provide for us. Eventually, with his army strung out along a single road, the Bastard will give us an opportunity to destroy him."

Some of the Thanes murmured their approval of the plan, and both Earls seemed happy with the outcome of the discussion, although Edric noticed that Abbot Thurstan had a worried look on his elderly face. All the talk of war and killing clearly upset the old man, although he raised no objections and, when the meeting broke up, left the room without a word to anyone.

Edric, though, had questions of his own. On the way back to Hereward's chambers, he asked, "Do you really think King Malcolm will aid us?"

Hereward shrugged, "I don't really care. I expect he'll be happy to take a chance to raid Northumbria, but I doubt he has the stomach to face the Bastard in battle. All that talk of catching William between our two armies is just so much fanciful nonsense as far as I'm concerned."

"Then why did you not argue more against the suggestion?" Edric wanted to know.

"Well, it might weaken the Bastard if he does need to send men north, but the main reason is that it gets Earl Edwin out of my way. He's obviously realised that his men need to help with the fighting now, so Barn and I can use them the way we want without Edwin interfering."

Edric warned, "But Earl Morcar will still be here. And he's been sleeping with the Lady Altruda."

"I doubt they've done much sleeping," Hereward grunted. "But you are right, we'll need to be on our guard. But I can handle Morcar easily enough. Altruda might try to plant ideas in his head when she gets her night-time claws into him, but he'll back down if Barn and I argue with him. After all, I am a rebel. I'm renowned for not doing as I'm told."

Edric laughed, but Hereward grew more thoughtful as he went on, "Still, Altruda is a sly devil, and we'll need to watch for her tricks."

"What sort of tricks?" Edric asked.

"Devious ones," Hereward replied. "For example, I have an idea she's behind that rumour about the witch woman."

"You think so?" Edric frowned.

"It's the sort of thing she's capable of."

"So there isn't a witch?"

"I don't know," Hereward admitted. "But it doesn't matter. Have you forgotten how Saint Etheldreda destroyed the bridge and drowned all those Normans?"

Edric shook his head as he replied, "I thought the bridge collapsed because our men weakened it."

Hereward laughed, "In my experience, Edric, God and his saints help those who help themselves."

Edric smiled, then asked, "But what about the Lady Altruda? If you know she's going to cause trouble, isn't there some way we can get rid of her?"

"I wish we could," Hereward growled. "But she's a noblewoman, and I can't have her sent away simply because I don't trust her. Locking her up isn't possible either. The Abbot wouldn't stand for it, and neither would Morcar."

"So we leave her alone?" Edric persisted.

"Yes, but that doesn't mean we don't watch for any of her ruses. I thought for a moment she might be behind Edwin's plan to fetch help from Scotland, but he's only taking three men with him, so it doesn't make a lot of difference to us and, like I say, it gives me more of a free hand, so she can't be the one who suggested it."

As always, talking to Hereward had buoyed Edric's confidence. The young Thane's assurances were easy to believe in.

"So you really believe we can beat the Bastard?" Edric asked him.

"Of course. If it was left to Barn or those two Earls, we'd simply stand in a shield wall and dare the Normans to attack us, but I'm going to fight dirty, lad."

"When you destroy the siege engines, you mean?"

"That's right. In fact, I think it's about time I took another look at them. First thing tomorrow, I want you to find Siward White. Bring some horses and one of the other lads, and we'll head down to Aldreth."

The following morning was another dull, cloudy one with the sky holding a layer of low, grey clouds, and with a damp breeze drifting in off the sea. Spring might have brought longer days and shorter nights, but there had been little sunshine. Even now, with summer fast approaching, the land was being battered by unseasonal squalls, a fact which had helped to spread the rumours of a storm being brewed by a witch. Despite Hereward's confidence, Edric knew that many of the farmers were shaking their heads and clucking their tongues as they surveyed the fields of newly-planted oats, barley and wheat which were being assailed by too much rain and not enough sunshine.

Now, though, Edric had a more personal matter on his mind. He was uncertain about riding a horse. He was comfortable enough around the animals because he had spent years helping his uncle in the smithy, so handling horses was an everyday task. But actually riding one was another matter. Only fine lords and their retainers rode horses, so Edric had never had the opportunity.

"There's nothing to it," Winter assured him as the two of them joined Hereward and White in the abbey courtyard. "Try to relax, and don't grip too tightly."

Winter selected a docile mare for him, and Edric mounted with trepidation, but the beast merely snorted and swished her tail when she took his armoured weight.

"We'll take it easy," Hereward promised, setting his own mount off at a slow walk.

Edric nudged his mare into motion, with Winter grinning at him as he rode alongside.

"It's not so bad, is it?" the big axeman chuckled. "We always used to ride to battle, you know."

Edric nodded absently, his attention focused on staying in the saddle. The horses were small beasts, stocky and strong, of the type which housecarls had traditionally used when following their lords into battle. But the English warriors had usually dismounted to fight, using the horses only as a means of transportation. It was the Normans who had mastered the art of fighting from horseback, and it was that which had gained them their victories. Edric could understand why. Perched on the back of the mare, he was higher and faster than any man on foot.

"Maybe we should learn to fight from horseback," he mused aloud as he slowly became accustomed to the motion of the horse.

"Horses won't charge a shield wall," Winter told him. "They're good for scaring a rabble and for pursuing a fleeing enemy, but they're not much use in the fight if men stand firm against them."

Edric deferred to Winter's experience. The big man had, after all, stood all day in the shield wall at Hastings, driving the Norman cavalry back time after time.

After a while, Hereward urged into a trot, an experience which Edric found both exhilarating and alarming as he bounced along the path towards Aldreth. A part of him wanted to go even faster, but fear of falling kept his enthusiasm in check. In any case, he told himself, a fast trot would cover the few miles to Aldreth soon enough.

When they arrived, Hereward rode through the sprawling Mercian encampment, their small group attracting curious glances from the scores of warriors who sat eating their breakfast by their cooking fires.

Hereward rode to the ramparts at the southern end of the island, a tall barrier of earth and timber, with a steep outer face and a ledge cut into the inner side from where the defenders could shoot down at anyone who dared cross the river to storm the defences.

Hereward exchanged a greeting with a barrel-chested Mercian Thane named Patton who commanded the men on the wall.

"They're still at their building work," he informed Hereward in a deep, gruff voice. "But it won't be long before they are ready."

Hereward dismissed the man's obvious concern with a cheery smile.

"I'll take a look," he replied before clambering up the makeshift steps to stand at the top of the rampart.

White, Edric and Winter followed him and gazed out across the river.

"No bridge this time," Winter rasped.

"A small mercy," Edric replied, remembering the slaughter and the sudden destruction of the bridge the last time the Normans had attempted to attack the island.

This time, the enemy were adopting different tactics. Edric could see the bustle of activity on the far side of the dark waterway where the Normans were working on their engines of war. There was a constant stream of logs being dragged through the fens, with dozens of men wielding axes and saws waiting to transform them into small boats and massive catapults. They made sure to do the work out of bowshot so the English defenders could not harass them with arrows.

Siward White chewed his lip anxiously when he saw the tall tower and huge catapults which were taking shape.

"They'll be able to bombard us and flatten the wall," he frowned. "And that tower means they'll be able to see what's behind our rampart."

Hereward's only reaction was to nod and smile.

"And they are building small boats," White added as he pointed further along the river to where the hulls of flat-bottomed boats were being assembled.

"So they are," Hereward agreed, still showing no concern.

"We should launch a raid across the river to destroy them," White continued.

"Not yet," Hereward replied calmly.

Patton, who had climbed the wall to stand beside them, frowned, "Then when? We will be at their mercy in a few days. We have no engines of our own."

"Soon," Hereward told him. "But let's give them time to finish their work."

The other men exchanged glances, and Patton wanted to argue, but Hereward cut him short.

"I will deal with them," he told the burly Thane. "You have my word on that."

Patton was not pleased, but Hereward would say no more, remaining tight-lipped even when White pressed him for an explanation as they rode back to the town of Ely.

"You seem almost pleased at the progress they are making," White accused.

"I am," Hereward agreed.

"Why?"

"Because the more progress they make, the more demoralised they will be when we destroy their engines. And the less time they will have to rebuild them."

"And how are we going to destroy them?" White persisted.

"You'll see," Hereward told him.

Chapter 9

When they reached the abbey, Hereward called Edric aside while Winter and White returned the horses to the stables. Standing outside the doorway of the guest quarters, Hereward looked around to make sure nobody else was within earshot, then leaned close to Edric and lowered his voice.

"I hear you know a potter," he whispered.

The unexpected question caught Edric by surprise and brought a flush to his cheeks when he realised Torfrida had betrayed his secret. He almost responded with an angry retort, but Hereward's penetrating stare showed the futility of denial.

Unable to speak because of his dismay, he gave a curt nod.

"Don't look so guilty," Hereward scolded. "I haven't told anyone else. But I'm not interested in your doxie. What I need are pots."

"Pots?" Edric blinked, taken by surprise.

"Pots. Lots of them. Clay pots. I particularly want some jars with lids. Jars we can seal up once we've filled them."

"Filled them with what, Lord?"

"A surprise for the Normans," Hereward replied with a grin. "Now, can you get hold of what we need?"

"Cecil has lots of pots," Edric confirmed bemusedly.

"Good. I want you to go and bring back a cart full of them. Get two dozen assorted pots and jars, but make sure some of them have lids."

Edric frowned uncertainly as he asked, "What for?"

Again, Hereward merely smiled and said, "You'll see."

He tugged out his purse and counted out several silver pennies, handing them to Edric.

"That should be more than enough," he said. "Get along now."

Then he went inside, whistling tunelessly to himself, leaving Edric more confused than ever. Realising he would learn Hereward's plan soon enough, he went to the back of the stables where he knew he would find a small, two-wheeled cart which the monks kept for transporting bulky loads. He dragged it round to the front of the stable building, then went inside to find a mule or

101

donkey to pull the cart. Instead, he found Winter who was still chatting amiably to one of the stable hands.

Edric hesitated. He had thought Winter would have gone by now, but the big man saw him and arched his eyebrows in question.

"What's up, lad?"

Edric tried to sound casual as he replied, "I need a donkey. Hereward has a small job for me."

"I'll give you a hand," Winter said cheerfully as he strode to one of the stalls. "There's a donkey right here."

"I can manage on my own," Edric told him.

"I've got nothing better to do," Winter said as he led the donkey out of the stall.

The stable boy was looking rather nervous but obviously had no wish to become involved in an argument between two large men who were decked in chainmail and wearing axes on their backs. He hurriedly found some important task which required him to scurry to the far end of the building.

Winter led the donkey outside, with Edric tramping after him and trying to protest that he needed no help, but Winter was adamant.

"If you need a donkey and cart," he said as he fastened the traces, "you'll probably need an extra pair of hands to load it."

Edric could find no excuse to deny Winter's assistance. Hereward had given him the task, but collecting pots was not really a secret mission. What had excited Edric about this was that it would, at long last, give him a genuine reason to see Ylva. Even if Kenton's son, Halfdan, did follow him, he had a genuine reason for visiting the potter, and Ylva would remain safe as long as she stayed out of sight.

But Winter could ruin everything.

"I really want to do this on my own," Edric told him.

"Do you now?" Winter grinned. "All the more reason I want to come with you, then."

"Please, Winter!" Edric protested.

The big man grinned at him, ignoring the plea.

"I suppose you could go on your own," he said. "But I feel I ought to tag along behind you just in case you run into any trouble."

"I won't fall into trouble," Edric asserted.

"Not if I'm with you," Winter agreed, struggling to keep a straight face. "You might as well face it, lad. I was charged with looking after you, and I don't like the thought of you going off on your own."

"I'm only going into town," Edric replied in exasperation. "It's the middle of the day, and there are plenty of people around."

"Then one more won't make much difference," said Winter.

Edric gave up. With a resigned sigh, he gestured helplessly towards the gates.

"Come on, then. But you can lead the donkey. If you're coming, you might as well make yourself useful."

Winter chuckled as he took up the halter rope.

"As you command, Lord."

Edric shook his head, setting a brisk pace as he headed to the gates and then followed the road into town.

"So what are we fetching?" Winter wanted to know.

"Pots. We are to buy two dozen clay pots of different sorts, but at least six of them must have lids."

"What for?"

"I have no idea. It's another of Hereward's schemes."

Winter nodded, "Ah, best just to do as we are told, then."

Edric sighed. The task itself was straightforward, but Winter's presence could ruin his meeting with Ylva. He was already feeling apprehensive enough about that without having the big axeman looking over his shoulder. He could already imagine the big man's lewd comments when he discovered Edric's ulterior motive for going to Cecil's pottery.

On top of that concern, he had another worry. As he and Winter plodded through the muddy streets, he frequently glanced back over his shoulder, searching for any sign of Kenton's son, Halfdan.

"What's bothering you, lad?" Winter demanded, giving him a sharp look. "You're as nervous as a virgin on her wedding night."

Edric sighed, knowing there was no way he could keep the secret of Ylva's whereabouts from Winter.

"There's a girl at the pottery," he told the big man.

"Oh, yeah?"

Winter said no more, letting the silence linger.

103

Eventually, Edric admitted, "You might recognise her."

"Yeah?"

Edric glanced at Winter and saw the axeman was grinning hugely.

"Just don't tell anyone about her."

"Me?" Winter asked, assuming an air of innocence.

"I mean it, Winter. If anyone finds out about her, she will be in danger."

Winter frowned, considered Edric's statement for a moment, then asked, "It's not Kenton's daughter, is it?"

In response, Edric gave a curt nod.

Winter let out a low whistle of astonishment.

"So that's where you hid her. I did wonder, but I thought she must have left the island. I mean, you never went to see her, did you?"

"No. I wanted to keep her safe. I still do. So make sure you tell no one. Swear it."

Winter's face grew serious. He gave a solemn nod as he placed his right hand on his heart.

"I'll swear it, lad. I can keep my mouth shut when need be. And I don't like the idea of that lout Kenton getting his hands on the girl any more than you do."

Edric nodded his thanks, but Winter went on, "So you haven't seen her since the day you magicked her out of the abbey last year?"

"That's right."

"How did you do that, by the way? Kenton was seriously pissed off about it."

Edric remembered Kenton's fury only too well.

He explained, "We took a boat out the sally port behind the infirmary, then walked the rest of the way through town. It was dark and raining, so nobody saw us go."

"Well, I can understand why you'd want to keep your distance in case her father ever found out, but it's a shame. She's a pretty little thing."

"She was just someone who needed help," Edric told him, receiving a sharp look as a reply.

"If you say so," Winter grinned.

"I do. It will be nice to make sure she is safe and well, but our main task is to collect the pots and jars for Hereward."

"I think we can manage that," Winter said. "As long as you don't walk into anyone. It's best to watch where you're going rather than keep looking back over your shoulder."

"Sorry."

"You think someone is following us?"

"Maybe. But it doesn't really matter today. We have orders to go to the pottery."

"Then stop looking so guilty about it," Winter told him. "We go there, we pick up the pots, and we walk back. Nothing to it."

Edric gave a weak smile, but he still took the occasional glance behind them. Fortunately, there was no sign of Ylva's half-brother, so he felt less anxious by the time they reached the potter's home.

Edric removed his helmet, placing it on the cart, then knocked on the door. After a few moments, Cecil's plump wife, Garyn, opened it.

She wore a plain dress of brown homespun and her dark hair was tied up beneath a white headscarf. She blinked at them, a brief look of concern on her face at the sight of two armed warriors standing in the street until she recognised Edric.

"It's you!" she gasped, her expression brightening into a smile. "Come in! Jetta will be pleased."

Edric held up a hand as he hurriedly told her, "We've come on business. We need to see Cecil. We need some pots."

He gestured to the cart behind them, which only made Garyn wrinkle her face in confusion.

"I'll tell Cecil," she said. "He's out back in the workshop. You come in and see Jetta."

Edric hesitated, but Garyn tugged at his hand and Winter gave him a gentle shove in the back, saying, "On you go, lad. I'll mind the cart."

Cecil's house was divided by a long hallway which ran from the main door to the yard at the back. There were small bedrooms to the right, with the main living area to Edric's left. He could smell the aroma of fish stew as he approached the door.

Moving briskly, Garyn led him into the room.

Ylva was there, standing over a bubbling pot on the hearth fire, but she looked around when Garyn brought Edric in.

"Jetta!" the woman said excitedly. "Look who is here!"

105

Edric stood in the doorway to the room, feeling awkward and apprehensive about how Ylva would react to seeing him again after so many months.

Yet the sight of her entranced him. He was dimly aware that the room was full of all the usual clutter that a large family gathered. There was a heavy table, a wooden chair and several stools, storage chests, a cupboard decked with plates and mugs, discarded toys lying on the rush-strewn floor, old cushions, woven baskets and the traditional crucifix on the wall.

But above all, there was Ylva.

He felt a wave of relief wash through him at seeing her. She had cut her long, auburn hair, and she seemed to have put on a little weight which was, he thought, a good thing, for she had been painfully thin and undernourished when he had last seen her.

She, too, had a headscarf covering her hair, with a plain blouse over a skirt of bright red and blue stripes. She was wearing a long apron which had tiny stains spattered across it.

Edric noticed all this in an instant, but it was her eyes that drew him. They were wide with surprise, their blue-green gaze showing her momentary confusion. Then she dropped the spoon she had been using to stir the contents of the pot and took a tentative step towards him.

"Edric?" she asked as if she could not believe what she was seeing. "Edric Strong? Is it really you?"

"Yes, it's me."

He sensed Ylva's hesitation, but he was unsure how to react, so he stood still, waiting for her to make the first move.

Garyn said to Ylva, "He came to see you. You could at least greet him with more of a welcome than that."

Ylva let out a long breath as she gathered her wits.

"I'm sorry, Edric," she said. "I just wasn't expecting to see you."

Yet she still made no move towards him, and Edric did not want to make any overt display of emotion while Garyn was looking on.

The older woman must have understood, for she told them, "I need to fetch Cecil. You two should talk."

Then she set off down the hallway to the back door of the house, her soft laughter clearly audible.

The two of them stood facing one another, a few feet apart, both of them silent. Edric did not know what to do now that he was here. He had expected more of a reaction from her, but she, too, seemed almost overwhelmed at seeing him.

Then the reason for her uncharacteristic reticence became clear when she asked in a serious voice, "Why are you here? Is something wrong?"

"No! Not at all!" he blurted. "Hereward sent us to get some pots. Winter is outside with a cart."

Ylva's sigh of relief was as genuine as any reaction he had ever seen.

"You should have come before now," she scolded. "Sending polite messages through Seaver and the Lady is not how I would prefer to talk to you."

"I know," he said feebly. "But I am here now. I didn't want to come in case I led your father to you."

A dark scowl marred her delicate face as she asked, "Is he still looking for me after all this time?"

"I'm afraid so. Your brother, Halfdan, has been following me."

"Poor Halfdan," she sighed. "He is too afraid to run away. I wish I could talk to him, but he lives in fear of our father."

Then a sharp edge of concern tinged her voice as she asked, "Did he follow you here today?"

"I don't think so. But it doesn't matter as long as you stay inside. He won't see you, and we have a reason to be here."

Ylva let out another sigh as her shoulders sagged. He was not sure, but she seemed to be trembling with emotion.

"What's wrong?" he asked, inching closer to her.

She waved a hand in a gesture of helplessness as she replied, "It was the thought that you might be coming to tell me he knows where I am. Sometimes I almost forget about him, but seeing you brought it all back."

"I'm sorry. I didn't mean to alarm you. But you are safe as long as you stay out of sight."

She gave a sullen nod as she said, "I do like it here, but I'm getting a bit fed up of constantly hiding."

"It won't be forever," Edric told her.

"Won't it? Are you going to kill my father for me, then?"

The harsh edge to her words made him smile. This was the Ylva he remembered. But he was forced to shake his head in response to her demand.

"I can't. He'd beat me in a straight fight, and I won't murder a man by attacking him by surprise."

"I know," she sighed. "But it is the only way to deal with him. I'll never be safe until he's dead. You know that. And if he does find me, I will need to run away."

Her harsh determination appalled Edric. He knew she meant what she said, and he wanted to offer some comfort and reassurance, but he could not find the right words.

As he struggled for a response, he heard voices in the hall. It was Garyn and Cecil coming from the back of the house. Grateful for the interruption, he turned to greet them.

Cecil had the sleeves of his tunic rolled up, and his arms, as well as the apron he wore, were streaked by dust and spots of clay. But he was smiling broadly, clearly pleased at the thought of selling so many of his wares.

"Hello, Edric," he said cheerfully. "I hear you need some pots?"

"That's right."

Edric quickly explained what he needed.

"I can manage that," Cecil smiled. "Garyn says you have a cart."

"Yes. It's out at the front."

"Edric has a friend with him," Garyn explained.

Cecil said, "All right. I'll get him to take the cart round the back so we can load it there. Seaver can help."

He bustled off to the front door, while Garyn gave Ylva and Edric a conspiratorial smile.

"I'll take the baby out of your way," she told them. "She's due a feed soon."

Edric had not noticed the tiny basket in the corner of the cluttered room from where Garyn now lifted a small child who made snuffling noises as she roused from sleep.

"The other children are out in the back yard or off playing somewhere," she told Edric. "You can chat for a little while without being disturbed."

She went off with a knowing smile, leaving Edric feeling both relieved and embarrassed. She obviously believed the two of them were having a romantic discussion, yet Ylva remained preoccupied with thoughts of her father.

Once Ylva was sure Garyn was out of earshot, she gave Edric a smile, although there was still a dark edge to her tone as she said softly, "I'm sorry, Edric. It's just that I swore I will never let that pig get his hands on me again. You know why."

Edric gave a sombre nod. He had been astonished and disgusted to learn that Kenton had forced himself on his own daughter when she was little more than a child. At the age of thirteen, Ylva had given birth to a baby son who had died after only a few days of life. It was, he supposed, no wonder she detested and feared the man.

Then the Ylva he remembered asserted herself once again. He saw her resolve hardening as she shook off the memories of her former life and forced a smile to her lips.

She said, "Never mind him. I don't want to think about him. Tell me about you. What have you been doing all this time? Fighting, I suppose?"

"Yes," he nodded before realising this might not be the response she wanted to hear.

Hurriedly, he added, "Although I don't do much actual fighting. My job is to protect Hereward."

"So you were with him when he stood at the end of the bridge?"

He could not deny that, but dismissed it with a shrug.

"Yes, but there wasn't a lot of fighting before the bridge collapsed."

"You are not very good at lying, Edric," she told him, the accusation softened by her smile.

Before he could reply, she went on, "People say there will be a lot more fighting soon. The Normans are coming again, aren't they?"

"Yes, but we'll beat them."

"And some say there is a witch woman who is going to cast a spell to drown us all."

"I've heard that too. I don't believe it."

Ylva grinned, "Neither do I. But some folk will believe anything."

Edric did not want to talk about the war. That was not why he had come here. Desperate to change the subject, he asked, "What about you? Lady Torfrida tells me you are happy here."

Now her face shone like the sun as she smiled, "Oh, yes. Cecil and Garyn are very kind to me. I have a room of my own, you know. I've never had that before. Seaver brought all his silver when he fled from your village, so he paid for extra rooms to be built on at the back of the house. And during the day I help look after the children."

"And you cook," Edric said, indicating the bubbling pot of fish stew.

"Oh, by Jesus!" she blurted, hurrying to the fire and scooping up a thick cloth to protect her hands as she lifted the pot from the flames.

She exhaled as she placed it on the stones that ringed the hearth.

"It'll be fine. I'll leave it there to keep it warm."

Turning back to Edric, she asked, "Will you stay for a meal?"

He was tempted, but knew Winter would present a problem.

"I need to get back," he told her. "Thank you, though."

She frowned her disappointment, but at last took those final steps and came over to him, reaching for his hand and clasping it between hers as she looked up at him.

"Tell me truly, Edric Strong, is my father causing you any problems?"

"No. He ignores me most of the time. All I get is a few stares. It's your brother I'm more worried about. I've seen him following me, so that's why I can't come here."

"So you do want to come and see me?" she asked, her eyes holding his gaze.

"Of course I do."

"And what about your woman and her child?"

"Aelswith is not my woman," he replied. "She's just a friend."

An impish smile played on Ylva's lips as she said, "But you want her to be more than that, don't you?"

Edric felt his neck and cheeks flushing red as he shook his head.

110

"No. Once, perhaps. Not now."

Even as he spoke the words, he knew they were not entirely true. Aelswith, for all her aloofness, still had the power to draw him like a moth to the flame.

Ylva seemed able to read his thoughts.

"You should learn to lie better than that, Edric," she said. "But I'm glad you haven't married her or anything like that. She's no good for you, you know."

"She's a friend," Edric repeated loyally, his thoughts confused.

"Just a friend? Then I suppose she can't object if I kiss you, can she?"

Before he could respond, she moved in close, stood on her tiptoes, put her arms on his shoulders and kissed him on the mouth.

He was so astonished, he barely reacted until the soft warmth of her lips on his drew an involuntary reaction. This was a new experience for him, and he was uncertain as to what he should do, but then he let his instinct take over and he placed his arms around her, holding her close as he returned the kiss eagerly.

Ylva's arms were now draped around his neck, her body pressed hard against him, her lips exciting his passion, but the sound of the back door opening and footsteps coming down the hall made them break apart.

Garyn appeared in the doorway, her baby daughter cradled against her shoulder.

She grinned, "You really ought to take your armour off first, Edric," she told him with a wink.

Edric flushed deeply once again, but Ylva laughed, "It wasn't very comfortable."

"Next time perhaps you will stay a bit longer," Garyn said to him.

"I will come when I can," Edric replied, unable to meet her amused eyes. "But it is not easy."

"Well, your cart is loaded, and Cecil is helping your friend take it back out to the street."

Edric glanced at Ylva, who gestured at him to go.

"Stay safe, Edric Strong," she said, her smile tugging at his heart.

"And you," he replied as he reluctantly headed for the outer door, his mind still reeling from the sensation of kissing her.

Outside, Cecil and Winter were standing beside the cart. Old Seaver was also there. He came to clasp hands and greet Edric like an old friend, even though they were so far apart in age that they had little in common other than their shared origin in Bourne.

"God greet you, Edric," said Seaver as he reached to clasp hands.

"And you," Edric replied warmly.

Seaver gestured towards Winter as he said, "Your friend tells us Hereward has a plan to defeat the Normans again."

"That's right."

Seaver sighed, "I hope you succeed. We hear so many stories. And I'm too old to run again. I don't want to live under Norman rule, but if they come, what other choice is there?"

"They won't beat us," Edric told him. "Trust in Hereward."

Seaver forced a smile, although Edric guessed he was not entirely convinced. Fear of Norman retribution was clearly a common concern.

Giving the old villager a confident smile, Edric turned to Cecil, tugging out the coins Hereward had given him.

"Is that enough?" he asked as he handed the small pennies over.

"It is more than enough," Cecil said.

"Keep it. We will take more from the Normans when we beat them next time."

Cecil seemed unconcerned. Unlike Seaver, he appeared to be one of those people who did not really care who was in charge. All he wanted was to be allowed to make his pots and earn a decent living for himself and his family. It was an attitude Edric found hard to comprehend, but it was far from uncommon even in the heartland of the rebellion.

They said their farewells, Edric placed his iron-bound helmet on his head, and the two warriors set off for the abbey.

Edric was in a contemplative mood, but Winter soon jolted him out of his reverie.

"Sorry we couldn't give you longer with the girl," the axeman grinned. "You barely had time for a quickie."

Edric snapped," It's not like that!"

"Isn't it?" Winter asked innocently. "More fool you, then. Have you even tried to kiss her yet?"

Edric's expression betrayed him, making Winter laugh aloud.

"Good for you. But you didn't go any further?"

"Shut up, Winter!"

"That's a no, then," Winter chortled.

Edric growled, "Just mind your own business and make sure you don't tell a soul about her. You swore."

"Aye, I did. And I'll keep my word. Kenton won't learn of her from me."

The mention of Kenton's name sent a shiver through Edric's body as he recalled Ylva's threat to run away if her father ever learned of her whereabouts. The memory of her kiss filled him with desire to see her again, yet he knew he could not, and that thought depressed him. Things would be different if only they could be rid of Kenton, but Edric knew that if anything were to happen to him, the person responsible would be punished. And facing the man in a fair fight was not a prospect Edric relished. Besides which, Hereward had explicitly ordered him not to meet the man in a duel.

Which left things where, he wondered? Despite his promise to make another visit, he knew he could not place Ylva in danger by going to see her again, and he could not remove the danger by killing her father.

It was, he concluded, a problem with no resolution.

He needed somebody to talk to, but he could not discuss it with Winter. Much as the big man was his closest friend as well as his mentor, Winter's advice would be to kill Kenton and claim Ylva for himself.

If only it were that simple, Edric reflected. No, he needed more practical advice than the blunt axeman could provide.

By the time they had returned to the abbey and stacked the pots behind the stables, Edric had decided he should seek out Brother John. The young monk had plenty of experience of the world and, despite being sworn to a life of chastity, he had an easy way with everyone and seemed to have a natural ability to understand women.

After returning the donkey to its stall, Winter went off to the dormitory, promising once again to keep Ylva's presence a secret. Edric made an excuse about needing to report to Hereward, but instead began wandering the abbey precinct in search of

Brother John. He looked in all the most obvious places without success and was beginning to feel frustrated. Brother John was not usually hard to find, but he was not in the refectory, nor the library, the scriptorium or the abbey. Wearily, Edric went back to the main courtyard where he found Auti walking back from the guest quarters, his turn as guard to Torfrida having just ended.

The tall, rangy outlaw gave Edric a nod of greeting, his smile never touching his eyes which were still haunted by the loss of his twin brother. Despite the months that had passed since his loss, there was always an air of grimness around Auti. He remained silent and withdrawn, as if a part of him had died along with his brother.

Edric always tried to treat Auti as normally as possible, so he asked, "I don't suppose you've seen Brother John?"

Auti gave a brief nod.

"He's in the guest chambers with Mistress Aelswith. Been in there a while."

Edric thanked him, although his heart fell at the thought of seeing Aelswith so soon after he had held Ylva in his arms.

Then he decided it would be good to see her knowing her hold on him had been lessened because he did know a girl who liked him. Ylva had kissed him; something Aelswith had never done. Spurred on by a new-found resolve, he strode into the long corridor and knocked on the door to Aelswith's chamber, pushing it open without waiting for an invitation.

The sight which met his eyes stunned him.

It was obvious that Brother John was helping Aelswith pack her few belongings into a large bag, and the startled expression on Aelswith's face told him that something was very wrong.

"What's going on?" he asked.

"Oh, hello, Edric," said Brother John with an easy smile. "We were hoping to see you before we left."

"What?"

"We are leaving," the monk told him with an almost casual air. "Ely is no longer safe, and I have a hankering to resume my travels."

"And Aelswith is going with you?" Edric asked accusingly.

114

Aelswith could not meet his gaze. She bent down to pick up baby Torfrida from the floor where she had been crawling, then hugged the child closely, while Brother John stood between them and Edric.

"We both think it would be best for her and the baby," the monk informed Edric. "This is no life for either of them, sitting in a small room for days on end, with the threat of attack hanging over them."

"But you can't just leave!" Edric protested. "Where will you go? Scotland?"

"Perhaps not," Brother John admitted with a smile. "That is a long way. But somewhere we will be safer than here."

"Together?" Edric glared.

"Edric!" Aelswith snapped, showing a flash of temper. But the look in her eyes told him his guess had been correct. Whether Brother John acknowledged the fact or not, it was evident to Edric that Aelswith wanted to be with the monk.

The unexpected realisation left Edric feeling as if someone had thrust a spear into his heart and twisted the blade to tear out his soul. He had always known Aelswith was unattainable, but for her to run off with Brother John was too much for him to take in.

Fighting to find words which might persuade her to stay, he took a step back, leaning against the door for support, his face pale and shocked.

"You can't leave!" he gasped, his voice little more than a whisper.

"I can go wherever I want, with whoever I want!" Aelswith declared defiantly.

She turned hurriedly away, fussing over baby Torfrida who had begun to cry on hearing her mother's raised voice.

"But how will you get past the Normans?" he persisted.

Brother John answered, "I am a man of God, Edric. They will not stop us."

Edric, lost for arguments, could only blurt, "You cannot leave!"

"It is for the best, Edric," Brother John said soothingly. "I will take Aelswith and young Torfrida somewhere the child can grow up in safety. Would you deny her that opportunity?"

Edric could not speak. He tried to summon some words, but all he could do was stare at the two of them in helpless

115

bewilderment. Brother John met his gaze with a calm strength, but Aelswith looked away, unable to answer the plea in his eyes.

"I am sorry, Edric," Brother John told him. "But we must do this."

Edric felt a silent scream of anger building inside him, but his voice still refused to work. With a supreme effort, he turned, flung the door open and stormed out, slamming the door behind him. He ignored the look he received from Ordgar who was standing further along the corridor on guard duty outside Hereward's room, and stalked out of the building as if a horde of demons were tormenting him.

Later, he stood in the shadowed doorway of the dormitory building, watching as Aelswith meekly followed Brother John out of the guest quarters and out towards the main gates and the town beyond. Brother John had his pack on his back and also carried Aelswith's bag slung over one shoulder, while she carried young Torfrida in her arms. Had it not been for Brother John's monk's habit, they would have looked like any young family setting out on a journey.

Edric sensed somebody moving up behind him and glanced round to see the bulky form of Winter regarding him with a grave expression.

"What's up, lad? Lost your girl, have you?"

"She's not my girl!" Edric snapped.

"Not now, at any rate," Winter agreed with grim humour. "I told you you should have shagged the redhead."

"Shut up, Winter!"

"Don't take it so hard, boy. That John has the looks women like. It's in his eyes, you know."

"He's a monk!" Edric protested.

"So? He wouldn't be the first to abandon his vows. And that Aelswith is a mighty fine young girl."

"I can't believe they are leaving," Edric sighed.

"They're not the only ones," Winter told him. "I hear the boatmen are earning a lot of money smuggling folk out."

"I don't care about that!" Edric snarled.

He thumped his fists against his thighs to vent his frustration as he watched Brother John and Aelswith leave the abbey and disappear from sight behind the high walls.

Neither of them looked back.

116

Chapter 10

Altruda was pleased at what she had accomplished over the past few months. The debacle of the collapsing bridge and the arrival of the two northern Earls had set back her plans considerably, but the tide was now beginning to turn. King William had at last begun his advance, building a roadway through the fens, while Abbot Turold was building siege engines opposite Aldreth, and a flotilla of ships patrolled the sea lanes to pen the Ely fishermen inside the marshlands.

For her part, she had been patiently weaving her webs of intrigue in her own unique way. As she had instructed, Kenton had spent weeks in the company of Earl Edwin's housecarls and had identified three who had been persuaded by handfuls of gold coins to change their allegiance. All she had needed to do was convince Earl Edwin that he should leave the island and attempt to bring help to the rebels.

That had taken time because her chosen tool for the task was Earl Morcar. She found him pompous and vacillating, never able to make up his own mind unless guided by his brother, but she had used the time spent in his bedchamber to plant the seeds of ideas and then encourage him to discuss them with Edwin.

Now everything was in place and, at long last, the end was in sight.

"It won't be long now," she assured Kenton when he reported that he had paid the three housecarls who had been selected for the task.

"I hope you have picked the right men," she told him.

"They won't betray us if that's what you are worried about," he assured her. "Now that the King has begun his advance, they know how it will end. They were at the battle of Fulford, so they have no trust in the Earls' ability to win a fight."

Altruda nodded. Four years earlier, Edwin and Morcar had tried to defeat Harald Hardrada of Norway when he had landed in England. He had defeated them easily, routing their army. On that occasion, King Harold of England had saved them when he had arrived a few days later and destroyed the Norwegian army and killed Hardrada, but the Earls' reputation had been severely damaged by their defeat. Things had not improved in the years

117

since then, for they had twice rebelled against King William and twice they had surrendered without a fight when confronted by the strength of the Norman army.

Naturally, the Earls' housecarls had become accustomed to their failure and, while most remained loyal to their lords out of habit, many were dissatisfied. With the aid of Altruda's gold, Kenton had found three who were willing to break their oaths.

"They'll do what you want," Kenton told Altruda.

She nodded and smiled, a sense of anticipation setting her nerves tingling.

"Good," she said. "Edwin leaves tonight. Then all I need to do is deal with Hereward. Have you discovered his plan?"

Kenton shook his head.

"Rumour is he's being very tight-lipped about it. All I've heard is that he's promised to destroy the catapults opposite Aldreth while Siward Barn tries to delay the king's road building."

With a sly smirk, he added, "I thought you would find out from Morcar."

Stiffly, Altruda replied, "He knows nothing of it. I have the feeling Hereward does not trust him."

Kenton snorted a laugh.

"I don't blame him. All I know is that he's got hold of a whole load of clay pots."

"What for?"

Kenton shrugged, "He and his gang have gone off to Aldreth with them. I can't see what use they will be against the catapults Abbot Turold is building."

Altruda frowned. Hereward, she knew, always had a reason for his eccentricities, but she could not fathom what he was up to this time. She considered sending a warning letter to the King, but decided against it.

"I can't tell the King to beware of pots," she sighed. "But the fact that he has gone to Aldreth is good. It means he is concentrating on the diversion, not on the King's main line of attack. Let him waste his time there."

She rose to her feet, picking up a small bag which she tossed to Kenton. He heard the jingle of coins when he caught it.

"A small reward, Kenton. Try not to drink it all away in one go. I may have need of you tomorrow."

"I am at your service, my Lady," he said in a tone that was little short of insolent.

Altruda dismissed him with a wave of her hand.

"Now, I must prepare to say farewell to Earl Edwin. He will be setting off shortly."

Kenton's only response was a feral grin.

The exodus of people from Ely was a trickle rather than a flood, but the boatmen were certainly kept busy. Most of the fugitives headed west, but Earl Edwin had hired a man to carry him to the north.

"That's dangerous, my Lord," the boatman told him. "I can only take you so far. You'll still need to walk a fair way, and there ain't no proper paths. Then there's the tides. You'll need to be well away before dawn, or you'll be cut off when the sea floods in."

"Then get a move on!" Edwin snapped as he stepped into the small boat.

The vessel was barely large enough to hold the Earl and his three housecarls, and it wallowed ever lower in the water as each of the heavily armed men stepped on board.

The boatman clucked his tongue disapprovingly, but said nothing as he gripped his long pole, ready to push off from the bank.

"Good luck!" called Morcar, who had come to see his brother off.

Edwin frowned. Morcar had the Lady Altruda clinging to his arm like some newlywed bride, a fact which seemed to make him inordinately proud, but which only irritated Edwin's fraying nerves. He knew how difficult his mission was, and knowing his brother would be hurrying to bed with Altruda as soon as he departed did nothing to diminish his anxiety.

Gathering his resolve, he gave the couple a peremptory wave as he told them, "I'll be back soon. With an army."

Morcar nodded, and Altruda gave a simpering smile of encouragement.

"We shall await your return eagerly," she assured Edwin.

Edwin gave her a frosty smile. He disapproved of Lady Altruda, although he could not deny that his feeling might be partly due to jealousy that such a gorgeous young woman had chosen his brother over himself. Not that he would have given in to her advances, of course, for Edwin was intelligent enough to know that, while Altruda was reputedly wealthy, she had no great political ties. When he married, it would be to seal an alliance with some powerful family, not simply to acquire a beautiful woman.

Still, he would have liked the opportunity to turn Altruda down, for then he could have basked in the sense of righteousness that not giving in to temptation would have brought him. The fact that she had not given him the opportunity only increased his dislike of her.

He had heard several rumours about her since arriving in Ely, but had dismissed most of them because Altruda gave every impression of being an empty-headed young woman with nothing to offer except the undoubted delights of her body. Morcar had insisted she was more intelligent than she let on, but Edwin doubted that claim. She seemed more concerned with finding a wealthy husband than with anything important. Even the growing threat from the Normans had not seemed to make any impression on her.

"I am sure you will protect us," had been her only response when Edwin had attempted to impress upon her the dangers facing them.

He shook his head. Morcar was welcome to the woman. As long as he did not marry the stupid wench, let him have his fun while he could.

As the boat pushed away from the hithe, Edwin took a deep, calming breath. He was committed now, and he suddenly realised that he was almost glad to be leaving. His mission might be full of risk, but remaining on the island was surely even more dangerous. Whatever Hereward said, Edwin feared what would happen when King William reached Ely.

Conscious that he must set an example despite his fears, he sat erect, looking dead ahead and ignoring the receding figures on the river bank. He told himself he had a mission to accomplish; a task which would bring him glory. He would summon an army and overthrow William. Edgar the Atheling would be placed on the throne of England, and the new King, naturally, would not forget the man who had made it all possible. When set against that prize, the risk of being captured by the Normans seemed worth the hazard.

Running through this ideal scenario in his mind, Edwin reckoned Malcolm, King of the Scots, might prove to be a more difficult problem if he decided to take advantage of the civil war in England to extend his own territory. But Edwin persuaded himself that, once William was defeated, the combined might of the English Earls would be sufficient to keep the devious Scotsman's interference at bay. If they paid Malcolm enough gold and silver as a reward for his assistance, he would no doubt retreat to his barbarous homeland to count his new-found wealth. Then Edwin would be free to guide the young Edgar in how best to rule England.

Determined to succeed in his quest, Edwin sat very still as the boat moved slowly away from Ely and entered the warren of channels which flowed sluggishly through the fens. His three housecarls also remained still and silent, as if aware of the magnitude of the task facing them.

All three of them were volunteers, Edwin knew. He could have ordered men to accompany him but, on Morcar's suggestion, had said he would prefer to be accompanied by men who knew the risks they faced. The three, Athelstan, Coenwulf and Egbert, had stepped forwards even before he had finished making his announcement. That was true loyalty, Edwin thought. Despite the dreams of glory he had imagined, he knew there was a very real danger of being captured before they could reach Scotland.

Now he was on his way, with no turning back, and he must believe he would succeed.

The sun sank slowly below the western horizon, and the boat moved at a snail's pace through the long shadows until the moon rose to cast its silvery light over the Fens. The boatman made better time then, pushing the flat-bottomed vessel along narrow waterways, with reeds towering over them on either side. It was an eerie, silent world of water and reeds, and Edwin prayed the journey would not take too long.

He was to be disappointed, for it was well after midnight before the boatman eased the blunt prow of the boat onto a low ridge of swampy ground and announced that he could go no further.

"You've still got about five miles to go," he informed them. You must head due North and cross the river before you are out of the Fens."

Edwin stepped ashore, feeling his boots sink into the marshy turf, and his housecarls stumbled out of the boat to join him. The boatman stepped easily along the boat, turned to face the way they had come, and used his long pole to punt the vessel backwards. He did not say a word, and was soon lost to sight in the silvery darkness.

"Due North," Edwin told his men. "Lead the way, Athelstan."

The journey quickly turned into a nightmare. The towering reeds and thick clumps of sedge grass blocked their view and impeded their progress. Mud clung to their boots, and their feet often sank into sticky, cloying pools of oozing liquid, icy water reaching almost to their knees as they splashed and stumbled through the wilderness. Edwin was soon exhausted, breathing heavily and wishing he could stop, yet knowing that to stop was to lose any chance of reaching dry land by daybreak. Five miles was a long enough way to walk in normal circumstances, but this hellish quagmire made every step an effort and slowed their progress so much he wondered whether they would ever escape the Fens.

Were they even heading northwards? He did not know. All he could do was trudge in Athelstan's wake, hoping the big housecarl was holding to the right direction.

Every so often they came across a small island, but these gave little respite because most of them were covered by trees and bushes which were almost as impenetrable as the marsh.

They plodded on, heads bowed and breathing hard with the effort of walking through the desolate wasteland.

Edwin was cold, wet and near exhaustion by the time he realised he could hear a familiar sound somewhere close at hand.

"Waves?" he muttered. "Is that the sea I can hear?"

"The river, I hope, Lord," replied Athelstan in a gruff whisper. "They say it is close to the sea here."

They staggered on for what seemed an age, water sloshing around their feet and reeds so densely packed that they were often forced to turn from a direct path. Then, almost without warning, they staggered into a more open stretch of ground which was bathed in pale moonlight.

Athelstan stopped, holding up a cautionary arm.

"We need to cross soon, I think," he said in a low voice. "The tide seems to be coming in."

Edwin had no idea how he could tell, but Athelstan had claimed to know something of the sea, which was another reason Edwin had been pleased to bring him on this journey.

"There are mud flats further along," the housecarl said, pointing inland.

Edwin could see nothing to denote a crossing place, but wearily trudged after the big man, with the other two men following doggedly behind him, the sound of their steps squelching and sucking in what seemed an inordinately loud heralding of their passage.

After plodding upriver for what Edwin felt was an age, they found what Athelstan claimed was a suitable crossing place, but the big man urged them to hurry.

"The tide is coming in fast," he warned as he set off across the broad expanse of mud which glistened in the moonlight like a pale mirror.

Edwin followed, no longer caring where they were going, only wishing the night's trek would end. His body was bathed in damp sweat and he was shivering beneath his sodden clothing. Every step was torture because his boots felt as if they were full of clammy water which was freezing his toes to numbness.

Athelstan led them through channels of water which rose almost to their thighs as they waded towards the next mud bank. Edwin thought he could feel the pressure of the incoming tide as the water surged around him, and he almost gave in to panic when he missed his footing and stumbled. Fortunately, Egbert was quick enough to grab his arm and steady him.

"Careful, my Lord," the housecarl said.

Edwin shook off the man's grasp and waded onwards, relieved to follow Athelstan as they emerged onto another low bank of mud with water cascading from their drenched trousers and cloaks.

They waded across two more channels and were barely twenty yards from the northern bank when, without warning, Athelstan hissed, "Down!"

Edwin was slow to react, but Egbert grabbed him from behind and hauled him down, both men splashing in the shallow water which was rippling across the mud flat. Edwin spluttered as his face struck the chilly water, and he tasted salt. He felt his fingers sinking into cold, oozing mud as he struggled to lift himself against the insistent pressure of Egbert's arm on his back.

"Quiet, Lord!" Egbert hissed in his ear.

"There are men on the far bank," Athelstan whispered.

Edwin peered into the gloom but could see nothing moving. There was certainly no sign of fire to mark where men might be, yet Athelstan seemed certain of the danger.

"What do we do?" Edwin asked. "Shall we go back?"

"Too late for that, my Lord," Athelstan told him. "The sea has already cut us off."

Edwin twisted his neck to look behind them and saw that, where they had passed only a few moments before was now a wide expanse of surging water. The four of them were lying on a slightly raised mud bank which was already beneath the surface and would soon be covered by a much greater depth of water as the tide continued to flood the broad channel.

Panic began to claw at Edwin's chest. He looked frantically at Athelstan as if the housecarl were his only hope.

"We must get out of here before we all drown!" he blurted.

He felt horribly exposed out here on the wide mud plain. Surely any Normans on the far bank must be able to see them? But facing the Normans, even being captured, was better than drowning.

Athelstan turned to face him, his eyes bright in the moonlight. The housecarl studied him thoughtfully, then slowly and deliberately looked at the other two men in turn.

"Very well," he said softly. "Let us do it now."

He stood up, water dripping from his clothing in a rippling cascade, then Edwin felt Coenwulf and Egbert each take one of his arms and hoist him to his feet.

"Have a care!" he snapped as they roughly yanked him upwards.

He tried to shake off their grip, but the two men held him tight and pressed close beside him, jamming his body between them.

"What is the meaning of this?" he demanded, his voice rising and his head snapping from side to side in fury. "Let go of me!"

Then he froze to immobility when he saw the dagger in Athelstan's hand, and he understood.

Chapter 11

Most of King William's men slept out in the open when on campaign. The nobles, of course, had tents to provide overnight shelter, and William, naturally, had the largest tent of all, a marquee where he could hold court each evening. There were few places to pitch such a tent in the Fens, so he had made his camp on the fringes of the marshland from where he would set out each day to examine the progress his men were making.

"It is too slow!" he complained to William Malet as the two men discussed the extent of the works over a late supper.

"I have sent for more wagons, Your Majesty," Malet replied smoothly. "But it is necessarily slow work, I am afraid."

William frowned but did not berate Malet. He had seen for himself that the task was an enormous one. Every day, tons of earth, gravel and rocks were being hauled into the marshes and dumped into the water, load after load building up until a wide path could be beaten flat on the uneven surface of the artificial roadway.

"We are following the local paths where possible," Malet explained, "and simply making them wide enough for our cavalry to use. That should speed things up."

William nodded. There were dozens of small islets dotted all through the Fens, low humps of land standing proud of the surrounding waters. Some of these were connected by swampy pathways, and these were providing the best route for his causeway. But it was slow, back-breaking work to create a wide path through the encroaching reeds, and some days saw the causeway barely increase in length as pools of deep water swallowed the earth and rocks like some ravenous sea monster.

William said, "We should bridge some of the gaps with boats."

"Boats, Your Majesty?"

"Boats, Malet. Lash together a row of small boats, then lay planks across them to form a bridge."

Malet gave an ingratiating smile as he nodded, "An excellent idea, Your Majesty. I shall see to it, although I fear we may need to build boats of our own. Still, that would be faster than trying to fill the streams with earth."

"The horses may not like it," William said pensively. "You should cover the planking with earth to make it resemble a path."

"It shall be as you say, Your Majesty."

William finished chewing on a joint of beef, then idly tossed the bone to one of the dogs which prowled the tables.

"What about the rebels?" he asked Malet. "Are they causing trouble?"

"A few minor attacks," Malet shrugged. "They come by boat and attempt to scare off the men driving the wagons, but I've got plenty of soldiers guarding the route. We've not had any serious issues."

"Good. But it is still too slow. It will be the end of summer before we reach Ely at this rate."

"If we are going to gather boats, perhaps we could use them to launch an attack by water," Malet suggested.

William frowned as he explained, "Any boats we use in these swamps need to be small in order to navigate the narrow channels. They may be suitable for raiding parties, but we could not transport enough men to make a full scale attack on the rebel defences. No, much as I want this ended, it must be done properly, which will take time."

"Perhaps Abbot Turold and de Taillebois will have more luck at Aldreth," Malet ventured.

William gave a snort of contempt.

"I doubt that very much. De Taillebois says his witch woman will summon a storm which will batter the rebels into submission, but I will believe that when I see it. The man is far too ready to believe any charlatan who claims to be able to perform magic."

"Perhaps God will send a storm anyway," Malet suggested. "The weather has not been pleasant so far this year, and I can well believe a storm might come."

The King nodded, his face serious. He was, Malet knew, a pious man who implicitly believed that God was on his side, yet the King often meted out savage reprisals against those who opposed him, and Malet suspected he lived in constant fear that, one day, God might turn against him and punish him for his unchristian deeds. So far, though, the King's prayers had obviously been accepted, for every endeavour he undertook was blessed with success no matter how formidable the obstacles facing him.

"Are you sure you can rely on Turold and de Taillebois?" Malet asked, knowing there was never a bad time to undermine the King's confidence in rival nobles.

William shot him a frown, then shrugged, "Turold is a man of drive and ambition, if little intelligence. He will do as I wish. As for de Taillebois, he is a fool, but a useful one, and he is completely loyal to me. I prize loyalty, as you know, Malet."

Malet inclined his head in a bow, acknowledging the implicit threat in the king's words.

"I live only to serve you, Your Majesty," he vowed.

Such flattery always pleased William, especially when there were plenty of other nobles in close attendance to see how he rewarded men who displayed devotion to him. The other men who shared the table were listening intently, each wanting to be noticed, but they could tell the King was in an irritable mood, so few dared voice any opinion for fear of being reprimanded.

The food was plentiful, the wine strong and invigorating, yet William still brooded over the time it was taking to build his causeway.

"If I may be so bold, Your Majesty," Malet suggested while they ate, "I can easily oversee the construction. You could return to London and I can send for you when we are ready to make the final assault."

William's eyes flashed dangerously, and Malet realised he had made a mistake.

"I want to see this rebellion put down!" the king declared. "I will leave nothing to chance, Malet. Nothing."

"I apologise, Your Majesty. I merely wished to relieve you of this burden while the matter of governing the country is also on your mind."

William's lips turned in a grimace as he scowled, "Do you know what makes governing the country easy, Malet?"

"The loyalty of your subjects, Your Majesty?"

"Precisely. But I do not mean my nobles. The Earls and Barons I have appointed will remain loyal because they know the consequences of disobeying my will. No, Malet, it is the common people we must keep in check."

"They are under control, Your Majesty," Malet observed.

"But only because they lack leaders. Our task is to keep the ordinary people in their place, Malet. We must convince them, by threat of punishment and by word spread by the clergy, that their place is to accept their lot in life and not to question their betters. They must be made docile. They must be persuaded that, whatever happens, they cannot expect more from life than we grant them."

"I understand, Your Majesty."

"Do you? Then tell me what happens if a nest of rebels stands up and opposes my rule?"

Malet gave a slow nod of realisation.

"The people may have ideas above their station, Your Majesty?"

"Exactly so. That is why all trace of rebellion must be wiped out, and why I must be seen to mete out the punishment. I was too lenient in my first years as King. I permitted some of the English nobles to retain their lands and titles, but that was a mistake. They do not have the right attitude towards government. They might have been of noble birth, but they did not impose themselves enough on their underlings. That must change. There are few enough Normans in England as it is. If the ordinary people ever realised just how few we are compared to them, they might rise up and kill us all. I will not permit that!"

Malet gave a respectful nod as he said, "As always, Your Majesty, your breadth of vision surpasses mine. You have my word, we shall destroy this nest of vipers."

"I know. And when we do breach their defences, Malet, I want this man Hereward killed without hesitation."

"I will attend to it personally, Your Majesty," Malet promised. "It will be a pleasure."

King William smiled, knowing Malet could best any man in combat. Hereward, he reflected, was as good as dead, although it might take some weeks before the final blow could be delivered.

As the meal was ending, one of the King's clerks entered the tent and strode to the high table.

Giving a bow, he announced, "Your Majesty, there are three men outside. They say they bring a message from Ely."

"A message? Then show them in."

The clerk retraced his steps, stepping outside but soon reappearing with three big men walking nervously behind him. Even in the flickering light of the many candles which filled the great pavilion, William could instantly see that the three were

Englishmen, wearing the long hair and drooping moustaches so favoured by the Saxon warrior class. They wore no armour, and William noticed with approval that their weapons had been taken from them. As an added precaution, half a dozen mail-clad Norman soldiers walked behind them, each man with a drawn sword in his hand.

The three Englishmen looked dishevelled, with their hair hanging lankly around their shoulders, and their tunics and leggings filthy with dried mud. They were clearly nervous, their eyes flicking from side to side as they took in the interior of the large tent, the seated nobles and the dozen or so servants and attendants who waited on the King. One of the hounds growled at them from beneath a table as they passed, but none of the nobles voiced any comment at the sight of these strange visitors.

"What is it you have to tell me?" William demanded when the men stood before him.

His clerk stepped forwards, acting as interpreter.

"They do not speak French, your Majesty, but they say they have a gift for you from the Lady Altruda."

"A gift? Then show me."

At a signal from the clerk, the leading Englishman swung a small sack from his shoulder. Without ceremony, he opened it, upturning it to empty the contents onto the ground at his feet.

A gasp went up from the watching Normans as a human head tumbled to the floor, rolling to stop with its blank eyes staring at the King.

"Edwin, Earl of Mercia," the English housecarl said, his words needing no translation.

"I recognise him," William nodded, barely reacting to the gruesome sight of the severed head.

He sat back in his chair, a thin smile playing around his lips.

Turning to Malet, he asked, "The Lady Altruda is truly remarkable, is she not?"

"She certainly is, Your Majesty," Malet agreed.

William suddenly sat erect, his gaze fixing on his clerk.

"These men killed him, I presume?"

The man nodded, "That is their claim, Your Majesty. They told me they were paid by a man who is in the service of the Lady

Altruda. He told them you would reward them if they brought the head to you."

"They are not in Altruda's service themselves, then?" the king enquired sharply.

After a brief interchange, the clerk replied, "No, Your Majesty. They were in Earl Edwin's service, but were persuaded by the payment of some gold to change their allegiance."

William's frowning gaze scanned the faces of the three Englishmen. They might appear ragged and more than a little in awe of him, but they were tough-looking, fierce men who obviously knew how to wield an axe or a sword. Men like this had stood against him at Hastings, and he knew their worth in a fight.

But there were other, more important considerations weighing on the King's mind as he surveyed the three housecarls.

He turned to Malet once again, his voice calm and conversational.

"What reward do you think I should give these men, Malet?"

"They have certainly done you a great service, Your Majesty," Malet ventured cautiously. "The rebels have lost their senior leader."

Then, recalling the conversation on loyalty from earlier, he added, "But, on the other hand, they have betrayed their own Lord."

The King's smile had no humour in it as he agreed, "They certainly have. And I cannot condone that sort of betrayal. I have no doubt these men stood with Earl Edwin the last time he and his fool of a brother rebelled against me. Yet now they have turned against him. How can I trust them not to betray me in turn if someone offers them more gold?"

"I doubt that you can, Your Majesty."

William rubbed his chin while he regarded the Englishmen with cold, dispassionate eyes. Then he signalled to the guards.

"Take them outside and hang them!"

The Englishmen did not comprehend his command, but they understood the rough actions of the guards who grabbed them and hauled them away at swordpoint. One of them shouted angrily, directing an accusation or insult at the King, while another struggled to free himself until he was struck on the head by the pommel of a sword. He staggered and would have fallen had the guards not held him upright and dragged him out with blood staining his long hair.

The Norman lords could still hear the shouts for a long time after the three men had been hauled outside to be given their reward. Then the cries were suddenly cut off, signalling that the King's sentence had been carried out.

"That is how disloyalty should be punished," William observed with satisfaction. Then he gave a cruel smile as he added, "It seems The Lord favours our enterprise, Malet. You never know, perhaps de Taillebois's witch woman may yet summon a storm to destroy our enemies."

Chapter 12

Edric could hardly believe what he was doing. Dressed in plain, ragged clothing like a peasant, he led the donkey through the horde of Norman soldiers and workmen as he trailed behind Hereward. The donkey was laden with sacks containing the clay pots Edric had purchased from Cecil, the weight of the burden reducing the beast's progress to a slow, grudging plod.

Hereward walked with a swagger, smiling as if he owned the camp, completely oblivious to the danger that surrounded them. If anyone saw through their disguise, they would be cut to pieces in a matter of seconds, for their only weapons were the knives they carried on their belts.

But nobody paid them much attention. Most of the Normans were too preoccupied with their own tasks to bother with a couple of ragged merchants and a donkey. The only challenge had come when they had first entered the camp, where a group of bored guards had been suspicious of Hereward because of his long moustache. Hereward, however, began chatting to them in fluent French, smiling, waving his hands and nodding his head. The guards relaxed after asking a few questions, then gave the donkey's baggage a cursory inspection before waving them on.

"What did you say to them?" Edric asked in a low whisper once they were beyond the guards' hearing.

"I told them I am a merchant, originally from Flanders, but now travelling throughout England selling the finest pottery to be found anywhere in Christendom."

"And they believed you?"

"It seems so," Hereward grinned. "At least they didn't break any of the pots."

He had wanted to bring the small, two-wheeled cart, but transporting its bulk through the waterways of the surrounding fens would have been difficult, so he and Edric had manhandled the protesting donkey into a fen boat which had taken them well clear of Ely. They had disembarked by night, just as they had done so often when carrying out a raid, but this time the grey, cloud-laden dawn had found them clear of the fens and able to join the trackway which led to the Norman camp opposite Aldreth. It had been a long, slow journey, their route having taken them in a wide circle to bring them back almost to where they had begun. Now, though, they were in the Norman camp instead of gazing at it across the river, yet Edric remained mystified as to what Hereward planned.

"Why are we doing this?" he had asked anxiously as they picked their careful way through the fringes of the marshland.

"Because I want to destroy those boats and siege engines the Normans have built," Hereward had answered.

"But why you and me?" Edric had persisted. "You should not do anything as dangerous as this, and I'm not the best fighter in the gang if you do run into trouble."

Hereward had smiled as he explained, "I am doing it because I speak better French than the rest of you."

Edric knew that was true, but he wondered whether Hereward's decision to undertake this mission might not be due to his ego. To walk into the enemy camp and destroy their siege weapons was a deed men would speak of for years.

If it succeeded, which Edric was beginning to doubt because there were so many Normans that even approaching the giant catapults without being challenged would be impossible. The three great weapons were lined up facing the earth rampart which Edric had helped to defend the previous year. The machines were set back from the river bank, just out of effective bowshot to allow the crews to work unmolested by the handful of English archers among the defenders. None of the siege weapons had been used yet, but dozens of large rocks had been gathered and were being piled near the catapults. This time, it seemed, the Normans intended to flatten the defensive wall by bombardment rather than storm it by weight of numbers. They had also constructed a tall, square-sided tower with a platform at the top from where they could look down over the earth wall to see what the defenders were doing.

Edric could not help feeling that Hereward had waited too long before taking action. He had watched from the ramparts as the machines took shape, but had waited until the work was virtually complete before setting off on this mission.

"The catapults are a danger," he had told Edric as they walked along the trackway towards the camp. "But the boats are our main target. They can hurl as many rocks as they like, but they can't cross the river without boats."

134

That made sense, but Edric was still none the wiser as to how Hereward intended to carry out his plan. He could see those boats now, nearly thirty of them lying upturned on the grassy bank at the extreme left of the Norman position. A curve of the river meant that any attempt by the defenders to strike at the boats would mean rowing past the front of the Norman camp where the English raiders would be exposed to arrows, javelins and catapult fire.

The Norman boats themselves were unimpressive. They were hastily-built, crude imitations of the flat-bottomed fen boats; little more than low, open-topped, rectangular boxes, but each of them was capable of carrying several armed men across the deep river in only a few minutes.

The boats were a sobering sight, but Edric had not been completely satisfied by Hereward's earlier explanation.

"You still haven't told me why you wanted me to come with you," he said. "Siward White speaks some French, and any of the others is better than me if it comes to a fight."

"White has something else to do for me," Hereward replied enigmatically. "As for fighting, I hope you and I will get away without needing to resort to that. But you are here precisely because you do not walk and act like a trained warrior. Bringing Winter or Ordgar would give the game away because they are so obviously fighting men. Also, as I have told you before, you are capable of thinking quickly and adapting to whatever happens. That is why I wanted you to come with me."

Edric was not sure whether he was being complimented or criticised, but he chose to accept it as a mark of the respect Hereward held for him.

In truth, he found it remarkably easy to slip back into the role of an artisan's apprentice. The disguise was crude, but Hereward had insisted that it was more about how they behaved than how they looked. Besides, other tradesfolk were in the camp, selling all sorts of goods to the soldiers. Hereward had explained that, with no towns or even villages within easy reach, the Normans would be relying on local traders to supply them. Since the camp could only be approached by a single pathway through the marshes, merchants would be able to charge high prices for their goods, so many had decided that the difficult trek would be worth their while.

135

Edric had seen for himself that Hereward's guess had been correct. Not only were labour gangs hauling timber, rocks and food supplies along the pathway, he had seen several merchants on the road as well.

"But pots?" Edric frowned. "Will they want pots?"

"I couldn't care less," Hereward chuckled. "But pots are what I need."

And now they were here, in the heart of the Norman camp which bustled with activity. Edric could hear men shouting, horses whinnying, pigs snorting and grunting, with the background accompaniment of carpenters at work.

But Edric's attention was on the soldiers. There were hundreds of them here, many of them in chainmail and carrying weapons, but others in tunics and leggings because they were involved in chopping or carrying wood, preparing food, sharpening weapons, tending the horses, making arrows or digging latrine ditches.

There were several large tents set up well away from the river, with pennons flying from the highest tent poles, and armed guards standing outside.

"Best keep away from there," Hereward said, although Edric caught a wistful look in the Thane's expression as he studied the tents. Then he shrugged and cast an expert eye over the rest of the camp.

He was not impressed.

"They're sloppy," he murmured, half to himself, half to Edric. "They think we are no threat because we haven't made any attempt to attack them. They think we are going to do no more than sit behind the wall and wait for them to cross the river."

There was certainly a relaxed attitude in the camp, with the men behaving as if the English forces on the far bank of the river were a hundred miles away rather than just beyond bowshot. Only a handful of guards patrolled the perimeter of the camp which had no defensive ditches at all. The Normans had simply spread out across this large patch of relatively dry land which was surrounded on all sides by peat bogs, reeds and water.

"They think they are safe here," Hereward said. "But that's what I am counting on."

They slowly made their way towards the river. A handful of bored guards stood near the great catapults to make sure nobody

136

got too close to the newly constructed engines of war, but Hereward stood for a long time, simply staring beyond the catapults and across the river to the English defences. It was strange, Edric thought, to see those ramparts from this side of the water. He could make out the dark shapes of men standing behind the earth wall, but the distance was too great to allow him to make out individual faces. Most of the defenders who manned the wall were Mercians, Edric knew, but Siward White and the gang were also there, and Edric wished he was with them, because being surrounded by so many Normans was making him anxious.

Hereward, apparently oblivious to his surroundings, stood there for a long time before turning away.

"We should get our wares set up," he declared.

He led Edric away from the river and headed towards the horse lines. The Normans had brought around forty horses, and had tethered them in rows by the simple expedient of hammering stakes into the ground and tying a long rope between them, then looping the horses' reins around the rope.

"Bloody daft dragging horses all this way through the marshes," Hereward commented. "They'll not be any use at all. But that's Norman lords for you. They don't like walking."

He told Edric to tether the donkey and unpack the sacks, then chose a patch of grass some distance from the horses where they set out their wares. Soon, Hereward was regaling the nearest Normans in an attempt to sell some of their pots and jars. He gained several potential customers, for the servants who had been charged with tending the Norman horses had little to do and were bored, so they wandered over to inspect the various pots which Edric had unpacked. Hereward did not gain much actual custom, but he spent a great deal of time talking to the servants.

"Everyone's waiting for this witch woman," he reported to Edric. "But we'd better keep our distance. It seems this place is under the command of Abbot Turold and Ivo de Taillebois. If either of them sees us, we'll need to make a run for it."

This news worried Edric a great deal. Abbot Turold would certainly recognise Hereward if he saw him, and might well remember Edric as one of Hereward's gang. But Ivo de Taillebois certainly knew him well because the Sheriff had been based in Bourne for several months.

He supposed they should have realised there was a chance of Hereward's nemesis being here, although Hereward had assumed that King William would send different commanders after the failure of the first assault on Ely.

"We'll be fine," Hereward assured Edric. "Those two won't have any interest in a potter's wares."

"I hope you are right," Edric sighed. "But what do we do if they come this way?"

"They won't," Hereward stated confidently.

"But if they do?"

"Then we run for the horses, grab a couple and gallop away."

"I've only ridden a horse once before," Edric told him. "And I never went at a gallop."

"Then I hope you are a fast learner," Hereward grinned.

Despite the Thane's confidence, Edric remained anxious, but when the two Norman commanders did put in an appearance, it was their companion who gave him the greatest cause for concern.

A group of men emerged from the tent which Hereward had identified as that belonging to Turold. The Abbot was among them, along with the large, fleshy figure of Ivo de Taillebois and a handful of senior knights, all of them dressed in chainmail, but there was also a woman with them.

She was dressed in a dark robe, with her grey hair tied back in a severe bun, and her thin face displaying a haughty air.

Edric gasped and lowered his head, tugging the hood of his cloak up to help disguise his features. The woman was fifty yards away and busy speaking to de Taillebois, but her presence left him feeling exposed and terrified.

"What's wrong?" Hereward asked sharply.

"It's Gytha! She's from our village. She's a witch!"

Hereward studied the stick-like figure standing among the burly men at the tent's entrance.

"So she's the one who is going to conjure up a storm?" Hereward grinned. "Don't panic, lad. Nobody is paying any attention to us."

It was true. Abbot Turold led the group down the gentle slope towards the high tower by the bank of the river, and everyone in the camp stopped to watch them pass.

When they arrived at the foot of the tower, Gytha reached out to grasp the rungs of a ladder which was attached to the rear wall. Slowly, tentatively, she began to climb, her every step watched by the men on the ground.

"Time for us to start, I think," Hereward remarked casually. "Bring the special sack, and let's collect a couple of horses."

They strolled the few yards to the horse lines, leaving their collection of pots sitting on the grass, with Edric carrying only one sack which contained half a dozen small pots with sealed lids. Nobody challenged them because everyone was intent on the spectacle of an elderly witch clambering up a wooden tower to cast her spells against the rebels.

While Hereward selected two horses and fastened saddles to their backs, Edric glanced nervously across the river. He could see the shapes of men lining the ramparts, could make out the pale ovals of their faces as they stared at the sight of a grey-haired woman standing on the platform at the top of the tower thirty feet above the ground. Those men had expected to be tasked with fending off armed soldiers, not magical spells, and Edric wondered whether they were feeling the same, stomach-churning anxiety that was now assailing his guts.

"Here we go," Hereward announced cheerfully. "Now, walk beside the horse, and keep it between you and the bulk of the Normans. We'll go in a slow circle around the edge of the camp."

"Where are we going?" Edric asked, accepting the reins and nervously fussing with the sack of pots.

"Down towards those boats," Hereward told him, jerking his chin to indicate the newly-built punts the Normans had assembled by the river.

Edric now understood Hereward's intention, but the thought of what they must accomplish left him horrified.

"But there are hundreds of Normans who will stop us!" he protested.

"So there are," Hereward grinned. "What we need is a diversion. Maybe something will happen soon."

He gave Edric a confident wink, then led the way in a wide circle, arcing to their left and skirting the edge of the islet which formed the Norman camp. With tall reeds on their left and the horses on their right, they gradually drew nearer the river bank.

Edric could see and hear Gytha now. The old harridan, who had tormented him ever since he had been a boy, was standing on the platform and screeching curses towards the Mercians on the far side of the river. She used one hand to hold onto a low railing which ran around the edges of the platform, but her other arm was waving theatrically as she spat her curses and summoned a storm to destroy the rebels. As she grew bolder, she released her hold on the rail and waved both arms aggressively while she continued to chant vituperative oaths. Then, giving the Mercians the ultimate insult, she turned to face away from them, bent over, lifted her dress and exposed her scrawny backside to them.

The Normans laughed and cheered at this, encouraging her to continue her antics. She did not disappoint, raising her voice even louder to hurl invective at the English defenders.

"Quite a performance," commented Hereward. "You say you know her?"

"She lived in Bourne. Nobody liked her."

Hereward's eyes took on a distant look as he searched his memory.

"Gytha, you say? Yes, I think I remember her. It was a long time ago, of course. One thing I do recall, though, is that she was never able to summon a storm."

Edric countered, "She's told the Normans she can."

Hereward looked up at the grey sky.

"It's been a miserable year so far," he commented. "We've already had a couple of storms, so I expect another one might come along soon enough."

"So you don't think she can make it happen?" Edric asked, seeking some reassurance.

"I expect she will be more able to wheedle silver from de Taillebois if she claims magical powers," Hereward shrugged. "Now, forget her and let's get on with what we came here to do."

Edric could still not shake off his nervous worry. They were now barely thirty yards from the tower, and he was sure somebody would challenge them at any moment.

Hereward stopped, turning to give him another reassuring smile.

"It's about time White put in an appearance," he whispered. "Watch the far side of the river."

Edric stared across to the other side of the water, but his view was obstructed by the hundreds of men who stood staring up at the spectacle of Gytha's bizarre ritual, so he heard the diversion before he could make out what it was.

Men began to shout in alarm, then the Normans scattered as they ran to pick up their weapons and armour. Edric caught a glimpse of fen boats speeding across the river as fast as they could go, warriors holding shields crouched in the prows of the boats to ward off the few arrows the Normans were able to fire at them.

It was like one of the night time raids the English had carried out the year before, but this time the boats were coming in daylight. It should have been a suicidal mission, but the Normans were unprepared, caught in a festive mood while they watched the witch woman. The boats were moving quickly, powered by several men in each vessel using short paddles to propel them across the waterway. As they thumped into the bank, warriors sprang out and hastily began to form a shield wall before advancing towards the nearest catapult.

"That ought to keep the Normans busy for a little while," Hereward said with a gleam in his eye. "They weren't expecting an attack."

The sudden assault had certainly caught the Normans by surprise. They had become complacent after several weeks of being left unmolested while they built their boats and catapults, and the camp was in uproar as they struggled to respond to the advancing shield wall. Edric saw Abbot Turold shouting at his men to form up and face the English advance, while Ivo de Taillebois was scurrying back towards the large tent near the horse lines. For a moment, Edric wondered whether Hereward might be tempted to chase the fat Sheriff, but Hereward contented himself with shooting an angry glare at de Taillebois's retreating back before turning his attention to his main task.

"Leave the horses here," he commanded. "Drive your knife into the ground and tether them to it. Then start breaking those pots open and spread the contents. I'll fetch a torch."

Edric obediently tethered the two horses, then hurried towards the Norman boats. They were entirely unguarded, every man having run off to confront Siward White's diversionary attack. Edric was aware of the sounds of shouting, of the rhythmic thump of the shield wall's challenge, and of Gytha continuing to

141

scream hate-filled imprecations from her lofty perch, but he ignored them all and opened his sack. Nestled in the depths of the reed stuffing, it contained six jars with sealed lids. He drew one out, broke the wax seal with his fingernails, discarded the lid, then swung his arm to spray the jar's contents out across the upturned hulls of the boats.

He had wondered why Hereward had wanted these jars filled with oil. Now he understood.

Fire. That was Hereward's weapon of choice. He had used it during the raid on Peterborough, and now he intended to use it to destroy the Norman boats. But to ensure the wood burned, they had brought jars of oil and fat which Edric was now spreading across the wooden boats. He broke the seals, flinging the oil over the upturned hulls as quickly as he could.

He emptied the last jar, then turned to see Hereward casually strolling back towards him, carrying a burning torch in each hand. With the nearby camp fires having been abandoned, he had simply walked up and lit the brands without anyone challenging him.

Careful not to alarm the horses by walking too close to them while holding flaming brands, Hereward moved to the boats. He grinned as he nodded at Edric's handiwork before setting a flame to the nearest boat. It caught immediately, the oil and fat sizzling into action so that even the new, green wood of the boats caught fire, emitting hungry flames and dark, oily smoke.

Hereward tossed one of the burning torches deeper into the assembled boats, waited to make sure it had caught, then turned and grinned again.

"Now for that tower," he said.

The tower was little more than twenty yards away, but there were no Normans nearby. The entire camp had now mustered into some sort of order and was facing up to Siward White's shield wall. Already, though, Edric could see a thin column of smoke rising from one of the huge catapults. White's men had obviously managed to set fire to it, and the threat was driving Abbot Turold to concentrate all his efforts on protecting the siege weapons.

Edric wondered how White and the others would get away, for they were severely outnumbered by the hundreds of Normans who were frantically mustering to face them. Only the unexpectedness of their raid had protected them so far, but Turold was gathering his men for a counterattack which would surely sweep the English shield wall aside in a matter of moments.

"Fetch the horses," Hereward commanded. "Meet me at the tower."

Edric dashed back towards the two horses. The noise from the fighting and the rising flames from the nearby boats had terrified them, so he took a moment to whisper soothing words to them. He may not have learned how to ride properly, but he was accustomed to dealing with nervous horses from his time in the smithy when he had helped his uncle shoe the mounts of the local Norman garrison. The horses, their ears flat against their heads, tossed their manes in readiness to flee, but Edric held tight to the reins as he recovered his knife and shoved it into his belt.

Still speaking soft words of comfort, he led the two horses towards the tower.

Hereward was already there, touching his flaming torch to the wood, making sure the flames had caught.

And still, Edric realised in wonder, nobody had seen them.

Beyond the tower, the Normans were huddling together, the men nearest the river bank now being peppered by arrows which the Mercians on the far bank were sending across in a series of small volleys. The Normans were compelled to raise their shields over their heads, a move which delayed them from advancing on Siward White's small band of warriors, while the Normans furthest from the river, although unmolested, had a greater distance to cover to reach the English raiders. Still, Edric knew, White and his men were in grave danger of being caught and surrounded.

Edric, desperate to see beyond the massed line of Normans, swung himself up into the saddle of the leading horse. He mounted clumsily, and the animal sensed his uneasiness, skittering aside and almost making him lose his grip on the reins of the second horse. He wavered unsteadily, then shoved both feet in the stirrups and wedged himself into the saddle, gripping the pommel with one hand while he clutched both sets of reins in the other. He knew the horse was nervous, yet he did not dare risk releasing his grip to offer it a comforting pat. He clung on desperately as he nudged the animal into motion and directed it towards the tall tower. At the same time, he shot a glance over the heads of the Norman lines and saw that Siward White's shield wall had not waited to be attacked, but had dissolved as the men turned and ran for their lives, pelting back towards the waiting boats. The Normans, in response, let out a great cry of victory and pounded after them.

Edric prayed the Englishmen would escape, but he had no more time to worry about them because, at last, somebody had noticed what was happening behind the Norman lines. A servant, one of the men set to tend the horses, was tugging at Abbot Turold's arm and pointing towards the dark cloud of smoke which was rising from the stack of boats. Edric saw the Abbot's mouth drop open in startled amazement, then saw other men turn as the Abbot began bellowing orders.

"Time to go!" Hereward called cheerfully as he tossed aside his torch and swung easily up into the saddle of the spare horse.

Just then, a screech from overhead impaled Edric as surely as a spear would have done.

"Edric Strong! I know you! God curse you for a rebel, a liar and a thief!"

He looked up, his heart pounding wildly, to see Gytha pointing down at him, her face contorted in rage which quickly turned to fear when she noticed the fire crackling around the base of the tower she stood on.

Edric could not speak. Gytha was a witch; a vindictive harpy who had tormented him for years, and he dared not move under the spell of her accusing finger. He knew Norman soldiers were hurrying towards them, but he was unable to react. All he could do was stare up at the old harridan in petrified horror.

"A curse on you, Edric Strong!" she rasped. "May you rot in Hell for your evil deeds!"

Still, Edric could not move. He managed to swallow, to create some saliva in his suddenly parched mouth, yet he could not say or do anything in the face of her accusations.

Hereward muttered a soft curse of his own as he stared up at the black-clad figure on top of the tower.

"Hold your tongue, woman!" he yelled up at her. "I suggest you save your breath because the fire is coming for you. If you have any sense, you'll jump into the water before the flames reach you."

Fear made Gytha screech a barely coherent curse at him as she became aware of the smoke wisping around her feet and the crackle of flames from the foot of the tower, but Hereward laughed.

"Come on, Edric, leave her. It's time we got away from here."

He tugged on the reins, wheeling the horse and nudging Edric's mount to turn and follow him. Edric, still with his eyes fixed on Gytha, barely noticed as his horse began to turn. Even as it did so, the old woman stumbled back, her face contorted by hate and fear at the realisation her route to the ground was being consumed by flames. With smoke drifting around her feet, she panicked, and in that panic she caught the back of her legs against the low rail which ran around the platform. Her hands flailed wildly as she toppled backwards, but she missed her grip and, with Edric watching on in horrified fascination, she let out a scream as she plummeted over the parapet. Her piercing wail was cut off when she struck the ground at the side of the burning tower.

Edric twisted, inadvertently turning his horse back towards the tower as he gaped down at the crumpled, twisted figure on the ground. Gytha did not move and, from the unnatural angle at which her head now sat on her shoulders, he could tell that her neck was broken.

"She missed the water, then," Hereward remarked callously. "Good riddance. It seems God disapproved of her, after all."

Then, more urgently, he reached out and tugged at the bridle of Edric's mount.

"Come on, lad! If we don't go now, we'll be joining her."

He forced both horses into motion, urging them into a fast canter which soon developed into a gallop. Edric, still dazed by the shock of witnessing Gytha's death, followed with no thought of what lay ahead. All he could do was cling to the pommel for dear life as he swayed awkwardly in the saddle, his whole body jerked and bounced by the unfamiliar motion. He was barely conscious of the shouts from the Normans who were now little more than twenty yards away and still charging towards them. Only the flashing of a javelin as it whizzed inches past his face registered on his numbed mind, but he ignored the danger and tried to concentrate on staying as close to Hereward as he could.

There was only one way they could go. The burning tower was behind them, the inferno of blazing boats to their right, and a swarm of enraged Normans closing in on their left. Hereward led the charge towards the southern perimeter of the camp, the horses soon outpacing the pursuing Norman foot soldiers. Hereward whooped in delight, disdaining the handful of arrows which flickered around the two riders, and looking back over his shoulder to grin his encouragement to Edric.

"Hang on, lad! We're not out of this yet."

Because the narrow neck of reasonably dry land at the southern limit of the camp, the only passable route through which the Normans had brought their baggage, was guarded by a small detachment of soldiers. They had not been able to see what was happening in the camp, but they could see the smoke and flames, and could hear the shouting, so they were ready for whatever might confront them.

When the two riders came galloping out of the camp, the dozen guards hastily formed a short line of shields and held their spears ready.

Edric knew that no horse would charge home against a solid line of men. Untrained men might break, and then the horses would gallop into the gaps between them, but men who stood firm could withstand a cavalry charge if their nerve held.

These men, although few in number, were obviously well trained. They would not break and run. Edric retained enough perception to realise that he and Hereward could not go around them, for they completely blocked the narrow isthmus which provided the only route off the peninsula.

"This way!" Hereward yelled, swinging to his left.

Edric's horse followed, more because it saw its companion turning than because Edric was providing any guidance. All he was able to do was hang on as the pounding, bone-jarring gallop swerved away from the Norman barricade. He swayed alarmingly in the saddle as the horse changed course, but somehow managed to cling on, too terrified even to offer up a prayer for survival.

"Come on!" Hereward called, his voice suffused with excitement as he leaned low over his horse's neck, kicking his heels to urge it ever faster. Clods of peaty earth flew from its hooves as it charged on.

Edric felt his heart quail. There was nothing ahead of them except a wall of tall reeds which marked the edge of the land. Beyond it, he could see the sparkling glint of afternoon sunlight reflecting on a wide stretch of dark water, with yet more reeds and marshland some thirty yards away on the further side of the pool.

Edric's mind registered this, but could not provide him with any suggestion as to why Hereward was racing towards the water. Perhaps Hereward had seen something he could not, but there was no time to do anything except hang on and try to follow. Gripping the pommel of the saddle even more tightly, he clamped his jaw shut to prevent himself biting his tongue as he bounced up and down.

A growing sense of alarm gripped him as they raced towards the reed-lined bank. Surely Hereward did not intend to gallop into the water?

But he did. Hereward's horse leaped high, its raised legs brushing through the tops of the wide cluster of reeds, then it crashed down into the water with an almighty splash which created a surge of ripples and sent a huge gout of water spraying in all directions.

Edric's horse refused to follow. As it reached the edge of the soft peat bordering the reed bed, it suddenly planted its hooves into the ground, sending Edric flying over its head in a high somersault. His feet left the stirrups, his hands were torn from the pommel and he arced into the air, careering over the thick hedge of reeds and crashing into the water with an impact which drove all the air from his lungs.

He landed on his back, slapping hard into the deep pond and sinking beneath the surface in a welter of panic. He had never learned how to swim, and he had always dreaded deep water.

His vision clouded, the sunlight vanished, and he lost all sense of where he was. All he knew was that there was deep, dark water all around him and that his lungs were burning, desperately pleading with him to open his mouth and take in a gasp of air.

He flailed wildly, arms and legs floundering as he sought something – anything – to grab hold of.

But there was nothing except the cold, wet, murky depths of the mere, and he knew he was about to drown.

Chapter 13

Torfrida thought her heart was going to break. She had never felt so alone in all her life, not even in those dark days in Flanders when one of her suitors after another had died, leaving her the subject of whispers and furtive glances from the other ladies of the court. There had even been rumours of witchcraft after her third betrothed had died. Nobody had openly accused her, but she had heard the rumours nonetheless. And, at the time, she had genuinely felt that she must be cursed and destined to a life of spinsterhood. After all, who would dare propose marriage to a young woman who had already seen three intended husbands suffer untimely deaths from accident or illness?

Of course, Hereward had dared. He had arrived at the court of Flanders as a penniless survivor of a shipwreck, but he had risen rapidly through the ranks of the Count's household until he had been appointed commander of the Count's army thanks to his astounding successes in battle. Women had vied for his attentions, yet it was Torfrida who had caught his eye, and he had laughed off the warnings men had whispered in his ear. In fact, Torfrida knew, the rumours surrounding her had only increased his desire for her.

So he had rescued her from the fate she had thought awaited her, but she had never forgotten the pain and misery of those earlier days.

Yet even those difficult times were nothing to the sense of loss she felt now.

"He will come back," Siward White assured her, although she could see from the look in his eyes he did not truly believe it.

Hereward's mission had been a success, but he and Edric had not returned.

Siward White's diversionary attack had achieved all its aims, and the warriors had successfully scrambled back into their flotilla of small boats which had brought them back across the river with only a few casualties to show for their audacious raid. They had burned one catapult, damaged the other two, and provided time for Hereward and Edric to destroy the Norman boats and the watch tower. White's men had returned to Aldreth full of excitement, but that had soon turned to concern when they saw the fires spreading on the far bank of the river.

The Norman boats had been laid on ground which was mostly peat, and that had caught fire, the flames soon spreading to the reeds bordering the Norman camp. Marsh fires were incredibly dangerous, sometimes burning for weeks, often spreading out of sight as the peat beneath the surface of ground or water smouldered, only to burst into life in another spot when it found the open air again.

The Normans had soon found themselves surrounded by flames as the inferno spread. Once again, panic had gripped them, and they had abandoned their camp, streaming away along the narrow pathway as quickly as they could, leaving tents and equipment behind.

Siward White and the rest of the gang had waited, hoping for some sign that Hereward and Edric had escaped both the conflagration and the stampede of fleeing men and horses, but they had waited in vain. It had been three days now, and still there was no sign of them.

"The fires are still burning," White told Torfrida, "so I expect they are trying to find another route back."

Torfrida tried to find some solace in his words, but her heart was aching so badly she could not throw off a deep sense of despair.

"He should never have gone!" she cried. "Now we have lost him!"

"He was the only one who could have done it," White replied, trying to explain Hereward's insistence on undertaking the mission. "But don't be too sure we have lost him. The Normans would have told us if they'd caught him. We have heard nothing, so he must be alive and free."

Torfrida wanted to believe him, but the more time that passed with no word, the more she convinced herself that Hereward and Edric had either been caught or had drowned in the marshes while attempting to escape.

The news of Earl Edwin's fate only served to reinforce her fear. She did not know how word of his death had reached the island, only that the rumours had spread among the monks and the warriors, and she could sense how much it had demoralised the men of Mercia and Northumbria.

Edwin's brother, Earl Morcar, was stunned. He had retired to his chamber, with the Lady Altruda keeping him company, but he had not been seen for two days.

"The lily-livered clown is probably trying to work out how to abandon us," was White's opinion.

Yet there was little chance of escape. Small numbers of men might evade the patrolling Normans, but the route to the sea was watched, and the causeway was inching ever closer. Now that there was no prospect of help coming from the Scots, and with their Earl dead, many of the Mercians were clearly having second thoughts about why they should remain at Ely, and that mood was spreading among the defenders. The threat of attack from Aldreth had been removed, but the king's causeway was still advancing and, without Hereward's leadership, the entire rebellion was in danger of crumbling.

"What else can go wrong?" Torfrida asked White. "I feel as if we have been cut adrift on a stormy sea."

Her sense of abandonment was compounded by other absences. Not only had Hereward and Earl Edwin gone, Torfrida's maid, Alice, had disappeared in mysterious circumstances. Ever since she had accompanied Torfrida on the journey to England from Flanders, Alice had been miserable. Torfrida could understand the girl's feelings because she, too, often felt isolated in this strange country with its unfamiliar customs, but she had never considered Alice might abandon her. Even now, she found it difficult to believe.

But what other explanation could there be for the girl's disappearance? The day after Hereward had burned the Norman camp, Alice had complained of feeling unwell. Torfrida packed her off to the infirmary to see Brother Richard. Alice had gone dutifully enough but had not returned. When Torfrida visited the infirmary later, Brother Richard confirmed that he had given the girl some herbal medicine to ease her stomach ache and told her to rest for a few days.

"I haven't seen her since then," the monk insisted.

In fact, it seemed nobody had seen her. Together with Martin Lightfoot, Hereward's taciturn manservant, Torfrida had searched the abbey for her, but Alice had vanished without a trace.

"Where could she have gone?" Torfrida asked Siward White when she turned to him for help.

"I'm afraid she must have run off," White suggested. "She was very frightened, wasn't she?"

"Yes, she was. She was frightened of everything. But she had nowhere to run to, and no friends other than me and Martin. She does not speak English well at all. Why should she run away, and where would she go?"

White had no answers for her except to say, "Fear does strange things to people."

Which was, Torfrida knew, no answer at all.

She sat in her room, nervously wringing her hands, feeling utterly helpless and lost. She had always managed to conceal her own fears, but now they threatened to overwhelm her. Earl Edwin was dead, Alice had vanished and, above all, Hereward was missing.

It had been a difficult enough year for Torfrida. She had never wanted to stay in Ely, but had reluctantly deferred to Hereward's desire to do something to help his fellow countrymen. When the Danes had arrived, he had been as joyful as she could ever recall seeing him, but things had gone wrong since King Sweyn's departure. Even the arrival of the earls Edwin and Morcar had brought as many problems as solutions.

All the time, Torfrida had tried not to complain. Hereward had been content to spend his days in Flanders when he had first met and married her, but Flanders had become a hostile place since the death of the old Count. She knew her husband's heart had always lain in England, yet she could not understand his stubborn insistence that he could free the country from the ravages and excesses of William's tyrannical rule. Hereward was a great man, she knew, but there were few left in England who would rally to join him. With Edwin's death and Morcar's unwillingness to fight, only the veteran Siward Barn remained. He, at least, was not prepared to give up the fight and had set off to the western fringes of the isle to prepare the defences against the encroaching causeway. Torfrida had never really taken to the crusty old Thane, but his departure left her feeling more abandoned than ever. Isolated from the monks by virtue of being female, she had spent over a year living in this small room, her excursions limited to walks around the abbey precinct or into the town of Ely. But everywhere she went, armed guards accompanied her, and she felt as if she were under siege. She had done her best to act the part of a dutiful wife, but had found little solace except in the times she had been able to spend doting on Aelswith's baby daughter.

But Aelswith, too, had fled, taking Torfrida's young namesake with her, and the memory of that additional loss added further weight to the burden of loneliness weighing on Torfrida's shoulders.

Martin Lightfoot was still with her, but he had always been Hereward's man first and foremost, and the ageing manservant offered no comfort. He had always been solemn and serious, his expression constantly dour, and all he could offer Torfrida was a half-hearted assurance that Hereward would return.

"He is a hard man to kill," he told her, although she could sense that Martin, too, was grieving.

The old man's loyalty was not in question, but Torfrida thought his words were uttered more out of hope than genuine belief.

There was only one person who could offer Torfrida any real comfort. That was the Dane, Ranald Sigtrygsson. He and Hereward had known each other for years, and their reunion when Ranald had arrived with King Sweyn's army had been a joyous occasion. Hereward had believed Ranald was in Ireland where he had a wife and children, but Ranald had travelled to Denmark to claim a share of his inheritance when he had heard of his father's death. When he had learned that his brothers had already divided the estate amongst themselves, he had gone to see King Sweyn. As recompense for his loss, the king had offered him a place in his expedition to England where Sweyn had hoped to either seize the throne for himself or at least return home with a great deal of plunder. He had achieved the latter objective, but Ranald had taken a serious wound to his leg during the raid on Peterborough and had been forced to remain in the infirmary at Ely where he had lain for weeks while he slowly recovered his health. Now, after several months of recuperation, he was at last able to walk and even run, only a slight limp remaining as a memento of the fight.

Seeing Torfrida's distress, he came to sit with her, reassuring her that Hereward would return.

"I have known him a long time," Ranald told her. "He is a remarkable man. You know that. He has fought bears and giants, has been exiled and shipwrecked, and he has always survived."

"Then why has he not returned?" Torfrida demanded.

"He'll be taking a long route to get back," Ranald insisted. "He'll need to avoid the Norman patrols, so it will take him some time, especially if he hasn't been able to find a boat."

"It has already taken him too long!" Torfrida exclaimed. "And every day the Normans get closer. He was the one with the plan for beating them, and now he's gone."

"Old Barn is no fool," Ranald replied easily. "Hereward's raid has secured the southern approach. Without boats, the Normans can't cross the river there. That means Barn can concentrate on the force coming along the causeway. And they only have one way in and one way out. Barn will chop them into pieces before long."

"He doesn't have enough men," Torfrida countered. "The Mercians and Northumbrians won't follow him unless Morcar commands it, and he's hiding in his room."

Ranald returned an encouraging smile as he told her, "You underestimate the warriors of the north, my Lady. When it comes to a choice between surrendering to the Normans or fighting them, I'm sure those men will pick up their weapons."

"It could be too late by then," Torfrida retorted. "Hereward always said he planned to destroy the Norman army before it reached Ely. If the Mercians wait until the causeway reaches us, they may not be able to stop the attack."

Many men would have dismissed her concerns because she was a woman and could therefore not be expected to appreciate the finer points of military strategy, but Ranald took her comments seriously.

"The defences are strong," he insisted. "We can hold them back. Believe me, my Lady, the Mercians know how to fight."

"But they lack a leader!" she persisted. "And holding the Normans at bay was never Hereward's plan. You know that."

"I know," he nodded gravely. Then, with a smile, he promised, "But I am sure Hereward will come back soon. You can count on it."

She nodded, struggling to hold back her tears. She felt foolish for giving in to grief, yet she could not help herself. More than ever, Ely felt like a small, isolated corner of a foreign land, full of strange customs and strange people, as well as being a place under siege. She hated it, and wanted to escape to somewhere she could live without the constant threat of attack.

But, above all, she wanted Hereward to return.

"What do we do if he doesn't come back?" she demanded in a low, fragile whisper, dismayed with herself for giving voice to her fear.

Ranald pursed his lips, then said forcefully, "We help Barn instil some backbone into the fighting men. Siward White will help us, too. He's a good man, and well respected. There are some other Thanes among the northerners who will stand up when needed."

As if afraid of her own words, Torfrida said softly, "You know that might still not be enough."

Ranald continued to smile, refusing to be downhearted.

"If the worst comes to the worst," he told her, "you and I will leave before the end. With a few good men, we could find a way out, then take a ship and sail to Ireland. I will take you to my home, where you will meet my wife and children, and you will be safe until Hereward is able to join you."

His unwavering belief in Hereward's survival was infectious, and Torfrida managed a faint smile as she asked, "How would he know where to find us?"

At this, Ranald laughed, "I fear your concern for Hereward is not helping you to think clearly, my Lady. It is quite simple. We will tell the Abbot where we have gone. Even King William will not dare harm an Abbot. When Hereward turns up, Thurstan can tell him where to find us."

"You really think he is still alive?" she asked.

"Of course he is!" Ranald assured her. "You must keep telling yourself that."

"I will," she promised, although she was not sure she would be able to dispel her doubts and fears.

"And in the meantime," Ranald went on, "you must take care of yourself. I know Hereward was concerned that someone might make an attempt on your life."

Torfrida's mournful expression turned suddenly hard as she spat, "Altruda! That bitch had better not come near me."

"I see you have not lost all your spirit," Ranald grinned. "But, with your maid having gone, you must have somebody taste your food for you. Just in case, you understand."

Torfrida gave a wan smile as she informed him, "Old Martin is already doing that. He feels Hereward's loss almost as much as I do, but he has sworn to keep me safe."

"Good. Now, you must try to keep your spirits up, my Lady. We are not beaten yet."

While Ranald was comforting Torfrida, Altruda met with Kenton in her old chamber, having managed to escape Morcar's self-indulgent misery for a short while.

"He is being stubborn," she informed the scar-cheeked warrior when he asked whether the Earl was prepared to give up the fight. "He's terrified of fighting the King, but even more afraid of surrendering."

"I can't blame him for that," Kenton grunted. "The King will have his head this time."

"That is what he fears," Altruda agreed. "But I will persuade him he is wrong."

"Good luck with that," Kenton muttered darkly. "Despite what's happened, it seems they are not beaten yet."

"They?" Altruda asked with open amusement. "I thought you were one of them, Kenton? An Englishman, I mean."

"I'm as English as you are," he growled. "But I'm not a bloody fool. I know which way the wind is blowing."

"So you do," she smiled. "The rest of them will realise it very soon. This is an ideal opportunity for us."

"It is?"

"Of course. We have dealt with Earl Edwin, and his brother is in my power, but the main obstacle we faced was always Hereward. Now he has conveniently removed himself, so we have a golden opportunity to end this futile war."

"Is Hereward dead, then?" Kenton demanded sharply. "Him and that boy, Edric Strong?"

"I have no news of them," she replied, amused by the hatred that still burned behind his eyes when he mentioned Edric.

"I wanted to kill that bastard myself," he muttered. "If he's drowned out there, I won't be able to hear him squeal when I gut him."

"Forget him," Altruda commanded. "What matters is that they are out of our way. Now we must act, and there are other people we must deal with."

"Hereward's wife, you mean?"

Altruda hesitated. Dealing with Torfrida had once been a personal issue, but Altruda had more important problems to address.

"She is irrelevant," she told the housecarl. "She has no power or influence, and all she is good for is serving as a prize for Ivo de Taillebois."

"The fat Sheriff?" Kenton frowned.

"The man is a buffoon," Altruda admitted. "But he is infatuated with Torfrida. If she is foolish enough to linger here when the final assault takes place, I am sure he will claim her as his share of the spoils."

Her nose wrinkled with distaste as she added, "That is not a fate I would wish on any woman."

"I thought you wanted rid of her?" Kenton persisted.

"That would be a tidy solution, but there is no need to take risks. I believe she is still having her food tasted, and she always has an armed guard with her. But, as I say, she is not important. I believe her own maid has deserted her."

"So I hear," Kenton smirked.

Altruda shot him a sharp look.

"Would you happen to know where the girl is?" she demanded suspiciously.

"Me?" Kenton grinned. "No. I expect she ran off somewhere."

Altruda did not believe him, but whatever he had or had not done to the maid was not important as long as nobody else suspected him. From all accounts, Torfrida had searched high and low for the girl without success.

Kenton returned her probing gaze with implacably hard eyes, so Altruda let the matter drop.

The housecarl asked, "So what are you going to do about Earl Morcar? You said you would persuade him to surrender. How?"

At this, Altruda picked up a folded parchment which lay on the table beside her.

"Fortunately," she smiled conspiratorially, "I have just received this communication which will help me apply additional pressure to the poor Earl."

"Your tame monk has been out and about again?" Kenton snorted.

"Brother Richard has his uses," Altruda agreed. "A man of God can travel anywhere. And this letter he brought me is what I need to end this siege."

"How?" Kenton asked again, his eyes narrowing suspiciously.

Tapping the small parchment with one finger, she patiently explained, "The King has written to confirm that he intends to strip the abbey of all its lands unless Abbot Thurstan abandons his support for the rebels, and aids the king in suppressing the revolt. When the Abbot reads this, he will help me persuade Earl Morcar to surrender, because losing wealth, power and influence is what the Abbot fears most in this world."

"Will that be enough to persuade Morcar?" Kenton frowned. "He'll still end up dead if the King gets his hands on him."

Altruda laughed, "Not so, Kenton. I have also been instructed to give the Earl the King's assurances that he will be well treated if he surrenders. He will lose his lands and title, but he will keep his worthless life and be permitted to live out his days in comfort."

"Truly?" Kenton gaped. "The King will pardon him again? I find that hard to believe."

"Surely you are not suggesting our King would break his word?" Altruda replied in a sarcastic tone.

Kenton bridled as he spat, "I have no dealings with kings. But will Earl Morcar believe it?"

Altruda smiled, "With Thurstan's aid, I am sure I can bring him around."

Kenton said, "So there will be nobody left who wants to fight except old Barn, and he hasn't got enough men to defend the whole island."

"Precisely," Altruda confirmed. "We shall give Thane Barn a couple of days to waste his energy combatting the King's army on the causeway, then, once I am sure he is fully committed to that fight and cannot interfere with my plans, I will speak to Abbot Thurstan and, together, he and I will convince Earl Morcar that his only real choice is to bend the knee to the King."

"And then we all get our rewards?" Kenton asked sharply.

"I did not think you would forget that," Altruda sighed. "Yes, Kenton, then we will all be rewarded for our loyalty."

A wide grin lit up Kenton's dour features, and his eyes took on a malicious glint. Altruda returned a smile, but her private thoughts were that it would be as well to dispose of Kenton once the rebellion had been firmly put down. He was, she reflected, too dangerous to keep.

But let him live a few more days, for that was all it would take for the revolt to be ended. She was certain of that now. With Hereward gone, there was no longer any hope for the rebels.

Chapter 14

"I suppose I should have realised you couldn't swim," Hereward said in an expression of regret.

Edric shrugged off the apology. He was too wet, cold and tired to talk. The memory of his near drowning was still vivid and he was trying hard to forget it, partly because his panic would have killed him unnecessarily.

He had been ready to surrender to the imperative of trying to breathe, even though he knew the act would kill him, when he had felt someone trying to find him. An arm swept across his chest, then fingers closed around the front of his tunic and he was pulled upright. Hereward had come back for him, diving under the water and grabbing him, then hauling him to the surface, dragging him into the reeds which masked them from the Norman soldiers who had come running after them. Edric, spluttering and gasping, was hissed to silence by Hereward. Despite the warning, he almost shouted aloud in surprise when he discovered his feet could touch the muddy bottom of the river and he could stand with his head above water. The realisation that he could have saved himself left him feeling stupid and embarrassed.

But they were not out of danger. Hereward's horse had swum across the pool and disappeared into the marshland, so the two of them were stuck, with a growing number of Normans gathering on the edge of the pool, barely five paces away. Only the tall hedge of reeds concealed the fugitives who stood up to their necks in water, trying to remain perfectly still so as not to create any ripples in the surface of the wide pool.

Edric was convinced they would be captured. He could hear the voices of the Normans, could almost sense some of them thrusting the blades of their swords into the thick hedge of reeds, and he nearly let out a cry of despair when he heard some of them begin shouting.

He was convinced they had been discovered, but Hereward grabbed his arm, squeezing hard to encourage him to silence.

"They are going away," Hereward whispered into his ear. "They think we must have drowned. And they have other things on their mind now."

Edric shot him a quizzical look.

159

"What things?"

"It seems the fire is spreading. Can't you hear the shouting?"

Edric cocked his head, rubbing at his ear to expel the last traces of water, then recognised the sounds of tumult which seemed to be growing louder.

"I think they are abandoning the camp," Hereward informed him.

They waited, and soon the unmistakable sounds of many men hurrying past could be heard. Edric could not understand the words, but Hereward was able to confirm that the Normans were leaving their camp as quickly as they could, and even Edric could sense the panic in the voices. He understood their fear when he saw a dark pall of smoke rising into the grey, cloud-laden sky and beginning to drift slowly towards the east.

Edric knew what that signified.

"Marsh fire!" he hissed. "We need to get out of here. Those things can spread very quickly."

"Follow me, then," Hereward agreed. "Stay as close to the reeds as you can. I doubt the Normans are looking for us any longer, but if they see us, they can still shoot us full of arrows."

So they had edged away from the fire, moving parallel to the fleeing Normans. The reeds were so dense it was impossible to see what was happening on the land, but there was little doubt that the enemy was in full flight. Horses were whinnying in fright, men were shouting, and Edric could imagine the chaos as the Normans pushed and jostled one another in their attempts to escape the fire. There was only one safe route through the marshes, and hundreds of Normans were now trying to reach that narrow path.

Edric and Hereward had problems of their own. Weighed down by their sodden clothing, they continued their slow wading until the pool came to a muddy end near a clump of willows.

Hereward glanced at the sky, judging the time.

"There are still a couple of hours until dark," he guessed. "I wonder if we can risk leaving the water and hiding beneath the trees?"

"If we crawl, the reeds should still keep us hidden," Edric suggested. "I'll go first if you like."

Hereward shook his head.

"I'll try it," he stated. "If they see me, get out of the water as quickly as you can and we'll make a run for it. They won't be able to chase us, but we need to get out of bowshot to be safe. If there's no alarm, we'll shelter beneath the trees for a while."

He inched forwards, bending low as he emerged from the dark, fetid pool, water cascading from his clothes. He cursed softly as his feet sank into clinging mud, forcing him to put enormous effort into every step, then he was free of the water, lying on his belly on the mud, and squirming towards the drooping branches of the nearest willow.

Edric followed, dreading to hear the shout of warning that would herald a volley of arrows, but Hereward reached the tree and wriggled beneath its screen of dangling branches.

Edric ploughed doggedly on, feeling his booted feet sink into the mud, grimacing at the clammy sensation of his clothes sticking wetly to his skin. As soon as he was able to lie down without having his face beneath the water, he crawled onto the strip of mud and wormed his way to the tree.

"We made it!" Hereward almost laughed once Edric had joined him under the shelter of the drooping branches. "It looks as if they are far too busy running away to bother about us."

Edric sat up and risked peering out between the hanging branches. Over the top of the reeds, he could make out the crush of Norman soldiers still trying to force their way onto the trackway which led away from the camp. Behind them, the smoke was darker and thicker, creating a screen which seemed to loom over them. Men in armour, men in tunics and men on horseback were jostling and shoving as they battled each other for the right to escape the encampment.

"What do we do now?" Edric asked.

He was beginning to shiver, his clothing still seeping water from every fold, and he was sitting in a widening puddle of water on the already damp earth.

"I think we wait until dark," Hereward replied calmly. "Then maybe we can sneak back to the camp and hail a boat to come and fetch us."

So they sat, cold, wet and miserable beneath the willow branches, watching the Normans abandon their camp. Neither of them spoke much, for there was little to say. Their mission had succeeded far better than even Hereward had hoped, and they were still alive, but their situation became increasingly difficult as the dull day edged towards dusk.

The smoke was seeping ever closer, and as the daylight failed, the glimmer of red fire could be seen to the north as the peat burned, devouring everything the Normans had left behind. A flare of hungry flames signalled the destruction of Abbot Turold's tent, and still the fire raged.

"We can't go back that way," Edric said despondently. "We'd never get through."

"We could maybe stay in the water," Hereward suggested.

Edric shook his head vehemently.

"I can't swim, and we don't know how deep the pool is at the other end. The river's too deep, that's certain. And those fires can spread under the ground."

Hereward gave a solemn nod. Everyone knew the dangers of marsh fires. The thick, compacted peat could smoulder beneath the ground for days, erupting into fire whenever it managed to reach the surface. Even under the water, a misplaced foot could plunge a man into a hot furnace of steaming peat.

"You're right," he sighed. "So our way north is blocked by fire, we can't follow the Normans because they'll soon get themselves organised and we'd be caught if we used the path."

He looked around, gesturing eastwards.

"So we go that way. The land seems a bit firmer there, and it will take us clear of the fire. With luck, we'll find a way to move back to the north."

Edric had no desire to trek through the fens at night, especially on a dark, cloudy night when the moon would struggle to illuminate their route, but he was so cold and wet that the thought of staying where they were was even more intolerable.

They emerged from beneath the willow and crept eastwards, following the firmer ground whenever they could. But the earth was treacherous, often becoming damp and yielding, sucking their feet down into oozing mud. They squelched their way along what turned out to be a narrow strip of land until they reached another water course edged by tall reeds. It was too wide to cross and it stretched away to their left as far as the gloom would allow them to see.

"Damn!" spat Hereward. "We'll need to go right."

162

Which was the opposite direction to the one they needed to follow, but there was no help for it. Behind them, the dull reflection of the raging fire was their only real landmark, and even that began to fade as they trudged ever deeper into the marsh.

Edric recalled the first time he had travelled any distance into the fens. It had been when he had left his home in Bourne and followed Hereward to Ely. That had been difficult enough, but this journey was even worse. They splashed and stumbled, making slow progress, often needing to turn around and retrace their steps when the way ahead was blocked by water or deep bog. Twice, Hereward almost sank into a deep pit of muddy water when the ground gave way beneath his feet, and each time Edric had to grab at him and pull him out. When they passed a small clump of shadowy trees, Hereward snapped off a branch, stripped it of twigs with his belt knife, then used it to probe the way ahead. It did not make their trek any faster, but it did make it a little safer.

The moon was curtained by the clouds, its silver light providing little assistance, so the two men blundered on, always trying to turn northwards and always foiled by the dangerous terrain.

Edric was exhausted, every step an effort, but Hereward seemed incapable of tiredness. Even he, though, eventually realised that they needed some rest.

"I think that could be a clump of trees up ahead," he offered. "Let's try to reach them. Maybe we can light a fire and get ourselves dry."

That seemed a forlorn hope to Edric, but he trudged his way in Hereward's wake, eventually splashing across a wide pool of water which reached only to their knees, then hauling themselves up onto what felt like a grassy islet which held a thick clump of trees.

Hereward plunged into the copse, pushing between branches and ploughing through snagging undergrowth until he stopped in a small clearing.

"Strip off your clothes and hang them on the branches," he ordered. "We will freeze to death if we stay in those wet things."

"We'll freeze anyway," Edric replied morosely.

"So let's get a fire going," Hereward declared as if this was the easiest thing in the world.

Edric struggled out of his sodden boots, then hauled off his soaking tunic, shirt, trousers and underclothes, draping them over low branches, moving more by sense of touch than anything else because there was barely any light at all under the crowding trees. His skin felt icily cold in the night air, and he began to shiver again.

Hereward, a mere shadow in the dark, said, "Let's find some wood to make a fire. We'll need kindling and a flat stone as well."

Edric thought he might as well have asked for the moon, but the two of them scrabbled around in the dark, on their hands and knees as they rummaged for whatever lay on the hard earth. Tree roots dug into their knees, sharp twigs scratched their exposed skin, but they soon had a collection of wood which could feed a fire if they could light one.

Hereward used his knife to shave kindling from some of the branches they had gathered, while Edric eventually located a large stone by the simple expedient of kneeling on it as he crawled through the trees.

"Have you done this sort of thing before?" Hereward asked him.

"Not like this," Edric replied. "I used to use a tinder box to light fires."

"Same here. I've seen it done, of course."

Edric had also seen fires lit using sticks and kindling, so he knew it was possible, but the equipment they had was far from ideal for the task. The fact that he could barely see what he was doing made it doubly difficult. Judging by feel, Edric tried to wipe away the mud and earth from the stone he had found, then they piled some scraps of kindling and shavings onto the stone's flattest surface.

"We really need a small hole to hold the kindling and the stick," he muttered.

Hereward said, "I'll try to hold everything together while you work the stick."

So saying, he took two small twigs and used them to create barriers on either side of the piled kindling. He held them firmly, confining the scraps of shavings into the centre of the stone's surface.

"Let's hope this works," he said.

164

Edric had selected a fairly straight stick of wood for the most important part of the task. He had lost his own knife somewhere in the swamp, so he used Hereward's knife to trim one end of the stick into a crude point, then placed the sharpened end in what he hoped was the middle of the kindling. Kneeling over the makeshift fire kit, he then held the upright stick between his palms. Taking a deep breath, he began to rotate the stick, twirling it as fast as he could while Hereward forced the wood shavings together to prevent them sliding away from Edric's pointed twig.

Edric's numbed hands soon began to protest as he rubbed faster and faster. He knew the best way to do this would be to use a second stick with a piece of cord which could be looped around the vertical twig, but they had no cord, so he had no option but to use his hands. His palms began to burn with pain as he rubbed them together with the stick between them, while Hereward knelt with his face close to the stone, offering words of encouragement.

"Keep going," he urged. "I think I saw a glimmer there."

Edric concentrated all his attention on turning the stick as quickly as he could, creating friction between its tip and the pile of loose shavings. He had no idea how long it took him, but eventually he heard Hereward gasp in triumph.

"Keep going!" the young Thane told him again.

Then Edric could see it. At the base of the stick, the friction had created enough heat to ignite the kindling. A solitary flame leaped upwards, then Hereward was feeding it, coaxing it into life. In moments, the kindling had caught, so Hereward fed larger twigs, saw them catch fire, then began to add ever larger pieces of wood to encourage the blaze to life.

Edric knelt back on his haunches, crossing his arms and tucking his hands beneath his armpits in an attempt to soothe his aching palms.

"You did it!" Hereward exclaimed in delight.

"It's not something I'd want to do again in a hurry," Edric replied, although he could not deny a sense of satisfaction that they had succeeded in creating a fire.

They both huddled close to the warming flames, the light flickering across their pale skin. Then Edric noticed some dark blobs on Hereward's arms and legs. Glancing down at his own legs, he saw that he, too, had collected a scattering of dark shapes.

165

"Leeches!" he gasped as he tentatively touched one of the fat, dark shapes which clung to his thigh.

"Best leave them," Hereward said. "If you try to pull them off, you'll leave a scar. They'll drop off when they are sated."

"Or we could burn them off," Edric suggested.

Hereward waved a hand in invitation.

"Go ahead. But you're just as likely to burn yourself."

In the end, they waited until the leeches dropped of their own accord, then took great satisfaction in flicking the beasts out into the shadows of the trees.

But Hereward still had marks on his arms, marks which drew Edric's attention.

Hereward saw him looking at the tattoos and smiled.

"Mementos of my youth," he explained.

"What do they signify?" Edric asked.

Tapping a finger of his left hand against the dark blue picture on his right forearm, Hereward said, "That's a boar. It was the first animal I killed on my own. I was fourteen years old."

"A hunting trophy?" Edric asked, knowing that hunting boar was an activity the upper class enjoyed.

"That's right. My father gave me a long spear, but told me to stay out of harm's way. I didn't listen to him, of course, because I rarely did. When the beaters flushed out a boar, I stepped into its way and drove the spear right through it."

He laughed as he added, "Damn thing knocked me off my feet, but it was dead before it could do me any serious damage."

He smiled in recollection of the memory, then pointed to the tattoo on his left arm.

"And that, as you can see, is a bear."

Edric saw the dark blue outline of a bear with a maw full of sharp teeth and with one huge paw raised, claws extended, ready to strike.

He said, "I think I know the story behind that one."

Hereward raised an amused eyebrow.

"Oh? Has someone been gossiping about me?"

"No, Lord. Someone told me about Lady Altruda. They said you saved her from a bear which had escaped from a cage. So I supposed that is why you have the tattoo."

"Not because of her!" Hereward said sharply. "I had the tattoo done to remind me of the feat. In truth, the bear was a

166

mangy thing, and half starved, but it's still not something I'd care to try again."

"How did you kill it?" Edric asked, seeking to keep the Thane from dwelling on thoughts of Altruda.

"I rammed my sword into its mouth," Hereward told him. "Shoved it right up into its brain."

He gave a rueful smile as he went on, "It didn't stop the bloody thing giving me these, though."

He raised his right arm, bending his elbow to reveal two pale, ragged scar lines on the back of his upper arm.

"And it nearly crushed me to death when it fell on me."

"It must have been a wondrous thing to behold," Edric commented.

"Some people thought so," Hereward recalled. "I only did what I thought necessary, but I sometimes wonder if it would not have been better to let the girl die."

Edric shook his head.

"You should not say such things, lord."

"No, I probably should not," Hereward sighed. "But Altruda had a vile temper even back in those days. She had been sent to Scotland to marry a young nobleman but, after I killed the bear, she decided she wanted me instead. When I turned her down, she swore revenge on me. Fortunately, I left once my wounds were healed, and I never saw her again until that day in Peterborough when we rescued her from de Taillebois."

Edric said, "I heard her husband died, and so did her second one. She's very wealthy because she inherited a lot of land, which is why the Normans want her."

Hereward nodded gravely, "I heard that too. A lot of Englishwomen are being forced into marriages to give Norman lords an excuse to seize land. Her story may be true, but I don't trust the woman. With Earl Edwin gone, we need to get back before she persuades Morcar to surrender."

"Even the Lady Altruda will not be able to persuade him to surrender," Edric asserted. "Everyone says he will be executed if the Bastard gets hold of him."

Hereward nodded glumly.

"That's true enough. But I still want to get back as soon as we can."

"How?" Edric asked.

"We could gather reeds, bundle them together and tie them with our belts. Then we could use them as floats to swim our way to Ely."

Edric was appalled by this suggestion. The thought of swimming in deep water terrified him, even if Hereward's idea did mean he would have something to hang onto. The memories of the Normans who had plunged to their deaths when the bridge had collapsed, and recollections of his own near drowning, were too vivid in his mind to ignore.

"We don't know which way to go," he pointed out. "We could wander here for days."

"We know where the sun is," Hereward countered. "Ely must be somewhere to the north of us."

"But the waterways do not run straight," Edric persisted. "We could become even more lost."

"Or we could die of thirst, cold or hunger," Hereward said softly. "But let us wait out the night and see what tomorrow brings.

Dawn filtered slowly through the branches, rousing Edric from what had been a restless and uncomfortable night. He had dozed occasionally out of sheer exhaustion, but the cold and damp had made sleeping nearly impossible. His clothing was far too wet to use as a covering, so he had huddled, naked and shivering, beside the fire, praying for the night to end.

The daylight brought little relief. Groaning as he sat up, he saw now that the clearing where they had made their camp was tiny, a small patch of relatively clear ground between several stunted trees and surrounded by brambles and tall weeds. It was a dull, gloomy space made little more appealing by the dim grey of the early sunlight.

He looked across the fire to where Hereward was stretching his back and legs as he stood, shaking off the cramps of the night. The Thane was filthy, his skin smeared with mud, his hair tangled and his body covered by dozens of insect bites. Edric's own itching skin told him that he, too, had suffered his share of bites. He stretched, feeling his body protest, and the old wound in his thigh inflicted by an axe which had almost ended his life, was throbbing with the familiar dull ache caused by over-exertion.

Worst of all, though, was the nagging hunger and raging thirst he felt. His dry tongue felt twice its normal size as if it filled his parched mouth, and his belly ached with the need for sustenance.

Hereward reached out to touch his tunic which hung in a shapeless huddle on a nearby branch.

"It's still sodden," he informed Edric. "We need to keep the fire going and place our clothes around it."

Edric nodded dully. He checked his own clothing and boots, discovering that they were so wet he could still wring water from them. Immersion in the pool had left them misshapen and filthy, yet he still wanted to wear something because the morning air felt chill on his naked body.

The only positive thing he could see about their situation was that there was plenty of wood to feed the fire. Hereward used his knife to hack more sticks from the stubby trees, adding them to the blaze, then held his tunic up beside the flames in an attempt to dry it more quickly.

Another faint sound caught Edric's ear; a pattering on the leafy ceiling above their heads.

Hereward grinned and put his wet tunic back on the branch where it had hung during the night.

"That sounds like rain," he said. "It won't help us dry our clothes, but it will give us something to drink."

They squeezed a careful way through the trees, emerging onto what proved to be a small islet of long grass and weeds. As Edric had guessed, it was another dull, miserable day, with the sun concealed by an endless layer of clouds. Today, though, he was thankful for the rain which was now drizzling down upon him. He turned his head skywards, opened his mouth and let the water relieve his thirst. He was still cold, and now growing wet again, but quenching his thirst was the most important thing, so he stood there for a long time, holding out his tongue to capture more of the tiny droplets, wetting the inside of his mouth and swallowing as much of the rain as he could. It was scarcely enough to satisfy his body's demands, but it was just enough to quell the danger of dying from thirst.

He had no idea how long they stood there, the two of them standing virtually motionless with their heads tilted skywards.

Eventually, though, Hereward said softly, "I wonder where we are?"

Edric looked at their surroundings. The copse where they had sheltered occupied one end of a long, thin patch of relatively dry land which rose like a small hump out of the marshland. The rest of the islet was a tangle of grass and tall plants, with a stand of reeds at the far end. On every side there was water, wide, slow-moving and probably very deep. More reeds lined the further banks, blocking his view of what might lie beyond them, but that hardly mattered since they could not cross the streams in any case. He could make out other small clumps of trees in the distance, but there was no sign of life other than the buzzing of insects and the chirp of the occasional bird.

"Not the most appealing place, is it?" Hereward asked conversationally.

He pointed to Edric's left as he added, "From where I think the sun is, I'd guess Ely is that way, but I have no idea how we can get there. The only way off this island seems to be back the way we came in."

"Maybe we should try to retrace our steps," Edric suggested. "The marsh fire might have burned down by now."

Hereward nodded, "I don't think we have much choice. But let's try to get ourselves a bit drier before we go anywhere."

They made their way back into the copse, treading carefully to avoid stepping on too many sharp twigs or stones. They passed their tiny campsite, then reached the other end of the tree line which bordered what they thought was probably the western edge of their island.

"Did we really come across that?" Hereward frowned when he saw the oozing, muddy swamp stretching out in front of them.

Getting back would, Edric saw, be a problem. Perhaps because of the rain, or perhaps because the fens always shifted, water was slowly seeping all across the path they had stumbled along the previous night. It was not yet very deep, but it was enough to make retracing their steps difficult and potentially dangerous since they might easily plunge into a deep pool if they did make the attempt.

"We are stuck here!" Edric groaned.

"We'll think of something," Hereward told him. "But we need to get dry, then find something to eat. Why don't you go and forage around while I set up some sticks to hang our clothes near the fire."

He phrased it as a suggestion, but Edric heard the order implicit in the young Thane's voice.

"I'll see what I can find," he nodded.

"Good. I'll try cutting some bark from a tree. Maybe I can fashion a cooking bowl out of it."

Edric had wanted to give up when he had seen they were cut off, but he knew he could not disappoint Hereward, so he endured another bout of scratches as he ploughed back through the copse and out to the other side of the island. It was barely thirty paces long, but he supposed there would be something edible growing amidst the profusion of plants. As a young boy, he had often helped his Aunt Edith gather herbs and weeds which she used to flavour her cooking. It had been a long time since he had needed to do anything like that for himself, but he reckoned he could still remember enough to find something they could eat.

Luck was with him. As soon as he emerged from the trees, he saw a dark shape to his left. A startled otter looked at him, then turned and splashed into the water, vanishing from sight. But it had left a barely eaten trout lying on the edge of the island. Edric knew that otters often ate only a portion of their catch, which meant the fish had been abandoned instead of being dragged away for later consumption. He picked it up by the tail, grinning to himself as he returned to the camp site. It was not a large fish, but it made a good start to his foraging.

"That was well done," Hereward said in amazement when he saw the catch. "I didn't think anyone could catch a fish that quickly. Did you have to take a bite out of it, though?"

"That was an otter," Edric informed him. "I thought I'd bring it back before I go looking for any more."

"I'll clean it," Hereward said as he took the fish. "Hurry back."

Edric headed out again, making a circuit of the island, stopping now and again to pull up plants he recognised as edible. When he reached the far end of the isle, he also pulled out handfuls of the tall reeds which crowded the river bank.

Feeling very pleased with himself, he returned to the camp site where he presented his haul to Hereward.

"I've got mushrooms, dandelion leaves, Fat hen and lovage. Also some reedmace."

Hereward grinned, "It sounds wonderful."

He had cleared the centre of their fire, revealing the stone they had used to light the flames. It now sat at the centre of the fire, and he had laid the meat of the fish on it to cook. He had also fashioned a very crude bowl of tree bark which he had partly filled with water from the river. This also sat atop the stone, the water beginning to bubble.

"The bark won't burn as long as there is water inside it," he said with a satisfied smile. "So I'm glad you've got some ingredients to cook in it."

He handed Edric his knife, the blade now sadly in need of sharpening. Still, it was enough to allow Edric to chop the various plants and drop them into the hot water.

"The reedmace needs some preparation," he told Hereward.

Without a proper chopping board, he knelt to use a thick tree root as a base. He quickly stripped the blade-shaped leaves from the stems of the reeds. This produced a slimy jelly which he smeared over his fingers.

"Put this on any scratches or bites you have," he told Hereward. "It will help heal them."

Hereward raised a quizzical eyebrow but joined in when he saw Edric rubbing the jelly onto his own body where he had been bitten or scratched.

"My Aunt Edith used this all the time," Edric told him.

Edric then returned to the task of preparing the edible part of the reeds. He cut away the top of the stems, leaving only four or five inches of the rounded base. He then sliced away the fibrous outer layers to reveal the white, pulpy inner.

"You can eat these raw," he said, "but I think we'd better boil them first. The water they grew in didn't look all that clean."

So saying, he dropped the chunks of pulp into the bubbling water.

They sat watching the sparse meal, their stomachs rumbling and their mouths filling with saliva in anticipation of food. The flames licked around the stone and the bark bowl, slowly cooking the eclectic meal.

Overhead, the drizzle continued, sending tiny droplets down through the leaves and branches.

"Our clothes won't dry well in this," Hereward said, "But at least we won't starve."

Using his knife and a sharp stick, he carefully lifted the fish and flipped it into the crude cooking pot.

"That will add some stock to the broth," he smiled.

Edric was feeling faint from hunger by the time they deemed the meal ready to eat.

"We should drink the hot water," Hereward decided.

Drinking from the clumsy, fragile bowl would not be easy, but they took turns in carefully lifting it to their lips to sip the hot liquid. It tasted awful, but Edric was so thirsty he did not care. At least, having been boiled, it would not make him ill. Or so he hoped.

Once the water had cooled sufficiently, they used their fingers to scoop out the leaves, reed pulp, scraps of fish and mushrooms, chewing hungrily and ignoring the odd tastes.

"That's the best meal I've had in a while," Hereward declared when they had eaten every last scrap.

Edric smiled. In truth, the food had tasted bland and had been difficult to chew, but it had staved off the worst of his hunger.

He made another foraging trip once the rain had stopped, gathering more of the same plants and discovering a duck's nest when he almost trod on it. The terrified duck gave him a fright when it suddenly burst from the nest, its wings beating frantically as it fled across the water. Edric felt sorry for it when he gathered up the newly-laid eggs, but he decided his need was greater than the bird's.

They rested all day, speaking little because there was not much to say, and dining on eggs and mushrooms.

Drying their clothing became the next important task, so they spent a long time holding their undergarments, tunics and trousers over the fire while they propped their boots at the edge of the flames. By late afternoon, they decided the ruined outfits were almost dry enough to be bearable, so they dressed again, feeling slightly more human when their nakedness was covered, although the damp, lumpy clothing had been ruined by the long immersion in the water. The stitching of Edric's trousers was coming loose, his tunic hung longer at his right side than at his left, and his boots still felt clammy when he thrust his feet into them.

Still, it was better than feeling like a savage, so he gave Hereward what he hoped was a confident grin.

"Should we try to go back now?" he asked.

Hereward shook his head.

"The day is almost over. Let's try to get some sleep tonight, then make the attempt in the morning."

He looked thoughtfully at the thin plume of smoke rising from their fire and said, "I wonder if anyone will notice that and come to see who's lit a fire out here?"

Edric replied dully, "I doubt if there's anyone within miles of us. Anyway, I think the trees will dissipate the smoke."

"You are probably right," Hereward agreed. "In that case, let's sleep on our problem and see if we can think of a way to get back to Ely. They probably think we drowned."

As plans went, it was hardly reassuring, but at least they were slightly warmer that night. They built up the fire, lay down in their drying clothes and managed to snatch some sleep until a downpour of rain woke them in the early hours of morning before the dawn. They again caught the rain in their mouths, often shaking branches to shake drops from the leaves to provide more to drink. Edric was almost grateful for the dreadful weather the summer had brought, but the rain produced another problem for them. When they ventured to the western edge of the copse to see whether they could escape the island, they found that the water had risen, making the path impossible.

Hereward stood there, scowling darkly and clenching his fists, his thoughts clearly racing as he sought a solution. Eventually, he said, "I think we will need to take to the water. If we bundle enough reeds, we can put our clothes on top of the bundle, then hold onto them while we kick our legs and swim."

Edric still hated this idea, but he had no other solutions to suggest.

"How will we know which way to go?" he asked.

"We will need to follow our noses," Hereward replied. "We can't stay here, that's for sure."

They gathered more plants for a meagre breakfast. Both of them were suffering stomach cramps now, although whether it was

174

lack of food or caused by their strange diet, Edric could not tell. Reluctantly, he went to the hedge of reeds at the far end of the island and began tugging them out of the water. It took a long time to gather a bundle large enough to satisfy Hereward. When he could barely encompass them with both arms, he used his belt to fasten the bundle together.

"That's one," he said, his face a mask of determination. "Now we need another one."

So Edric pulled yet more reeds, all the time wishing he could think of some other way to escape this island prison. The thought of immersing himself in leech-infested water filled him with dread. He had visions of them clinging desperately to sodden reeds which would slowly sink, leaving him helpless and ending up at the bottom of a dark waterway.

Hereward must have sensed his fear, for he kept trying to reassure him.

"The reeds will float, Edric. All we need to do is hang onto them. And we will find other bits of land just like this one, so we can stop to find food and make fresh bundles of reeds for the next stage."

His attempts at reassurance did not convince Edric, but he knew he must do as Hereward said. They could scrape a living here on the tiny island for a few days, but they were already hungry and needed to make the effort to return to Ely before they became too weak to try.

They gathered up a second large bundle of reeds which was lashed together using Edric's belt, then Hereward said, "I suppose we may as well get started."

Edric could feel desperation welling inside him. He wanted to argue, to do anything other than take to the water, but his mind refused to provide any other solutions. Not wanting to meet Hereward's eyes, he took another look around at their surroundings, silently praying for inspiration.

Then he blinked in astonishment as he saw a miracle.

Because a small boat had appeared, edging around a bend in the reed-lined river.

Chapter 15

There was a man sitting in the stern of the small fen boat, using a crude paddle to propel the vessel through the water. He, too, stopped and stared in disbelief as his boat glided towards the island.

"Saint Etheldreda has answered our prayers," Hereward chuckled, unable to hide the relief he felt.

Grabbing his belt and fastening it around his waist once again, he walked to the edge of the islet and waved to the man in the boat.

"Well met, friend. Would you be able to help some stranded travellers? We need to get to Ely."

The man, whose wild hair and long, ragged beard framed a tanned and weather-beaten face, continued to gawp at them. He made no effort to come close to the island, using his paddle to hold the boat some ten yards from its shore while he quickly scanned the bare islet for any sign that it might be harbouring more people.

Once he was satisfied they were alone, he asked, "Who are you?"

His accent was coarse, and his words sounded stilted as if he were unused to speaking to other people.

Suspicion dripped from his voice as he added, "And what are you doing here?"

"We are lost," Hereward told him. "My name is Toki, and this is Edric. Our horses ran away, and we blundered after them during the night, but somehow ended up here."

He gave the explanation glibly, but the man was not convinced.

"Nobody comes out here," he said with the certainty of one who knows.

"Yet here we are," Hereward replied. "And we are in sore need of a drink before we die of thirst. Could you save some fellow Christians? We can pay you well if you take us to Ely."

Whether it was the appeal to provide Christian charity or the lure of reward, the man gave a slow nod, then eased the boat towards the island.

As he approached, Edric noticed that the front section of the flat-bottomed boat contained a crude net which held several gleaming fish. Whoever this man was, he clearly knew how to survive in the fenland.

The boat had a single bench seat where the man sat, but the two exhausted warriors were forced to kneel in the flat-bottomed forward section next to the fish.

"Thank you, my friend," Hereward said as he settled into the tiny vessel. "What is your name?"

"Wilfred," the man grunted, still obviously uncertain as to whether he should be helping them.

"May God reward you for your kindness, Wilfred. I see you have a sack of ale there. Could you save us from thirst?"

After a slight hesitation, Wilfred handed over the bulging sack which lay at his feet. Hereward passed it to Edric who removed the stopper and drank deeply before returning it to Hereward with a gasp of relief.

After they had both eased their thirst, Hereward thanked Wilfred again.

"Now, can you take us to Ely? And we would prefer to avoid meeting any Normans."

Wilfred's suspicion flared again as his eyes scanned both men.

"You are fighting men?" he asked.

Hereward gave a relaxed laugh as he replied, "Do we look like fighting men? We have no armour or weapons. Edric here is a blacksmith's apprentice. I am a potter. But we need to get to Ely, and we hear the Normans are stopping anyone from going there."

Wilfred, now using his paddle to turn the boat, gave another grunt which could have meant anything.

Then he said, "Can't go to Ely today."

"Why not?" Hereward asked.

"I only go on market days."

"What day is this?" Hereward asked, looking at Edric.

"Tuesday?" Edric guessed. "Market is on Thursday."

Wilfred nodded, "That's right. Two days until market."

"But we need to go now," Hereward said. "It can't be all that far."

Wilfred shrugged, "It is a long way if you want to avoid the Normans. They are everywhere. They have been sending boats into the fens for a few days now."

Hereward scowled, making Edric wonder whether the Thane was considering overpowering Wilfred and seizing the boat. But that would do them little good if they could not find their way to Ely. Without a guide, they could easily blunder into the Normans or become lost in the maze of streams.

"All right," Hereward sighed. "So where are we going, then?"

"Home," Wilfred said flatly.

His home was on another small island. It was a tiny shack built of timber, turf and reeds, barely distinguishable from its surroundings. Beside it was a chicken coop where half a dozen hens clucked and scratched. There was also a large, covered pit which turned out to be a stone-lined tank where he kept his catch fresh before taking it to market.

"Mostly eels," he explained when Hereward asked what he would be taking to sell in Ely.

The main things he was able to provide were warmth and food. His home may have been a filthy hovel, but it was better than the meagre shelter of the trees they had slept under for the previous two nights.

Taking a block of dried peat from a small pile which lay in one corner of the hut's single room, Wilfred fed the embers of the fire which glowed in the stone-lined hearth, then hung an iron pot over it and made a fish stew, using two of the fish he had been carrying in his net. He cleaned and gutted the fish with practised precision, then added a few beans from a small sack which comprised his meagre larder.

For their part, Hereward and Edric huddled close to the fire and tried to ignore the protests from their hungry bellies as the smell of the stew began to fill the hut.

"Have you no family?" Hereward asked their wild-haired host.

"I had a wife," Wilfred replied. "She died."

His words sounded almost uncaring, but Edric supposed life in the depths of the marshes must be tough, where death was something to be accepted. Many people died young in every village, whether as a result of disease, childbirth or accident, and the risks must be even greater out here in the wilderness of reeds and water.

Edric tried to estimate their host's age, but could only place it at somewhere between thirty and fifty. There were grey flecks in his matted hair, and his ragged clothes stank of fish and sweat, but Edric tried not to judge him too harshly because the man had undoubtedly saved their lives. There was still an air of suspicion between them, but Wilfred grudgingly shared his food even though he constantly watched them with wary eyes as if he feared they might still seek to overpower him and steal his boat. He tried to conceal his concerns, but his words revealed more than he intended.

"I have nothing here that is of any value," he told them.

"You have a fire and proper food," Hereward replied. "To men who have spent two nights in the fens, those are a treasure beyond value."

Wilfred gave a pensive nod, then said, "I will take you to Ely on Thursday. You won't get there without me. It is easy to get lost in this part of the fens."

Hereward ventured, "We can pay you well if you take us there tomorrow."

"You have silver?" Wilfred asked dubiously.

"Not with me," Hereward admitted. "I lost my purse in the water. But I can get coins when we reach Ely."

"I will take you on Thursday," Wilfred repeated stubbornly.

Edric could see Hereward struggling to retain his temper, so he said, "We could do with a day's rest anyway. I think I could sleep for a week."

Hereward relaxed a little, but still looked unhappy.

Wilfred dipped a wooden spoon into the pot, sipped at the stew and then picked up a ladle which he used to fill a small, wooden bowl.

"I only have one bowl," he told them. "You can eat from the pot."

He rummaged in a worn chest of ancient, warped wood which seemed to hold all his earthly possessions, producing two more spoons, one of which had a broken handle.

Protecting his hands with an old rag Wilfred passed him, Edric lifted the pot from the hearth, setting it on the ground where he and Hereward could dip into the stew. It was poor fare, watery and with little real nourishment, yet it was infinitely better than the sparse meals they had been able to forage the previous day, and it revived their spirits considerably.

Wilfred had only one threadbare blanket, but Edric was grateful to sleep beside the fire, so he stretched out on the hard-packed earthen floor, pillowing his head on his arm, and closed his eyes. He was aware of Hereward's tension and of Wilfred's unease, but he was so tired he soon drifted into a deep sleep.

He awoke with dull sunlight poking through the many gaps in the hut's dilapidated walls. Wilfred was already awake, feeding the fire and preparing a breakfast of eggs.

"Only four today," he muttered as he indicated the morning's clutch.

Hereward was also awake, a brooding expression clouding his features as he sat cross-legged on the hard floor.

"Are you sure you cannot take us to Ely today?" he asked once again. "It is important that we get there soon."

Wilfred hesitated, clearly torn between a desire to be rid of his visitors and the compulsions of his own life.

"I still need to empty some nets," he explained. "And I can't take my catch to market until Thursday. It will go off and will be worth nothing. I need to buy bread, grain, meat and beans, so I need my catch."

"I will give you more than enough silver to fill your boat with whatever you need!" Hereward said in loud exasperation.

"Show me this silver," Wilfred responded dogmatically.

Hereward slumped back, muttering dark curses, knowing the fisherman would be persuaded only by the sight of coin, not by promises which might prove empty.

None of them spoke during the meagre breakfast. Wilfred ate two of the eggs, giving one each to his guests. Then he stood, donned a cloak and said, "I will be back later. You will find fresh water from the spring beyond the chicken coop, but do not take anything else."

Then he was gone, pulling the rickety door shut behind him.

Hereward growled, "Perhaps we should take his boat."

"We would need to take him with us to guide us," Edric pointed out. "He probably wouldn't help us if we stole his boat."

"I know," Hereward sighed.

180

"Why did you not tell him who you are?" Edric asked. "That might have persuaded him."

"If he knew that, he might be tempted to hand us over to the Normans. He said they were patrolling the fens. Even if he is completely trustworthy, if we run into any of them while he's taking us to Ely, I'm not sure he'd be able to act innocently. I can't take that risk. No, we'll just need to wait another day."

His words suggested he had accepted their fate, but Edric could see that the Thane was still angry. To distract him, he gestured at Wilfred's paltry belongings.

"I think we can trust him to take us to Ely tomorrow," he said. "As he said, he has nothing of value, yet he shares his home and his food with us."

Hereward gave a reluctant nod.

"I wouldn't mind wringing the neck of one of his chickens, but I suppose we'll need to go hungry again today."

They ventured outside into a dry but dull day, scanning the horizon for any sign of other habitation. There was nothing but a few gulls soaring high over the fens and the gentle ripple of flowing water from the broad stream which bordered Wilfred's island home.

They found the spring, although it provided little more than a trickle of water which burbled down to join the marsh water, but the island held little else of interest. An old hand axe had been stuck into a large tree stump which obviously served as a chopping block, and there were piles of wood and peat stacked against the side of Wilfred's home. The stone-lined fish tank was covered by thick planks of wood, and the area around the place where Wilfred beached his boat was marked by a well-trodden path, a pile of old nets and a couple of damaged creels for catching lobsters and eels.

The island was no larger than the one they had lived on for the previous two days and was even less abundant in wild plants. Edric did find a few mushrooms and picked more reed mace which he cut and stripped using the axe, frying them on a skillet he found in the hut, using a dribble of fish oil which was one of the few plentiful items in Wilfred's larder.

"It's at times like this I miss the abbey refectory," he said as he jostled the reed pulp on the pan. "I could eat a whole goose right now, and a loaf of fresh bread would be welcome."

They shared the strange meal, then passed their time sitting outside, leaning against the wall of the shack and gazing out at the seemingly endless marshes surrounding them.

"I wonder what is happening in Ely," Edric said wistfully.

"Barn will be harassing the Normans who are building the causeway," Hereward said. "If he can persuade Morcar to give him men now that the catapults and boats at Aldreth have been burned, he can make life difficult for the Bastard."

Edric could sense Hereward's unspoken concerns, so he observed, "We've only been away for a few days. The causeway won't have reached Ely yet."

Hereward nodded, "I know. But Torfrida will be worrying. And so will your girl."

Edric normally responded to such comments with an automatic denial that he had a girl, but he held his tongue. Hereward knew all about Ylva and, in an odd way, seemed to approve of her more than he had ever done of Aelswith. Or, at least, he approved of how Edric had protected the girl from her vicious father.

"We'll be back tomorrow," Edric said.

For that day, though, they sat, dozed and sipped at water from the spring which they caught in crudely made wooden beakers they found in Wilfred's hut. The time dragged, the only thing of note being the occasional glimpse of a duck or a ripple in the water as a fish tried to catch an insect which hovered on the surface.

There was no sign of Wilfred. Mid-day passed and the afternoon wore slowly on. Hereward began pacing up and down, his impatience almost bursting as he strove to use some of his pent up energy.

Edric decided to pass some time by chopping more wood for Wilfred. There were some large logs already piled against the hut, so he yanked the axe free from the tree stump and began splitting them into smaller pieces which would feed the fire more manageably.

He was dimly aware of Hereward moving up and down, impatiently pacing the afternoon away, then he heard the Thane's hiss of warning.

"Normans!"

Edric looked up in alarm. Hereward was already beside him, taking the axe from his unresisting hand and passing him his blunted knife in exchange.

"Stay calm," Hereward whispered urgently. "Follow my lead."

Hereward tucked the axe into his belt behind his back, and Edric copied the move with the once sharp knife, then he followed Hereward past the hut and down to the edge of the island where Wilfred usually berthed his small boat. As they walked slowly towards the stream, Edric saw a small fen boat moving towards them. Two Normans knelt at the prow, each holding a large, kite-shaped shield to form a defensive barrier, with a long spear held upright in their other hand. In the stern sat two more men, one behind the other, each using a large paddle to propel the boat towards the island.

And then Edric saw the second boat. It was empty, floating along behind the first, the tether now clearly visible.

"That's Wilfred's boat!" he rasped.

Hereward gave a grim nod.

"I know."

Which meant, Edric realised, that the Normans had either killed the old man or abandoned him somewhere in the fens. That thought roused his anger as he glared at the approaching boat.

The boatmen were not wearing the chainmail armour which was so common among Norman troops, but they wore thick leather tunics over padded wool. It served as some protection against blades, and it might just be light enough to prevent them drowning if they fell into the water.

When the boat was within ten yards of where the two Englishmen stood, one of the leading Normans called, "You have a boat?"

His accent was typically French, but the words and their meaning were plain enough. If they had a boat, the Normans intended to take it.

"Our boat is being repaired," Hereward replied, waving a hand to indicate some point behind the hut.

"Stand back!" the Norman commanded, gesturing with his long spear.

Edric copied Hereward as he took a couple of small steps backwards, seeming to comply with the order but moving only a short distance from where the boat would land.

The blunt prow of the vessel bumped against the edge of the landing site, and the two leading Normans stood up, stepping onto the land, their shields still held close to their bodies and their spears clutched firmly in their right hands.

Hereward moved so suddenly that he caught Edric by surprise. In the instant when the Normans were slightly off balance as they made the transition from the floating boat to the firm ground, he launched himself at them with the small axe now in his hand. He aimed at the man on his left, swung the axe in a vicious arc to knock the Norman's spear aside, then crashed into the shield, shoving the man backwards. Still off balance, the soldier toppled over, crashing violently into the boat, bringing shouts of anger and alarm from the two men who sat holding their paddles.

Hereward swung his axe to ward off the second spearman, but leaped forwards, landing on top of the fallen man, stamping his booted feet down onto the man's face while he swept his axe in an overhand arc which ended when the blade smashed into the skull of the leading boatman.

Edric reacted at last, whipping the knife from behind his back and jumping forwards to fling his left arm around the throat of the second spearman who had, naturally, turned to follow Hereward's movement. Edric yanked the man's head back as he brought up his knife. The blade was far from sharp having been used for cutting food and chopping firewood over the past few days, but he sawed it viciously across the front of the man's neck, seeing the spurt of dark blood. The Norman jerked and kicked, but he was encumbered by his spear and shield, and he could not reach Edric who was holding him tightly around the neck while he killed the man as quickly as he could.

At last the Norman slumped, his lifeblood flooding from the awful gash in his neck. Edric dropped the knife and grabbed at the Norman's spear as it toppled from his dying grasp, then he leaped over the fallen body and went to help Hereward.

But the only aid Hereward required was in returning to the island. The Norman boat had tipped to one side with the violence of the struggle, and water was filling it, making it sink lower into the stream. From what Edric could see, all three Normans were dead, their bodies sprawled in unnatural positions as the water crept into the boat to claim them. Hereward had severed the tether which held Wilfred's boat and was now hauling it closer as he, too, sank into the dark water. One of the large paddles was floating on the surface near him, so he threw the axe to the shore and grabbed at the paddle while he continued to cling to the rope tether.

The Norman boat lost its futile attempt to stay afloat as the stream drowned it. The bodies went down with it, leaving Hereward treading water as he clung to the rope which was fastened to the prow of Wilfred's vessel.

Awkwardly, Hereward tossed the paddle ashore, then reached for the end of the spear which Edric extended out over the water. He grabbed at it, almost missed his grip, then took a firm hold.

Edric hauled him to the bank, first using the spear shaft, then reaching down to grab Hereward's wrist and help him from the water.

Hereward emerged dripping and cursing.

"Help me pull the boat onto the bank," he gasped.

Together, they dragged Wilfred's boat clear of the water, then Hereward gestured to the dead Norman lying at their feet.

"Get rid of that one," he said brusquely. "Dump the weapons, too. We don't want to be caught with them."

Edric dutifully rolled the heavy body to the edge of the stream, watching it as it fell into the water and slowly sank from sight.

"Will they stay hidden?" he asked Hereward. "They might float."

"As long as they stay under for a little while," Hereward replied. "We are leaving."

"But you are soaked!" Edric protested. "Again. You'll catch a fever."

"Then I'll dry myself as best I can while you pack the boat. Take the axe. Kill a couple of chickens and fill one of those old nets with fish from the tank. We will be fishermen heading to market. but we need to go. We have a war to fight."

Chapter 16

Hereward's clothing was still sodden by the time he boarded the fen boat, but he shook off Edric's protestations.

"I'm not staying here a moment longer than we have to," he explained. "Have you loaded everything?"

Edric, who was sitting on the bench in the stern, indicated the items he had brought from Wilfred's home. He had felt guilty at first, believing they were stealing, but the sight of dried blood on the boat's bench told him Wilfred would not be returning. The old fisherman must have objected when the Normans demanded that he hand over his boat, and they had killed him for it.

He told Hereward, "I brought Wilfred's plate, a couple of mugs, some spoons and a tinder box. The axe, of course, and a few small bits of firewood. His ale sack was almost empty, so I poured it out and filled the sack with water from the spring. There's a small amount of beans and some flour. And the chickens, of course. We've got plenty fish and eels now, too."

He scarcely needed to point out the bulging net which lay at the front of the boat. The smell of the fish was strong enough to fill his nostrils and was already attracting a small flock of gulls who were circling overhead in hope of stealing a meal.

Hereward sat in the centre of the boat, creating a small puddle on the planking of the bottom of the hull as water continued to seep from him.

"Then let's go," he declared. "The sooner we return to Ely, the better."

"Which way?" Edric asked with a frown.

Waving a vague hand, Hereward told him, "Northwards and westwards whenever possible."

"We could get lost," Edric reminded him.

"So we could, but we need to try. So use that paddle."

Edric dutifully plunged the large, clumsy paddle into the water and pushed off from the landing spot. He did not look back at Wilfred's home, for there was nothing there except an abandoned shack. As for the boat, he was glad it was smaller than most fen boats. Using a single paddle would have been difficult in a broad vessel where two men could sit side by side, but Wilfred, a lone fisherman, had used a narrow boat which would allow him to go where wider vessels could not, so Edric was able to alternate his strokes to keep the boat on a more or less straight course. Still, it was hard work and he was soon sweating with the effort of propelling the boat along the reed-lined waterways.

Their route twisted and turned, with Hereward always telling him to follow the broadest course which headed in what seemed like the right direction, although Edric was soon confused as to whether they were actually going northwards. Hereward kept looking to the clouds, trying to estimate the location of the sun, but the fens were like a maze, often turning them in completely the wrong direction. Several times they were forced to laboriously turn the boat around or move slowly backwards when the stream they were following ended in a stretch of boggy ground or an impassable hedge of reeds or tall sedge grass.

As dusk approached, they began to look for a place to make camp. There were few islands in this part of the fens, so they eventually beached the boat on a small patch of squelching marshland. Using the flint from Wilfred's tinder box, they managed to light a small fire, but their supply of firewood barely lasted long enough for them to roast one of the chickens over the feeble flames. Hereward attempted to dry his clothes, but Edric could see that the Thane was already shivering with the damp and cold. There was, though, nothing they could do except huddle together on the wet, marshy ground and try to snatch some sleep until dawn.

It was a long, uncomfortable night, and they ate no breakfast, simply launching the boat and setting off again as soon as it was light enough to see.

At one point, Edric thought he could hear the breakers of the sea off to their right, but he could not be sure. If it was the sea, he knew they had come too far eastwards.

They continued to follow the winding streams in a roughly northwards direction, but again found they often needed to retrace their path.

Hereward took a turn on the paddle, insisting that Edric should not do all the hard work, so they exchanged places several times to allow one another to rest.

Later in the day, Edric was back at the stern when he saw Hereward sit upright, peering ahead and to their left.

"Is that smoke?" he asked, pointing an excited finger.

Edric followed his directions, narrowing his eyes as he sought to make out what the Thane had spotted through the murk.

"Our marsh fire could still be burning," he suggested, although he could not make out anything against the drab grey of the sky and the persistent drizzle of rain.

"No," Hereward said. "That looks more like a smudge of smoke over a town."

To Edric, Hereward's words seemed driven more by hope and desperation than reality, but he dutifully followed the next stream which headed in the direction Hereward insisted would lead them home. After a while, though, the rain ceased and Edric was able to discern the slightly different smear of grey which seemed to hover in the air beneath the low-hanging clouds.

"It could be smoke," he agreed tentatively.

"It's the best landmark we have," Hereward decided. "Let's try to get there."

Edric paddled more vigorously as the thought of reaching Ely spurred him on. Twice more, though, they were compelled to retrace their route, and found themselves moving further away from the faint smear of wood smoke they hoped indicated the site of their intended destination.

They were growing hungry, but there was no point in stopping unless they could find firewood to cook a meal, so they pressed on, drinking water from the ale sack until that, too was finished.

The day dragged on, and still they seemed to draw no nearer to their hoped for destination. Then Hereward held up an urgent hand, signalling for silence.

Edric stopped paddling, merely trying to hold the boat's position as Hereward held a finger to his mouth, urging him to make no sound.

Edric tensed, straining his ears, then he heard voices.

French voices.

There seemed to be some sort of argument going on as at least three men exchanged angry views. They sounded horribly close, perhaps just on the other side of a bank of tall reeds which delineated the edge of the stream Edric and Hereward had been following.

Edric's heart began to beat rapidly. Wilfred had told them the Normans were patrolling the fens now, and it was clear from what had befallen Wilfred and from their own encounter that the aim was to seize as many fen boats as possible. Despite Hereward's attempt to disguise them as fishermen, Edric doubted whether the Normans would let them pass unmolested. But the prospect of a fight on the water terrified him. He was likely to fall in and drown if it came to a hand to hand struggle between two boats.

They waited for what seemed an age before the voices began to diminish.

"They are heading back to their fleet which is out at sea," Hereward informed him in a whisper. "I think they were part of a small raid on Ely, but they were driven off and became separated from the rest of their group."

"So we must be close," Edric remarked.

Hereward nodded, "Let's hope so. But we still need to find our way. Still, if that lot are heading to our right, then we should be able to get to Ely if we follow the stream to our left."

Edric needed no further encouragement. He dug in the paddle and propelled the boat along the stand of reeds until they reached a confluence of two waterways. Following Hereward's signals, he turned to the west.

Soon, after a few more twists and turns, the narrow stream joined a much broader stretch of water, and Edric could feel a strong current slowing them. He exerted all his energy, pushing the boat onwards, still unable to see for any great distance because of the tall reeds, but knowing they were now on one of the main routes, perhaps even the Ouse itself.

The dark smudge in the sky was now clearly visible and drawing much nearer.

Almost without warning, they rounded a bend and found themselves at another junction in the watercourse. They bobbled and swayed as they moved into another arm of the river, this time with the current in their favour, then they turned again and found they had reached the Isle of Ely.

Hereward let out a rasping cry of triumph, turning to grin at Edric, but their dangers were not over.

A group of horsemen were watching them, all armed with spears, and the open stretch of ground on the bank had been barricaded by a wall of peat and timber.

"Keep going," Hereward told him. "Let the current carry us to the town. There's still an open hithe there."

So Edric paddled on, using less effort now that the stream was guiding them. Hereward waved at the horsemen who trotted along, keeping pace with them and continuing to eye them with deep suspicion.

Up ahead, the town of Ely soon came into view, its thatched roofs and the pall of shimmering smoke one of the most welcome sights Edric could ever recall. He began to anticipate being warm, dry and well fed, the expectation providing him with the strength to keep paddling.

A few minutes later, they made landfall at the hithe near Ely. There were dozens of armed men here, Northumbrians who regarded them with a mixture of suspicion and scorn when the two bedraggled men wearily clambered out of the boat.

A group of boatmen and a handful of passing townsfolk watched with amusement as the two men were confronted by the Northumbrians.

"Who are you?" the leader of the warriors growled suspiciously, keeping his long spear pointed directly at them. "You don't look like you're going to the market."

"I am Hereward, son of Asketil," Hereward replied, his voice still hoarse. "And we need a drink. We have been lost in the fens for the past four days."

The man with the spear stared at them, his expression dubious.

"Hereward, you say?" he frowned. "Can you prove that?"

In response, Hereward tugged at the sleeves of his tattered shirt, revealing the tattoos he bore on his forearms.

"The bear and the boar," he told them. "Anyone who knows me will recognise them. Now, put down your weapons and stand aside. I need to get to the abbey."

The Northumbrian remained uncertain and suspicious.

"Everyone says you are dead," he said with a frown.

"It takes more than a few hundred Normans to kill me," Hereward assured him.

The confrontation was now attracting a great deal of interest as some of the boatmen ventured nearer.

The leader of the warriors was still trying to make up his mind what to do when one of the boatmen exclaimed, "It is Hereward! My Lord, you are alive! They said you were dead!"

"No, but I might die of thirst if I don't get a drink of ale soon," Hereward responded.

His words produced a flurry of activity as boatmen scurried to their beached vessels, several returning with skins or clay jars of ale.

Hereward and Edric drank deeply and gratefully, although Edric felt his head begin to spin a little as the ale hit his empty stomach.

"Easy, lad," Hereward warned. "Don't guzzle it and make yourself drunk on top of everything else."

The boatmen were asking questions, wanting to know where they had been and how they had survived, but Edric was barely aware of what was happening. He felt as if he were in a dream, scarcely able to believe they had reached safety at last.

Hereward, though, almost seemed to be enjoying himself. Unshaven and filthy, with his clothes hanging in sodden shreds, he nevertheless began issuing orders.

"There's a pile of fish in that boat," he told the boatmen. "Share it out among yourselves. Take the damned boat as well if you like."

The boatmen grinned and laughed when they heard this, several of them scurrying down to where Edric had abandoned Wilfred's tiny fen boat.

Turning to the Northumbrians, Hereward said, "The Normans have boats coming in from the sea. You should build a barricade here. But make sure you can open and shut an entrance so that the fisherfolk can come and go."

The Northumbrian commander gave a thoughtful nod.

"We heard there was a raid near Aldreth earlier, but we've seen no sign of anyone here."

"If the Normans find an unprotected landing spot, they'll be here soon enough," Hereward told him. "So get your lads to work straight away."

The Northumbrian seemed on the point of arguing, perhaps thinking that he should take orders only from his Earl but, despite Hereward's ragged appearance, the Thane retained his air of authority, so the man nodded and said, "I'll see to it."

"Good. Now, my young friend and I must go to the abbey. We need to tell everyone else we are alive."

Edric was incredibly tired, but the relief he felt was enough to keep him going. A gaggle of boatmen followed the two men, and townsfolk soon came to stare at their unexpected return and the sorry state of their clothes. They looked more like beggars than warriors, yet their short walk turned into something akin to a triumphal parade as word of their survival spread. A couple of young boys ran ahead, shouting the news that Hereward had returned, and people came rushing out of the abbey to meet them. In the oncoming crowd Edric saw Siward White, Winter and the others, all of them with expressions of delight and amazement on their faces. Then Torfrida appeared, her face a picture of relief as she pushed through to throw herself at Hereward and cling to him, her tears unrestrained.

"I thought you were dead!" she sobbed.

"Not me!" Hereward assured her. Then, repeating the boast he had given to the Northumbrians, he added with a laugh, "It takes more than a few hundred Normans to kill me."

"But what happened?" Torfrida demanded.

"It's a long story," Hereward replied. "I'll tell you all about it, but first I need a bath, some food and a comfortable bed."

"Martin will prepare a bath," Torfrida said, wiping tears of joy from her cheeks with the backs of her hands. "And you can eat as much as you like."

Edric, who had been watching this exchange in a detached way, feeling he was intruding on a private conversation despite the very public setting, almost stumbled when he was pounded on the back by a meaty hand.

Winter boomed in his ear, "By God, you're like a scarecrow, lad! We'll need to get some fresh clothes for you, I think."

Edric turned away from Hereward and Torfrida to find the rest of the gang clustering around him, all of them clamouring a welcome.

"Food and drink first," he gasped in response to Winter's greeting.

The gang were grinning like idiots and firing questions at him, asking what had happened and why it had taken so long for them to get back.

Edric soon found himself separated from Hereward and Torfrida who were now surrounded by a gaggle of well-wishers which included Ranald Sigtrygsson, the two Siwards, Martin Lightfoot and Abbot Thurstan. In spite of the attention he was receiving, Hereward still found a moment to glance over at Edric and wave him off, clearly telling him to allow himself to be taken care of by the gang. That was a command Edric was happy to obey.

"I need some decent food," he told Winter again. "Lots of it."

"You need a bath," Auti observed, wrinkling his nose. "You stink of fish and muck."

Edric was so glad to be back among friends he could not protest as they half carried him to a water barrel. Wulfric drew out a full bucket, Ordgar handed him a chunk of tallow soap, and Winter stripped off his tattered rags, then they ordered him to wash. By the time he was clean, Winter had produced a set of mismatched clothing for him.

"It's mostly Ordgar's and mine," he explained. "We'll need to burn your old stuff. But I've got your good boots here. It's just as well you didn't wear them, because those other ones are ruined."

"I doubt any of his stuff will burn," Ordgar chuckled. "It's too wet."

Auti handed Edric a comb of fine antler, so he tugged at his wet hair until it was reasonably straight, Then he was led to the dormitory where he consumed a mug of ale and devoured a leg of lamb, some eel pies, half a loaf of bread and a large chunk of cheese before washing the food down with another mug.

"Careful, lad," cautioned Winter. "You'll make yourself sick."

Edric certainly felt full, his stomach gurgling and his head spinning with the effect of the ale, but he had been so hungry he felt he could have eaten all day. By this time, though, the gang were demanding answers to their questions, so he gave them an account of what had happened.

"That's a tale and a half," Ordgar commented when Edric had finished the telling. "You're bloody lucky, boy."

"Lucky I had Hereward with me," Edric replied. "I would have died out there if not for him."

193

"You should get some sleep now," Winter suggested.

Edric shook his head.

"No. There's somebody else I need to see first."

"Who?"

Edric hesitated, then muttered, "A friend."

Winter clearly knew who he meant, but Wulfric guessed, "A girl?"

Edric gave an embarrassed nod, much to the amusement of Wulfric and Ordgar.

"Then you'd better get along," Winter told him. "But take your gear."

"Why? What's happening?"

"There's been a fair bit of action out near that causeway," Winter explained. "It's getting a lot closer, and Siward Barn's lads have had some tough fighting. There was a raid by some boats probing our defences near Aldreth, too, so we're all expecting more trouble from the Normans soon. Now Hereward is back, he'll be wanting us ready, I expect. So take your gear, just in case."

Edric did not have the strength to argue. He pulled on his chainmail byrnie, strapped on his axe, slung his Norman shield over his back and placed his helmet on his head.

"You look almost like your old self," Winter nodded approvingly. "A few hours sleep will get rid of those bags under your eyes. Not that you'll get much sleep if you're going to visit a girl. Whoever she is."

He ended his pronouncement with a wink which promised Edric he would keep the secret of Ylva's identity.

To the accompaniment of the gang's raucous laughter, Edric headed outside and made for the town. He felt light-headed and knew he was exhausted, but his only thought was to see Ylva. By now, she would have heard that he was missing, and he knew he needed to tell her he was still alive, so he plodded wearily into the town.

It was market day, so the streets were busy. Even the threat of the Norman attack could not prevent the people going to market. For many of them, market day was when they obtained much of the food they would need for the coming week. Tradesmen and artisans like Cecil could produce goods people wanted, but they could not eat the pots they made. Trade was vital for everyone, so the town was thronged as people crowded the marketplace.

Edric knew Cecil and Seaver would be in the town square, and he was tempted to go there first, but decided to head for the potter's home. He remained cautious in spite of his eagerness to see Ylva, taking several sudden turns, then backtracking to make sure nobody was following him. Satisfied, he hurried on his way.

He knew it had only been a few days since he had last been here collecting the pots he and Hereward had used to destroy the Norman boats, yet it seemed he was returning from a long exile as he rapped his hand on the door.

Cecil's wife, Garyn, opened the door, her lips forming an astonished circle when she recognised him.

"We thought you were dead!" she gasped.

Then she seized his hand and tugged him inside, turning as she did so to call excitedly, "Jetta! Jetta! Come quickly!"

Responding to her assumed name, Ylva appeared in the passageway, standing at the door of the kitchen, her apron dusted with flour which also smudged her hands and cheeks. She stood very still, her eyes wide with disbelief, then ran to meet him, flinging her arms around him and pulling herself up to plant kisses on his cheeks while Garyn stood laughing with delight and her children clustered at the kitchen door to stare in bemused wonder.

"You're alive!" Ylva almost screamed. "They said you were dead!"

"It takes more than a few hundred Normans to kill me," Edric told her, borrowing Hereward's earlier boast.

Ylva disentangled herself and took a step back, studying his face as she wiped a tear from her cheek with her flour-smudged hand.

"You look awful!" she announced in a voice thick with emotion.

"I've felt better," Edric admitted. "But I'm really just tired."

"And you've got flour all over you," she sniffed happily, using her apron to wipe her own face clean.

Edric rubbed a hand against his cheek and saw smears of the white powder on his fingers. He licked it off, grinning back at her.

Garyn, obviously feeling she was intruding, decided, "Why don't you two go and talk? I expect you have a lot to tell each other."

195

The twinkle in her eye clearly suggested she thought they would want to do a lot more than talk, and Edric felt a blush begin to rise on his cheeks, a reaction which brought a wide smile to Garyn's lips.

Ylva said, "But what about the baking? And the children?"

"I can cope with them," Garyn told her firmly. "I managed fine before you came to stay here. Go on, lass. Take the poor lad to your room and let him rest. Cecil and Seaver will be back in a couple of hours. Then we can all have dinner together and hear Edric's story."

Ylva did not wait to be told again. She seized Edric's hand and led him out through the kitchen, taking him into the yard, then guiding him to the door leading to the small room which, originally intended as a store, was now where she slept.

It was a tiny place, with a mat of woven reeds for a mattress, a couple of blankets and a small, flat-topped wooden chest which contained Ylva's few personal belongings, and doubled as a table on which she had placed a candle.

She lit that candle now, for the room had no windows and was plunged into darkness when the door was closed. Then she turned, untied her apron and cast it into a corner where it fell into a rumpled bundle.

"Take off all that armour," she instructed. "Unless you plan on fighting anyone."

Edric was not entirely sure what she intended, nor what he was hoping for, but he struggled out of his byrnie and propped his axe, shield and helmet into the same corner near the door where her discarded apron lay.

"Come and sit beside me," she said, indicating the reed mat. "And tell me everything that happened to you."

So they sat down, Ylva's hand reaching for his, their bodies touching at shoulder, thigh and knee, and he recounted the tale of his adventure once again.

"Poor Edric," she smiled when he had finished. "I am so glad you are safe, but you must be exhausted."

He nodded, "I could sleep for a week."

Ylva shifted away from him, then reached up and gently eased his head towards her.

"Come and lie down, with your head in my lap. You can rest until Seaver and Cecil get back from market. Just sleep and let me look at you."

Edric was not sure whether he was supposed to do as she said or make some other, more intimate move. Yet lying with his head on her lap was more intimate than anything she had previously permitted, so he decided to lie down and see what developed.

She gently stroked his head and face, closing his eyes and whispering softly to him, as if he were one of Garyn's children she was attempting to coax into falling asleep.

It should have felt silly and childish, but Edric relaxed, enjoying the soothing sound of her voice and the gentle brushing of her fingers on his skin.

He needed no coaxing, and fell into a dreamless sleep within moments.

Chapter 17

Edric had been too tired and too overcome by relief to notice that someone else had been watching his arrival at the abbey.

Altruda stood beside Kenton, casting furious eyes over the scene as Hereward and Edric were mobbed by warriors and monks clamouring to hear their tale.

Altruda kept her distance, but her eyes remained fixed on Hereward. She folded her arms beneath her bosom and took several deep breaths while her mind raced with calculations. From her own personal perspective, she was pleased to discover that Hereward had survived his ordeal, yet his return had ruined the timetable she had mapped out for the rest of her plan.

Without looking at Kenton, she said softly, "I have things to do. I must write a letter. Find Brother Richard and tell him I need him."

"It's urgent?" Kenton guessed.

"Very. We are running out of time. With Hereward back, the whole situation has changed. We must act before he has time to rally the defences."

"You will need to act fast, then," Kenton observed.

"So go and find Brother Richard. I had hoped we had a few more days, but this changes everything."

The scar-faced man turned to go, but Altruda called him back.

"One other thing," she told him. "Make sure you are up early tomorrow. I will need you at daybreak."

Kenton regarded her with his scheming, calculating gaze before asking, "Will you need me again before then?"

She shook her head.

"No. Just be ready by dawn tomorrow."

Kenton nodded, "I'll be ready. As long as I have the rest of today to do what I need to do."

"And what is that?" she asked sharply, distrusting his manner.

In response, Kenton merely grinned and tapped a finger to the side of his nose.

"Personal stuff," he told her in a patronising voice.

As he spoke, his eyes moved, flicking to where Edric Strong was being dragged towards a rain barrel by the other members of Hereward's gang.

Altruda warned, "Don't touch him! I don't want Hereward being alerted to my plans by your need for revenge. You can wait one more day."

Kenton spread his arms, adopting a look of innocence.

"Me, my Lady? I won't touch a hair on his head. No, I have other things I need to attend to. Personal things. Important things."

With a smirk, he turned and swaggered off towards the infirmary, whistling tunelessly like a man who had no cares in the world.

Which, Altruda reflected grimly, boded ill for someone.

With a shake of her head, she dismissed Kenton's mysterious plans, for her own strategy was in danger of failing again. When Hereward had gone missing, she had sent Brother Richard to the King with an important message. It had been a dangerous journey, for the fens were now the scene of fighting as the Normans forced their way towards Ely, but Brother Richard was a man of God, and so had been able to travel unmolested. He had done an excellent job, returning with a letter signed and sealed by the King himself, offering immunity from punishment to Abbot Thurstan and Earl Morcar. Altruda's task was to convince those two fools to believe the promises. She had intended to wait a few more days to allow the causeway to draw even nearer and give the King's naval force time to gather more small boats, but Hereward's return meant she could no longer delay. Brother Richard would need to go out again, this time to urge the King to strike without delay.

Bringing forward the plan posed some risk, Altruda knew, but the danger of delaying was even greater.

She looked over to where Hereward was surrounded by a throng of well-wishers, and once again she found her emotions conflicted. Hereward's return threatened to thwart her victory, yet she was glad he still lived, because that meant her desire for revenge could still be satisfied. He was the only man who had ever refused her advances, and that was something Altruda needed to remedy. She wanted to see him on his knees, begging her to help

199

him. Now, if she acted quickly enough, perhaps that would come to pass sooner than she could ever have hoped.

"Enjoy your moment of happiness, Hereward," she whispered softly to herself. "It will not last long."

Kenton's plans did involve Edric, but not in the way Altruda suspected. Once he had found Brother Richard and told him to report to the Lady, Kenton left the monastery and headed into the town. He wore his byrnie and had his axe slung on his back, but he carried no shield and left his helmet behind. He needed to look intimidating, but he was not expecting to fight anyone.

His son, Halfdan, saw him and came ambling after him, but Kenton sent the boy away.

"I don't need your help with this," he snapped.

Later, he almost regretted sending the boy away because it would have done Halfdan good to see what his father was going to do. But the task required patience and a long wait, and Kenton had no wish to have Halfdan hanging around him all afternoon. The boy had become increasingly morose and withdrawn over the past few months, never smiling and rarely speaking. He did as he was told and took his beatings without complaint, but something inside him had changed. There was an air of sullen defiance about the boy now, but Kenton supposed that was probably to do with the lad growing up. Whatever it was, the boy's attitude irritated him, so he chased him away and tried to forget about him. He had more important things to occupy his mind this day.

He grinned at the memory of how he had learned the truth about his daughter. It was all down to that stupid little French girl he had killed.

Torfrida's maid had been terrified when he had grabbed her, clamping a hand over her mouth and dragging her behind the infirmary. She had kicked and struggled, naturally, but he had overpowered her easily, and the sight of his dagger held to her throat had ended her resistance and kept her quiet.

It had been an impulsive deed, but Kenton had been constrained by Altruda's injunctions for so long he needed some release. He had often watched Hereward's wife, Torfrida, flaunting herself around the abbey, but he had more sense than to make any attempt to injure her. Altruda, too, was a woman who enjoyed teasing him, and he longed to teach her how a woman ought to behave, but he understood that his future lay in her hands, so all he could do was dream about the things he wanted to do to her.

Which meant he had been confined to paying the tavern sluts to satisfy his lusts, and those degraded women were hardly in the same league as the noble ladies.

And then he had seen the maid, walking alone across the courtyard. There was nobody else in sight, so Kenton had followed her, then waited until she had left the infirmary.

It had been almost too easy to drag her out of sight and force himself on her. She had sobbed and moaned, feebly tried to ward him off, but she had been too afraid to offer much resistance. Kenton liked it when women surrendered to him, and he had enjoyed seeing her frightened anguish as he used her to sate his desire.

She knew he intended to kill her once he was finished. She had seen the look in his eyes, and so she had begged for her life, offering up a secret if he would let her go.

"What secret?" he had demanded, finding her tear-stained desperation amusing.

He had merely wanted to prolong her agony before killing her, but she had surprised him with her tale when she told him about the meetings Torfrida held with the potter and the old man from Bourne on market days.

"Your daughter lives with the potter," the maid had blurted through her misery.

"What? She's a potter's wife?" Kenton had snorted.

"No. He has a wife already. But he's sheltering her. She has cut her hair and goes by the name of Jetta now, but she is alive and still in Ely."

Kenton had struggled to follow the explanation because the girl's English was not good, and her accent was unfamiliar, but he made her repeat the secret until he was convinced.

"Where is the potter's home?" he had demanded roughly, shaking her shoulders as if to force the answer from her.

She had cried and sobbed, shaking her head as she told him, "I don't know. The Lady always meets them in the town square on market days."

He believed her. She could tell him no more, so he had killed her. It had made him laugh to see the hope flare in her expression when he had put his dagger away, then turn to horror when he had grabbed her by the throat.

In the end, he had killed her quickly, snapping her neck with one vicious twist of his hands. It was the least he could do after what she had told him.

Once he had dragged her lifeless corpse out of the small gate behind the infirmary and dumped her in the river, he had wanted to rush into the town and find every pottery, but he decided to wait until market day. He would find the right man, follow him home, then he would take his daughter back. That would show Edric bloody Strong what it meant to go up against a real man. He would parade Ylva through the monastery, then have her locked up until the siege was over. After that, he would need to decide how to punish her for running away.

Anticipation of what he would do sustained him while he wandered the town square, seeking out the potter. The place was the usual heaving mass of people, with stalls jammed close together and the narrow aisles between them full of men and women who were browsing or bartering. There were cows, pigs, sheep, goats and chickens for sale; there were bolts of cloth, leather hides, fish, birds, eggs, bales of wool, wooden platters and mugs, household items made of tin and pewter, and, above all, there were clay pots.

He found the stall, noted the jovial man bantering with potential customers, and saw the older man helping him.

Kenton grinned to himself. He had found them. Now all he had to do was wait.

As the afternoon eased towards early evening, Edric was woken by Ylva gently shaking his shoulder. He stirred, mumbled something incoherent, then blinked his eyes open and came alert.

"I fell asleep!" he said as he pushed himself up from her lap.

"I know," she smiled. "But I hear Cecil and Seaver coming back. It's nearly dinner time."

She stood, grimacing slightly as she stretched her legs.

"I'm sorry," Edric told her shyly. "I didn't mean to use you as a pillow."

"I don't mind," she assured him.

Edric stretched his body, rubbed his eyes, and yawned. Then, not sure what to do, he hesitated.

The dim light of the solitary candle was insufficient to show him Ylva's expression, yet he sensed a tension in the way she stood, her delicate frame poised and alert as if waiting for something.

But what?

It was too late to find out now. The sound of voices in the yard told Edric that Cecil and Seaver had come in through the back gate and were packing away their unsold goods, stacking the clay pots and jars in a small outhouse. Something made Edric stay quiet, not wanting to alert them to his presence. He was not certain whether he would be more embarrassed at being found in Ylva's room or by the fact that all he had done while there was sleep. Either way, he did not relish encountering his friends at that precise moment.

Then he heard a loud crash which brought shouts of alarm from the two men, and a third voice angrily demanding, "Where is she, you bastards?"

Edric heard pots shattering, furious threats being uttered, and the frantic, bewildered denials of Cecil and Seaver.

Edric did not hesitate. Grabbing his axe, he pulled the door open, admitting a blaze of evening sunlight which momentarily dazzled him. As he blinked his vision clear, he could make out Seaver sitting slumped against the high fence that surrounded the yard, while a man in chainmail had grabbed hold of the front of Cecil's tunic and was furiously shaking him.

Kenton!

Edric recognised him and took a step outside, but the scarred axeman moved much more quickly than he had expected. In the short time it had taken Edric's eyes to adjust to the daylight and take in the scene, Kenton had tossed Cecil aside like a rag doll, spun on his heel and rushed at Edric like a wild bull.

Kenton's shoulder struck him on the chest, knocking him back against the outer wall of Ylva's chamber. His head struck the wood with a violent crack, dazing him and forcing him to release his hold on his axe. The weapon clattered to the ground, with Edric sliding down beside it, his senses dulled by the impact.

"Thought you were clever, did you?" Kenton snarled.

Edric's vision was clouded, bright lights dancing before his eyes. He thought he could hear Ylva screaming, but the sound was vague and distant, as if she were shouting from the far end of a long tunnel.

Kenton's voice, on the other hand, was much closer and much more threatening.

"You tried to make a fool of me, boy! Now you're going to suffer. I don't care what that high and mighty whore says, I'm going to break your fucking neck."

Edric tried to struggle upright, but Kenton lashed out with a heavy boot and kicked him on the side of the head. Edric saw the kick at the last moment and attempted to roll with the blow, but pain exploded in his head and he tumbled sideways, lying hunched on the ground with his back against the wooden wall.

A second kick caught him in the belly, driving all the air from his lungs and sending another explosion of pain coursing through his body.

"How do you like that, you stinking bag of shit?" Kenton growled.

Edric winced, expecting another kick, but he heard Ylva shouting at her father, yelling at him to leave him alone. Groggily, he pushed himself up on one elbow and scrabbled for his axe, his hands fumbling in vain as he blindly searched for the weapon.

Kenton had half-turned to face Ylva who had picked up Edric's kite-shaped shield. She held it in front of her, thrusting it towards her father as if she intended to knock him over, but Kenton merely laughed, flashing out his arms to grab the rim of the shield, wrench it from her grasp and toss it aside. It smashed into the fence at the far side of the yard, the sound loud and echoing like a clap of thunder, while Ylva fought to regain her balance and leap away from her father's reach.

She was too slow. Kenton seized her by the shoulders, his fingers digging into her flesh and causing her to cry out loud. She tried to kick him, but he merely laughed as he twisted her around.

"I'll deal with you in a minute, you slut," Kenton promised with a snarl.

Roughly, he shoved the protesting Ylva through the door of her room, pushing her so hard that she fell sprawling on the floor. Then he turned back to Edric who was now on his hands and

204

knees, retching and coughing, but desperately trying to climb to his feet.

"You're pathetic!" Kenton snorted. "Call yourself a warrior? A jumped up farm boy is what you are."

Edric could sense another kick coming for him, but the blow never landed. Instead, he heard a scuffle and caught a glimpse of a small figure rushing up behind Kenton and leaping high to land on the axeman's back.

Kenton was caught off guard by the unexpected attack. He stumbled forwards as he tried to recover his balance and fling his arms up to push away his new assailant, but he was too slow. The small figure had wrapped its legs around Kenton's torso and flung one arm around his throat as it clamped itself onto him. The scar-faced man's instinctive reaction was to grab at the arm which threatened to throttle him and force it away, but his attacker had no intentions of choking him. Instead, it was the dagger in the other hand which dealt the fatal blow.

Edric struggled up in time to see a hand stab at Kenton's neck, driving the knife deep, then yanking it back and stabbing again. Blood gushed from the wound, flooding down Kenton's neck and chest, covering his arms and soaking his chainmail tunic.

Wild-eyed with horror, Kenton twisted savagely, threw off his killer, then swayed, clamping a hand to his neck in a futile attempt to staunch the massive flow of blood. Then he sank to his knees, a look of disbelief on his face, before his arms fell to his sides and he toppled forwards onto the hard ground, his head striking the earth barely a foot in front of Edric.

There was silence in the yard. Several dogs were barking nearby, but nobody had come to investigate the sounds. Cecil's neighbours obviously had more sense than to get involved in what was obviously a serious brawl.

Edric was still dazed, taking a considerable time to understand what had happened. He lurched to his feet, feeling sick as a bout of nausea assailed him. Staggering, he reached out to steady himself against the wall of Ylva's room.

Ylva!

Focusing on the doorway, he saw her appear, a slight, trembling figure who stared down at her father's corpse. The expression on her face held a mixture of horror, revulsion and hatred.

Beyond Kenton's body, Cecil was emerging from behind his store where he had scuttled to avoid danger. He was rubbing the back of his head, grimacing in discomfort.

Seaver, too, had been slightly hurt. There was blood oozing from a cut, swollen lip, and he was gingerly rubbing his cheek, but he managed a wan smile in Edric's direction.

Finally, there was the boy who had killed Kenton.

It was Halfdan, his dark hair awry, his left arm soaked by the blood his dagger had drawn from his father's neck. He was sitting up, his face pale, his chest heaving as he gulped in air, his eyes wide and bulging. In his right hand, he still held the dagger he had used, and its blade was dark with Kenton's lifeblood.

Ylva ran to Halfdan, kneeling down beside him and wrapping her arms around his shoulders. Gently, she prised the dagger from his clenched fingers, letting it fall to the ground.

"You killed him!" she gasped. "You saved us."

"I hate him," Halfdan said, his voice high pitched and urgent.

Then he buried his face in Ylva's shoulder and burst into tears.

Seaver helped Edric carry the body away. They did not go far, but dumped it in a narrow alleyway only fifty yards from Cecil's home.

They left the axe beside the body. Cecil did not want it, and Halfdan, to whom Edric had offered it, refused to accept it.

"I want nothing of his!" the boy spat.

He did, though, take a share of the surprisingly large amount of money held in Kenton's purse.

"Rewards from the Lady Altruda, I expect," Edric muttered.

He split the money between Halfdan and Ylva, although she gave most of her share to Cecil.

Looking down at the crumpled, blood-stained corpse, Seaver observed, "People will think robbers killed him."

Edric did not really care. His head ached, his belly was bruised, and he felt as if he had been kicked by a horse.

"He must have followed you from the market," he suggested to Seaver.

"Aye. I suppose he heard about Ylva from someone. It was bound to happen eventually."

Edric frowned, his mind automatically thinking of Winter. Had the big man inadvertently revealed the secret of Ylva's whereabouts?

Not that it mattered now. Ylva was safe, and Halfdan had released himself from his father's tyranny.

"He says he's known where I was for a long time," Ylva told Edric once she had persuaded Halfdan to tell his story. "He kept it quiet because he knew what my father used to do to me, and he wanted to keep me safe from that."

"He has a good heart," Edric nodded.

"Only because he spent so much time watching you," Ylva smiled. "He was in danger of being turned into a copy of my father until he began following you. He says he is terrified of someone he calls, 'That Woman', and that he wanted to run away like I had done, but could never summon the courage."

"That Woman is Altruda," Edric explained. "She's not a pleasant person. She's very beautiful, but she's evil inside."

"She certainly frightens Halfdan," Ylva agreed. "So what do we do now?"

That was the question they all asked. Garyn had prepared fish stew for dinner, and they sat around the table, although none of them had much appetite after what had happened.

Halfdan joined them, although he hardly spoke and kept his eyes downcast, never meeting anyone's gaze. Ylva sat beside him and tried to act normally, but there was a strained, sombre atmosphere hanging over them. Cecil's children had heard the noise of the fight and a couple of the older ones had seen Kenton's body. The sounds and sight had terrified them, so Garyn bustled them off to bed as soon as dinner was over.

Everyone looked to Edric, clearly expecting him to make the decision about what to do. His head was still throbbing in protest at the treatment Kenton had meted out, but he did not take long to make up his mind.

"Halfdan will need to stay here," he told Cecil. "I'm sorry, but Altruda will miss Kenton and would no doubt ask Halfdan what has happened to him."

He saw a shiver of fear flash across Halfdan's face at the mention of Altruda, so quickly added, "That means he needs to stay away from the abbey for the time being."

Cecil gave a reluctant nod, but Seaver put in, "Will anyone come looking for Kenton, do you think?"

"Perhaps. He was not a popular man, but if Altruda wants him found, she may pay people to search for him."

Neither Cecil nor Seaver appeared happy with the arrangement, but Garyn returned from putting the children to bed to make the decision for them.

"Of course he must stay here!" she insisted when she heard Edric's proposal. "He can sleep in the kitchen."

Nobody would dare argue with one of Garyn's decrees, so Ylva helped her move another reed mat and a couple of old blankets into the kitchen where they set up a bed beside the clay oven. Halfdan, still in a daze, went along without protest. Ylva sat with him for a long time, speaking softly to him and stroking his hair, while Edric was compelled to once again relate the story of his recent adventure to Cecil and Seaver. Cecil was horrified at the account of fighting and Edric's ordeal in the marshes, but Seaver had other concerns.

"You did well," the old man remarked. "But will it be enough? The Normans won't be put off by that setback, will they?"

Edric insisted, "They don't have enough boats to launch an attack from the water. With their camp at Aldreth destroyed, they can only come at us along their causeway, and Hereward will deal with that soon enough. After that, he'll destroy their army."

"I pray you are right," Seaver said sombrely.

It was growing late by the time Edric decided he should return to the abbey. When he went into the kitchen to say farewell to Ylva, he found her sitting cross-legged on the floor, staring down at her younger brother who was fast asleep.

"He was so frightened of our father," she whispered to Edric as she stood up to greet him. "Now he doesn't know whether to be relieved at what he has done, or terrified of what will happen to him because of it."

"Nothing will happen to him," Edric assured her. "Tell him that when he wakes up. I owe him my life, so I'll make sure he

208

stays safe. And once people become accustomed to your father not being around, you can both return to the abbey."

Ylva smiled up at him, her eyes warm and grateful.

"You are a good man, Edric Strong," she told him.

"I try to be," he shrugged. "I'm not always sure I manage it."

Taking his hand, Ylva indicated that he should follow her. Moving quietly, they went out the back door of the house, walked along the edge of the yard and went to her small room. She opened the door and tugged at Edric's hand, guiding him into the room.

He released himself from her grip and said, "Can you light the candle? I need to gather up my things."

Instead, she reached out and pulled him round so he was facing her in the gathering darkness.

"Forget that stuff," she said softly. "You won't need it."

"Yes, I will," he frowned.

Ylva stood on her tiptoes and reached up to pull his face down towards hers.

"No," she breathed as she gently kissed him on the lips, "you won't need them tonight. You are staying right here. With me."

Chapter 18

The cocks were still crowing to greet the early dawn when Edric left Ylva. She gave him a kiss and demanded a promise that he would return soon.

"I will," he grinned, attempting to snatch another kiss from her, a move she batted away with a laugh.

"Go and join your friends," she told him playfully before adding more seriously, "But be careful. That Altruda woman will be angry if she finds out my father is dead."

"I'm not going to tell her," Edric decided. "In fact, I'm not going to tell anyone. If you can keep Halfdan out of sight, people might think the two of them have run away to avoid being here when the Normans attack."

"That's probably the best thing to do," Ylva agreed, although Edric could tell she was worried about her younger brother.

"I'll be back as soon as I can," he told her.

She gave him a forced smile as she said, "Take care, Edric Strong. I know there will be a lot of fighting. Make sure you don't go and get yourself killed."

All he could offer her in response was a smile of his own as he waved farewell. Dressed in his byrnie and helmet, with axe and shield on his back, he left by the back gate, feeling a sense of loss tugging at his heart as he walked away from Cecil's home. The night with Ylva had filled him with joy and confidence, yet leaving her behind was a wrench he had not expected.

But he knew where his duty lay, so he made his way through the almost deserted streets as the sun slowly inched its way into the heavens and banished the shadows of the night.

The day promised to be dull and cloudy, but that prospect did not concern him in the slightest because his mind was filled with thoughts of Ylva. Knowing she was waiting for him made him feel as if he were walking on air. He was tired but happier than he could ever recall, and he knew now why Winter and the other men were always going on about women. His one night with Ylva had left no room in his mind for thoughts of anything other than seeing her again.

By the time he reached the abbey, he had no real recollection of how he had got there, but he was jolted back to reality when he saw Ranald Sigtrygsson hurrying out of the gates, one hand purposefully clasping the hilt of his sword. The Dane saw Edric and urgently beckoned him over.

"What's wrong?" Edric asked, seeing the worried expression on Ranald's face.

"That's what I'm trying to find out," Ranald told him enigmatically. "Come with me and let's see if we can learn what is going on."

Bemused, Edric fell into step beside the fair-haired Dane as Ranald led the way out of the abbey and headed along the road that led towards the river and the hithe.

Edric had not spoken to Ranald very often. The man had spent a long time in the infirmary recovering from his wound, and had later been ensconced in the guest chambers where he had spent much of his time speaking to Hereward and Torfrida. He was, after all, a Lord, albeit one who had been stranded far from his home without any followers. From what little Edric knew of him, he was generally affable and easy-going, but his face now wore a worried expression.

"I was woken before dawn by the sound of people moving in the corridor," Ranald explained as they walked. "I wondered what was going on, so I poked my head out the door and spoke to your big friend, Winter, who was on duty outside Hereward's room."

Frowning, Ranald continued, "He told me that Earl Morcar and the Lady Altruda had left, taking all their guards with them."

"Left?" Edric frowned. "To go where?"

"Winter apparently asked the same question. Earl Morcar rarely rises before the third hour, especially when Altruda is sharing his bed. But, for some reason, today they are both out and about before sunrise."

"That is odd," Edric agreed, privately wondering whether Kenton's disappearance might have something to do with the Earl's unusual behaviour. Had Altruda called out a search party?

But Ranald informed him, "One of the guards told Winter that the Earl was going to meet with the Abbot."

"With old Thurstan?"

211

"That's what they said. Winter wasn't sure whether to wake Hereward or not, but I told him to let him sleep. He's bound to be exhausted after your adventures in the Fens."

At this, Ranald shot Edric a probing look and said, "You look rather tired yourself. Where have you been?"

"Visiting a friend," Edric replied, although he was unable to keep a grin from his face, divulging his secret.

"Good for you!" Ranald chuckled. "But, to get back to Morcar and Altruda, I told Winter I'd follow them and find out what was going on. They'd disappeared by the time I got dressed, but they aren't in the church. The monks are all there, chanting those droning prayers of theirs to greet the dawn, but the Abbot isn't among them."

"So where have they gone?"

Ranald told him, "I found a servant who said he'd seen them all leaving the abbey and heading towards the river. So I'm going down there to see what they are up to."

Edric tried to make sense of what Ranald had told him. He could come up with no explanation for the Earl's odd behaviour, but his knowledge of Altruda's cunning made him fearful that this was another of her plots.

It did not take long to reach the hithe. Ranald raised an arm, indicating that they should stop by the side of one of the houses which flanked the open space. Then the two of them peered around the edge of the building to catch a glimpse of what was happening. As soon as they did so, Edric's worst fears were realised.

"Mother of God!" he breathed.

Because the Northumbrian defenders who were supposed to be guarding this approach to the island had laid down their weapons and were standing sullenly by the side of the road, while Earl Morcar, Altruda and Abbot Thurstan, together with a small group of monks and Thanes, had gathered by the river to greet the men who were crossing the stream in a small flotilla of boats.

"Normans!" hissed Ranald. "Hundreds of the swine! We have been betrayed!"

Standing by the bank of the river, Altruda maintained a tight hold on Morcar's arm. She knew that, without her insistence, he would still have backed out of this, and she could feel him trembling as the Normans drew nearer. For her, though, this was the culmination of a year's work, the moment when the rebellion would be brought to a sudden and very final end, and she felt the thrill of exultation as she watched the boats draw nearer.

She had been mildly irritated that Kenton had not kept his word, but it no longer mattered. The man was expendable. She had intended to dismiss him from her service as soon as the King had gained control of the Isle of Ely, but that small pleasure would need to wait. It was Kenton's loss that he was not here to see the final stage of her work coming to fruition.

"That's him!" Morcar breathed softly. "That's the king!"

"Of course it is," Altruda replied, squeezing the Earl's forearm. "He would not leave this to other men to oversee."

"Will he keep his promise?" Morcar gulped, his voice barely audible because of his fear.

"You saw his letter," Altruda replied.

She did not reveal that she had burned the letter once Morcar and Abbot Thurstan had agreed to submit to the King. Now there was no evidence that any promises had been made.

But the letter had accomplished its purpose. The first boats were landing, disgorging their passengers onto the hithe. Norman soldiers, dressed in chainmail, wearing helmets and carrying cumbersome shields and swords, were clambering awkwardly out of the vessels and forming a cordon at the river's edge. The boats instantly moved off, heading back across the river to where hundreds more men and horses waited to be ferried to the island. There were not enough boats to stage a landing if the island's defenders had opposed them, but the Northumbrians were standing idle in obedience to their Earl's command. Altruda could tell that few of the warriors were happy about their surrender, but the Norman incursion was, so far, proceeding without difficulty.

Still, the Normans were nervous. They had undertaken a long and difficult night march to reach the far bank, and they would be horribly outnumbered until the rest of their column had been ferried across the river.

But one among them showed no fear at all. A large man, his close-cropped red hair marking him out, stepped ashore, cast a scornful look at the mute English warriors, then placed his helmet on his head. Around the iron was a band of gold, shaped to form a crown. The big man grinned a smile of triumph, then strode

213

forwards, the cordon of soldiers moving with him in a protective circle.

Altruda saw that Abbot Turold and Ivo de Taillebois were with the King, along with another lean, dark-haired man she did not recognise.

But her attention was on King William.

Dressed in chainmail, he looked like an invincible giant of war, a man who expected his every command to be instantly obeyed. Exuding supreme confidence, he marched up to them as if he had every right to be there, as if there were no hint of danger in landing in the midst of a rebel army.

If anyone among the English had the nerve to fight, William was horribly exposed. The few men who accompanied him could not hope to hold off a determined assault, but Morcar had forced his men to swear they would not oppose the King, and their oaths to their Lord bound them to watch impassively as the Normans came ashore.

Altruda bowed her head reverentially when William drew near, and she felt Earl Morcar free himself from her grip as he fell to his knees in front of the King.

"My Lord!" he spluttered. "Your Majesty! Forgive me!"

"Of course I forgive you, Morcar," William responded in a loud, confident voice.

He held out his hand, gesturing to the Earl that he should stand.

When Morcar had risen to his feet, the King went on, "I am glad you have come to your senses. Now, there is more I need you to do for me."

"Anything, Your Majesty!" Morcar blurted, eager to prove his newly regained loyalty.

William's cold eyes sought out Abbot Thurstan, who stood a few yards away, apprehensively fingering the crucifix that hung at his chest while he waited to hear his fate.

Beckoning the Abbot forwards, the King addressed both men.

"The two of you will go with Abbot Turold. As soon as we have sufficient horses brought across the river, my men will provide an escort. Together, the two of you will visit every part of the island. You will order your men to lay down their arms and surrender to me."

214

Morcar nervously licked his lips, and seemed about to protest, but William cut him off, his voice suddenly harsh.

"Tell them you have given your word that the rebellion has ended," he told them. "Tell them it is God's will. And tell them my army is already in possession of the town. Tell them anything you need to, but make them lay down their weapons. If they surrender without a fight, I will let them go free, but if they resist, I will have every last one of them executed as outlaws. Is that clear, Earl Morcar, or do I need to carve it on your forehead?"

The menace in the King's voice was unmistakable, and all Morcar could do was gulp, "It is clear, Your Majesty."

"Lord Abbot?" William demanded, his expression merciless.

"I will do your bidding, Your Majesty," Thurstan said in a cracked, defeated voice.

"Good. Now, both of you get out of my sight."

As Morcar and Thurstan, dismissed like disobedient children, skulked away, William beckoned to Abbot Turold.

Leaning close to the mail-clad churchman, he said softly, "Watch the Earl closely. I don't expect him to give you any trouble, but kill him if he tries anything stupid, or if the Englishmen do not obey him."

"Yes, your Majesty," Turold nodded. "What about the Abbot?"

"He is a man of God," William responded harshly. "His presence should ensure the English offer you no harm. But I want no churchman's blood on my hands, Turold."

"I understand, Your Majesty."

"Good. Now, once all the defenders have surrendered, round them up and bring them here. Then have Morcar put in chains until I decide what to do with him."

"As you command, Your Majesty," smiled Turold. "And Abbot Thurstan? What should I do with him?"

"Nothing. He is of no consequence. Once he has helped persuade the rebels to surrender, let him return to his abbey. I will deal with him later."

"It shall be as you say, Your Majesty."

William dismissed the Abbot with a flick of his hand, then called de Taillebois to him.

The fat Sheriff bobbed his head subserviently when he stood in front of his King.

"I am putting you in charge of the prisoners," William told him. "Have any nobles kept under guard. Put them in shackles as soon as we have sufficient men here to quell any trouble."

"Yes, Your Majesty."

"You can let all the rest go free. Have them taken off the island, though."

"You were serious about that, Your Majesty?"

De Taillebois blinked in surprise at the unexpected leniency. William was not renowned for his forgiving nature.

A cruel grin tugged at the King's lips as he explained, "Yes. But first, make sure each of them loses a hand or a foot. That ought to ensure they can't rebel against me again."

De Taillebois beamed as he said, "It will be a pleasure, Your Majesty."

"I know it will," William murmured scornfully, before adding, "Wait until Earl Morcar and Abbot Thurstan have left with Turold before you start any of your fun. I don't want them knowing what I intend."

De Taillebois smiled happily, but William had already turned his attention away, switching his gaze to Altruda, who stood patiently watching him. He signalled to her to join him as he moved away from the group so they would not be overheard.

More and more men were flooding ashore, and now a handful of horses were being ferried across the river. William surveyed the preparations with an approving eye before addressing Altruda.

"You have done well, my Lady," he told her. "I am grateful. The English are still expecting another attack along the causeway. My brother, Odo, is making a show of preparing just such an attack, but they have no idea we are already behind them. I am sure Earl Morcar will have no trouble persuading most of them to lay down their arms. And it is all thanks to you."

"I live to serve you, Your Majesty," Altruda assured him.

William eyed her speculatively, and she guessed he was thinking that she probably served herself rather than anyone else, but he was too much in her debt to say such a thing openly.

Instead, he asked, "Where is the man called Hereward?"

"Sleeping. He is in the abbey."

"Then I shall send William Malet to deal with him once and for all."

When she heard this, Altruda gave the King a startled look which he could not help noticing.

"What is it?" he asked her.

Quickly gathering her wits, Altruda said, "Your Majesty, in one of my letters, I requested that you spare Hereward's life."

"Did you?" the king frowned. "De Taillebois must have forgotten to mention that."

Altruda's normally unflappable poise almost deserted her, but she managed to hold back the angry outburst which threatened to escape her lips.

"Then may I formally make that request now, Your Majesty? I would ask that Hereward's life be spared."

"Why? Do you still believe you can bring him round to be a loyal subject?"

"I would like to try, Your Majesty."

"I sense there is something personal behind your request, my Lady."

Altruda conceded the point with a slight nod.

"I once asked Hereward to marry me," she admitted. "He refused."

"So you want to ask him again?" the King enquired with an amused smile.

"I doubt he would agree unless he was compelled to," Altruda replied coldly. "But I want to see him beg me."

William's eyebrows arched as he asked, "Do you think he is the sort of man who will beg for his life?"

"Not for his own life, Your Majesty. But for the life of another. I will grant it, but at a price."

"You are a devious woman, my Lady," William chuckled. "But I will let you have your way in this. Provided we can take Hereward alive, of course."

"He is sleeping. It will be simple enough to capture him. Brother Richard will be able to lead your men to him."

"Very well. Malet!"

The dark-haired swordsman inclined his head as he stepped boldly up to them. Altruda thought he looked like an animal on a leash, ready to strike at a word from his master. He

217

was lean but powerful, radiating an air of supreme confidence in his own abilities.

"Your Majesty?" he asked.

"Take thirty men and go to the abbey. Lady Altruda will find you a monk who will act as your guide. Capture the rebel leader, Hereward. I want him alive if at all possible. Kill anyone else who offers resistance."

"His wife is with him," Altruda put in. "If you take her alive, Hereward will surrender."

"Bear that in mind, Malet," William said.

Despite the King's words, the look in his eyes told Malet that, whatever Altruda wanted, the command William had given him several days earlier was the one he should obey.

Hereward must die.

Edric was gasping for breath and sweating profusely by the time he staggered up to Cecil's door and began pounding on it for admission. He had run the whole way, weighed down by his byrnie of heavy chainmail, his axe and his shield. Sweat ran down his face from beneath his iron helmet, and his entire body felt clammy with exertion and fear. He knew he must have made an odd sight as he had run through the streets, but he had ignored the curious looks on the faces of the people he had passed because he had not wanted to start a panic by announcing the arrival of the Normans. The townsfolk would find out soon enough.

Cecil opened the door, gasping with shock as Edric pushed past him and ran into the house.

"The Normans are coming!" he called. "Ylva! Where are you?"

She was in the kitchen, helping Garyn prepare breakfast. Halfdan was there too, looking more composed than he had the previous evening but still silent and watchful. Seaver appeared, his face anxious, as Edric bustled into the kitchen.

"The Normans are on the island!" Edric told them urgently. "We have been betrayed! We need to get away."

Every one of them stared at him in shock.

Seaver muttered, "I'm too old to run again, lad. I'll stay here, I think."

Garyn nodded defiantly, "I'm not leaving my home. Not for anyone."

Edric looked pleadingly at Ylva.

"I must go," he told her. Hereward is my Lord, and I must follow him. He will not surrender. Will you come with me?"

Ylva looked across to Halfdan who, to Edric's surprise, responded with a definite nod.

"Yes," she told Edric. "I will come with you. Both of us will."

"Then grab whatever you must bring, and come now!" he blurted, too aware of how little time they had to be pleased by her response.

"I only need my cloak," she said, untying her apron and tossing it aside.

As she hurried to fetch her cloak, Edric said to Cecil and Garyn, "Thank you for looking after her. We will always be grateful."

"You should stay here," Garyn told him, her face full of concern. "You would be safe. You could find work in the smithy."

Edric shook his head.

"I can't do that, Garyn. I pledged my service to Hereward."

"Other men have gone back on such words before now," Garyn told him insistently.

"Maybe. But I am not other men. I will keep my word."

Seaver patted him on the back.

"I wish you luck, Edric. May God grant you good fortune."

"Thank you," Edric managed to say, his throat suddenly constricted by emotion.

Then Ylva was back, her cloak fastened around her shoulders, her jaw set tight with determination, and it was time to go. She hugged Garyn, Cecil and Seaver, blew kisses to the frightened children, then grabbed Halfdan's hand and said to Edric, "Lead the way!"

Edric did not know it, but they were already too late. Ranald, after failing to persuade Edric to return to the abbey with him, had run there to rouse Hereward's gang, the only warriors left inside the abbey precinct.

219

He knew Hereward must still be cocooned in the deep slumber of exhaustion, but he hammered on the door and shouted for Torfrida to wake him.

Turning to Winter, he quickly explained what he had seen.

"Wake the rest of your gang," he ordered. "Hold the gates as long as you can."

Winter did not waste time on questions. He merely nodded and ran out of the building, heading towards the dormitories.

Ranald bustled into Hereward's room as soon as Torfrida opened the door. Hereward was awake, dressed in a nightshirt and with his eyes bleary with sleep, but he came alert as soon as he heard Ranald's tale. He leaped out of bed, telling Torfrida to help him dress and don his byrnie.

"That scheming bitch Altruda has betrayed us!" he cursed savagely as he scrambled into his clothes.

"Never mind about that," Ranald told him. "You need to get away! Take Torfrida and sneak out the back way. Find a boat and get clear."

"You must come too," Hereward told him. "You have a wife and family waiting for you in Dublin."

"God willing, we'll all get away," Ranald agreed. "But get Torfrida to a boat before you do anything else."

With that, he dashed out of the room and ran to the gates.

Winter was the only one there. He was frantically trying to haul one of the two huge gates shut, but the heavy wood moved agonisingly slowly on its hinges, squealing in protest as Winter put all his weight into swinging it closed. Ranald dashed to help him, but hesitated when he looked beyond the entranceway and saw a large group of Norman soldiers hurrying along the road towards them. Even with two of them, there was no way the gates could be closed and barred before the Normans reached them.

"Where are the others?" Ranald asked urgently.

Grunting with the effort of moving the heavy gate, Winter replied, "They're coming."

"They're too late," Ranald rasped, drawing his sword.

Without another thought, he stepped through the gateway and advanced to confront the onrushing Normans.

"What are you doing?" Winter shouted as he finally swung the left-hand gate into position. "Get back here!"

Ranald ignored him, slashing his sword in the air to show the Normans he was ready to resist them.

To his amazement, the charging men slowed their advance as one of their number shouted something in French. Ranald did not understand the words, but their effect was clear. The heavily armoured men gratefully slowed to a walk as one of them pushed his way to the front and continued the advance on his own, walking steadily to confront Ranald. He carried a long shield on his left arm, and a glittering sword held easily in his right hand, the blade lowered as if he expected no trouble.

The man stopped when he was only a few paces away. It was difficult to make out his features because he wore a helmet with a nose guard, but his eyes were bright and intelligent, and his manner was that of a man accustomed to command.

"I am William Malet," he announced in English. "You are Hereward?"

In response, Ranald merely grinned and readied his sword. He instantly realised the man had mistaken him for Hereward because he, too, had fair hair and moustache. The longer that confusion remained, the more time Winter had to close the gates.

But Winter, now standing in the open space with his great axe held in both hands, would not shut the gate while Ranald was outside.

"Get back in here!" the big Englishman growled.

"Shut the gates!" Ranald called back without looking round.

The Norman knight gestured with his sword, indicating that Ranald should lay down his own weapon.

"Surrender!" the man invited.

Ranald still said nothing, but continued to smile at Malet while his heart thumped in his chest and his mind prayed for Hereward and the rest of the gang to arrive.

The Norman uttered a scornful exclamation, turning away as if to leave Ranald to his madness, but then he suddenly whirled and launched a blisteringly fast attack, using both sword and shield to drive Ranald backwards. At the same time, the Norman shouted a command, and his men surged forwards, rushing past Ranald to reach the gates.

Ranald heard Winter's roar of defiance, but he had no time to worry about what was happening behind him, for the Norman

221

facing him was the most dangerous opponent he had ever encountered. Malet was faster than any man Ranald had ever seen, and it was all the Dane could do to ward off the swinging blows of the heavy sword that came at him again and again. Unencumbered by armour, he tried to use that to his advantage by dancing away from the pummelling assault, but it was no use. There were other Normans dashing past him on either side, hemming him in, although none of them attempted to harm him. They were plainly content to leave him to their leader.

Which was, Ranald instinctively understood, a sign of just how good this man was. He was facing the fight of his life.

Standing alone in the half-open gateway, Winter bellowed as he swung his axe, beginning the figure of eight sweeps which so terrified the Normans. The first man to rush at him was driven back by a thundering blow which carved a chunk from the wood of his shield, and the second man was sent back, screaming in agony as the razor-sharp tip of the constantly moving blade tore away one side of his face.

But there were too many Normans for Winter to have any hope of keeping them out. He stepped into the attack, lashing at them, keeping them at a distance, and few were brave enough to attempt to close with him, but they were beginning to surround him, and he knew he would end his life here.

Then he heard shouts and saw the looks of alarm on the faces of the men in front of him, and he grinned, smashing his axe into another shield as he screamed a war cry in response to the arrival of his friends. The Normans were wary enough of one English axeman, and now they would face half a dozen of the feared housecarls.

The two Siwards were there, with Auti, Ordgar and Wulfric charging in beside them. Their unexpected arrival drove the Normans back, and Winter howled in delight as he saw two of the armoured men go down.

Siward White shouted, "Get back! Close the gates!"

Winter, still grinning manically, called back, "The Dane is out there!"

White cursed, but still imposed some order, drawing the gang back to form a barrier where the right-hand gate should have closed the gap.

"We must close the gate!" he decided.

"We can't leave him out there!" Winter shot back.

White was in a quandary. There were too many Normans for them to reach Ranald, yet he did not want to abandon Hereward's friend, even though he knew their survival might rest on closing the gates.

"Shut the gate!" he decided.

But it was too late. They heard Ranald scream as a sword gouged into his belly, and saw his fair hair vanish from sight as he fell. At the same time, the Normans charged again, this time forming their own line, shields interlocked, as they barged into the entranceway, preventing the Englishmen from closing the gates.

Winter fought desperately, smashing his axe against shields, against swords, against armoured bodies. The axe was a terrifyingly powerful weapon and carved havoc among the Normans. Men fell in front of him, and other Normans were driven to the ground, but the English were taking casualties as well.

The first to fall was Siward Red. He had lost a finger of his right hand in the fight at Peterborough, so his grip on his sword failed him. The blade was knocked from his grasp by one Norman, while a second soldier cut at his neck, killing him with savage efficiency.

Auti was next. He leaped from the line, screaming at his enemies, shouting to his dead twin that he was coming to join him. His axe whirled, taking down one Norman and forcing another backwards, but there were too many of them, and Auti was struck down by several blows. His chainmail absorbed much of the impact, but his arm was broken, his leg slashed, and he fell to the ground where he was easy prey for the Normans who surrounded him.

"Bastards!" yelled Winter as he frantically drove back another attack.

It could not last. There were too few of them, and the Normans were gradually forcing them back into the abbey precinct. Once beyond the gates, the attackers had more space to circle round them.

Wulfric was barged to the ground by a ferocious assault from two Normans, and Siward White, whirling round to ward off two more Normans who had run behind him, was smashed down by a hammer blow which split his helmet. His last vision as he

223

crumpled was the sight of Hereward, sword in hand, running to join the fight.

Edric could hear the sound of fighting as they drew closer to the abbey. Several townsfolk had scurried past them, running away from the danger, while most stayed inside their homes, barring the doors and windows.

"There are Normans at the abbey gates!" one terrified man blurted in response to Edric's question as he ran past.

Edric signalled to Ylva and Halfdan to stay behind him, then he slowly edged towards the last house in the street and peered around the corner. The sight that met his eyes made him groan aloud.

"What is it?" Ylva demanded in a low whisper.

"Stay here," he replied, taking hold of his axe and shield.

Ignoring him, Ylva leaned forwards to look out at the abbey's entranceway. She let out a stifled gasp and whirled to Edric.

"We are too late!" she blurted in dismay.

She stood facing Edric, neither of them speaking, and he could see the conflict in her eyes. They both knew they could turn around and seek refuge with Cecil. If Edric threw away his weapons and armour, they could live in relative peace, making a life together even if that life was under Norman rule.

But the look they exchanged told him that she knew he would not agree to turn and run. If he did that, he would not be the man she believed him to be. Her father had been a housecarl, and her mother had been a Dane, so Ylva understood the code of honour which drove Edric.

Yet he also saw that she understood the odds facing him, and that he would be giving up his life in a futile gesture.

She raised her chin proudly as she told him, "Do what you must, and may God protect you."

Edric could not find the right words to answer her. He gave her a grim nod, wishing he had time to tell her everything he felt, but knowing that time was running out. His friends were dying, yet to join them, as he must, meant he would be giving Ylva up, and that knowledge threatened to break his heart.

With a great effort, he succeeded in squeezing some half-strangled words through his constricted throat.

"Go back to Cecil's house. Stay safe."

He glanced at Halfdan who was standing, pale-faced, with his hand clasping the hilt of his long knife.

"Take care of your sister," Edric told him.

Halfdan, his expression grim, gave a nod as solemn as a spoken vow.

His mind made up, Edric forced a smile for both of them, gripped his axe in his right fist, and stepped around the corner.

The scene that confronted him was almost enough to stop him in his tracks. Bodies lay strewn on the ground, some moving feebly, while around fifteen Norman soldiers had fallen back to form a loose cordon facing the abbey. In the gateway, Winter and Ordgar stood back to back, both of them with blood streaming from cuts and gashes, but both still standing and still holding their axes as if daring the Normans to come at them again.

And, in the centre of the tableau, stood Hereward.

William Malet had been disappointed. He had heard so much about the vaunted skill of the man named Hereward, yet it had been relatively easy to kill him. In the end, he had proved to be no better than an average swordsman, while Malet knew that he himself was so far above average that the fight had been almost unfair. But he had accomplished his mission, for the rebel leader was dead, and that would please the King. Malet knew it would be a disappointment to the Lady Altruda, but he could think of several ways he would be able to console her. He had heard so much about her as well, and the sight of her had sparked a keen interest in getting to know her much better. She was a beautiful and talented woman, and he had noticed her reaction when she had first seen him. Yes, getting to know Altruda would be a delight.

First, though, he must complete his mission, and it galled him to see how many of his own men had been killed or wounded by the small band of English rebels. Two of those defenders still stood in the open gateway, axes swinging in ferocious arcs, but they could not survive much longer, for they were about to be surrounded.

Then another armoured man burst onto the scene, charging into the fray like a demon, his sword swinging left and right to fell two more Norman soldiers before he barged into a third and sent him sprawling.

225

Malet gripped his own sword tightly as a thrill of expectation tingled throughout his body. Was this a man worthy of his own skill?

As the remaining Normans fell back, he heard one of the giant axemen call, "You should go, Lord. We'll hold them until you escape."

Being half-English himself, Malet spoke the language fluently, and the words made him smile. The fact that the newly arrived warrior wielded a sword instead of an axe denoted his status, but the reaction of the two axemen told him much more. This powerfully built, fair-haired warrior was a leader they respected and admired.

"Lord, is it?" he asked as he took a few paces forwards.

Switching to French, he ordered his men to stand back and allow him to deal with the newcomer. He did not bother turning to see whether they had obeyed him. He knew they would form a cordon behind him. Now he would be able to demonstrate his mastery of the sword in single combat with a worthy opponent.

Addressing the English swordsman again, he said, "You are Hereward? Yes, of course you are. Your friend tricked me into believing I had already killed you. Still, it will not take long to rectify that."

In response, the man growled, "Who are you, you smug bastard?"

Malet shrugged off the taunt. Such words were, he knew, intended to unsettle him.

"My name is William Malet," he replied confidently. "Perhaps you have heard of me?"

Hereward shrugged, "No, I can't say I have. But I rarely bother learning the names of minions."

As he spoke, Hereward took several paces forwards, taking care not to stumble over any of the bodies which lay around him. His intent was clear, and that pleased Malet because, in spite of himself, the Englishman's words had irritated him.

He sprang to the attack, launching a series of blows which would have overcome most opponents. Hereward, though, blocked and parried every cut and thrust, his own sword flashing with expert speed. Then he counter-attacked, forcing Malet to block a stunningly powerful blow which forced the Norman to take a step back.

Malet almost laughed at the joy of discovering a skilful opponent, but he took the opportunity to deliver a taunt of his own.

"Not bad for a landless peasant," he said sarcastically. "But if that is your best, you won't last much longer than your friend."

His eyes never left Hereward's face, and he saw that his words had no effect. He had hoped to goad the rebel into making an angry attack which would leave him open to a counter, but Hereward's next slash was fast and deadly, forcing Malet to make another lightning parry.

Malet was not concerned. He had the measure of his man now, and he knew he could beat Hereward. It was only a matter of time.

He attacked again, delivering blow after blow, driving Hereward backwards in a frantic defence, the sound of their clashing swords echoing across the corpse-strewn grass.

Hereward dodged aside, disengaging from the combat, then lunged at Malet in a desperate attempt to catch him off guard. Malet knocked the rebel's blade aside with contemptuous ease.

He readied himself again, knowing he had won this fight.

Then he saw Hereward glance over his shoulder and smile.

Malet grinned. It was a sign of Hereward's desperation that he should attempt such an obvious ruse. Malet would not be distracted. Instead, he moved into the attack once again.

Edric's heart was pounding, but he forced himself to walk at a steady pace. Rushing into a charge too soon would only exhaust him and give the Normans warning of his approach.

So he plodded on, his eyes taking in the appalling scene ahead of him. It was reminiscent of the fight at the end of the bridge, where so much death had been dealt in a confined space. Bodies sprawled on the ground among discarded helmets, swords and shields, some of the men still feebly trying to move.

It was a bizarre scene. With so much death and bloodshed surrounding them, everyone had ceased fighting to watch two men battle each other to the death. Edric, recalling what Hereward had told him about the need to fight dirty and not obey the rules, instantly realised that this gave him a slim chance of surprising the Normans, none of whom had seen him yet.

227

Gripping his axe and shield tightly, he continued walking, his eyes constantly scanning the Normans in case one of them should turn around and see him.

It seemed unreal, as if he were in a dream, but the reality of the situation struck him when he noticed a monk cowering some sixty or seventy yards from the gateway, crouching down on the ground at the side of the rutted roadway which led to the river. It was Brother Richard, the monk from the infirmary. Edric's anger flared when he understood the man's treachery. He had brought the Normans here, and they had killed Edric's friends.

Brother Richard caught sight of Edric at almost the same time, his mouth dropping open in startled amazement. The monk rose to his feet, pointing, his lips moving as he shouted a warning, but the sound was drowned by the clash of steel as Hereward and his opponent exchanged furious blows, both men hacking and slashing for all they were worth. Even then, Edric realised that Hereward had seen him, and he thought he detected a faint smile on the young Thane's face.

But Hereward was in trouble. For all his skill, the Norman knight was able to block every attack and returned the blows with murderous cuts of his own. The watching Normans shouted their encouragement and approval, but one or two were turning to look at Brother Richard, who was now waving his arms and yelling at the top of his voice.

One of the soldiers glanced back, saw Edric, but then turned back to Brother Richard with a puzzled shake of his head. Edric realised that the Norman shield he had taken from the battle at Aldreth had momentarily disguised him. Yet he knew it would not be long before one of the Normans recognised the significance of the axe he was carrying.

But it did not matter, for he was close enough now.

He broke into a run, covering the last yards in a few paces and swinging his axe in a great sweep to bring it crashing down on the neck of the nearest Norman. The man died without knowing what had killed him, the great blade carving its way down through his body with terrible force. At the same time, Edric used his shield to barge the man to his left, knocking him off balance and sending him crashing into a third soldier. Both men fell in a tangle of limbs and weapons.

"Etheldreda!"

Edric yelled the war cry as he yanked his axe free of the dead Norman, then swung it in a ferocious backhand arc to bury it in the chest of another soldier, felling the man instantly.

He ran on, but men were alert to the danger now. They were turning, coming for him, shields raised and swords ready. He rushed at two of them, smashing his shield against theirs, using his massive body weight to drive them backwards as he slashed at them with his axe.

A sword hammered off the iron rim of his shield, but he kept moving, cutting again and again, terrifying the Normans with the speed and power of the weapon they dreaded above all others.

It was madness, but he could not stop. All his thoughts were on killing as many of these invaders as he could before they surrounded him and cut him down. He was dimly aware of noise behind him, of shouts and screams, and of Winter and Ordgar yelling as they charged into the fray.

Then, incredibly, the two men facing him backed off, crouching behind their shields for a moment before turning and running away as fast as they could.

Edric whirled, suspecting some sort of deception, but all of the surviving Normans, fewer than a dozen of them now, were fleeing, running down the road towards the hithe and safety. Brother Richard had hoisted up his robe, revealing his pale legs, to pound along with them.

Malet broke off his attack when he heard the fighting behind him. He had believed Hereward had been trying to trick him, but he knew the sounds of battle, and the deafening war cry told him of danger behind him.

He would not have been human if he had not turned to see what was happening, but even as he twisted his head, he knew he had made a fatal error. That brief moment of distraction was all the time Hereward needed. The Englishman lunged forwards, driving the tip of his sword into Malet's belly with ferocious power.

Malet's chainmail armour gave him some protection, but the savage blow was delivered with such force that it drove the breath from his lungs and knocked him off balance. His feet scrabbled as he tried to recover, but he was not fast enough. Hereward's sword came down, its edge smashing into Malet's right wrist, breaking bones and shattering the links of the

229

chainmail on his sleeve. His sword dropped from his numbed grip, and he knew he was about to die.

"No!"

It was impossible! Nobody could best him with a sword. But his strangled cry was silenced when Hereward's blade slashed upwards, catching the side of his head. The blow knocked his helmet off and gouged a deep cut in his temple. Dazed and stupefied by shock, Malet stumbled, his legs barely able to support him. He never saw the final blow, a savage, two-handed cut of Hereward's blade which clove the top of his skull.

Edric's breath was coming in great, lung-bursting gasps, but he almost laughed aloud at the sight of his fleeing enemies.

Winter and Ordgar were beside him now, bloody and bruised but grinning like idiots because Hereward was standing over the corpse of the man who had challenged him.

"Thank you for distracting him," Hereward said to Edric as calmly as if he had been discussing an annoying dog rather than an armed man. "He might have been difficult to beat if he hadn't turned to see what was happening behind him."

He gave the body of the Norman a kick, then spat, "That was for my friend, Ranald, you poxy bastard!"

Ranald Sigtrygsson lay only a few yards away, his belly ripped open by a savage wound, his sightless eyes staring up at the sky. Edric felt simultaneously saddened by his death and relieved that he himself had somehow survived the uneven combat.

Hereward managed a wry smile as he nodded behind Edric and said, "I see you brought an army with you."

Edric turned to see that Ylva and Halfdan had followed him into the fight. Each of them had picked up a fallen sword, and they stood over one of the Normans Edric had felled. Edric's axe had smashed into the man's chest, but had not killed him thanks to his chainmail armour, but he was breathing hoarsely, blood bubbling at his lips, and he was barely able to move. He had hauled himself to his knees, but his hands were clamped around his ribs, and he swayed unsteadily as he gazed up at the young woman and boy who confronted him.

As Edric watched, Ylva gripped her stolen sword in both hands and, with a supreme effort, managed to raise the heavy blade high enough to swing it down onto the back of the man's neck. It was a clumsy blow, with little strength behind it, but the sword was heavy enough to inflict a fatal wound.

Ylva had to place one foot on the dead man's back before she was able to jerk the blade free again, and only then did the savage look in her eyes fade.

Hereward grunted his approval before asking Edric, "That's Kenton's girl, isn't it?"

"And her brother," Edric confirmed.

"So where is their father?"

"Dead."

"Good riddance," muttered Winter.

With Halfdan in close attendance, Ylva strode up to Edric, dragging the heavy sword behind her with the tip trailing along the blood-stained ground. There was a defiant look in her eye as she faced him.

"I wasn't going to stand and watch you die without trying to help," she told him before he could voice any protest at the way she had placed herself in danger.

"You've got a tough one there, lad," Winter chuckled grimly. "You'd better not argue with her."

Edric decided to take that piece of advice. He simply asked Ylva whether she was all right.

"I'm fine," she nodded grimly, surveying the bodies that lay around them. "But we shouldn't linger here. More of them will come soon."

"She's right about that," Hereward agreed grimly. "Martin and Torfrida are waiting with a couple of boats. We'd best join them."

He wore a troubled look as he gazed on the bodies of his friends, but they all knew there was nothing they could do for any of the fallen. If they did not flee now, they might never escape, but their departure was delayed when Ordgar signalled to them to join him near the scattering of bodies which lay in the open gateway. A few of the Normans were groaning feebly, begging for aid, but Ordgar had other concerns.

"Wulfric's still alive," he told them, his face set in a stony frown.

They gathered near Wulfric, who had suffered several wounds, one of which was still pumping a great pool of blood onto the ground beneath his long legs.

231

"I'm gone," he whispered hoarsely, his eyes holding a desperate look. "Leave me here. I won't last long."

Winter, kneeling to examine the wound near Wulfric's groin, gave a sad nod of agreement.

Wulfric coughed, blood seeping from his mouth. He gave a weak grin and said, "We showed them, though. Didn't we?"

Winter nodded, "Aye, I reckon we did."

"Good. Now bugger off and leave me to die in peace. You're blocking the sun, and I'd like to feel it on my face one last time."

"Farewell, friend," said Hereward. "We'll meet again one day."

All six of the survivors bowed their heads in respect. Hereward made the sign of the cross over Wulfric, then gestured for the others to follow him as he turned away, striding purposefully across the courtyard, his face set in a grim expression.

The others followed, hurrying to match Hereward's pace. Edric offered to take Ylva's sword, but she refused to let go of the weapon, even though she was struggling under its size and weight.

"If we meet more Normans, I want to be able to fight them," she announced with steely determination.

"If we meet more Normans, stay behind me," Edric told her.

The pale, nervous faces of several monks were peering out from behind half closed doors, watching them go, but nobody made any effort to dissuade the sad remnants of Hereward's gang from leaving.

"Make sure my men receive Christian burials!" Hereward shouted to the monks as he marched towards the small gate which lay beyond the infirmary.

Edric could not tell whether any of the monks had heard, nor whether they intended to obey if they had, but there was no time to linger.

"Where are we going?" he asked Hereward when he caught up with him.

"Away from here," was the gruff response. "Anywhere away from here."

Edric was dismayed by the defeat he heard in Hereward's voice, but he could not argue. Because Ely was lost, and the rebellion was over.

Part 2: The Refugees

Chapter 19

It was a strange feeling to walk through the village again. Around half of the residents of Bourne had left with Hereward the previous year, resulting in the place having a desolate, abandoned air. Edric had worried whether those who had fled would be safe now that Ely had fallen, but the sight of Bourne's forlorn homes made him wonder whether the few who had stayed were any better off.

That thought almost made him laugh aloud. The chances were they would be a lot safer than Edric and his companions. The fugitives had reached the sanctuary of the dark forest, skulking deep within the trees, yet they all knew that, if the Fens had not protected them from the Normans, the woods were unlikely to be a safer haven.

It had been a miserable fortnight since they had fled from Ely. Thanks to Martin's memory, they had eventually located one of the small huts the two Siwards had used, and they had turned it into a temporary home. There was running water from a nearby stream, and plenty of wood to burn, but there was no food except what they could forage and hunt. Yet with no bows, nor any of them having the skill to use one even if they had possessed such a thing, meat was largely absent from their meagre diet which consisted mostly of berries, roots and herbs. Ordgar had set some snares and caught a few rabbits, but those catches were not enough to stave off the constant hunger. For Edric, the experience was reminiscent of the days he and Hereward had spent lost in the fens, and he began to wonder whether he was destined to always be hungry.

Torfrida had retained enough presence of mind to bring a fat purse of silver coins when she had left the abbey, but they could not eat silver. Nor was their new home a comfortable one, because the hut was dingy, damp and teeming with crawling insects. Torfrida and Ylva were especially miserable, bemoaning their inability to stay clean, and all of them were saddened by the deaths of their comrades. They spoke in low whispers, the weight of their failure and loss heavy on their shoulders.

Despite Torfrida's insistence, Hereward appeared to have lost his capacity for making decisions. His dream of a rebellion, of freeing England from the Norman yoke, had collapsed thanks to the treachery of Altruda, Earl Morcar and Abbot Thurstan, and this had struck him hard. Worse, though, was the loss of his friends and kinsmen, especially Ranald and Siward White. He had been forced to abandon their bodies to the unkind mercies of the Normans, but it was the loss of their company the young nobleman felt most.

"I have never seen him grieve so much," Torfrida confided to Edric and Ylva one evening when they accompanied her on a short stroll through the forest after she had insisted she would not remain cooped up in the hut any longer.

"I spent a year stuck in that tiny room in Ely," she grumbled. "I have no desire to exchange that prison for another, less comfortable one without at least taking some exercise."

Ylva had appointed herself as Torfrida's unofficial maidservant, and had done her best to wash and mend their ragged clothing, as well as brushing Torfrida's long, dark hair, but Edric could tell that both women were frustrated and impatient to do something other than sit around moping.

"He will come out of it soon," Torfrida assured them. "Hereward is not a man who gives up easily. But he seems to have caught a chill after your adventure in the marsh, and that is not helping his mood."

Edric could sympathise. He, too, had suffered a short cold which even now had left him with a dry cough. It had not helped his brooding over the loss of his friends, nor wondering what fate had befallen the men like Thorkel, Wulfstan and Horgar the cook. Were they still alive? Had they been imprisoned or, worse, executed? He knew how brutal the Normans were when anyone dared resist them, and the men on Ely had been the fiercest rebels of all.

But brooding would not solve their problems, he knew. Hereward knew it as well, but the young Thane had, so far, been unable to reach any decision.

"I hope he makes up his mind soon," Ylva remarked. "We will all starve to death if we don't find more food soon."

Torfrida had nodded thoughtfully, then shot Edric a searching look.

"What do you think we should do?" she asked him.

"Me, my Lady?"

"Who else? I respect Winter and Ordgar as fighting men, but they are hardly the sort who use their brains overly much. Until Hereward shakes off his gloom, the three of us need to think about what we should do."

Edric shrugged, "All I know is we can't stay here much longer. There are thieves and brigands in these woods. Sooner or later, one of them will tell the Normans about us."

"I agree," Torfrida stated firmly. "But where do we go?"

It was Ylva who put in, "We cannot stay in England. The King will hunt us down."

Edric felt slightly shocked, although the truth of her statement could not be denied. Nevertheless, it was depressing to acknowledge that he would be forced to leave his homeland. He wanted to protest, but he knew that a man like Hereward, let alone the two women, could never live life as an outlaw in the forests.

He ventured, "What are our options, then? Wales? Scotland?"

"Perhaps," Torfrida nodded, raising a hand to push back a protruding branch which overhung the path they were following. "But both are easily within William's reach. How do you think King Malcolm would respond if he were threatened with war unless he handed Hereward over? He could not oppose the Norman army if William turned against him, and I doubt he would risk his kingdom for the life of a single refugee. The same, only more so, goes for the Welsh Lords."

Edric's stomach, already growling in protest at his hunger, gave another lurch as he guessed, "Then you think we should cross the sea?"

"It would be safer," Torfrida nodded. "As long as we avoid Normandy."

"What about Ireland?" Edric suggested tentatively. "Ranald Sigtrygsson said he had a wife and children there."

The memory of the Dane's death was still vivid, and Edric felt they ought to make some attempt to inform his wife that she was now a widow, but Torfrida shook her head.

"Ireland is not a safe place. Ever since Brian Boru made war on the Danes, there are few welcomes there for outsiders. Some still cling on in Dublin, but we would find few friends there, I think."

235

"The sons of King Harold are in Ireland," Ylva put in. When the other two stopped and looked at her quizzically, she explained, "Seaver heard tell of it in the market. King Harold's sons fled to Ireland, but they have been raiding the south coast of England."

"Raiding," Torfrida sighed, "is not the same as invading. I doubt they have much support. The Irish will not provide them with an army."

Ylva shrugged, "I don't know much about it. But we heard they were chased away, so I suppose you are right."

Torfrida nodded at this confirmation of her view.

She said, "Even if we did want to go to Ireland, it would mean crossing England to find a port. That would be dangerous."

There was a moment of contemplative silence before Edric suggested, "Then I suppose we could go to Anjou."

Torfrida regarded him with a look of some surprise.

"Do you know much about Anjou?" she asked.

"Not really," he admitted bashfully. "But I know the Normans don't rule there. It's where Brother John came from. He told me about it once."

Thinking of the young monk whom he had once regarded as a friend, Edric felt another pang of loss. Even though Brother John had abandoned them, he wished the monk was with them now. He, at least, would have had some suggestions as to where they might go.

"It is an idea," Torfrida smiled. "But there are many places we could go. There are Spanish rulers who would welcome Christian fighters to aid them in their wars against the Moors. Or there is Rome, although it is a lesser place than it used to be, so I have heard."

Ylva said, "There is always Miklagard."

"Where?"

Edric had never heard the name before and neither, it appeared, had Torfrida.

Ylva explained, "That is what the Danes call it. My mother was from a Danish family, and she used to tell me stories about Miklagard. One of her brothers went there, or so she claimed. In English, it is called Constantinople."

Torfrida laughed, "Oh, yes! That is a fine idea. I hear the Emperor has a permanent Guard of Northmen. No doubt he would welcome some English volunteers as well."

The only thing Edric knew about Constantinople was that it was supposed to be even further away than Rome, but that single fact was enough for him to interrupt the women's pleasure by pointing out, "The first thing we need to do is find a boat. I doubt we will find a captain who will be willing to take us all the way to Constantinople."

"You are quite right, Edric," Torfrida acknowledged with a nod of her head. "So, we must find a boat which will take us anywhere but Normandy, then decide where to go after that. So, where do we find a boat?"

"The Normans will be watching all the ports," Edric frowned. "They'll be looking for us."

Torfrida smiled, "And, with all due respect, you, Winter and Ordgar are not easily missed."

"There are plenty of small fishing villages, though," Ylva put in. "The Normans cannot watch them all."

"True," Torfrida nodded, "but most fishing vessels are too small to carry all of us."

There was a short, reflective pause, then Edric, suddenly more sure of himself, declared, "Then we should go to London."

"London? Why?"

"Because, from what I have heard, it is a big place. We will be able to lose ourselves in the crowds."

"Have you ever been there?" Torfrida asked, obviously taking his suggestion seriously.

"No, but Brother John used to tell me about it. He went there often, or so he said."

Torfrida stopped, turning to face him.

"How far is it to London?" she asked.

Edric shrugged, "I don't know. I think Brother John mentioned it took several days for him to walk from there to Peterborough."

Ylva frowned, "Isn't that where the King lives?"

"Yes, but it is also where we are sure to find a boat and where there are so many people we may not be noticed."

237

After a moment, Torfrida nodded, "I think that is a good idea. Each choice is as dangerous as the next, but the King may not expect us to venture so close to his lair."

Ever pragmatic, Ylva said, "Well, if we are going to walk all the way to London, we will need provisions."

Torfrida nodded, her expression once again serious.

"That will not be easy," she murmured.

There was another short silence which Edric broke by saying, "I know where we can get some food."

The following day, Edric set off on the long walk to Bourne, the village where he had grown up and where Hereward had begun his ill-fated rebellion. He had wanted to go alone, but Ylva had insisted she would accompany him, and Halfdan refused to be separated from his sister. Nor, it seemed, was Winter prepared to remain behind.

"I'm not letting you wander these woods without some protection," the big axeman had announced when he learned of their intention.

Edric had left his armour and weapons behind, believing that marching into Bourne dressed as a warrior might create unnecessary antagonism. He wore only his tunic and leggings, with a long-bladed knife at his belt. Winter, though, wore his chainmail and carried his huge axe in his hands.

"I'll stay out of sight," the big man promised. "But only after I've checked whether there are any Normans in the village. If there are, you can't go in."

Edric foresaw an argument brewing about that, but the problem was resolved when they left the shelter of the woodland and reached the outskirts of the village. Winter led them on a wide detour to a low, wooded rise from where they could look down over the fields and the northern edge of Bourne.

They could make out the tiny figures of people busy with hoes and rakes in the fields, but they concentrated their attention on the castle the Normans had built around what had once been the Thane's house.

The wooden tower built by de Taillebois still stood on its artificial mound of earth, and the high perimeter fence still marked out the bailey of the castle, but they could see that the place was deserted. Nothing moved, and the main gates were standing wide open, with the charred remains of the Thane's house providing a reminder of Hereward's raid.

"It looks as if they've abandoned the place," Winter grunted. "I expect they are all on the isle of Ely now."

"Wherever they are, it means we can safely go into the village," Edric replied.

They retraced their steps, finding the narrow, rutted and partly overgrown track which marked the northern road out of Bourne.

Winter said, "I'll wait for you here. Don't be long."

He stepped beneath the spreading boughs of a large chestnut tree, wishing them a successful and, above all, speedy journey.

The closer they came to the village, the more Edric began to doubt whether they were doing the right thing. The Normans may have left, but there were other things for him to worry about. Returning as a fugitive after leaving with Hereward's gang the previous year was not how he had envisaged his homecoming. He had believed they would free England from the Normans and he would return to Bourne as a hero. Yet now he was almost skulking in, seeking help and succour like an errant child who had run away from home but quickly discovered he could not survive on his own.

Ylva interrupted his moody thoughts by saying, "You know we don't need to go back. It is Hereward who is being hunted, not us. We could find a new home anywhere in England."

Edric shot her a look of concern, his emotions fraying as he said, "I cannot do that."

To which she smiled and replied, "I know. That is why I love you, Edric Strong."

Her words silenced him. He had never considered that she might love him. She had made love to him, of course, that night in the tiny room behind Cecil's house, and he knew in his heart that he had loved her for a long time, but he had never dared hope that she might feel the same about him.

"What's wrong?" she asked.

He reached out and took her hand in his, matching the gentle swing of their arms to their stride.

"I'm feeling guilty because you are right. We could be safe if we left them and went our own way."

"But we won't do that, will we?"

"No. They are my friends."

"Then that is settled," she said firmly. "We will take back some food, then we will walk to London and find a boat to take us somewhere King William will never find us."

"To Miklagard?"

"Why not? But anywhere would do, as long as we are together."

"Always," he promised.

It would, he knew, be a difficult promise to keep, because his loyalties were torn between his desire to be with her and his devotion to Hereward. But the immediate future at least held a plan, so he was determined to find a way to keep his vow.

And now they were in Bourne, where half the houses had a gloomy, deserted look, and the other half were quiet because most people were out in the fields. It was a bright day, warm and sunny, with bees buzzing all around the hedgerows and a lazy feel to the almost empty street.

One of the first cottages they passed was Gytha's home. Edric felt nervous as they approached the old witch's lair. He had been afraid of Gytha ever since he had first come to Bourne as a small boy, and the knowledge that she was dead did little to remove the dread the sight of her house inspired. The place looked deserted, but a dark, beady-eyed crow sat on the thatched roof, cocking its head as it seemed to study the three people walking past.

Edric gave an involuntary shudder. He was sure Gytha was dead. He had seen her fall from the Norman tower only three weeks earlier. But had her spirit returned in the shape of an evil-eyed crow? Stooping, he picked up a pebble and hurled it up towards the bird which flapped away in panic, cawing in protest as if vanished beyond the cottage.

"Why did you do that?" Ylva asked.

"I don't like crows," Edric mumbled, not wanting to explain his fear that Gytha's spirit might haunt him.

The next cottage had once belonged to Seaver. Edric hoped the old man would be safe. There was no reason why he should be in danger, for he was no threat to the Normans, but remembering him was another cloud in Edric's mind.

A door opened in the cottage on the opposite side of the road, and a young woman stepped out, holding a baby against her shoulder. Edric gave her a smile as he and his two companions passed her door. She hesitated when she saw the three strangers, then her eyes widened when she realised one of them was not a stranger. Her eyes fixed on Edric, her expression a mixture of fear and startled amazement which his smile did nothing to allay. Then she made the sign of the cross and hurriedly went back inside her home, shutting the door behind her.

"That's Cyneburg," Edric told Ylva. "Her husband, Alfnoth, will be out in the fields."

"Will she tell anyone you are here?" Ylva asked nervously.

Edric shrugged, "Probably. But there won't be many folk around just now, so unless she runs off to fetch folk from the fields, we should be gone by the time anyone else hears about us."

"At least she can't fetch any Norman soldiers," Ylva said as she squeezed his hand.

"I doubt she would have done that anyway," Edric replied. "Hardly anybody liked the Normans being here. Putting up with them because you have no choice is not the same as liking them or supporting them."

He hesitated, then frowned as he added, "There was only one person in Bourne who ever tried to curry favour with them."

"Your uncle?"

"That's right."

"The man we are going to see?"

Edric told her, "No. We are going to see my aunt. With luck, Uncle Ethelred won't even know we are here until it's too late."

He spoke confidently, yet his heart was beating fast, and his nerves were on edge. The thought of confronting his uncle was playing on his mind. The blacksmith may have been married to the sister of Edric's mother, but that blood tie had not made him an easy taskmaster. Edric had lost count of the beatings he had endured as a boy and, even as a man, he was not sure he would be able to stand up to his Uncle Ethelred.

Part of him was telling him to turn around and leave Bourne, yet he knew they could not do that. They must have food for their journey, and there was nowhere else they could obtain what they needed.

When they reached the crossroads, Edric could not help turning his head to look at the remains of the abandoned castle. Storming that place had been his first act of rebellion, and he had felt so proud when he had helped Hereward sack de Taillebois's stronghold. Yet the fence and the tall tower remained intact, and he knew the Normans would come back one day. That thought did nothing to alleviate his already anxious state of mind.

"Calm down," Ylva told him, squeezing his hand once again. "You are more nervous than when you attacked all those soldiers on your own."

"You don't know my uncle," he replied with a forced smile. "I really don't want to bump into him today."

"Then let us be quiet and careful," Ylva stated, her chin thrust out in determination.

They moved deeper into the village, the thatched cottages now closer together, each with its little patch of ground where the villagers grew vegetables or kept goats and pigs. Still the place seemed deserted but, a few yards further along the track, they passed three young children who were playing at the roadside, tossing small pebbles into a large puddle which had been left behind by some recent rain. The boys stopped to look at the three travellers, their expressions curious, but they soon returned to their game when Edric and his companions continued down the roadway.

Edric could feel the tension building inside him. The village seemed to crowd in on him as he drew nearer to the smithy. He heard the clacking of a loom from within one of the cottages they passed, and further along the road he could see an old woman sitting at the door of her home spinning wool on a hand-held spindle. He recognised her as an elderly spinster named Aeldgifu, so he was not worried about her noticing anything. Her eyesight was known to be very poor, and her cottage was over a hundred yards away. Even if she noticed three shadowy figures, she would not recognise Edric unless he was standing right in front of her. Yet that knowledge did little to alleviate his mounting anxiety.

That feeling rose to a peak when they reached the smithy. The wide doors were open, and he could hear the harsh sound of metal striking metal as his uncle hammered at some hot iron on the anvil. He hesitated, knowing he would probably have turned back if he had been on his own. But Ylva was here, and so was Halfdan, both of them looking to him to protect them from hunger. Summoning his resolve, he quickly ushered the others past the doors when the next bout of hammering began, for that was when Uncle Ethelred's attention would be focused on his work.

Edric let out a long sigh of relief once they were beyond the doors. Then, signalling for the others to be as quiet as possible, he led them up the side of the building to the rear yard.

It was as he remembered it. Chickens pecked at the grain Aunt Edith had scattered for them, the rain barrel still stood against the rear wall of the smithy, and the old, two-wheeled cart was propped near the back of the yard as if it had not moved since the day he had left.

And there was the door to the house, sitting open and inviting. He could smell food cooking, and the aroma brought another rumble from his empty belly.

Ylva let out a nervous giggle, clamping her free hand over her mouth to stifle the sound.

Edric sighed, took another step, then froze into immobility when a figure appeared in the open doorway.

"Edric!" his aunt exclaimed, her mouth and eyes wide in astonishment.

She was holding a tray of pies which she almost dropped, only catching hold when the tray began to slip from her grasp. She whirled, placing the tray on the table behind her, then ran across the yard, her arms wide, to embrace him.

"Oh, Edric! You are safe! We thought ..."

He knew what she had thought. Word of Ely's fall must have reached them days ago.

Aunt Edith kissed his face, tears rolling down her cheeks, then she stood back, holding him at arm's length and studying him.

"You've changed," she observed. "But you look well."

"We are hungry," he told her. We came to buy some food."

"Buy?" she objected. "You don't buy from family!"

Then she turned to regard Ylva and Halfdan.

"Who is this you have with you?" she asked.

"This is Ylva. And her brother, Halfdan."

Wiping away her tears, Aunt Edith smiled, bidding them welcome, then said, "Oh, come in and have something to eat. You all look as if you could do with a decent meal."

Edric held up a hand.

"We are going on a long journey," he told her. "We need as much food as you can give us. We have silver to pay for it."

"You're going away again?" she asked, her face crumpling in dismay.

"We must. The Normans are looking for us."

"But where will you go?"

"Scotland," Edric told her, hoping Ylva and Halfdan would keep any surprise from their faces. He need not have worried. All his aunt's focus was on him and his words.

"Scotland? But that is so far away. A foreign land, full of savages."

"No," he assured her. "There are lots of English men and women in Scotland now. Plenty of people who don't want to live under the Normans have gone there."

She shook her head, fighting back more tears, then looked aghast as the rear door of the smithy was flung open to reveal the bulky figure of Edric's uncle.

"What are you doing here, you traitor?" Ethelred barked as he strode out into the yard, his heavy hammer firmly gripped in his right hand. He held it low at his side, but Edric knew he could easily have left it behind. He had brought it out for a reason.

Ethelred's face was flushed with anger, his eyes blazing and his mouth twisting in fury as he stepped towards them.

He was a big man, with muscles which had been developed by a lifetime of work in the smithy. His face, broad and flat, was streaked with sweat, and his eyes burned with a fierce malevolence Edric knew only too well.

"Scotland, is it?" Ethelred snapped. "You're running away again, are you?"

Edric instinctively ushered Ylva and Halfdan behind him. He waved a hand at the boy, warning him to keep his knife sheathed. If Uncle Ethelred saw the glint of a blade, there would be even more trouble.

"Get off my land!" Ethelred ordered, brandishing his hammer threateningly. "Get away before I do what the Normans should have done to you when you murdered all those men in the castle!"

Aunt Edith squealed, "Put the hammer down, Ethelred! They only came to get some food."

Ethelred's angry face grew redder as he snarled, "Food? They'll get nothing from us! Who are these others anyway? A whore and a thief you picked up in Ely?"

Edric had been telling himself to remain calm, but that insult was more than he could bear. He closed the gap between them in two strides, sweeping his left arm to knock his uncle's hammer aside, then driving his right fist into Ethelred's belly. Winter had taught him that hitting a man on the jaw was likely to result in broken fingers, but a good punch to the belly could end a fight quickly.

Ethelred, though, was as strong as an ox. The blow winded him, but he did not double over as Edric had hoped. But the blacksmith was so stunned that Edric had dared strike him that it took him a moment to react. That moment was all Edric needed. Winter had taught him more than one thing about fighting during their practice bouts, and Edric put the lessons to good use. He stepped in close, smashing his forehead against his uncle's nose, sending the big man reeling backwards to crash against the rear wall of the smithy.

Still he did not fall, so Edric followed up with another blow to the man's belly, then jerked his knee upwards to catch Ethelred between the legs.

At last, the blacksmith slumped to the ground, groaning in pain, his hands clamped over his groin. He lay, dazed and stunned, twitching feebly while blood streamed from his broken nose.

Aunt Edith let out a soft, half-stifled scream, but she quickly regained her composure. It seemed to Edric that the expression on her face was a mixture of pride and pleasure as she looked down at her husband's hunched figure. Then her features settled into a look of grim resolve.

"Come into the house," she told them. "I'll give you all the food you can carry."

Edric looked down at the groaning figure of his uncle. Ethelred was trying to stand, but could only manage to struggle to his knees. That, Edric thought, was appropriate. Ethelred had spent his life on his knees, especially in the years since the Normans had come to England.

The battered smith blinked furiously as Edric leaned down and hissed, "Go back into the smithy. Stay there until I have gone, or next time I won't be so gentle. I don't want to kill you, but I will if I must. I have learned how to do that, you know."

He had never expected to see genuine fear in his uncle's eyes, but he saw it now, and the sight brought a smile to his lips.

Turning to Halfdan, he told the boy, "Watch him. If he tries anything, call me."

Halfdan nodded, drawing his dagger and placing himself between the fallen blacksmith and the door of the house.

Taking Ylva's arm, Edric led her after his Aunt Edith. He felt better than he had done in several days. He had stood up to his uncle for the first time in his life, and had taken some small revenge for the years of insults and beatings. Now he knew what he would do next. They would pay for their food, then he would say farewell forever.

Because they were going to London, and then to wherever the seas would take them, perhaps even as far as Ylva's fabled Miklagard.

Chapter 20

London amazed Edric. It was far larger than he had ever imagined, a noisy, bustling, crowded place with enough sights, sounds and smells to overwhelm the senses. He had thought Ely was a large town, but that was only because he had little to compare it against. London, he instantly understood, made Ely look like a tiny village.

There were all sorts of street vendors and shopkeepers, selling anything people might ever want and, in Edric's opinion, some things few people would consider owning until they saw them. There were butchers, bakers, saddlers, silversmiths and goldsmiths selling intricate jewellery, cloth merchants and wool merchants, weavers and drapers, cobblers and coopers. There were also street musicians and men loudly proclaiming entertainments such as cock fighting and bear baiting.

The streets were also full of ordinary citizens, of clerics in their long robes, of scribes whose fingers were stained dark with ink, and of men, women and children from all levels of society. Some wore clothing that was even more ragged than Edric's own travel-stained tunic and breeches, while others were decked out in fine cloth and a dazzling array of colours.

Every street seemed to reveal yet more wonders as he, Ylva and Halfdan edged their way through the town. The narrow lanes were lined with shops of all trades, with inns, warehouses, tanneries, churches, and houses of all descriptions, from lowly hovels to large, imposing and brightly painted mansions bedecked with banners and pennons.

Edric could only gawp in amazement at each new revelation.

"No wonder Brother John talked about London so often," he murmured.

Ylva, a look of wonder on her face which matched his own, could only nod, but Halfdan wrinkled his nose and muttered, "It stinks."

"It certainly does," Edric agreed with a soft laugh.

Halfdan was still quiet and withdrawn with most people, but he had become more relaxed with Edric during their long walk to London.

It was a journey that had taken an entire week, even though Martin had visited Peterborough where he had purchased a small cart and a donkey to carry their baggage. That baggage consisted of the men's armour and axes which they had concealed beneath ragged bundles of sacking alongside the swords Ylva and Halfdan had taken from the Normans. Their shields, far too large and obvious to carry even in the cart, had been abandoned, so the cart held enough space for Torfrida and Ylva to ride in relative comfort while the men walked.

Hereward insisted on wearing his sword, and he led the way, walking alongside Martin, who guided the donkey by means of a short halter rope. Winter, Ordgar and Edric, playing the role of hired escort, trudged along behind the cart, each of them carrying a stout piece of wood to deter any bandits who might believe the cart contained valuables.

Edric had been more concerned at the thought of encountering Norman soldiers than with any fear of brigands. They did see one or two patrols, but only one group stopped to interrogate them, and Torfrida had a story prepared for them. She explained that she was a widow, on her way to London to take ship to Flanders where her family lived. The Normans eyed Hereward suspiciously, for his sword marked him out as a man of status, and his moustache suggested he was an Englishman, but Torfrida told them he had been sent by the Count of Flanders to escort her, a lie which the Normans accepted when Hereward confirmed the story in his Flemish French. Knowing few Englishmen could speak French, the soldiers bobbed their heads, then rode on.

"Bastards!" muttered Winter under his breath as the horsemen trotted past him.

One of the riders must have understood the sentiment, if not the word, for he guided his horse towards the big Englishman, forcing Winter to step off the trackway and into the roadside ditch, before laughing and riding on.

Winter cursed loudly, but Ordgar also began laughing at him, and Winter soon joined in as he stamped his feet to shake the mud from his boots.

"You're a bloody idiot," Edric told him. "Next time, keep your mouth shut."

Winter shot him a chastened smile as he sighed, "I'll try. But it's hard to look at those stuck up pigs riding around our country as if they own it."

"They do own it," Edric reminded him sourly. "So if we meet any more of them, do as Halfdan does, and stay quiet."

Halfdan had permitted himself a slight smile at that. Remaining quiet was never a problem for him. He barely uttered a word to anyone except Ylva, but he had refused to ride in the cart because he had insisted he was nearly a man, so he had walked with the men, uncomplainingly putting up with the resulting blisters on his feet.

Gradually, he had relaxed sufficiently to say a few words in response to Edric's gentle prompting. The boy never mentioned his father, and would clam up whenever Edric broached the subject, but he at least opened up enough for the two of them to develop the beginnings of a relationship.

There was only one topic on which Halfdan was remotely eloquent, and that was his sister.

"Are you going to marry her?" he asked Edric one day as they brought up the rear of the small caravan.

The question caught Edric by surprise, but he knew there was only one answer he could give.

"If she'll have me," he nodded.

"She'll have you," Halfdan asserted. "She thinks the world of you."

"I just hope I can keep her safe," Edric sighed.

"I'll help you," Halfdan promised.

"Thank you," Edric smiled.

He knew Halfdan was not stupid. The boy had merely been subjected to years of brutality and scorn, an upbringing which had left its mark, making him suspicious of everyone. He rarely spoke to Winter or Ordgar, and never dared open his mouth when Hereward was nearby, but he was alert and watchful, traits which Edric reckoned would prove useful if they were to escape England.

That thought still left him feeling more than a little apprehensive. Hereward and Torfrida spoke as if journeying across the sea to foreign lands where people spoke strange languages and had odd customs was nothing to be concerned about. Winter and Ordgar, though understanding Edric's fears, did not share them.

249

"We'll stay with Hereward wherever he decides to go," was Winter's attitude.

Even Ylva seemed unconcerned.

"Anything will be better than the life I've led up until now," she told Edric. "Apart from those last few months on Ely, I've had little to make me believe there is happiness to be found in England."

Edric could understand why she felt that way. His own life as an apprentice to his uncle had hardly been a joyful one, but the long walk to London had shown him more of the countryside, and he had been remarkably happy as they tramped the long miles southward. Sometimes they followed an ancient road which Hereward said had been built by the Romans, a cobbled roadway which ran straight as an arrow for mile after mile, but this route was busy, increasing the likelihood of meeting more Norman patrols, so they often took slower roads which were little more than muddy tracks barely wide enough for the cart. Yet still Edric was content. Even the frequent showers of rain could not dampen his love for the natural world around him. Hedgerows buzzed with bees, birds chirped in the trees, cattle and sheep grazed in meadows, and the ploughed furrows near the villages were sprouting with barley, oats, rye and wheat which would soon be ready for harvesting.

It was so wonderful, the thought of leaving it all behind was the only thing preying on his mind.

Not wanting to upset Ylva, he merely said, "Other places might be even worse."

"Or they might be better," she countered. "But staying here means being hunted, and I don't want that."

He could not argue with her on that point. So they had come to London, the guards on the city gates allowing them through without challenge once they heard Torfrida's concocted story. Martin had soon found lodgings for Hereward and Torfrida above a large inn, with the rest of them being provided with old palliasses in the tavern's common room, quarters they shared with half a dozen other travellers.

"It's not great," Hereward admitted. "But it's out of the way, and we won't be here long. Martin and I will go to the docks to see if we can find passage on a ship. The rest of you, stay out of trouble."

Torfrida had refused to remain indoors and had ventured out into the city, the others tagging along with her. She spent the morning browsing through the shops, where she spent some of her silver to buy a new dress. The dressmaker had been putting the final stitching to a new gown of dark blue velvet which had been ordered by a rich merchant's wife, but Torfrida used her persuasive powers and the temptation of several pennies to entice the woman to adjust the dress for her.

"You can always make another one for your first customer," Torfrida had smiled when she had tried the dress on. "That way, you sell two dresses. But if you insist on keeping it for your first customer, I won't be back."

They had returned to the tavern around mid-day, but Ylva was desperate to see more of London, so she persuaded Edric to accompany her on another expedition into the teeming streets. Halfdan, inevitably, insisted on going with them. Edric could not begrudge the boy, but he had rather hoped for some time alone with Ylva. Since that one night in Ely, they had had no opportunity to share any intimacy, and the enforced celibacy was playing on both their minds. Still, Edric was content to be with Ylva and to walk through the streets with her on his arm, even if he did not share her interest in the goods on sale in the multitude of shops. Instead, he spent most of his time looking at the people who inhabited this amazingly crowded city. Even so, he needed to look twice when he spotted someone who, against all expectation, looked familiar.

A man had emerged from a large, two-storey house just as Edric and his companions were nearing the main door. Something about the way he moved drew Edric's attention. He stopped in his tracks, staring and blinking as he took a closer look.

The man he had seen wore a smart outfit of tunic and breeches, with a cloth cap on his head. He carried a leather satchel instead of the old backpack Edric had been accustomed to seeing, but there was no doubt as to his identity. From a distance of only ten yards, Edric could not be mistaken.

"Brother John!"

The man looked up in surprise. He, too, froze.

"Edric?" he gasped, unable to keep a startled look of guilt from his face.

"Is it really you?" Edric asked.

251

The former monk quickly gathered his wits. A beaming smile replaced his expression of astonishment, and he hurried over, weaving his way around passers-by and extending his hand in greeting.

"Edric! I never thought to see you here! And you have some friends with you!"

He bowed his head in greeting to Ylva, who gave him a hesitant smile in return.

"Ylva," Edric began, "this is Brother John."

The reminder of his title made Brother John wince slightly as he informed them, "No, my name is John of Brissac. I am a scribe and tutor."

This response raised so many questions, Edric was not sure where to begin. To gain some time, he introduced Ylva and Halfdan, then asked, "Where are Aelswith and young Torfrida? I thought you were taking them to Scotland?"

"They are here in London," John of Brissac replied smoothly. "We changed our minds."

Edric wanted to ask whether they might be able to see Aelswith and her daughter, but he hesitated, thinking Ylva might take exception to him asking about another woman, especially Aelswith.

While Edric dithered, John said, "Come, this is no place to stand and talk. There is a tavern at the end of this street. We shall sup some ale, and you can tell me all about what happened. I've heard the official version, of course, but I never trust reports which come from those in charge."

So saying, he led them along the busy street to a large inn which looked rather more prosperous and well maintained than most of its rivals.

Most of the lunchtime diners had left, so they had no difficulty finding a table near the open window from where they could look out onto the busy street. John ordered mugs of ale and bowls of broth, insisting he would pay for everything.

"Now," he said, "tell me what really happened on Ely."

Keeping his voice low, Edric recounted the story of the final days, explaining how they had escaped after the island had been betrayed.

"The King is said to be furious that Hereward got away," John grinned. "Is he here in London as well?"

252

Edric hesitated, the delay confirming his answer.

"You can trust me, Edric," the former monk said. "I am no lover of Normans, as you know very well. I will not ask any more questions except one. What will you do next?"

"We are leaving England," Edric told him, hoping his response was vague enough to leave some doubt as to whether they were leaving with Hereward or making their own way abroad. The amused expression in John's eyes suggested the former monk had not been fooled.

"I wish you a good voyage," John smiled, raising his mug in a toast. "I'm sure you'll have no difficulty finding a ship's captain who will be willing to take you across the sea."

"As long as we can avoid any soldiers," Edric murmured softly.

John waved a lazy hand to dismiss his concerns.

"There are tax officials at the docks," he informed them, "but few soldiers. Most of them are garrisoned at the King's Palace at Westminster or at the castle they built further east along the river."

Edric nodded cautiously, saying, "I noticed we haven't seen any of them patrolling the city streets."

"Why should they? All the King wants is taxes. As long as people pay, he has no need to send his thugs to enforce his will."

"What if people don't pay?" Ylva put in. "Or if there is trouble of any sort?"

"Then," John told her with a serious expression, "you will see more Norman soldiers than you would like. They pretty much stick to their strongholds, but there are enough of them to put down any trouble if need be. They slaughtered a few hundred people a couple of years back, and that was enough to quell any potential stirrings of revolt."

"That sounds like the Norman way," Edric muttered. Then, thinking he had probably revealed too much of their own plans, he asked, "What about you? How did you end up here? And why are you John of Brissac now?"

John sighed, took a sip of ale, then reached up to scratch beneath his cloth cap. After a moment, he removed the hat and laid it on the table beside his mug.

"I wear it to disguise the tonsure," he explained. "But my hair has grown over the past few weeks, so it is hard to see unless you are very close."

Ylva said, "Edric told me you were once a monk."

John forced a wan smile as he sighed, "Once? Well, I suppose it is only fair that I tell you my secrets now that you have told me yours."

"Secrets?" Ylva smiled, inviting him to continue.

Edric recalled how Brother John had always adopted this habit of exchanging news and information, yet the mention of secrets made him feel a little uncomfortable despite his curiosity. He wondered whether the monk would have told him anything of significance if he and John had been on their own, but John had always had a liking for pretty women, just as they warmed to him, and Ylva's presence was enough to loosen the man's tongue.

Looking Edric in the eye, John sighed, "Since you are leaving and it is unlikely we will meet again, I think you ought to know the truth."

"What truth?" Edric asked warily.

"You know I am from Anjou," John began. "I was born in a place called Brissac. That is why I use that name now. My father was a rich man, a nobleman, although a fairly minor one in the great scheme of things. He had a small castle and owned some land and a couple of tiny hamlets, but he had little real power or influence outside of his own domain."

"But your family are rich?" Ylva prompted. "So why did you leave?"

John raised his eyes to the ceiling as he sought for the right words to frame his story. After a short pause, he explained, "I have a sister and two brothers. I was the middle son. Do you understand what that means?"

"Your older brother would inherit your father's title and lands?" Ylva ventured.

"That's right. That left only two choices for my younger brother and myself. We could follow a career in the Church, or we could go to war."

His lips parted in a wide, mocking smile as he went on, "My young brother, Gaston, was always belligerent. He would not have made a good cleric."

"So you became a monk?" Edric asked.

John paused again, chewing his lower lip while he sought a response. Then he exhaled slowly as he shook his head.

"I was educated by priests," he told them, "but I never fancied the life. And, to be honest, locking myself away in a monastery when there are so many beautiful girls in the world was not my idea of a fruitful life."

He shot an admiring look at Ylva as he spoke, a glance which again reminded Edric of how easily women were attracted to the young man. That memory roused a stirring of jealousy, especially when Ylva giggled in response to John's glance.

"Did you do something awful?" she guessed.

John could not conceal a grin as he admitted, "Alas! My older brother was supposed to marry the daughter of some wealthy baron. Of course, when I met her and saw how lovely she was, I could not help myself."

Edric was shocked by this admission, but Ylva seemed to be highly amused.

"You seduced her?" she asked with a sparkle in her eye.

John showed no contrition as he nodded, "She became pregnant. That, of course, brought down all sorts of trouble. Her father was furious, but he had sense enough to demand that either the marriage should go ahead as planned, or that I should step in and marry her instead. However, my father and brother refused to contemplate either suggestion. I could not marry her because they knew she would bring a great deal of land as her dowry, and it was my brother, Robert, who was supposed to inherit the wealth, not me. But Robert had no wish to wed a woman who had deceived him. He was furious at her and, naturally, at me. In fact, he was so enraged that he decided to have me killed."

Ylva let out a soft gasp, and even Halfdan showed his surprise.

John continued, "So I ran away. I reached the coast, took ship and ended up in England. But I had very little money and no prospects at all. Faced with starvation or turning to thievery, I decided to put some of my learning to use. So I had my head shaved in the tonsure, wore an old robe, and took on the guise of a mendicant friar."

"You were never a monk?" Edric exclaimed in hurt surprise.

"Anyone can become a monk," John replied. "I know more about the Bible and canon law than many who do follow that life, but I confess that I was never ordained as a priest."

Edric could only stare at his former friend in dismay.

John sighed, "I see from your expression that you are wondering why I would do such a thing. It is quite simple, if not very honourable. You see, I knew very well that nobody turns away a man of God. By moving around the country, I was able to satisfy my love of travel without fear of being waylaid by bandits, and I was able to obtain lodgings and food wherever I went."

Edric sat, his hands clasping his pewter beer mug, his mouth agape, as he listened to the confession, but Ylva began to laugh.

"You tricked people into feeding you?" she grinned. "That was clever."

John smiled back at her, adding more jealousy to Edric's confused emotions and provoking his anger.

He said, "But you carried out baptisms and marriages. How could you do that?"

The accusation silenced Ylva's amusement, and John had the good grace to look guilty.

"How could I not?" he said defensively. "I tried to avoid those situations if at all possible, but it wasn't always easy to find an excuse."

"But the babies were not properly baptised!" Edric protested. "And those you buried might not find their way to Heaven!"

Ylva placed a hand on his, leaning close to whisper, "Keep your voice down, Edric. This is difficult enough for your friend, I think."

His cheeks flushing at her reprimand, Edric peered around the dim interior of the tavern, noticing that one or two of the patrons were casting curious glances in their direction. He shook his head, annoyed that he was being made to feel in the wrong when what he had heard from Brother John – no, from John of Brissac – was as serious a sin as he could imagine.

John told him, "Edric, I understand your anger. But I truly believe that, if God is as omnipotent and omnipresent as our churchmen insist, he will have no trouble identifying which children are truly deserving and which souls have lived a good

256

enough life to enter his kingdom. I don't think they will be denied simply because I deceived them. The fault is mine, not theirs. A loving God will know that."

Edric looked down, unable to meet John's eyes. He was confused by what he had heard, and did not know what to say. For as long as anyone could remember, the Church had exerted its power and influence over every aspect of people's lives, yet John had flaunted the edicts and rules, and had seemingly escaped divine retribution. This was another baffling realisation which only added to the confusion and doubt Edric felt over the contrast between Church doctrine and what he had witnessed over the past year. For all the churchmen's talk of a divine plan and God's mercy, war, violence, lies, deceit and betrayal seemed to go unpunished.

Ylva apparently had no such concerns. She asked John, "So you left Ely with Aelswith and her baby. Why did you come here?"

"Ah, that is a long story," sighed John. "But, put simply, I persuaded Aelswith that an England under the thumb of King William would not be a pleasant place. I decided we should go to Paris. It is probably a safer place than London. Also, I confess I had hopes that I might be reconciled with my family. The King of France nominally claims suzerainty over Anjou, although his power is generally ignored by men like my father. But I thought that, if we were closer to my old home, we might learn what has happened in Brissac since I left. Then, if I were able to find favour with some wealthy French Lord, perhaps he could put in a word for me. If not, Paris is a pleasant enough city, with many prospects for a man of learning."

Edric frowned, mentally adding Pride to John's list of sins, but Ylva stuck to her interrogation.

"But you are still here," she pointed out.

John nodded sadly.

He explained, "I spent some time seeking news from the continent. I spoke to a great many sailors and merchants while I was seeking safe passage. One of them had news from Brissac."

He fluttered a hand as he went on, "The sailor did not know me, of course, but it turned out his sister had married a man from Brissac and he had heard the news when he had visited her."

"What news?" Ylva asked gently.

257

John took another deep breath before revealing, "It seems my father died a few years ago. Not only that, my older brother, Robert, is also dead. A hunting accident, apparently."

Ylva said, "I am so sorry."

John shook his head.

"There is no need to be sorry. My father had disowned me, and Robert wanted me dead for the shame I had brought on him. My chances of being able to return to Brissac were slim to begin with, but this news makes it impossible for me to go back."

"Why?"

"Because my younger brother, Gaston, is now the local Baron. What do you think he would do if I turned up and tried to claim my place as the rightful Lord?"

Nobody responded, for they all understood.

John said, "Gaston was always a bloodthirsty little monster. I would not be surprised to learn he had a part in Robert's death. As for me, I certainly wouldn't survive a day in Brissac. Even Paris would be dangerous if he ever learned of my presence there."

"So you stayed in London?"

"It's only been a few weeks," he nodded. "I found employment as a tutor. There are plenty of wealthy Englishmen who want their children to learn French now that the Normans are in charge. You know what merchants are like. They always want to take advantage of new situations. So I am teaching a few of them how to speak, read and write French."

"What about Aelswith and the baby?" Ylva asked, making Edric feel grateful that she had broached the subject.

A cloud briefly flickered across John's features, but he forced a smile as he replied, "They are both well. Our present lodgings are not ideal, for they are above a carpenter's workshop, so are very noisy during the day, with constant hammering and sawing. But I am earning more money now, so we will soon be able to find better lodgings."

Rather more sharply than he had intended, Edric asked, "Is Aelswith happy?"

John's smile faded as he shrugged, "She has a hankering to return to Bourne, but I think that is partly because our home is very close to the castle the King built. She looks out of her window and sees Norman soldiers, and it frightens her."

"So why not take her back to Bourne?" Edric pressed. "There are plenty of empty homes now."

John looked almost horrified as he retorted, "And become a farmer? No, my friend, I can earn a better living here. Besides, do you really think the people of Bourne would welcome me back? Don't forget they knew me as Brother John. What do you think they would say if they knew the truth?"

"That's easy!" Ylva insisted. "Tell them you renounced your vows. They don't need to know the whole truth."

"And if the Normans discover who young Torfrida is?" John countered. "The niece of Hereward the Outlaw?"

"She is your daughter now," Ylva stated. "Who will tell the Normans otherwise?"

"In Bourne?" John snorted. "I could think of a few whose tongues would wag."

"There are other places nearby," Edric pointed out. "Peterborough, for instance. Or even Ely."

"Perhaps," John shrugged. "But London is where the future lies."

"At the cost of Aelswith's happiness?" Edric challenged.

"I see you have not lost your concern for others," John said with a conciliatory smile. "Well, perhaps you are right. I will think on what you have said. Once I have earned enough money, it may be that we could return."

Edric wondered whether John was merely saying this to placate his simmering anger, but he knew there was nothing he could do about it in any case. He would be leaving England, while Aelswith had made her own decisions. He wondered whether her unhappiness might be with John himself rather than with London. A small part of him could not help feeling self-righteous that Aelswith's choices had not turned out the way she must have hoped. He recalled Ylva's opinion of Aelswith, that she had merely been using Edric, and he knew now that Ylva had been correct. He had once thought he was in love with Aelswith, but she had chosen to go with John, and he told himself she must live with the consequences of her decision, just as he must live with his.

Then he felt guilty for having such an uncharitable thought, and decided to do some penance. Delving into his purse, he took out two silver pennies which he pushed across the table to John.

The cleric looked down at them in surprise.

"What is that for?" he asked. "I have no need of money, my friend. I told you, I am earning quite well as a scribe and tutor."

"Take it," Edric urged. "It is a gift. For the baby."

"Are you sure?" John asked.

"Yes. Take it. Please. And tell Aelswith I wish her every happiness."

"I will," John nodded as he slowly picked the coins from the table. "Thank you, Edric. You have always had a noble spirit."

Edric shrugged off the compliment. He had been tempted to ask John to take him to see Aelswith, but had decided against it. A meeting would only complicate matters. She was no longer a part of his life, he decided. He was leaving England and would make a new life for himself and for Ylva.

"We should get back," he told her.

They rose from the table, making their way into the street. There, John embraced each of them in turn, wishing them health and prosperity.

"Take care of your friends, Edric," he said as the two of them clasped hands. "And I promise I will look after Aelswith."

It was as good a promise as Edric could hope for.

"May God guide your choices," he replied, bringing a soft grin of embarrassment to John's boyish face.

Their farewells felt awkward, but John eventually gave them a broad smile then turned away and walked off down the busy street, soon disappearing from view.

"Do not be too harsh on him," Ylva told Edric as she squeezed his hand. "Life is difficult, and we each do what we can to survive."

Edric let out a soft sigh as he said, "I don't know what to think of him now. He is not who I thought he was, and that is difficult for me."

"I know. But it does not matter now. We will be leaving soon."

Slowly, the three of them made their way back to the inn where they had left Torfrida in the care of Winter and Ordgar. Ylva, wanting some time alone with Edric, told Halfdan to go on ahead. The boy was reluctant, but scampered off when she threatened to withhold his dinner that evening.

Ylva laughed as he darted ahead, winding his way through the crowd.

"It's been an interesting day," she observed happily as she clung to Edric's arm.

Edric was grateful for her closeness, but he was still preoccupied by what he had heard from John.

He sighed, "It certainly has. I still can't believe what Brother John told us."

"You'll need to stop calling him that," Ylva chided.

"I think he'll always be Brother John to me," Edric admitted.

"He certainly fooled a lot of people," she remarked with a grin.

"Everyone liked him. Well, most people did. I suppose they still do."

"He has a nice smile, friendly eyes and seems trustworthy," Ylva said.

"But he's a fraud," Edric reminded her.

"All the best fraudsters appear trustworthy," she laughed.

Edric shook his head as he said, "I worry for his soul."

Ylva squeezed his arm as she told him, "I don't think you need to worry about that. I'm sure John could talk his way into Heaven without too much trouble."

Edric could not help but smile at the thought of John pleading his case to Saint Peter. He supposed Ylva was probably right.

He was debating whether to turn the conversation around to discussing Aelswith when Ylva's grip on his arm tightened and she gasped, "Here comes Halfdan! Something is wrong."

The boy was weaving his way along the street, running as quickly as the busy lane allowed, his face pale with shock and dismay. As he reached the two of them, he gasped his message between gulps of air.

"The Normans came to the inn. They have taken Hereward and Torfrida!"

Chapter 21

Altruda had grown more frustrated the longer she stayed in London. After a year of being cooped up in Ely, she had hoped for rather more freedom once the rebellion had ended, but King William had insisted she accompany him to London where she was allocated an elegant set of rooms in the palace. She enjoyed the comfort, of course, but when she asked leave to visit some of the new lands he had granted her as a reward for her pivotal role in ending the rebellion, the King had merely told her that he wanted her to remain close at hand for a while longer.

"I may have need of you soon," he had told her enigmatically.

Altruda had accepted his command, supposing he had some plans in mind to ensure his iron grip on England was retained, yet his injunction irritated her. For one thing, she felt that her current task was not yet complete. The rebellion may have been crushed, its leaders, Earl Morcar and Siward Barn, might have been imprisoned, the army of warriors may have been mutilated, but one man remained at large.

Hereward.

Where was he?

As was becoming a habit for her, Altruda sat by an open window overlooking the main courtyard of the palace complex, her mind focused, as it so often was, on pondering Hereward's whereabouts.

She had seen the bodies lying in a cluster at the gates of the abbey, and she knew he was not among them. She had recognised his cousins, the two Siwards, along with the Dane, Ranald Sigtrygsson, and another couple of Hereward's men. Yet, unlike most of the Normans who saw the dreadful result of the bloody combat, she was not surprised at how many of their enemies the English warriors had slain. She had always known Hereward and his gang were fearsome fighters, and it was almost amusing to see the shock on the faces of the Normans when they learned that William Malet was dead. They had believed him to be invincible, yet there he was, his head almost severed, and Hereward had escaped him.

For her part, Altruda felt a slight regret at Malet's demise. She had noticed the spark in his eye when he had met her, and she reflected that he might have been a useful man to know more closely. As always, though, she did not waste time dwelling on lost possibilities.

"It was not to be," she had told the gory corpse. "You failed me. And Hereward is gone."

She had interrogated Brother Richard, and had spoken to other monks who had watched the fight from a safe distance, so she knew that Hereward had evaded capture by taking two fen boats and stealing away into the marshes.

She had been amused to learn from the witnesses that Edric Strong had been among the surviving fugitives, and that he had been accompanied by a red-haired girl and a teenage boy. Edric, it seemed, had not only fooled her, he had suborned young Halfdan into the bargain. She could scarcely believe that Kenton's dimwit son had sufficient courage and guile to betray her, yet he had clearly done so. Appearances, she reflected, could be deceptive. That was a lesson Altruda vowed not to forget.

As for Kenton's disappearance, she dismissed it as irrelevant. Knowing the man's venality, she doubted that he had sneaked away on his own. If he lived, he would have presented himself in order to collect his reward. The fact that he had vanished, and that Edric Strong had been hiding Kenton's daughter, told Altruda that her henchman must be dead.

"That is no loss," she mused.

But, while they were interesting, thoughts of Edric Strong and Kenton's fate were mere distractions. It was Hereward she wanted to find.

But where had he gone?

King William had puzzled over the same question. Once he was sure Ely was secure, he had sent groups of knights to every nearby port, but none of them had found any trace of the fugitives. The King had also set Abbot Turold the task of scouring the area around Peterborough and Ely, but that was a difficult task given the dense forests and the wide expanse of the fens. Still, it was always possible Turold's searches might yet flush Hereward out of hiding.

Except that Altruda did not believe Hereward would skulk in hiding like a common outlaw. With no allies, and the rebellion ended, he was more likely to go somewhere he could offer his services to another king.

263

The question was which king?

Edgar the Atheling had a claim to the throne of England, but he was a boy who had no support within England. Yet Hereward might still be tempted to use him as a symbol to raise another revolt. That would mean travelling to Scotland where Malcolm, King of Scots, had welcomed many English nobles who had fled after William had seized control of England.

But the more Altruda considered this, the less she was inclined to believe Hereward would go north. Nobody in England really wanted Edgar the Atheling as their king and, while Malcolm might be happy to cause mischief and raid the north of England if an opportunity arose, he was not foolish enough to pit his full strength against the might of William's army. This was evident from the fact that he had refused to provide young Edgar with anything more than a place to live. His English wife might have persuaded Malcolm to welcome refugee nobles, but few of the men who had fled north were as notorious as Hereward. Besides which, Hereward was not a noble, but a landless renegade. Malcolm would surely not risk his kingdom to protect him. No, Altruda decided, the King of Scots might send Hereward on his way with some kind words, a bag of silver and a warning not to return to Scotland, but he was just as likely to put him in chains and send him to William as a token of friendship.

So, if not Scotland, then where? Ireland was a possibility, she supposed. The Northmen there had their hands full with the natives, so they might welcome a man like Hereward. Yet somehow that seemed an unlikely destination. Hereward would, she reflected, probably prefer to serve someone who was openly opposed to William.

That, she decided, probably ruled out Sweyn of Denmark. Sweyn had harboured dreams of uniting England and Denmark under one king just as Cnut the Great had done, but Sweyn was not made of the same stuff as his famous forebear. He had accepted gold to abandon his claim, and William had told her Sweyn was sending a peace delegation to seal a treaty between them.

No, Altruda decided, serving King Sweyn was unlikely to hold much attraction for Hereward.

Who else was there?

She smiled as realisation dawned.

Philip of France, the boy King who was now a young man, had designs on bringing all the French-speaking regions of Europe under his control. That included Normandy.

Yes, Philip of France was the obvious choice. His domain was relatively near, and he was implacably opposed to William, especially now that the Duke of Normandy ruled England as well as his home duchy. For a man like Hereward, Philip would be the ideal overlord.

So he would try to reach France, which meant he would need to use a port on the eastern or southern coasts of England.

That did not help her very much. The King did not have enough troops to watch every port, but cavalry patrols were making random visits in search of the fugitives. Altruda had even gone so far as to pass the word to her network of informants in London itself, asking them to be on the lookout for Hereward or any members of his gang. She doubted whether they would be foolish enough to come to the capital, but she was always thorough in her planning, so she had greased the palms of some dock workers, gate guards and other less reputable citizens. So far, it seemed that money had been wasted, for she had heard nothing from any source.

She shook her head, telling herself she should forget about Hereward. Yet, even if she ignored the personal nature of her obsession with the only man who had ever refused her, she knew that locating him would add to her prestige in William's court; prestige she badly needed in spite of her recent success. Her mission on Ely had taken too much time and had kept her isolated from the burgeoning flock of noble men and women who now fawned around the King. Despite the success of her mission, those newcomers tended to look down their noses at her. Rumours of the untimely deaths of her husbands had circulated, resulting in most men being very wary of her, while the women were envious of her beauty and her influence with the King.

But the main problem was that she was English; a member of the defeated race who no longer ruled this island. To a Norman, she was therefore a second-class citizen no matter what services she might have rendered to the King. Indeed, in aiding the Normans against her own people, she had somehow managed to reduce her status even further, for she had betrayed her own people. Who would trust a woman like that? The King might, she knew, but few others would.

An Englishwoman, a turncoat and without allies or friends, she understood that she needed to take steps to alter her fortunes. With the King rapidly gaining full control of the country, he would surely have less need of her as a spy. He might have other ideas, but she convinced herself that she should seize the initiative and consolidate her position.

Reluctantly, she came to the conclusion that she needed a husband. It would need to be a man who could bring her power and influence, yet who would not prove obstructive to her wishes. A man who attempted to dominate her would never do.

But were there any such men available? And would the King permit her to marry a powerful nobleman? William was always wary of betrayal, and would no doubt baulk at giving Altruda too much power in case she took it into her head to persuade her husband to make a play for the throne.

Not that Altruda was foolish enough to believe such a thing would be possible. William's position was now virtually unassailable, and he had sons who would inherit the kingship after him. Only a fool would attempt a coup against him, and Altruda was far too grounded in realism to be tempted into such a dangerous ploy.

She would need to give the question of a husband considerable thought, she knew, but she was distracted by a flurry of activity in the courtyard below her window. The clattering of many hooves announced the arrival of several dozen visitors. Altruda did not need to look outside to know who they were. She recognised the Danish tongue being spoken, and she knew this was the peace delegation come to offer gifts to William. She was tempted to stand in the open window and study the new arrivals, but she held back, remaining in the shadows.

"When the Danes arrive," the King had told her, "I think it would be best if you remained out of sight."

He had phrased it as a suggestion, but Altruda understood. Some of these men had probably been on the isle of Ely with King Sweyn. If they saw her at William's court, they might begin to ask questions about the role she had played in their king's decision to leave England so unexpectedly.

266

She risked a glance out of the window, seeing a small army of attendants rushing to take horses to the stables and assisting the visiting Danes. The newcomers were gazing around at the impressive palace complex which William had inherited from his Anglo-Saxon predecessor, all of them dressed in brightly coloured tunics and cloaks, and each man weighed down by glittering jewellery of gold and silver. They were, she mused, like so many peacocks.

Standing near the edge of her window, Altruda clucked her tongue when she recognised a few of the faces. These men had come in war only the year before, but now they were back on friendly terms. And they might stay here for weeks.

She sighed. She had no wish to be confined to her rooms for days on end while the King entertained his former enemies.

It seemed to Altruda she had escaped the prison of Ely only to find herself trapped in a more luxurious prison. Perhaps she should have insisted that she wanted to visit some of her estates, but William seemed determined to keep her close at hand. Could it be, she wondered, that he had heard some of the less flattering rumours circulating around the court, and that he wanted to keep her where he could see her in case she was plotting against him?

She shook her head, telling herself not to succumb to feelings of paranoia. William trusted her, she was sure. But why, then, had he insisted she stay in London, especially when he did not want any of the Danish ambassadors seeing her?

She needed time to think, but the noise from below was almost as distracting as the knowledge that she must avoid meeting these men while they stayed in the palace.

She made a decision.

Turning to the maids who stood like impassive statues on the far side of the room, she said, "I am going out for a walk. Fetch my brown dress and my old cloak."

The two girls who had been assigned to her were startled out of their silent watchfulness by her words, but they knew better than to delay in obeying her commands. They were, Altruda thought, stupid, dull-witted girls, but they were competent enough to help her change. Before long, she had discarded her elegant dress and was wearing a plain, brown outfit covered by a long, rather worn cloak. Her long hair was bound up on her head and covered by a plain headscarf, and her only concession to her status was to wear a pair of sturdy shoes. This was the shapeless, undistinguished costume she wore when she wanted to wander the streets of London without drawing attention to herself.

Quietly, she made her way through the corridors to a back entrance, then left the palace and headed for the bustle of London.

She normally enjoyed the subterfuge of wandering the streets in disguise. It forced her to concentrate on the people around her, and it had always been a highly profitable pastime. She had spent a lifetime quietly gathering information and using what she had learned to aid whichever Lord she happened to be serving. Even with William securely on the throne, she had not been able to abandon those traits which had served her so well. During previous visits to the city, she had liberally dispensed silver in order to cultivate the allegiance of merchants, street vendors and other less worthy inhabitants because she knew that information was one of the key valuables in life, and developing a network of informants was always useful.

This day, however, she merely wanted time to think. She hoped that moving amongst the ordinary citizens of London might distract her from the numerous concerns preying on her mind. What it brought instead was the change in fortune she had been in need of.

She was idly watching a street performer juggling a set of wooden balls, her mind still preoccupied with thoughts of how to improve her standing at court, when one of her spies, a young street urchin named Alban, sidled up to her, his expression suggesting he had news for her.

Alban was a dark-haired, pock-faced, light-fingered thief who roamed the city in search of unwary strangers. Altruda had caught him attempting to steal her purse on her very first venture into London but, instead of having him mutilated or hanged, she had recruited him.

"I found yer man, My Lady," Alban grinned.

"Which man?" she asked distractedly.

Alban held out a grubby hand as he gave her a gap-toothed smile.

Reluctantly, Altruda handed over a silver penny which the youth snatched before she could change her mind.

"He was down at the docks this morning," he told her. "A stocky man, with fair hair and a moustache. I didn't see his tattoos on account of him wearing long sleeves, but he had a tall, grey-haired servant with him, just like you said he would, so I followed them."

"You mean you planned to rob them if they didn't turn out to be the men I am seeking?" Altruda guessed, thinking the young thief was merely attempting to wheedle more coin from her.

Alban's grin was as good as an admission, but he did not dwell on the matter.

"They're staying at Guthred's Inn," he continued. "I asked around, careful like, and I reckon it's them. There's two women with them. One's a redhead, the others a posh lady with very dark hair."

Altruda felt her pulse quicken. Had Alban really found them?

"Who else is with them?" she asked, suddenly more interested in the boy's tale.

"Two or three hired men, so the tavern girls say. And a young lad as well. They reckon he's a servant."

Altruda nodded to herself. Everything matched.

"Do you know which boats they visited at the docks?"

"No," Alban shrugged. "They were on their way back when I spotted them."

"And they are at the inn now?"

"They were half an hour ago," the young thief confirmed.

"You have done well, Alban," Altruda told him.

She took another two pennies from her purse, giving the boy more money than he had ever possessed before. He would probably squander it on strong ale, she knew, but that did not matter to her. What mattered was that Hereward had been found.

It must be him, she told herself. A tall, grey-haired servant, a dark-haired lady, and two or three surviving gang members. The presence of a red-haired girl confirmed it. It must be them.

She considered returning to the palace, but it was a long walk back to Westminster. Besides, King William was entertaining the delegation from Denmark, and it would not do to alert those visitors that their one-time ally, the famous rebel Hereward, was at large in the King's capital.

No, she decided, the new castle William had built on the riverside was much closer. Not only that, she knew she would find a man there who would help her; a man who held a grudge against Hereward.

Walking briskly, she hurried through the streets to find Ivo de Taillebois.

Chapter 22

As soon as Hereward entered the room, Torfrida knew something was troubling him. He tried to appear relaxed, and he smiled broadly when he saw her new dress of fine, dark blue velvet, but she knew him well enough to recognise the tension underlying his apparent good humour. She also understood that it would be unwise to challenge him straight away. He would reveal whatever was troubling him in his own time.

"The dress suits you," he told her admiringly.

"Yes, I was very fortunate to find it."

"You didn't go out alone, did you?" he enquired.

She knew he was delaying, but she played along.

"Of course not. Ylva came with me, and so did Edric and Winter."

"They must have enjoyed that," he murmured sarcastically.

"Ylva didn't mind," she smiled.

He returned a quick smile of his own which soon vanished. Then he strolled to the room's solitary window, his boots loud on the bare wood of the floor. Pushing open the shutters, he stared at the city outside. Not that there was a great deal to see, Torfrida knew. The view from this upper floor was restricted to the tavern's back yard, the stables and a succession of rooftops stretching away to the river, all of it shrouded in a fug of smoke from the city's many hearth fires. Torfrida had looked out earlier but had soon lost interest because there was very little to see, yet Hereward stood, his hands clasped behind his back, staring out as if he were surveying the entire city.

"We found a boat," he informed her without looking round.

"That is good news," she replied. "Where will it take us?"

"Hedeby."

"In Denmark?"

"That's right."

"I don't think it would be wise to linger in Denmark," she observed cautiously. "King Sweyn might not welcome us."

Hereward turned away from the window, nodding slowly to acknowledge her remark.

"I know. He may think I bear a grudge after the way he abandoned us."

"You do," she said with a soft smile. "And Kings don't like people who harbour grudges against them."

"It was the best I could do," he shrugged. "The other boats were sailing too close to Normandy for my liking. But we won't stay in Denmark. From Hedeby, we can take another ship to anywhere we like. It's a major trading port."

Torfrida nodded, knowing they were soon to become exiles, and she wondered whether it was this thought that was troubling him.

"When does it sail?" she asked.

"On the dawn tide. The Master is loading goods today, and his crew will be visiting the inns this evening. He said we should board today and spend the night on the ship."

"So soon?" she asked. "That is good."

Hereward gave a vague nod, but the expression in his eyes told her that he did not agree with her.

She was desperate to know what was troubling him, but she confined herself to saying, "I don't care where the ship takes us. Anywhere will do. The sooner we are away from here, the better."

Hereward's face remained grave, a frown clouding his features. He stood facing her, saying nothing, but Torfrida declined to fill the silence.

His admission, when it came, surprised her.

He said, "The Bastard is here."

"What? What do you mean?"

"I mean," he muttered darkly, "that the Bastard is here in London. He's staying at his palace out at Westminster."

"That is hardly a surprise," she replied carefully.

Hereward scowled, "I thought he might still be chasing us around the Fens. I didn't really think he'd come back here so soon."

It took Torfrida a moment or two to grasp the meaning behind Hereward's words. When she suddenly understood his intention, the blood drained from her face.

"No!" she insisted. "Hereward! Do not even consider it."

His reaction confirmed that her fears were correct. His face was stern, his fingers clenching into fists of anger.

"He killed my friends!" he spat. "He stole my country from me! Those things require answering."

"No!" she repeated.

Crossing the tiny room, she placed her hands on his arms, clinging to him as if the touch of her fingers would bind him to the spot.

"There is nothing you can do!" she told him. "I understand that you want revenge, but this is madness."

"I must try," he replied, his voice hard. "Winter will help me. The rest of you must go to the boat today. We will come later. If we are delayed, wait for us in Hedeby."

"Delayed?" she almost shouted. "Delayed? Are you mad? You will not be delayed, Hereward. You will be killed."

"Someone must deal with him," he insisted. "He is a monster."

"Yes, he is. But killing him would solve nothing. You know that. He has too strong a grip on the land, and there is nobody who will stand beside you."

She could see the tightness in his jaw as he sought to retain his resolve, but she did not allow him peace.

"I gave in to you when you said you wanted vengeance against de Taillebois," she reminded him, her words hot and angry. "I helped you then, because you promised we would leave England once he was dead. But he escaped you, and still I stood by you when you decided to lead all those refugees to Ely. Then I agreed to stay when the Danes came to Ely, because I thought you had a chance of victory. I even stayed once King Sweyn had abandoned you, because I believe in you."

She stared into his eyes, not allowing him to refuse her as she went on, "But I have had enough. It is over, Hereward. The Earls betrayed you, and there is nobody left. Even if you had William here now, bound hand and foot, and on his knees in front of you, I would say you should not kill him."

"Why should I not?" he demanded, a flicker of confusion briefly flashing in his eyes.

"Because his Barons hold all the land. He has sons, and the Barons would either rally behind the eldest, or would squabble among themselves for the right to become King. If that happens, you would be responsible for condemning England to years of strife."

"The alternative is perpetual Norman rule," he argued.

"Yes, and I know how cruel that will be. But killing William will not prevent it. The very best you could hope for is that his eldest son becomes King and rules less harshly than the father."

She leaned close, lowering her voice, forcing herself to speak more calmly, while remaining insistent.

"England is lost to the Normans, my love. You did your best, but there is not enough help. All those who could have aided you are dead. I do not want you to throw away your life in a futile and pointless sacrifice which will achieve nothing except to satisfy your thirst for vengeance. Please! It is time to make a new life for ourselves."

Her words had struck home. She could see the conflict raging inside him; the desire to avenge his friends, the need to strike a blow against the Norman lord who had stolen the crown, and his private acknowledgement that he would lose his life in the attempt.

"If you do this," she assured him, "I will not wait for you in Hedeby. I have had enough of waiting around, Hereward. I want a new life, away from this cruel land. I want you to share that life with me, but I will no longer wait for you. If you insist on doing this foolish thing, I will make my life without you."

She continued to stare into his eyes, telling him that she meant every word. They gazed at one another for a long, silent moment, then she felt the muscles of his arms relax and he let out a long, slow sigh.

"I have never lost before," he told her in a mournful whisper.

"I know. But you have not lost this time. It is others who lost England, not you. You tried, but you were betrayed by people who are content to bend the knee rather than stand up for their way of life. That is not your fault. And you can still win. By escaping, by making a new life, you will have defeated William."

"You are clever with words," he said with a sad smile. "But I feel the loss in my heart."

"I know. But you know I am right. This war is over, and killing William would only make things worse."

He pursed his lips, frowning to himself, then gave a reluctant nod.

"Very well," he sighed. "We will board the ship together and sail to Hedeby. I hate it, but you are probably right."

Torfrida kissed him, letting him know how much his concession meant to her.

"Thank you," she whispered.

She was not entirely sure that she had convinced him, and she privately vowed to stay close to him to prevent him slipping away and carrying out his suicidal plan. She briefly considered asking him to swear an oath that he would not attempt to kill the King, but she decided it would be better to display some trust in him.

"Thank you," she said again.

They embraced, holding one another for a long time, before Hereward gently eased her away and said, "I sent Winter and Ordgar out to the stables to prepare the cart. Martin is downstairs, tucking into a lunch of beef stew and bread. We should join him."

"That would be nice," she agreed, attempting to return to some semblance of normality, and hating herself for distrusting him.

For his part, Hereward still seemed torn and unsettled but he, too, made a show of acting as normally as their circumstances allowed.

"What about Edric and his girl?" he asked. "I didn't see them downstairs."

"They went out for a walk," she informed him. "Halfdan is with them. Don't worry, they'll be back in plenty of time."

Hereward nodded, "Come. Let's go down. I don't expect the food will be any better than it was yesterday, but you never know."

Torfrida forced a smile, deciding to repeat her injunction once they were eating. Despite his apparent acceptance of her argument, she understood that a part of him would always want vengeance against William. She knew it was vital that she prevent him acting on that desire until they were safely out of London.

They left the room, heading down the narrow flight of creaking, wooden steps which led to the main room of the inn. Hereward led the way, with Torfrida only a step or two behind him. She could hear the chatter of conversation and the clatter of wooden platters coming from the kitchen, sounds of reassuring normality.

That normality was shattered when they were almost at the foot of the stairs. The front door of the tavern suddenly burst open with a violent crash which made Torfrida jump in alarm. She watched, horrified, as a squad of Norman soldiers thumped their way into the inn, swords in their hands, barking shouted commands for everyone to remain still.

A frightened silence fell over the inn's common room. The few patrons sat very still, not daring to meet the gaze of any of the Normans who were flooding in through the door, clearly intent on searching for somebody.

Nobody dared voice any protest or question. The innkeeper, the sallow-faced Guthred, stood with a half empty mug in his hand, gaping at the Normans in pale-faced terror, and even Hereward was brought to an abrupt halt.

Torfrida wanted to flee, but there was nowhere to run to, and a feeling of dread washed through her. She retained sufficient presence of mind to place her hand on Hereward's shoulder, squeezing tightly to tell him not to react too soon. She half hoped the unexpected commotion was down to something more mundane than their own presence, but that hope was dashed when she saw the plump, odious figure of Ivo de Taillebois stride in behind the leading soldiers.

De Taillebois saw Hereward instantly and pointed an excited finger at the staircase as if he could scarcely believe his luck.

"That's him! Arrest him!"

Torfrida felt Hereward's arm moving as he reached across his body for his sword, so she squeezed his shoulder more tightly, gripping him with fingers like talons.

"No," she hissed in his ear. "They'll kill you."

It was too late anyway. The tips of two swords were at Hereward's throat, and the Normans were reaching for him, ushering him down the final steps to where they surrounded him.

"Bind his wrists!" de Taillebois ordered in a voice that was too loud and excitable for Torfrida's liking. "And take his sword!"

Then the fat Sheriff turned to her, his saturnine features alive with delight, and his fleshy mouth splitting in a lascivious grin.

"Good afternoon, my Lady. We meet again. Sadly for you, I don't think you will enjoy our acquaintanceship quite so much this time."

"I didn't enjoy it the last time," she replied, amazed at how calm her voice sounded. "You are a revolting slug, Lord Sheriff."

The insult could not dampen Ivo de Taillebois's good mood. His men had bound Hereward's wrists behind his back and had confiscated his sword. He was glaring at his captors, muttering promises of retribution, but it was, she knew, false bravado. They had been found, and there was no escape.

She resisted the temptation to turn round. Martin Lightfoot would be sitting somewhere in the room, supping on a bowl of stew. He could not help them defeat the Normans, for there were at least twenty soldiers crowding around the inn's door, many of them still outside in the street. She hoped Winter and Ordgar would not come rushing in with their axes, because that would only result in a bloody death for all of them.

Holding her chin high, she stared de Taillebois in the eye and demanded, "What are you going to do with us?"

He leered at her as he replied, "We have a very strong castle, My Lady. You will be held there until the King has time to decide your fate. Until then, you will be my guest. My very special guest."

He laughed in anticipation of what he would do to her now that she was in his power at last, then he signalled to his followers.

"Bring them!"

Chapter 23

Edric looked at the grim, tight-set faces of his companions. They had gathered in the inn's stables because Guthred, the innkeeper, had told them to leave his tavern. The Normans had not concerned themselves with Hereward's followers, perhaps because Ivo de Taillebois was so jubilant at the ease with which he had found and captured Hereward and Torfrida, but Guthred knew who they were and he wanted nothing to do with them.

"Those Norman bastards would happily string me up if they knew I was harbouring you," he had told them gravely. "I'm sorry, but you must leave."

Once the gang had assembled in the barn, Martin, who had witnessed Hereward's capture, quickly explained what had happened. Then all faces turned to Edric.

He felt helpless. What did they expect him to do? They could not storm a Norman fortress on their own.

Martin appeared lost, like a child who has been abandoned by his parents, while Winter and Ordgar were angry but unsure of what to do. It was Ylva who provided the strength Edric needed.

"Hereward is your Lord," she stated. "And we all love the Lady Torfrida. We must try to help them."

"But how?" Edric wondered.

"We rush the gates and cut down anyone who tries to stop us," growled Winter. "We'll bring them out or die trying."

"I don't want anyone to die," Edric told him. "Trying to storm a Norman castle would only end in us being killed."

"I don't care!" Winter exclaimed angrily, clenching his fists as he spoke. "It's our fault they were taken. If Ordgar and I had been inside instead of out in the stables, we would have got them away."

"Don't be daft," Edric told him. "You would have been killed. There were too many of them. You're just lucky they didn't come looking for you as well."

Winter subsided into a sullen mood, fidgeting and muttering oaths under his breath, but clearly expecting Edric to devise some way of freeing the captives. Edric had never seen this new fortress, but John had mentioned it as one of the King's principal bases in the city, and he knew from experience how formidable Norman castles were.

"We need to take a look at this place before we attempt anything," he decided.

Martin said, "I've seen it. Lord Hereward and I passed it earlier today."

In response to Edric's questioning look, the old retainer went on, "It's like most of their castles. A wooden fence taller than a man, a mound of earth with a big wooden tower on top. It's much bigger than the fortress at Bourne, though, and they've dug a moat around it so the river water has turned it into an island."

"Which means," growled Winter, "that the gates are the only way in."

He fingered the long shaft of his axe, making his preference clear, but Edric waved a hand to silence him.

"Let me think," he said.

His eyes scanned the group once again. Three warriors, an ageing manservant, a young woman and a teenage boy had no chance of breaking their way into a defended fortress. If William's castle followed the usual pattern, the tower would not be the only building inside the perimeter fence, and the other buildings would house a garrison of soldiers. It would take an army to storm the place.

But perhaps there was a way. An idea began to form in his mind; an idea so outrageous he hardly dared mention it. It was dangerous in the extreme, foolhardy beyond belief, but he could not shake off the thought that it might just be possible.

He shook his head, telling himself it could only end in disaster, but still it nagged at him, insisting that he must try something drastic if Hereward and Torfrida were to be saved.

"You've thought of something," Ylva said with a soft smile.

Edric exhaled a long breath. He ran over his idea in his head, recognising its flaws but knowing the only alternative was to abandon Hereward and Torfrida to whatever fate the Normans had in store for them. When looked at in that light, he knew what he must do.

He jabbed a finger at Winter as he began issuing his orders.

"Winter, fetch my byrnie and helmet from the cart. I'll need one of the swords, too. Then bundle up Hereward's armour and a spare sword. Wrap them inside some of the sackcloth."

Allowing no time for interruptions, he turned to Martin Lightfoot.

"Take everyone else down to the docks. Load the baggage and wait for us."

Martin nodded, and Edric rapidly turned to Ordgar.

"You make sure everyone stays safe. If we don't arrive by the time the boat is due to sail, go without us. Stay in Hedeby for as long as you can, but if we haven't joined you in a couple of months, you can assume we're not coming."

"I'm not leaving England without you," Ylva declared.

"You won't have to if my plan works," Edric told her, avoiding the implications of her words.

"And what is your plan?" she wanted to know.

Winter, carrying Edric's byrnie in his arms, added, "I'd like to know what you're up to as well."

"It's simple," Edric replied. "Do you remember the first time we met? When we tricked our way into Ivo de Taillebois's castle?"

Winter's craggy face rumpled in a frown.

"You think you can simply walk into a Norman fortress because you're wearing armour?" he asked dubiously.

"It's better than trying to fight our way in," Edric told him.

Winter said, "Well, if you're daft enough to try it, I'll get my own byrnie and join you."

"No," Edric told him sharply. Running a finger across his top lip, he explained, "With that moustache of yours, you'll never pass for a Norman."

Edric had often felt irritated by his inability to grow the facial hair which marked out the English housecarls, but now he realised it would aid his disguise.

Winter bristled, "You're not going without me, lad. If need be, I'll shave the damn thing off."

"There's no need," Edric assured him. "You are coming with me, all right, but not as a Norman soldier."

"Then what am I supposed to do?" Winter grumbled.

Edric could not help smiling as he explained, "Martin said de Taillebois boasted of holding Hereward and Torfrida as prisoners. What's the best way for me to get into a prison without being challenged?"

Winter gave a helpless shrug, but Ylva had grasped Edric's meaning.

"You need a prisoner," she offered.

"That's right. Winter, we'll wrap some bindings around your wrists to make it look as if you are tied, and I'll take you in at the point of a sword. It means you won't be able to take a weapon, but at least you'll be in there with me."

"I'll tear the place down with my bare hands if I need to," grinned Winter, happy that he would be included in Edric's stratagem.

Ordgar was less pleased. He growled, "Two prisoners would be better than one. I should come with you."

Edric shook his head.

"No, that won't work. They might just believe a solitary prisoner would have a small escort, but two prisoners would need a whole squad of soldiers. Besides, I need you to make sure that the ship's master doesn't take it into his head to set sail early. And I also need you to keep the others safe if we aren't able to join you."

Ordgar was unhappy, grumbling about the need to act as a nursemaid, but Edric snapped at him to obey his orders.

"Hereward put me in charge of what is left of our gang," he told the big axeman. "Whether I'm right or wrong, I need you to follow my plan."

Ordgar subsided with poor grace, but it was Ylva who raised the next objection.

"You will never get into the fortress," she pointed out. "You don't speak French. They won't let you past the gates."

"That's not a problem," Edric replied confidently. "Because I know somebody who speaks excellent French and will get us inside."

"Who?"

"Brother John."

It was growing dark and rain had begun to fall heavily by the time Edric and Winter found the carpenter's shop and the tiny apartment above it. Edric, wearing his armour and with a sword at his side, was sweating in spite of the rain because he was now having doubts about whether his plan had any hope of success. His damaged leg was aching as if his body had decided to protest at the danger he was about to place it in.

It was too late to back out now, of course. He had said farewell to the others, promising them he would bring Hereward and Torfrida to the boat before dawn, but he could tell they did not truly believe him.

Ylva had wanted to come with them, but he had insisted that she go to the boat and wait for him.

"If you came with us, I'd be too worried about you to concentrate on what we need to do," he had explained. "Besides, if you came, Halfdan would follow us, and I don't want to be worrying about him as well."

He had thought she would argue, but she had simply nodded her acceptance before stepping close and kissing him tenderly.

"Come back to me, Edric Strong," she had whispered.

"I will," he had promised.

"You had better. In all my life, you were the first person who was ever kind to me, and I don't want to lose you now."

"I don't want to lose you either," he had assured her.

She smiled, "I wish we had had more time together. And I pray that the one night we did have will bring me a son to remember you by."

The thought that she might be pregnant had never occurred to Edric, but the reminder made him realise how much he stood to lose by undertaking this rescue attempt.

"I will see you before dawn," he had assured her.

She had given him a weak smile as she said, "I wish I could help you."

"You could always pray for us," he suggested.

"I gave up praying a long time ago," she had told him. "I used to pray for my father to stop abusing me, but the prayers were never answered. No, Edric, I have more faith in you than in God."

Before he could protest at this blasphemy, she kissed him again, then turned away, hiding her face from him to conceal her tears.

The thought that he might never see Ylva again tugged at his heart and made his footsteps heavy, but he could not turn back now.

"This must be the place," he told Winter who stood behind him, a heavy bundle of sacking held in his huge hands.

"It's bloody impressive," Winter murmured.

"What?"

Edric turned to see that Winter was not looking at the houses which lined the street but at the fortress King William had constructed near the river.

He followed Winter's gaze and saw the tall, earthen ramparts topped by the usual palisade, with a deep, water-filled moat running around the perimeter, making it impossible to enter the fortress except through the one gateway; a gateway which would no doubt be guarded by several soldiers.

Beyond the walls rose the tower of the keep, looming like a patch of darker shadow against the cloud-laden evening sky. It was much larger than the tower in Bourne's castle, and the faint glimmer of candlelight showed several slits of windows which seemed to him to be so many eyes glinting at him with brooding menace.

This was the fortress William had built to awe the people of London.

This was the place Edric must overcome.

"Come on," he sighed. "Let's find John."

They clumped up the narrow, creaking stair which clung precariously to the outer wall of the building, the steps slick with rain, and reached an unpainted door. Edric knocked, thumping his fist on the wood, wondering whether he had found the correct place.

He had.

John of Brissac, formerly Brother John, opened the door a short way, nervously peering out through the crack, his head silhouetted against the dim light of candles from within.

Edric saw a flash of fear on the man's face and realised his own features were masked by his helmet, the heavy rain and the gathering gloom of evening. He probably made a terrifying sight standing there in the shadowy alleyway in the guise of a Norman soldier.

"John? It's me, Edric."

"Edric?"

"Open the door and let us in. Winter is here with me."

Plainly bewildered by their unexpected arrival, John opened the door and stepped back, allowing them to enter. The two of them clumped inside, John hurriedly closing the door behind them.

Edric stopped, staring at Aelswith who was sitting beside a wooden cot which she was gently rocking. She shot him a disapproving frown, as if his arrival had interrupted her efforts to get baby Torfrida to sleep.

Taking off his helmet, Edric said, "Hello, Aelswith. I hope you are well."

"You see us as we are," she replied with what seemed a forlorn, helpless shrug.

"And the baby?"

"Teething," she replied curtly, as if she did not want to speak to him.

He continued to stare at her. She was still pretty, but he could see the tiredness etched on her features, the dark shadows under her lacklustre eyes, and the weariness of her half-slumped form as she sat rocking the cradle. She looked, he thought, utterly miserable.

John interrupted his thoughts by asking, "Why have you come here, Edric?"

He seemed embarrassed at the poor quality of the lodgings. The room was basic, with a table and chairs, a small dresser and a bed which seemed scarcely large enough for one person, let alone two. There was no fire, the only heat coming from the two candles which stood on the otherwise empty table. An assortment of clothing, much of it obviously belonging to the baby, was hung on pegs along one wall, and the room smelled of damp wool. If this was what John considered decent lodgings, Edric wondered what a poor room would look like.

But that was not his concern. Dismissing the state of the room, he said to John, "I need your help."

John's eyes were darting to and fro, studying both men and scanning the heavy bundle Winter had eased to the wooden floor, allowing rainwater to slowly ooze from the sack to the creaking floorboards.

"What sort of help?" he asked warily.

Adopting a matter-of-fact tone, Edric calmly outlined what had happened to Hereward and Torfrida, and what he needed John to do.

The former monk's face barely registered any emotion, but Aelswith was horrified.

Speaking in a low, angry whisper so as not to wake her child, she spat, "You cannot ask this! Why don't you go and leave us in peace?"

"Because Hereward and Torfrida helped us when we needed it," Edric told her plainly. "Because your daughter is their family, and it is our duty to help them if we can."

"But you'll be killed!" she protested, her face marred by her anguish. "I'll be left alone here!"

Edric could not help comparing her distraught reaction to Ylva's dignified acceptance of his decision. As he had come to learn, Aelswith's first thought was always for herself. Ylva had warned him to expect this sort of response and, while he had half hoped she might be wrong about Aelswith, he had come prepared. Fortunately, the Normans who had taken Hereward and Torfrida had not bothered to search their room. Martin Lightfoot had rescued the purse of money they had concealed within the mattress. Edric had given half of the silver to Ylva, but had brought the other half with him. Now he took the fat purse from his belt and placed it on the table.

"With that," he said, "you will be able to do whatever you like. You could return to Bourne, or anywhere."

Aelswith studied the purse through narrowed eyes, clearly reluctant to reveal just how much Edric's offer meant to her. Slowly, she reached out, picked up the damp purse and weighed it in her hand.

"It's all I have," Edric told her. "It is yours, whether John helps us or not."

He switched his attention back to John and said, "If you do not help us, Winter and I will try anyway. The very least you can do is teach me a few French phrases to help me reach the keep."

"You're mad!" John breathed, shaking his head. "Quite mad!"

"Perhaps I am. I'm not much good at pretending to be something I'm not. But you are. That's why I want your help. All you need to do is get us past the gate and into the keep. Then you can leave while Winter and I find Hereward."

Gesturing to the bundle at Winter's feet, he added, "We have a byrnie and helmet for you. It's probably a bit too large, but it will serve. Now that it is growing dark, nobody will look too closely."

John stood like a lost soul, his eyes closed and his face pale.

After a moment, he opened his eyes and asked plaintively, "Is this your way of taking revenge on me for my deceptions?"

"No," Edric replied. "This is my way of helping my friends who are in trouble. We tried to stand up to the Normans, but we failed to save our country from them. The least we can do is try to save our friends."

Shooting a sidelong glance at the cot, he added, "And family."

John sighed, "You do realise that we will be hanged if we fail?"

"You won't," Edric told him.

"What do you mean?"

"You know the right phrases to say in Latin. You can quote scripture. If this goes wrong, all you need do is tell them we threatened to kill your wife and child if you did not help us. Then you claim the right to be tried by Church justice. If you can recite the words, you can prove you are a cleric. You'll be given a much lighter sentence than Winter or I can hope for."

John gave him a rueful smile when he heard this. Everyone knew that Church law was more forgiving because it only applied to those who had been ordained as priests or monks, and the Church rarely inflicted severe punishments on its fellows. Yet to escape formal justice and be tried by an ecclesiastical court, the only proof required was the ability to recite the Lord's Prayer and some passages from Scripture in Latin. If anyone could do that, it was John of Brissac.

Shaking his head, John acknowledged, "You have thought all this out, haven't you?"

"I have tried," Edric agreed. "You are our best hope, Brother John. You spent years walking into Norman castles under false pretences. You persuaded them to give you shelter and to feed you. You pretended to perform marriages and baptisms.

Compared to that, talking your way into a fortress when we have a ready-made prisoner will be simple."

John gave a low chuckle, a spark appearing in his eyes as he shook his head once again.

"Edric Strong, I never cease to be amazed by you."

"So you will help us?"

Edric was aware that Aelswith was sitting very still and tense, her eyes boring into John, but the former monk gave a resigned nod.

"Yes, my large friend, I will help you. Not because of the money, or your pleas about helping family, but because, if I let you go without me and you are caught, I would always wonder whether I might have made a difference."

Aelswith let out a soft gasp, but made no protest.

Once his decision was made, John acted quickly. He crossed to Aelswith, embraced her, promised he would return, then asked Winter to help him don the armour.

Aelswith sat in stony silence, refusing to meet Edric's gaze while John was dressing. Nevertheless, Edric moved across the room and gazed down into the cot at the sleeping child.

"She is very beautiful," he said softly. "Take good care of her and, whatever happens tonight, teach her about her true heritage."

Aelswith at last raised her eyes, regarding him coolly, but she rewarded him with a faint nod.

"I will."

He smiled at her, then turned away when Winter announced that John was ready.

Hereward's byrnie was slightly too large for him, the shoulders sagging down his arms, but it was a passable disguise.

"Let us go before I change my mind," John told them once he had strapped the sword around his waist.

Edric nodded, then turned back to Aelswith.

"I have always wished you well," he told her. "May God watch over you."

Her face remained impassive, and he could not tell what she was thinking. She sat with one hand still gently rocking the cradle, the other clasping the purse of silver in her lap.

Looking at her now, Edric wondered why he had ever felt he was in love with her. Her beauty, it seemed to him now, was only skin deep.

"Come on, lad," Winter said softly, tugging at his arm. "We have work to do."

Chapter 24

Torfrida had tried to remain defiant, yet the weight of her fear and an almost overwhelming sense of helplessness threatened to crush her spirit.

It had seemed almost unreal as Ivo de Taillebois and his squad of soldiers had marched her and Hereward through the town, the fat Sheriff at the head of the column striding out with undisguised glee, and his soldiers surrounding their prisoners in a wall of chainmail and drawn swords. Torfrida had noticed how the people of London moved aside to let them pass, some stopping to watch, a few making the sign of the Cross, but most hurrying away while casting frightened glances at the prisoners and their escort.

There had been no possibility of escape. Hereward's hands were bound behind his back, and de Taillebois had taken the extra precaution of having his ankles hobbled by a short length of rope. Yet now, looking back, Torfrida realised that their only hope of escape had been during that humiliating walk. Once they were inside the Norman castle and the great gates had been barred behind them, they were truly lost.

The castle sat beside the river Thames, a wide channel having been dug around its perimeter to allow the river water to flood in and create a moat which sealed the castle off from the rest of the city. Behind the moat was a high rampart of earth topped with a tall palisade of thick timbers. There was only one way in or out, and it was guarded by another squad of heavily armed soldiers.

Within the wide perimeter were several long, low, wooden buildings. Torfrida supposed these housed the garrison, servants, horses and stores, but her attention was seized by the tower which stood at the far end of the bailey.

As with all Norman castles, a mound had been created using the earth from the excavation of the moat. Atop this stood a square-sided wooden tower which dominated the lower bailey. There were narrow window slits on the tower's upper levels, but only one door, and this was set high in the centre of the side facing the fortress's main gate. To reach the door, they had to climb a long set of wooden stairs which rose up the side of the steep mound. The steps were wide enough for two armed men to walk side by side, and railings not only provided support and guidance for their hands, they prevented anyone leaping down or, as Hereward had no doubt considered, pushing anyone else off the stairway.

Two guards stood at the door which opened as they approached, revealing the slender figure of Altruda.

It took a moment before Torfrida recognised the woman, for she was dressed in a simple, brown dress of cheap wool, but there was no mistaking her scornful voice as she greeted them.

"Welcome, Hereward. Here you are at last. I was afraid we would not see you again."

Hereward, who had remained silent throughout the march through the city streets, simply glared at Altruda, his lips clamped tightly closed, but his eyes blazing a promise of retribution if he were ever able to break free.

Altruda merely smiled at his useless anger. She had won, and she knew it.

"And Torfrida!" she beamed. "How nice to see you again. I know Sir Ivo has been very keen to find you."

De Taillebois let out a sadistic chuckle which Torfrida tried to ignore.

Under her breath, she muttered, "Bitch!"

Altruda stepped back inside the narrow doorway to allow them to enter the keep. It was only once both prisoners had passed through the door that she shot an angry glance at de Taillebois.

"Where are the others?" she demanded.

"What others?" de Taillebois replied, his saturnine features crumpling into a confused frown.

"Their servants and henchmen!" Altruda shot back. "Where are they?"

De Taillebois did not take kindly to being reprimanded in front of his soldiers. He glared back at Altruda as he blustered, "You said nothing of any others. All you told me was that Hereward and his wife were at the inn. I went there and captured them, as you can see."

Altruda rolled her eyes, then shrugged, "Well, I suppose it does not matter. They can do nothing now. And there is little point in going back to the inn. They will have fled by the time you get there."

"I don't care about a handful of servants!" de Taillebois insisted. "We have the people we wanted."

"Very true," Altruda conceded. "Then I suggest you send a messenger to the King to advise him that we have Hereward here. A discreet messenger, mind you. The King has guests from Denmark, and he would not want them to know about this."

"Very well," de Taillebois agreed. "And what do we do with them in the meantime?"

"I will take Hereward down to the lower level. I'll need two of your men to stand guard over him, but we shall also tie him up to keep him secure. I suggest you take the woman upstairs. But do not harm her. The King will decide her fate."

Despite herself, Torfrida felt a pang of relief and gratitude when she heard this. She had no illusions about de Taillebois's reasons for wanting her. Altruda's warning would at least delay that fate. She glanced at Hereward to confirm that he, too, had understood the implications, but he was ignoring the conversation and was looking around at the interior of the tower.

Torfrida smiled to herself, knowing he was still trying to work out how to escape. It was useless, of course. More than a dozen Norman soldiers still stood outside on the long stairway, while several more were inside watching over them. They were trapped.

Even so, she took heart from Hereward's example. Stifling her mounting terror, she took a moment to glance around at their new surroundings.

The interior of the keep was dimly lit by candles and the limited daylight admitted by the narrow arrow slits in the wooden walls, but there was sufficient light to allow her to see they were in a large, square room which occupied the entire breadth of the tower. There was little furniture other than a broad table and several stools, but scores of weapons of various sorts were stacked neatly around the edges of the room. There was also a brazier glowing with hot coals, and some cooking implements stacked neatly on a long shelf against the rear wall. A narrow flight of wooden stairs was on the right, leading up to a trap door in the ceiling, while a similar door was set into the floor to their left. This, it soon became apparent, led to the tower's cellar. One of the Normans heaved the heavy door upwards, letting it swing back against the far wall, then took a candle and led the way down another flight of steps. Another man shoved Hereward towards this gloomy pit. He went, but he turned his head, making eye contact with Torfrida.

"Stay strong!" he managed to tell her before he was roughly shoved down the steps and vanished from her sight.

Altruda followed the guards down into the cellar to oversee their handling of the prisoner, leaving de Taillebois to carry out the rest of her orders. The Sheriff was clearly irked by her manner, but he quickly detailed one man to take a message to the King at the palace, told four more to remain in the main room of the tower, then dismissed the rest of the squad.

"Send a servant to light the upper room," he told them as they left. "And have some food and wine brought."

Then he turned to Torfrida with a chilling smile as he indicated the stairs which led to the upper floor.

"Come, my Lady. We have a lot to talk about."

Torfrida climbed the stairs slowly, following one of the soldiers who heaved open the heavy trap door at the top. He waited until both she and de Taillebois had ascended the steps, then went back down, pulling the door shut behind him.

The upper level was, to Torfrida's surprise, much more elegantly furnished than the spartan room on the central level. There were comfortable chairs, a brazier in one corner, a desk stacked with writing materials, a table with elegant dishes, glasses and jugs, and, set against the far wall, a bed piled high with thick furs and blankets. The wooden boards of the floor were covered by heavy rugs, deadening the sound of their footsteps and making the room feel almost warm and comfortable.

"This is where the King stays when he is in residence," de Taillebois informed her. "It is the safest room in London. As you saw, nobody can reach this far unless they are invited. And uninvited mobs cannot reach us even if they break down the main gates. That stairway we climbed can be collapsed by the guards with only a few blows of a hammer. Then there is no way for anyone to reach the door without a ladder."

Torfrida made no reply. There was nothing she could say.

He indicated one of the chairs, telling her to sit down.

Torfrida sat but remained tense, her back straight and stiff. She was determined not to engage in conversation with him.

De Taillebois, full of self-importance, did not appear to notice her silence. He continued to expound on the virtues of the fortress.

"Of course, this castle was built quickly to provide a safe place for the King to stay. But he has plans. I hear he is already thinking of having a stone keep built here, and high, stone walls will replace the wooden fence. Once that work is complete, this will be one of the strongest fortresses in Europe."

Despite herself, Torfrida could not help saying, "A king who must seal himself in a castle to keep himself safe from his subjects must be a very insecure ruler."

De Taillebois glowered at her as he retorted, "The peasants respect power! They must know their place. And this castle will demonstrate the power of the king!"

Torfrida turned her head, deliberately snubbing him. He was, she knew, a loyal lapdog to William. Arguing with him was a waste of her time.

Time. It continued to pass, and each moment would bring her closer to the fate she dreaded. Through the narrow slits of the small windows, she could see that the afternoon was waning. The light seemed dull outside, as if another of the summer's frequent rain showers might soon arrive, but it was difficult for her to tell, for the windows, designed to allow archers to loose arrows if the tower were ever to be attacked, admitted little light.

That situation was soon remedied. A servant arrived with a glowing candle. He used this to light several other candles which were placed around the walls and on the desk and table. Then he spent a few moments lighting the fire in the metal brazier before departing. Two more servants arrived soon afterwards, bringing platters of bread, meat and cheese which they set on the table. One of them poured wine from a jug into two of the glasses.

De Taillebois flicked a finger, dismissing the servants, and telling them to close the trap door behind them. Once they were gone, he invited Torfrida to join him at the table, his earlier outburst forgotten.

"You may as well eat," he told her. "There is no point in starving yourself."

Reluctantly, Torfrida had to agree with him. She rose from her chair, crossed the room and sat at the table, taking a seat as far from him as possible.

"You are not quite as friendly as the last time we ate together," he commented drily.

Torfrida ignored him, helping herself to a leg of chicken and some bread. She took a sip of the wine, finding it excellent, but decided she would only drink one glass. Getting drunk now would not help her, she knew. But draining the glass might give her an opportunity to smash it on the table and use the jagged remains as a weapon.

She gave a mental sigh. That desperate measure might allow her to savage de Taillebois's face, but it would not save her in the long run. Even if she somehow managed to overcome the Sheriff, escape from this prison was impossible.

De Taillebois, tucking into the food, continued to talk even while chewing.

"The last time, as I recall, you chatted all evening, although I fear that was solely to distract me from your husband's intent. He came to kill me. But you know that, of course."

"He nearly succeeded," Torfrida responded sharply.

"Yes, he killed all my men and burned down my home, but I escaped him all the same. And now he is my prisoner."

Torfrida, unable to resist a chance to goad him, remarked, "It seems to me he is Altruda's prisoner."

De Taillebois gave a careless shrug.

"She seeks to ingratiate herself with the King, as always. But he will know it was I who captured your husband."

He paused, taking time to allow his eyes to rove over her features before adding, "And I am sure he will reward me."

"Hereward will kill you if you touch me," she hissed in warning, gripping her glass tightly to prevent him seeing how her hands were trembling.

De Taillebois laughed aloud.

"I hardly think he is in a position to do anything like that. No, My Lady, your husband is a dead man. I know Altruda desires him for herself, but the King would never allow such a dangerous rebel to live."

He paused again, his expression thoughtful. Then, as if an idea had suddenly come to him, he beamed, "Unless I could persuade him that Hereward's good behaviour could be assured. If, for example, you were to be held as a hostage for his loyalty."

Torfrida understood him only too well.

294

"You want me to be your concubine?" she said. "Under pain of death if Hereward should cause any more trouble for your King?"

De Taillebois smirked, "I would not have put it as crudely as that, My Lady, but I see you have grasped the essence of my proposal."

Torfrida said nothing, lowering her eyes to stare blankly at the plate of food in front of her. All of a sudden, she had lost her appetite.

"What do you say, My Lady?" de Taillebois asked her. "Do I need to point out the alternative?"

Still Torfrida refused to look at him.

He sighed, "Without your cooperation, your husband will surely die. I expect he will be hanged as a common criminal."

There was another long pause before he added meaningfully, "And you will be mine anyway. You cannot escape that. Except that, with Hereward dead, I will have no need to keep you alive should you fail to please me."

Torfrida shivered. Through the narrow windows, she could hear the patter of raindrops which soon grew into a constant drumming as the sky darkened. Gusts of wind flitted through the room, making the candles flicker. De Taillebois stood up, stretched his back ostentatiously, then moved around the room, closing the small shutters to seal them from the world beyond the walls.

And still Torfrida sat in miserable silence, knowing what Hereward would want her to do and knowing, too, that she would never allow him to die if there was a way she could save his life.

But it was the cost that appalled her.

De Taillebois seemed oblivious to her pain.

"It is growing dark outside," he informed her casually. "I expect we will receive the King's response to my message before long."

Still Torfrida sat, her stomach churning, the sight of the food making her nauseous. She set aside her glass, abandoning all thought of using it as a weapon, and stood up, returning to one of the large, comfortable chairs which was set beside the glowing brazier.

She slumped into the chair, another desperate thought coming to her. The brazier was made of iron, and set on a thick, metal plate on the floor. But if she could knock it over, the burning coals would scatter across the thick rugs. Could she set the whole tower ablaze? Would that provide an opportunity for her and Hereward to escape? The brazier appeared to be very heavy, and she doubted whether she would be able to overturn it without seriously burning herself. Even if she did succeed, it might only result in all of them being consumed in an inferno as the wooden tower burned to the ground.

Perhaps, she mused miserably, that would be a preferable end to the one that awaited her.

She glanced up as de Taillebois sat down facing her, his plump frame filling the chair.

"I see you are still considering your answer," he said inanely. "Do not take too long to make up your mind. As I said, I will have you either way. All you need to decide is whether you wish to save your husband's life."

"You are an animal!" she spat.

She saw his cheeks flush with anger. With the glow from the brazier reflecting in his eyes, it made his brooding features seem as demonic as his demands and threats.

"Mind your tongue!" he barked. "I can have it removed if it pleases me."

She saw that this threat was very real, so she lowered her head and clasped her hands in her lap, desperately trying to think of some way she could escape.

De Taillebois leaned forwards, reaching out to grasp her knee with one hand.

He squeezed hard as he told her, "You are trying my patience, My Lady. I think I should teach you a lesson."

He rose from his chair, grabbing her by the arms as he did so. Torfrida tried to fend him off, but he hauled her to her feet. Her knee came up, aiming for his crotch, but he had clearly been expecting the move, and he blocked it with his leg. In response, his right hand released its grip on her arm and came up in a vicious slap which knocked her head sideways as it struck her left cheek in a stinging blow.

Then he seized her with both hands again and was pulling her close, crushing her against him as his lips sought hers.

She twisted her head away, trying to scream but finding no voice except a hoarse, terrified whisper.

"No!"

"Yes!" he laughed as he tightened his grip on her, making it difficult for her to breathe as he embraced her.

He was shuffling his feet, moving them closer to the bed which stood against the far wall, and she knew with horrifying certainty that he intended to ignore Altruda's warning.

And there was nothing she could do to prevent it. He might be an almost comical figure with his fat belly and lack of martial prowess, but he was still too strong for her.

"Lord Sheriff!"

The voice was muffled, but the banging on the trap door was loud enough that de Taillebois could not ignore it.

"Go away!" he barked angrily.

"Lord Sheriff!" the voice repeated urgently. "The King is here!"

Those were probably the only words that could have prevented him from continuing. Torfrida felt him falter, then he shoved her away, making her stagger and almost fall to the floor.

As she regained her balance, de Taillebois straightened his tunic and glared at her.

"It seems my pleasure will be delayed," he rasped. "But only for a short while, I am sure."

He spun on his heel, moved to the trap door and reached down to pull it up.

A soldier was on the stairway.

"The King is here!" the man repeated.

De Taillebois signalled to him to come up into the room.

"You stay up here," he ordered. "Watch the lady and make sure she does nothing stupid. I will be back once I have spoken to the King."

The soldier nodded his understanding. He climbed up into the room, glanced around curiously, then took a couple of steps to allow de Taillebois to descend the stairway.

Torfrida was breathing hard, terror and relief mixing in equal measure. Slowly, she moved back to the chair beside the brazier and sat down, clamping her legs together in an effort to stop her knees from trembling. She felt weak, exhausted and sick at heart. De Taillebois would be back, she knew, and then he would carry out his threat.

She was dimly aware of the sound of voices from the lower level drifting up through the open trap door, but her mind would not focus on what they were saying. All she knew was that King William was here, and he had the power to dispose of her like a common chattel.

And still there was only one way she could save Hereward's life.

Chapter 25

The keep's lower level was so dark, damp and oppressive that it rivalled any dungeon a stone fortress could have offered, and Hereward felt he was descending far beneath the earth even though he knew the tower stood well above ground level.

He felt utterly helpless as he trudged down the wooden stairs. With his hands bound and a sword held close to his throat, he had no chance of overpowering the two guards who took him down into the darkness. The man behind him seized a fistful of Hereward's hair as they descended the steps, gripping tightly to prevent the Englishman throwing himself down the stairs in an effort to knock over the leading soldier who was holding a candle aloft to light their way. But the feeble flame barely illuminated the vast chamber of the tower's cellar. There were no doors or windows leading to the outside from this bottom level of the three-storey keep. This not only prevented any attacker finding a way in without climbing to the next level, it also provided a huge storage space where supplies could be kept. Hereward could see enormous barrels, stacked wooden boxes and piles of heavy sacks stretching into the shadowy distance.

A flash of green eyes reflected momentarily in the candlelight, then a dark, four-legged shape slowly emerged from between two piles of crates. The black cat stared at the intruders who had come down into its realm, then slinked off into the blackness. At least, Hereward thought ruefully, he did not need to fear being bitten by rats. Not the four-legged variety, anyway. He supposed that, with such a huge quantity of food being stored, it was important to keep rodents at bay, yet the sheer scale of the supplies told him something else. William the Bastard was still afraid of being overthrown by his new subjects, and had made this place a bolthole for himself.

There was an open space near the foot of the stairway. It was barely large enough for half a dozen people to stand closely together, and an immense wooden pillar occupied part of the space. Various narrow paths between the piled boxes and barrels led off into the gloom, but Altruda, who had also brought a candle, gestured her free hand towards the huge post.

"Tie him to that," she told the two guards.

The first man placed his candle on top of a huge barrel, then circled behind Hereward while his companion held the tip of his heavy sword close to the Englishman's throat.

Hereward tensed, knowing this could be his last chance to escape. To secure him properly, they would first need to untie his hands which were behind his back. That might be his only opportunity to overpower them. What he would do after that, he had no idea, but he quickly discovered that they were not going to give him any chance at all. The guard behind him hauled him back towards the pillar, then grabbed his chin and smashed his head back against the solid oak, stunning him. He almost fell, but the Norman shoved him against the column of wood, cut the ties around his wrists, then brutally yanked his arms back, one on either side of the wide, round pillar. By the time Hereward had shaken off the effects of the blow to his head, he was securely tied once more. A second rope passed around his ankles held him firmly against the massive column which was one of the supports for the floor above. He tugged uselessly, feeling how expertly the knots had been tied and how impossible it would be to move the pillar.

Satisfied with their handiwork, the two soldiers moved away from him. The man facing him leaned against one of the barrels, while the other took up position at the foot of the stairs. Both now held swords in their hands, and both studied him with the intensity of raptors, their expressions as hard and uncaring as the iron of the armour and helmets they wore. They were both big men, Hereward noticed as he tried to shake off the throbbing pain in his head and blink away the lights that flashed in his eyes.

The guard facing him was young, barely into his twenties, while the second man was much older, clearly a veteran. Hereward noted these things, but it was difficult to think of them as men; they were the enemy. And he was in their power.

He dismissed them from his mind when Altruda stepped into the faint pool of light from the candles and stood facing him. The soldiers might present the physical threat to him, but he knew it was this woman who held the real power here.

She spoke to him in English, a language the Normans would not understand, as she regarded Hereward thoughtfully.

"We will hear from the King soon," she informed him. "But he has guests, so we have some time to talk, I think."

"If all you are going to do is repeat your offer of marriage, my answer is still the same," he rasped, his expression showing nothing but contempt.

She treated him to a smile that was almost a sneer as she said, "It is far too late for that, Hereward. I asked you twice, and you refused me twice. To ask a third time would be an act of desperation, don't you think? But there is only one of us who is desperate, and it is not me."

"So you have merely come to gloat?" he challenged.

"I have come," she told him coldly, "To hear you beg for your life. I want you to plead with me to save you, and to save your precious Torfrida from Ivo de Taillebois. I expect he is already forcing himself on her in spite of my injunction. He likes that sort of thing, you know."

"Then that is another reason for me to kill him," Hereward replied calmly, refusing to react to her goading. "He already owes me a life for the murder of my brother. If he harms Torfrida, I will take my revenge slowly."

"You are in no position to do any such thing," Altruda scoffed. "Brave words will do you no good here, Hereward."

"Why? What are you going to do to make me beg?"

She regarded him with a cruel smile as she said, "The King will decide what is to be done to you. I am sure it will not be pleasant. I will soon hear you beg, be sure of that."

"Will it do me any good?" he shot back.

"No," she admitted.

"Then I won't waste my breath. At least I'll have the satisfaction of going to my death knowing I've not given in to your sick games."

"We shall see!" she snapped, irritated by his refusal to show fear.

His only response was a smile, which angered her even further and forced her to look away.

"I will return once I know the King's decision," she said irritably.

Switching back to Norman French, she told the two guards to remain alert, then she retrieved the candle she had placed on top of a pile of boxes, and climbed the steps. The trap door slammed heavily shut behind her, cutting off what little light had filtered down from the main level of the keep.

301

If Hereward had hoped that the darkness would intimidate his guards, he was sorely disappointed. The two men continued to watch him, although both lowered their heavy swords to rest the tips of the blades on the wooden floor.

None of the men spoke, and if the cat was busy hunting, it did so silently.

Hereward tried not to think about what Ivo de Taillebois was doing to Torfrida, but he put little faith in Altruda's warning to the Sheriff. King William was unlikely to be annoyed by one of his followers raping a woman who was known to be a rebel, so there was nothing to prevent de Taillebois doing whatever he wanted. That thought made Hereward's guts churn with helpless rage, but all he could do was stand with his back pressed against the cold, hard wood of the pillar and wait for others to decide his fate.

Altruda was annoyed at Hereward's refusal to be intimidated, but she concealed her frustration from the four soldiers who garrisoned the main floor of the keep. None of them knew her, but they had seen how Ivo de Taillebois deferred to her, so they treated her with a measure of respect despite her plain, drab clothing.

Now all she could do was wait. It promised to be a long evening, but the monotony was broken when a servant brought a candle to light the upper floor. He was soon followed by several more bearing plates of food.

Out of curiosity, Altruda listened intently when the servants went to the upper level to deliver the food they had brought, but she could hear nothing. Perhaps de Taillebois was taking his time and attempting to woo Torfrida with a meal. Altruda briefly considered climbing the stairs to see for herself, but she decided against it. She really had no interest in Torfrida's fate except in so far as having the woman in de Taillebois's power provided her with a lever against Hereward. The fact he had refused to give in to that pressure annoyed her intensely, so she decided to let de Taillebois have his fun. That would teach both Hereward and Torfrida the consequences of opposing her will.

The arrival of the food did, though, prompt another response. She realised she was very hungry, so she ordered the servants to provide refreshments for herself and the soldiers. It was a while before they returned from the castle's kitchens with more plates of bread, cheese and meat, but Altruda waited patiently, doing her best to ignore the surreptitious glances the soldiers were casting in her direction. None of them said very much, for her presence clearly unsettled them. They were unsure of her status, so dared not say anything out of turn.

The food, when it arrived, provided a distraction. Altruda ate slowly, enjoying her first meal since early morning, then she settled back to wait for the return of the messenger who had been sent to the palace.

Outside, the evening waned into full darkness, bringing rain which grew steadily heavier, drumming on the thick, wooden walls of the keep. One of the soldiers closed the shutters on the narrow windows, while another lit more candles to banish the shadows in the huge room.

And still they waited.

The two guards who had been standing outside at the top of the long stairway which led to the tower's entrance came into the chamber, barring the door behind them. Both were soaking wet, rain dripping from their helmets and chainmail to make small puddles on the wooden floor. They hurried to stand beside the iron brazier which provided a sliver of warmth, muttering about the futility of remaining outside on such a miserable night.

"Typical English weather!" grumbled one of them as he rubbed his chilled hands together to warm them.

Altruda was beginning to think the messenger had been unable to speak to the King when she heard a thump on the door. Two soldiers immediately sprang up, one of them opening a tiny view port in the door and barking a question to whoever stood outside. Altruda could not hear the response which was drowned by the drumming of the rain, but the soldier hissed a warning to his companions as he closed the view port and hurriedly unbarred the door.

"The King!" he told them in a surprised whisper.

Altruda rose to her feet, as did the rest of the guards. The door was swung open, admitting a large, broad-shouldered man who was wearing a broad-brimmed hat and a thick cloak, both of which were sodden with rainwater. He pulled off the hat as soon as he was inside, passed it to a young squire who had followed him through the doorway, then shook off his cloak, adding it to the boy's load.

"Hang them to dry," he commanded.

"Yes, Your Majesty!" the drenched squire bobbed, scurrying to the brazier near the table.

William, Duke of Normandy and King of England, was dressed in a plain tunic and leggings of dark wool, with long, leather boots which reached just below his knees. Other than a few golden rings on his fingers, he wore no ostentatious displays, although his damp clothes were of the finest wool. He quickly took in the scene. Ignoring the soldiers who stood erect and immobile, he focused his eyes on Altruda.

"You have him?" he demanded.

"He is downstairs, Your Majesty," she responded. "And his wife is upstairs. With Sir Ivo de Taillebois."

"Tell de Taillebois to come down," William commanded brusquely, sending one of the soldiers hurrying up the wooden staircase to the upper level.

Then the King turned back to Altruda and said, "Once again you have served me well, My Lady. I thank you."

Altruda felt a moment's amusement at the thought that the soldiers around her were probably giving silent thanks that they had been respectful towards her. A woman who had been personally thanked by their King was not a person to be treated lightly.

De Taillebois came scurrying down the stairs, leaving the trap door which led to the upper level open.

"Your Majesty!" he blurted. "I did not expect you to come in person."

"The Danes were boring me," William grunted dismissively. "They are still drinking, so I made an excuse and left them to it. Now, let us go and talk to our prisoner."

Altruda took up a candle, placing it on a wooden holder, and crossed the room to the trap door. De Taillebois, not wishing to be outdone, grabbed another candle and followed.

Altruda waited until one of the soldiers had dragged the trap door open, then she led the way, with William following her and de Taillebois bringing up the rear.

"Here he is, your Majesty," she said when they reached the foot of the stairs.

The open space was crowded now. Altruda moved aside, taking up a position beside the wooden stairway and placing her candle on top of a pile of crates. De Taillebois scuttled over to stand beside her, putting his own candle on top of a huge barrel which stood near the foot of the steps.

The two soldiers stood alert, greeting the King with deferential bows as he passed them to stand in front of Hereward, the two men coming face to face for the first time.

Altruda found she was mesmerised by the sight as the pair studied one another. Physically, William was taller, more imposing, and had close-cropped hair, while Hereward's long, blond locks, moustache and shorter, stockier build could hardly have been a greater contrast.

Yet, for all their physical differences, they were similar in manner. Both men exuded an air of confidence mixed with a capacity for violence, and both were obviously accustomed to being obeyed.

William planted his hands on his hips as he stared silently at Hereward. The King carried no weapons, but that only seemed to enhance his authority. Bare-headed and heavily muscled, the dim, wavering light in the chamber had the effect of making him appear larger and more imposing than ever.

There was a long silence before William spoke.

Addressing Hereward in French, he said, "You caused me a great deal of trouble. And for what? Because your brother was killed?"

Altruda wondered whether Hereward would maintain a defiant silence, but he retorted, "Is that not enough? Your lackey, de Taillebois, still owes me *weregild* for that death."

"Not under my law," William shot back.

"I do not recognise your laws," Hereward replied insolently. "You stole this land from its rightful King."

William's face glowed red in the flickering light, and his fists bunched as he barked, "I am the rightful King! The throne was promised to me by King Edward! Your precious Harold was a usurper!"

"Your anger cannot conceal your guilt," Hereward told him, smiling to reinforce his insult.

Altruda began to wonder why the King had come here. She had expected him to remain at the palace to entertain the Danish ambassadors, but he had crossed the city as soon as night fell.

And for what? To argue over past events with a rebel?

305

William, though, took a deep breath as he regained a measure of composure.

"You intrigue me, Hereward," he said more calmly. "You are a fool, of course, but I will admit you are a brave fool. I am a soldier, so I can recognise courage when I see it. There is little enough of it left among your countrymen, but now I see why you created so much trouble for me. I do believe that I might not have won the crown if there had been three men like you in England."

Then, with a slight sneer, he added, "But there are not. Harold died in battle, and all his best men with him. His sons are but a nuisance with the raids they make from Ireland, and the remaining English nobles are, as you have witnessed for yourself, more like old women than men."

Hereward snorted, "Did you come here to bore me to death or to kill me?"

William let out a throaty chuckle of amusement.

"No, I came to see what sort of man you are. I thought you might provide more interesting company than the petty fools who normally cluster around me."

Altruda briefly wondered whether the King had aimed that comment at de Taillebois, but she could not take her eyes from the confrontation between the two enemies.

Hereward said, "I am the kind of man who, if our positions were reversed, would kill you without all this talking."

"Indeed? To what end? I can understand you wanting to kill de Taillebois. He has that effect on most people."

Ivo de Taillebois, standing close to Altruda, barely moved a muscle when he heard this insult.

He is such a lickspittle, Altruda thought to herself. She almost pitied Torfrida when she thought of the fat fool ravishing the poor woman.

Almost.

Ignoring everyone except Hereward, William continued, "Even if you did somehow manage to kill me, it would do you no good. My men would cut you down and one of my sons would become King in my place. They may hate me, and one another as well, but their claim to the throne is better than that of anyone else."

"The Witan elects our Kings," Hereward argued.

306

"The Witan knows what is best for it," William derided. "With swords held to their necks, that spineless bunch of bishops and thanes will elect whoever is the strongest."

"The words of a bully," Hereward scoffed.

"No," William shot back. "They are the words of a man who has power."

"That is all you care about, isn't it? Power. You care nothing for the people."

"The people?" William snorted. "The people are sheep to be shorn. They will do as I wish, or they will be punished. God has ordained that the strongest should take what they want, while the weak will only serve."

"I am no cleric," Hereward retorted, "but did our Lord not say that the meek shall inherit the Earth?"

"Ah, you must be speaking of that child, Edgar the Atheling. They do not come much meeker than him. No, he will inherit nothing. I may keep him as a lapdog, but he will never be King."

"So you will use England as your personal property?" Hereward demanded, his voice growing angry in spite of the vulnerability of his position.

"It is my right," William nodded. "I have always had to fight for everything in my life. I built up Normandy, I fought for England and won. God has rewarded me for my hard work and devotion to him, and nobody can take that away from me!"

"The people will not stand for it," Hereward told him. "You may kill me, but others will take my place."

The argument had been in danger of becoming heated enough to warm the chill of the basement, yet William now seemed more amused than angry.

He took a step back, spreading his arms expansively as he smirked, "No, they will not. I control an army of soldiers, and I control the Church. Between these two, the people will be taught the futility of resistance. More than that, they will be taught that to resist the natural order of things is a sin. Soon, I will have them grovelling and fawning, begging me to keep them in their place. They will never dream that there is any other way to live."

He gave Hereward a mocking smile as he went on, "The problem men like you have is that you do not see the wider picture. You think everything can be solved by brave words and wielding a

307

sword. That may help you seize power, but it takes more than that to hold on to a throne once you have it. People must be persuaded not to challenge the order of things. Swords and speeches are important, but so, too, are other things most people never even consider."

"What sort of things?" Hereward scowled, clearly intrigued in spite of his hatred for the man taunting him.

William could not hide his smugness as he explained, "Take coins, for example. My name and face is already appearing on every new coin that is minted. Old coins are being withdrawn, melted down and minted again with my stamp on them. Soon, every time anyone looks at a coin, they will see my name, and they will know who their rightful Lord truly is."

He waved a contemptuous hand as he added, "Fools like you never think of things like that. So you see, even if you kill me, you will change nothing. The old Saxon ways are dead, and the Norman ways will prevail from now on."

Hereward fell silent, and Altruda thought she saw a look of despair in his eyes. That was understandable because the King's speech had been delivered with such conviction that even Hereward had felt the truth of it. All the leaders of England, all the nobility, were either dead or exiled; all the priests and bishops were in thrall to William, and there was nobody for the people to rally behind. The Norman grip on power was absolute, with every aspect of life under William's control.

"You cannot change destiny," William went on.

Hereward growled, "And you cannot change the fact that you will burn in Hell for your crimes."

His accusation, spoken in desperation, had a startling effect on the King.

"That is a lie!" William snapped, his voice rising almost to a shriek, as if Hereward's words had stung him. "The Pope himself blessed my mission to claim the throne of England! It is you who will be condemned to Hell!"

Again, Altruda saw Hereward smile, his eyes regarding the King as if he could see deep into the man's soul and recognise the blackness that lurked there. William, Altruda knew, was secretly terrified of divine retribution, and Hereward's jibe had clearly frightened him.

As she had expected, William responded to his fear by resorting to violence. With a savage slash of his hand, he signalled to the nearest guard.

"You have a knife?"

"Yes, Your Majesty," the younger of the two guards replied.

"Then take out one of his eyes. I want to hear him scream before we execute him."

Chapter 26

The rain was heavier now, hammering down and turning the streets to mud. It had also extinguished the torch John had been holding up to light their way, so the three men stumbled along in darkness as they made their way towards the castle.

The closer they came, the more Edric saw the flaws in his plan. He had gathered up his long hair and stuffed it under his helmet, but he became convinced the guards would recognise them as imposters as soon as they reached the gates. And if one of them spoke to him, he would have no answers because he knew only a smattering of Norman French.

"I'll tell them you are a Breton," John assured him. "They have their own language. And the Normans think Bretons are stupid anyway, so just act simple."

The former monk had spent a few moments trying to teach Edric a handful of short phrases, but Edric struggled to recall any of the words.

"Then I'll tell them you are a mute and an idiot," John sighed in frustration. "But if you want to call this insane idea off, that's fine by me."

Winter growled, "It's either this or I fetch my axe and fight my way in."

John shrugged, "Then let us give this foolishness a try."

So they inched carefully down the quagmire of the narrow lanes towards the river and the brooding Norman castle. They did not have far to go, but they stopped when they heard the sound of horses coming up behind them. John led them into an alleyway between two tall buildings where they huddled together and watched as a dozen riders trotted past. They were unmistakably Normans, but it was too dark to make out any details of who they might be.

Once the column of horsemen had passed, John edged his way to the end of the alley and peered out into the rainy night.

"I think they are going into the castle," he reported in a whisper.

"We'd best wait a few minutes," Edric decided. "Let's give them time to get themselves and their horses indoors."

So the three men stood in the spurious shelter of the buildings while the rain fell, plastering Winter's hair to his head and soaking his clothes. Edric and John were comparatively dry because their armour covered their tunics, but they were almost as miserable as the big axeman. Rain trickled down Edric's neck, and his boots squelched in the mud. It also rang off the iron links of their chainmail and the heavy sword Edric carried. Yet it also meant that the streets were empty. Every house had its door and shutters firmly closed against the rain, and not even a dog would venture out in this sort of weather without a good reason.

Edric counted to a hundred, then repeated the count four more times before he decided they should continue.

"Let's go!" he told the others.

John led the way, with Winter, his hands loosely tied behind his back, following close behind, and Edric holding a sword at Winter's back, bringing up the rear. He had no need to remind Winter to look downcast, for the big man was trudging through the puddles with his head lowered, looking totally abject with misery.

There was just enough light to make out the dark shadow of the high fence which surrounded the castle.

"Keep well clear of the moat," John warned as he led them down the gentle slope to the main gate.

Then they arrived, and there was no turning back.

John thumped a fist on the thick timbers of the iron-bound gates, repeating his knock several times before a hatch opened and a querulous voice spoke in French.

John began to gabble away, gesturing to Winter as he did so. Edric could not understand more than a handful of words the former monk said, but he knew John was telling the guards that they had captured another of Hereward's gang and had brought him here as ordered by Sir Ivo de Taillebois. Using the Sheriff's name would, they hoped, gain them access to the fortress. Martin Lightfoot had recognised de Taillebois when the Sheriff had captured Hereward and Torfrida, and Edric was gambling that the Norman would want to stay close to his prisoners.

They stood there with the rain still falling, for what seemed an age, then one of the gates swung open. John turned to Edric and grinned, gesturing him inside with a curt word of command in French.

Edric's heart was pounding as they passed under the enormous gateway, but he soon realised that only two guards had come to open the gate. The rest had obviously remained inside the nearby gatehouse. As soon as the gate had been closed, one of the two men darted back into the shelter of the building while the other signalled to the three men to follow him.

Edric could make out very little of his surroundings. It was too dark and wet to see more than the vague outlines of buildings which were closed against the elements. He did notice what was obviously a stable, where wide doors stood open and faint light showed a handful of soldiers tending to horses. They must have been part of the column that had passed them on the road.

Their guide led them to the foot of a wide stairway which climbed the side of the castle's mound and led up to the keep. There he left them, saying something to John before hurrying back to the main gates in search of warm shelter.

John stepped close to Edric and said softly, "He says the King is here."

"The Bastard himself?" Winter snarled expectantly.

"He just arrived," John confirmed. "That was his escort we saw riding in."

He gave Edric a forlorn look as he asked, "What do we do?"

"We go in," Edric replied. "What else can we do?"

John made the sign of the cross as he sighed, "May the Lord preserve us."

"Did you find out how many men are in the keep?" Edric asked him.

"No. The guard did say that most of the King's escort went into the barracks, but he doesn't know how many came up here with William."

"It doesn't matter," Winter asserted. "We must go in."

"It matters to me," John said with a sigh. "There could be a small army up there."

"You needn't worry," Edric told him. "Keep out of the way when the fighting starts. You can always tell them we forced you into this by threatening your family. You'll be able to talk your way out of it."

John simply shook his head, but he took a deep breath and led the way up the long stairway. The steps were slick with rain,

312

but they were broad enough to provide a reasonably safe ascent to the tower's high door.

John was breathing hard by the time they reached the entrance, and Edric thought his friend was too afraid to go any further, but the former monk composed himself, then rapped loudly on the door.

Once again there was a pause before a viewing hatch opened; once again John told his story and, once again, the door was pulled open.

John stepped hurriedly inside, speaking volubly in French as he made space for Winter and Edric to follow him.

Edric blinked water away from his eyes as he quickly took in their surroundings. By the light of several candles, he could see they were in a large room which occupied the entire length and breadth of the keep. At the far end of the chamber, three soldiers sat at a table playing dice, while a boy of around twelve years of age stood beside a glowing brazier, holding aloft a large cloak as he attempted to dry it. Two more men had opened the door and were now closing it behind Edric.

Five armoured soldiers and a servant. It was fewer than he had feared and more than he had hoped.

To his right there was a staircase leading to an open trap door which gave admittance to an upper floor, and he saw stacks of weapons arranged around the walls, but most of this level was open. There was plenty of room to swing a sword, but it also meant that the three men at the table were a lot further away than Edric wanted.

John was still talking to the men who had opened the door, and they were gesturing towards Edric's left where, in the faint light of the candles which illuminated this vast room, he noticed a large, heavy door set into the floor.

They must act now, he knew. Winter caught his eye and nodded, then made his move.

The axeman shook off the loose cords which had appeared to be binding his wrists behind his back. Then he grabbed at John, shoving the smaller man into one of the guards who had opened the door. As he did so, he swept John's sword out of its scabbard, swinging it free. In an instant, he was pounding across the wide room towards the table.

313

Edric reacted as soon as Winter attacked. With his sword already in his hand, it was a simple task to sweep it up and smash it into the neck of the nearest guard. The man fell before he knew he was under attack, his head almost severed by the heavy blade. Blood gushed from the awful wound, but Edric was already moving, dragging the sword clear and swinging it towards the second guard.

This man was already off balance because Winter had pushed John into him. As the former monk scrabbled desperately to get out of the way, Edric smashed his sword onto the Norman's head, crushing the iron and leather of his helmet. The man went down, clearly stunned, and Edric kicked him in the belly before aiming a vicious slash at his neck. He missed his target, the blade inflicting a terrible wound in the man's lower face, taking away most of his jaw and spraying blood and teeth. Edric kicked him again, this time on the side of the head, and used the tip of the sword to end the guard's life quickly.

Gasping with exertion, Edric spun around to watch Winter. The big man had crossed the room with amazing speed, making barely any sound as he dashed towards the three seated soldiers. The ringing clash of Edric's attack on their comrades, and a shriek of panic from the squire brought the men to their feet, but Winter was on them before they could draw their weapons. He gripped his sword in two hands as he reached the table, sweeping it left and right in rapid succession, each strike taking down one of the Normans. Then, with a shout of "Hereward!" he leaped onto the table, lashed out his right foot to kick the third man in the face, sending him sprawling to the floor. Winter was on him in an instant, jumping down and slashing his sword to silence the man's shouts. With barely a pause, Winter spun round and quickly finished off the two men he had wounded with his initial attack.

He grinned ferociously, holding up the bloodied sword.

"Not as good as an axe, but it does the job," he declared happily.

Soaking wet and now spattered with blood, he looked like a monster out of legend standing over his fallen foes.

But he had left one Norman standing.

"Look out!" Edric shouted as the squire, who had dropped the cloak he had been holding, drew a long knife from a scabbard at his waist.

314

The boy took a scared, tentative step towards Winter, but the big axeman whirled, knocked the knife from the squire's hand with one casual blow, then drove the lad back against the wall.

"Sit down or I'll spill your guts for you!" Winter snarled.

The squire, visibly shaking with terror, obeyed, sliding down the wall to slump on the wooden floor. His face crumpled in embarrassment and he tried to hold back tears as his bladder gave in to fear.

"Stay there!" Winter ordered.

Edric could scarcely believe they had succeeded, but the noise of their fight had alerted others to trouble. John, picking himself up from the floor, pointed upwards to the open trap door at the top of the stairs. The entrance to the upper floor revealed yet another Norman soldier.

Edric cursed. There was no way to reach the man before he closed the door or, worse, summoned help from any others who might be up there with him and came charging down the steps. Grimly, Edric dashed to the foot of the stairs, ready to attempt the climb, but he stopped when the soldier gave a frightened yelp as someone pushed him from behind. The Norman lost his precarious balance and toppled down head first. He came in a clatter of armour, his sword bouncing clear to fall over the side of the steps and thud into the thick planks of the room's floor while his body bounced and thudded down the wooden steps to land in a sprawl at Edric's feet.

Edric suspected the soldier had broken his neck, but he stabbed down with his sword to make sure he was dead, then looked up, ready to face more enemies.

Instead, he saw Torfrida, looking down in wide-eyed amazement at the carnage the two Englishmen had wrought.

"Edric? Winter?" she gasped, holding a hand to her chest as if to still her racing heartbeat. "Is it you?"

"We are here," Edric confirmed unnecessarily. "Where is Hereward?"

"Down in the cellar," she said as she hurried down the steps.

Winter had already grabbed John once again and was hauling him roughly to the trap door. Over his shoulder, he told Torfrida to watch the squire who was cowering in a corner of the room, sitting with his eyes closed, his lips moving in silent prayer.

315

"Make sure he stays quiet!" Winter barked. "Edric! Come on!"

They were only just in time. Someone was coming to see what had caused all the noise, and the three men reached the trap door just as it began to open.

Edric hissed to John, "Tell them we have a prisoner who tried to escape!"

John did not respond. He looked bewildered by what had happened, so Winter shoved him aside and reached down with one meaty hand to haul the door open quickly.

In the dark rectangle of the entrance, Edric saw the pale oval of another soldier's face peering up at them. The man held a sword in one hand, but he was off balance as a result of Winter yanking the door open.

Edric took advantage, smashing his sword down on the man's head. The blow dislodged the soldier's iron helmet and Edric heard bones being crushed. The man fell away, almost taking Edric's sword with him as he collapsed into the darkness below.

Winter flung the trap door aside and leaped into the shadow-filled space, pounding down the steps as he uttered a wordless challenge to anyone who dared face him.

Edric followed, desperately trying to make out what awaited them. The cellar was a nightmare of ghostly, flickering images and dark, forbidding shadows, with only a few pinpricks of light to help make sense of what lay below him. But he knew speed was essential. They could not afford to give any Normans who lurked down here time to react to their attack.

In a few reckless, bounding steps, he had reached more than half way down the wooden stairs. Looking down to his left, he could make out Hereward standing against a huge wooden pillar, while several other people stood around him, all of them staring upwards in horror.

Winter was almost at the foot of the stairs, lashing out at the corpse of the fallen guard and frantically trying to clamber over the body.

Edric decided to take a shorter route. He vaulted over the side of the staircase, landing on top of a man who was already shouting aloud in panic as he gaped up at the unexpected attack.

Edric's boots caught the man in the chest, knocking him to the floor. Edric tried to stamp on his face, but he lost his balance and felt himself beginning to fall. He was aware of another figure behind him, but the principal danger came from one of the two men who were standing close to Hereward.

One of these was a soldier in chainmail who was holding a long-bladed knife in his right hand. Even as he fell, Edric saw the guard whip his arm back, then hurl the dagger at him.

It was the Norman Edric had jumped on who inadvertently saved him. The man tried to roll away, making Edric topple sideways just as the knife flashed over him.

He heard a sickening thud as the blade of the knife struck flesh, and he heard a strangled cry of shock as he struck the floor hard, losing his grip on his sword.

He was tangled with the man he had knocked over, and now another heavy weight landed on top of him, pinning him to the floor.

Desperate, he roared an incoherent challenge as he pushed himself upwards, kicking his feet to drive away the two bodies entangled with him.

He glanced up, seeing the soldier now held a sword and was advancing on him, while the other man, little more than a bulky shadow in the gloom, stepped backwards to give the swordsman more room.

Another ferocious yell filled the dark chamber as Winter arrived. He leaped past Edric, charging recklessly at the Norman soldier who twisted to face him, his sword swinging in an arc which almost slashed Hereward's face. Winter, though, knocked the blade aside and back-handed his own sword to smash into the guard's chest. Staggered by the enormous blow, the soldier stumbled backwards. He collided with a stack of heavy, wooden crates with a loud crash, then Winter's sword was bludgeoning him repeatedly, driving him to the floor with a savage fury Edric had rarely witnessed.

Eventually, long after it was clear the man was dead, Winter stood erect, turning to face the others.

There was only one Norman left standing. Dressed in tunic and leggings, this large man raised his hands to show he was unarmed as Winter advanced on him. For a moment, Edric thought Winter would cut him down anyway, but Hereward's peremptory shout held everyone still.

"No! He's mine! Cut me free and I'll deal with him."

317

Edric managed to extricate himself from the tangle of limbs around him. Finding his sword, he hauled himself to his feet. He looked back to see that the Norman he had landed on was now huddled on his hands and knees, moaning in fear. The other figure, he saw with horror, was Altruda, and she was quite dead. The knife thrown by the soldier had thudded into her chest, driving deep and finding her heart. She lay in a sprawl of limbs, her eyes staring at Edric in unblinking horror.

He stood, frozen by the sight of the woman's corpse, thinking of all the times he had wished her dead, but shocked by the sight of her lifeless beauty lying crumpled and misshapen on the floor. It was only when Hereward repeated his command that he was able to tear his gaze away from her.

"Edric! Cut me free!"

With a shake of his head, Edric turned, stepping to the pillar. He could barely see the ropes fastening Hereward, but he felt carefully for them, then sawed through them with his sword.

Hereward stumbled free, rubbing his wrists and stamping his boots to bring blood back to his numbed hands and feet.

"Torfrida is upstairs," he told Edric urgently.

"She's safe!" Edric assured him. "We killed all the guards."

Hereward gave him a grateful smile, then his eyes grew hard and he bent to retrieve the sword the Norman guard had dropped.

He stood up, his fingers gripping the sword hilt as he stared at the shadowy bulk of his nemesis.

"Well, Bastard," he rasped. "Now the tables are turned."

Chapter 27

Edric watched in fascinated horror as Hereward stalked towards the King, his sword raised as if to strike.

William stood motionless, his hands still raised, his eyes showing no fear as he fixed his gaze on Hereward. It was as if he was prepared to accept his fate now that he had lost.

He said something in harsh, bitter French as if encouraging Hereward to cut him down, but Edric saw the Thane hesitate. For a long, silent moment, Hereward regarded the King thoughtfully, then uttered a soft curse.

"Tie him to that pillar," he told Winter abruptly, as if dismayed by his own decision. "Edric! get that grovelling worm de Taillebois to his feet and keep an eye on him."

Edric had not realised the man he had landed on was the Sheriff. Turning, he saw that the Norman was still on his knees, his hands clasped imploringly together as he stared in horror at Altruda's blank, sightless eyes. He was mumbling something in French and seemed oblivious to everything around him except Altruda's corpse.

Edric grabbed him by the collar, hauling him to his feet.

De Taillebois let out a whimper of fear which Edric stifled by shoving the man roughly against the side of the staircase. He held up his sword, growling at his captive to be silent. He spoke in English, but the Norman Sheriff clearly grasped his meaning even if he did not understand the words.

While Winter bound William's wrists behind the pillar, Hereward asked, "Where are the others?"

"Waiting on the boat," Edric replied without taking his eyes from his prisoner.

"So the two of you did this all by yourselves?"

"It was Edric's idea," Winter said proudly as he tugged on the knots, making sure they were secure.

"John helped," Edric replied. "He's the one who talked his way past the gates."

"Who?" Hereward asked.

"Brother John, although he's no longer a monk. He's upstairs, keeping an eye on the King's servant, I hope."

319

Hereward shook his head, obviously bemused by their explanation.

"You can tell me the whole story later. Watch these two until I get back."

Satisfied that William was securely bound, Hereward hurried to the stairs and began climbing. He had barely reached half way when Torfrida's anxious face appeared in the open doorway.

"Hereward!" she gasped, tears filling her eyes as she came down to meet him.

The couple embraced, holding one another tightly for a long time before Hereward led her down the steps. When Torfrida saw Altruda, she made the sign of the cross, her tear-streaked face sombre. Then she caught sight of William.

"You didn't kill him!" she breathed.

"Not yet," Hereward grunted. "I wanted to, but I remembered what you said earlier. I'm still tempted to spill his guts, though. Or maybe take an eye. He was going to do that to me. As for de Taillebois, he owes me a life. I intend to take it from him."

He paused for a moment before adding, "But they might be useful hostages for the moment. We still need to get out of here, and we could have an army of Normans coming up to the keep any moment."

"I doubt they will have heard anything," Edric told him. "It's very late, and the rain is very heavy. Even if anyone is still awake, we're a fair way from the nearest buildings down in the bailey."

Hereward nodded pensively.

"So you have a plan for getting away?" he asked.

"I'm not sure," Edric was forced to confess. "I was hoping we could simply walk out, just as we walked in, but I don't know how we could talk our way past the sentries with three people who are supposed to be the King's prisoners."

"Three?" Hereward asked.

"Winter and you can't pass for Normans," Edric explained. "Your moustaches will give you away. And the lady can't be disguised either."

He felt foolish, because he had been so intent on finding a way into the castle that he had given little thought to what they would do if they did succeed in freeing Hereward. The truth was that he had not really believed they would be able to get as far as they had.

There was a brief, concerned silence, then Torfrida took a deep breath and spoke up.

"I think there is a way we can walk out."

All eyes turned to her as she explained, "We need to take de Taillebois with us. He will get us past the guards."

"How?" Hereward wanted to know.

"I doubt they would question his authority," she replied. "But, if they do ask, he can tell them that the King has ordered us to be taken to Westminster."

"Why would the Bastard issue such an order?" Hereward frowned.

"He might do that if you had submitted to him and pledged your loyalty," Torfrida replied.

Hereward's eyes sparked dangerously at the very idea, but then he gave a slow nod.

"That might work, I suppose," he said doubtfully.

Torfrida added, "Not that I think anyone will challenge us if de Taillebois tells them it is by the King's command. The guards know William is here, and they also know de Taillebois is close to him. None of them would dare question the King's orders."

Hereward looked at each of the others in turn.

"Does anyone have a better idea?"

Winter suggested, "If we're going to try it, why not take the Bastard with us? He'll order them to let us out."

Torfrida shook her head.

"No, that's too dangerous. He came with his own bodyguards and wouldn't leave without them. Besides, he's likely to order the sentries to turn on us while he takes his chances of escaping. De Taillebois is too much of a coward to try that."

"She's right," Hereward agreed.

Winter shrugged, and Hereward looked to Edric.

"Do you have any ideas?"

Edric shook his head.

"Then we'll give it a try," Hereward decided. "De Taillebois still owes me a life for my brother, but if he gets us out of here, I will consider that debt paid."

321

Torfrida held up a hand as she said, "There is one other thing, Hereward."

"What is that?"

"It means you must leave William alive."

Again, Hereward's expression darkened, but Torfrida did not allow him time to argue.

"I gave you reasons earlier," she reminded him. "I did not imagine you would ever have him at your mercy, but what I said still holds true. But there is another reason we must let him live."

Winter growled, "The Bastard killed our friends, and plenty others besides."

"And he'll kill more if he lives," Hereward agreed.

Torfrida said, "But de Taillebois must be given a reason to help us over and above the threat to his own life. If he knows William has been killed, he will be less likely to perform the role we need him to play. If we set de Taillebois free once we are away, he can return and free the King. That is his incentive."

Hereward glared at the two Normans who stood, one bound to a pillar, the other held in place by the threat of Edric's sword. Neither of them could follow the conversation, but both of them obviously understood that their fate was being determined.

Hereward argued, "But if I kill the Bastard, de Taillebois might be frightened into helping us to avoid the same fate."

"He might," Torfrida nodded. "But keeping William alive gives him a much greater incentive. Especially if you explain it to both of them."

After a long, reflective silence, Hereward snarled, "All right! I will let the Bastard live. But I'll tell de Taillebois that I'll cut his heart out if he doesn't get us safely out of here."

He began speaking in quick, angry French, outlining what he needed de Taillebois to do. The Sheriff shot a terrified glance to the bound figure of his King, and William gave a curt, furious nod, uttering a few low words which seemed to Edric to be confirmation that de Taillebois should do as he was ordered.

His speech delivered, Hereward moved to one of the fallen Norman guards and unbuckled the man's sword belt. Tugging it free, he sheathed his sword and fastened the belt around his own waist.

"That's better!" he declared. "If I'm a free man now that I've pledged my loyalty to this murderous piece of shit, I'm entitled to carry a sword."

"Me too?" Winter asked.

"You're not a nobleman," Hereward told him. "You'll need to make do with a knife."

Winter blew a raspberry to show what he thought of that, but did not argue.

Hereward asked Edric, "You said your friend is upstairs with a servant?"

"With a squire, yes."

"Then bring them down here. And find some cloth we can use to gag mouths."

Edric stepped away from de Taillebois, but the fat Sheriff was so petrified he dared not move even once the immediate threat of a sword at his throat had been removed.

Hurriedly, Edric climbed to the main floor where he found John sitting on the floor beside the young boy. The lad had obviously been crying and, just as obviously, was doing his best to conceal the fact. John, sitting beside him with his back against the wall, was carrying on a one-sided conversation in low, encouraging tones, but the boy looked utterly miserable.

John looked up when Edric approached.

"This is Gaston," he said, indicating the pale-faced squire. "He's eleven years old."

"Is he going to cause us any trouble?" Edric asked.

"No. He's terrified of what we are going to do to him."

John gave Edric an accusing look as he added, "I tried to reassure him, but I don't see how we can let him stay alive."

"Tell him he'll live as long as he does as he's told," Edric said. "But bring him down to the cellar. And Hereward wants cloth to use as a gag for the Bastard."

"We have the very thing," John said with a forced smile.

He picked up a heavy cloak and began hacking away a long strip from the hem while he spoke to the squire. His words did little to reassure the boy, especially when Edric hauled him to his feet and bustled him towards the trap door.

The three of them descended into the gloomy cellar, where Hereward told Edric to tie the squire's wrists and ankles.

"Then gag him," Hereward added.

323

John had caught sight of Altruda and, as Torfrida had done, he made the sign of the cross as he looked down at her.

"She was an evil woman," he sighed. "Now God has punished her for her crimes."

"And he may yet punish us if we don't get out of here soon," Hereward said sharply.

John gave him an apologetic smile, then set to work. He cut several long strips from the King's cloak which Edric used to truss the distraught boy. He propped the lad against one of the huge barrels, then stood back.

To John, he said, "Tell him we'll send someone back to free him once we are clear of pursuit."

John dutifully translated the words, patting the boy on the head as he did so. Then he shot Edric a meaningful look as he switched back to English.

"I hope you'll be freeing me as well."

"What's that?" Hereward asked.

Edric explained, "We forced John to help us. We told him we would kill his wife and child if he did not help us. Can you make sure de Taillebois knows that?"

Hereward grasped his meaning instantly. Jabbing a finger at John, he delivered what seemed to be a long series of threats in French.

John bowed his head in apparent resignation, while Edric clamped his jaw tightly shut, hoping the dingy light had masked his amusement. Hereward, though, had done all he could to give John an excuse for helping them. If they did manage to get free, Edric hoped it would be enough to allow the former monk to escape retribution.

With the young squire secure, Hereward took a strip of the cloak and bundled it into a tight wad. He stood facing William, his expression hard. Then he suddenly punched the king in the belly, giving him a ferocious blow which would have doubled him over had he not been held up by the cords pinning him to the pillar. Still, he gasped and coughed, wheezing and retching as he struggled for breath. Hereward grabbed at his face, gripping his head with one hand while he rapidly stuffed the torn cloth into William's mouth.

"Can't have you calling for help, can we?" Hereward growled. "I doubt anyone would hear you down here, but I'm not going to take that chance."

"He might choke," Torfrida warned.

Hereward shrugged, "I don't care."

With a jerk of his thumb to indicate de Taillebois, he added, "It's another reason for this fat slug to get us out of here quickly. The sooner we are away, the sooner he can come back and free his master."

William continued to retch and moan behind the improvised gag, hanging limply against the pillar as he fought for breath, but Hereward turned his back on the man and told the others, "Now, it's time to go."

They filed up the stairs, with Edric staying close to de Taillebois. He had sheathed his sword, but drew his knife which he showed to the Sheriff with a meaningful gesture.

Once they had all climbed to the main floor, Winter closed the trap door behind them, sealing the captives in the cellar.

"I hope the Bastard rots down there," he muttered. "May God curse him."

Grimly, Hereward told him, "If you want God to do something, you'd better pray nobody finds them until we are well away."

Even as he spoke, his eyes were taking in the scene of carnage in the main chamber.

"That's a fight I'd like to have seen," he remarked. "You did well. But I think it's time we left this stinking cesspit."

Edric thought they made a poor showing. They were tired, their clothes rumpled, and all of them, particularly Winter, was spattered with blood. But they had no choice except to hope that the rain and the darkness would disguise the stains of combat.

Torfrida found a shabby cloak hanging on a peg near the door. It was short enough to fit her, so she wrapped it around her shoulders and pulled up the hood.

"I'm ready," she said softly.

Ivo de Taillebois led the way, with Hereward and Torfrida close behind him. Then came Edric and Winter, with John bringing up the rear.

The rain seemed to have lessened, and Edric caught sight of a handful of stars shining between rents in the low clouds, but

325

even this lighter rainfall added to the danger of descending the wet stairs. They went down slowly, with Hereward chatting amiably to Ivo de Taillebois, and Torfrida joining in. By the time they reached the foot of the long flight of steps, Hereward's prompting had strung a few words of response from the Sheriff.

They made their slow way across the bailey, passing between dark buildings. Edric's nerves were on edge with the knowledge that dozens of Norman soldiers were sleeping close at hand, but the only sounds he could hear were the falling rain and the low conversation of the three people who walked just ahead of him.

He gripped the hilt of his sword tightly as they approached the gates. De Taillebois, his voice tremulous, called out a sleepy guard who blinked in surprise when he saw the shadowy group, but nevertheless called a second guard to help him unbar the great gates.

Edric dared not look at the guards as Hereward led the way outside. His throat was dry and his heart pounding, but Hereward strolled out as if what they were doing was perfectly normal.

Moments later, the gates shut behind them with a solid thump, and Edric began to breathe easily once more.

They had to resist the temptation to break into a run, but Hereward kept them under control until they reached the nearest buildings and had turned out of sight of the castle's entrance.

Then, just as they were beginning to relax, two figures emerged from the shadowy recess of a doorway where they had been waiting and watching.

Winter uttered a low curse of warning, but a soft voice called, "Edric?"

"Ylva? I told you to stay on the boat."

He saw the flash of her teeth as she smiled, "If you thought I was going to leave England without you, you don't know me that well."

She was grinning, and so was Halfdan who had, inevitably, accompanied her. Their smiles were infectious, and soon the whole gang was grinning like fools.

Ylva shot a suspicious look at de Taillebois.

"Who's this?" she asked. "Did he help you?"

"Not willingly," Edric told her.

He explained what had happened as they made their way through the darkened streets towards the river.

"I knew you'd do it!" she exclaimed happily.

At the riverside wharf, they found Ordgar and Martin waiting and fretting, along with the ship's captain who frowned when he saw de Taillebois.

"What's going on?" he wanted to know.

"Nothing you need worry about," Hereward told him. "We have a couple of extra passengers who need to be dropped off further down the river."

The captain scowled but dropped any objections when Martin passed him another handful of silver.

"When can we set sail?" Hereward asked impatiently.

"Not for another couple of hours," the seaman informed him. "I don't want to risk sailing downstream in the dark. Besides, we'll catch the turning tide if we wait."

Hereward suggested, "You might catch a bit of trouble if you are still here in a couple of hours. I think you ought to rouse your crew and cast off as soon as you can."

Angrily, the captain demanded, "What have you done? I want no trouble here."

"Too late, I'm afraid," Hereward told him. "But this fellow has a fat purse, so I'm sure he will reward you well for setting off immediately."

He gestured towards de Taillebois as he spoke. Then, switching to French, he held out a hand to the Sheriff who reluctantly relinquished his purse.

Hereward examined the contents and handed over several gold coins.

"Can we go now?" he asked the captain. "I am sure the King will be very grateful if we leave without delay."

The sailor looked from Hereward to de Taillebois, then down at the shining coins in his hand. He pursed his lips, frowned deeply, then sighed.

"All right. We'll go now."

He turned away to summon his sleeping crew, telling the passengers to keep out of the way. They clustered near the starboard side as they watched the grumbling seamen begin their arcane duties.

327

De Taillebois glowered at everyone from beneath his dark eyebrows, and John managed to maintain his charade by looking suitably miserable. He took off the byrnie and helmet, glad to be out of them, and made a good show of objecting to the way he was being treated.

The boat cast off, the sail was raised, and the ship slowly edged downriver, soon passing the black, brooding outline of the King's castle.

"I wonder if the Bastard has choked yet?" Hereward mused as the ship glided on.

Dawn was still some way off when they put John and de Taillebois ashore some miles beyond the city's walls. The Sheriff looked as if he wanted to issue some curses but was too afraid to speak. He scrambled ashore as quickly as he could, muttering to himself but offering no resistance.

John, still maintaining his role as a victim of threats, did manage to whisper a kinder farewell to Edric.

"Take care of yourself, my friend."

"And you. Will you stay in London?"

John shook his head.

"I doubt it. Even if de Taillebois believes the story about your threats, it might be too dangerous. Besides, the truth is that Aelswith hates the city."

"Then take her home to Bourne. Make a life there."

"I think I will," John nodded guardedly.

"And look after the baby. She carries a proud name and a proud heritage."

"I will," John promised. He grinned as he added, "Perhaps I will grow a moustache and become a proper Englishman. I might even change my name. What do you think?"

"I think you could achieve that if anyone can," Edric smiled.

"Leofric, do you think? Do I look like a Leofric?"

"You can be anyone you want," Edric told him. "But you'll always be Brother John to me."

"I shall miss you, Edric Strong," John said softly.

"And I you."

Then the captain was calling for him to step ashore or be carried across the sea, so John hurried down the long plank the sailors had placed over the ship's side. Once ashore, he turned and shook his fist at Edric, uttering a stream of curses. He did, though, give a broad wink at the same time.

Edric laughed and waved back. Then the boat pushed off once again, soon leaving the two men behind. Even so, Edric continued to stare at the night-shrouded spot long after the two figures had vanished from his sight.

Beside him, Ylva wrapped her arm around his and snuggled into him.

"Are you happy?" she asked.

"Yes," he nodded, "I think I am."

"You will probably never see England again," she reminded him.

"It's not my country any longer," he shrugged. "It's a Norman land now. But that doesn't really matter. We will make a new life somewhere else. Somewhere we can be safe."

Ylva said, "The world is an unsafe place, Edric Strong. Wherever we go, there will be troubles to face."

He smiled, "But at least we will face them together."

"Yes, we will. You cannot get rid of me now."

"I don't want to," he told her.

Staring out into the night, the land distinguishable only as a dark patch against the star-studded sky, she asked, "Where will we end up, do you think?"

"I don't know. That is up to Hereward. France, perhaps. Or Italy. Maybe even Miklagard."

"I'd like to see Miklagard," Ylva murmured.

"Maybe we will."

Towards the east, the sky began to lighten, the dull, rosy streaks of dawn slowly edging up beyond the widening sea.

Edric looked out at the woods and meadows of England as a new day began, and the enormity of what they were doing struck him. But he had made his decision on that fateful day when the Siwards had found him in the forest and taken him to meet Hereward for the first time. He vowed that he would not regret that decision, no matter what happened.

So he turned, facing away from the land, looking out beyond the ship's prow to the sea and the unknown future.

"I don't know whether Hereward was right to leave the King alive," he said. "But whatever happens, the England we knew has gone. It will never be the same again."

329

Ylva remarked, "I suppose all things must come to an end."

Edric turned to her, clasping her hand in his.

"This is not an ending for us, though," he told her. "It is a beginning."

Author's Note and Acknowledgements

Many people have heard of Hereward the Wake, but few know much more about him than his name. He is a character who has fascinated me for a long time, yet tracking down the real Hereward is a difficult task. In many ways, he is like Robin Hood because many of the stories told about him are almost certainly fictional, yet there was a real man named Hereward, and he was so famous in his time that the Anglo-Saxon chronicle could name him without needing to explain who he was. Unfortunately, that leaves huge gaps in our knowledge, with the genuine history being further clouded because the other sources which tell of Hereward usually contradict one another. All that can be said for certain is that he led the resistance on the isle of Ely and that he disappeared without trace after the Norman army quashed the rebellion. There are several versions of his tale which give mutually incompatible reports of what happened next. Perhaps the best known version is that, having divorced his wife, he married a woman named Aelftruda, and, having sworn allegiance to King William, was subsequently ambushed and killed by a group of Norman knights who held a grudge against him. As far as fictional heroes go, that's not a very satisfactory ending, but it doesn't ring true in any event. Many English nobles did submit to William the Conqueror, but Hereward does not come across as the sort of man who would bend the knee to anyone. Given his fame at the time, it seems likely the Normans would have boasted about his conversion from rebel to loyal subject, but there is no authentic record of that happening. Nor is there any record of his death, so it seems probable that he escaped from Ely. He might even have ended up in Miklagard, better known as Constantinople, where the Byzantine Emperor had a guard of Northmen and, after 1066, Englishmen.

In terms of disentangling a kernel of truth from the many stories and legends, historian Peter Rex has done a huge amount of research on Hereward, and I am indebted to his book, "The Last Englishman", for much of the background included in my own story. Anyone wishing to know more about the real Hereward should read his book.

One thing that must be said is that Hereward was never known as "The Wake" in his lifetime. This name was added centuries later when the Wake family wished to stress their origins by reference to an English hero. Also, he was not, as most legends maintain, the son of Earl Leofric of Mercia. As Peter Rex demonstrates in his book, Hereward was almost certainly the son of a Thane named Asketil. However, although Hereward held lands around Peterborough, he was exiled in the early 1060s for "stirring up dissension among the people", whatever that means. He very probably ended up in Flanders where he learned his trade as a fighting man. He was probably not in England in 1066, but returned at some point shortly afterwards. He was certainly based on the isle of Ely, and he and his "Gang" carried out a raid on Peterborough Abbey in conjunction with a force of Danes led by King Sweyn of Denmark. Sweyn did have some claim to the English throne but decided not to take his chances and returned home, taking most of the plunder from Peterborough with him.

The story of the final days of the rebellion is very confused. King William certainly took charge after his lieutenants failed to overcome the resistance. It is claimed that he built a causeway through the marshes, but the precise location of his final assault is unknown. There is a strong suggestion that the defenders were betrayed by the monks who showed William the best route through the marshes. There is a (possibly fanciful) report of a bridge collapsing under the weight of the attackers, although it is unclear when this took place. It is, though, a great story, so I decided to incorporate it as the closing part of the first of my Edric Strong novels, "Last English Hero".

After the fall of Ely, Hereward simply vanishes from history. Some legends about him are strongly reminiscent of the tales of Robin Hood, and have him carrying out raids from a base in the forest before the claims become even more confused and contradictory. He may have submitted to the king, or he may have been taken prisoner, then been rescued by his gang. The latter version, even if it is very possibly an invention, suited my own narrative best. I had hoped to place the final confrontation between Hereward and William in the Tower of London, but construction work on that had not begun by the time of the fall of Ely. There is, however, evidence of wooden structures on the site of the Tower, so it is entirely plausible that a standard motte and bailey Norman castle was the first fortress on that site.

As far as the broader aspects of the story are concerned, the fact that so little is actually known about Hereward, and that the various tales often contradict each other, allowed me to weave a fictional narrative which incorporates the latest historical research by Peter Rex with some of the more legendary parts of the Hereward tales. This means that my version almost certainly bears only a passing resemblance to what actually happened, but I set out to write a fictional novel, not a history book. Of course, the less that is actually known about the genuine history, the more scope there is for fictional writers to create a story, and I hope that genuine history buffs will forgive me for twisting events to fit the narrative, and for omitting several characters who are alleged to have been associated with Hereward. Sadly, the story has more than enough characters as it is, and I felt adding more would only clutter the book unnecessarily.

As usual, I have others to thank for getting this book published. Moira Anthony, Stuart Anthony, Ian Dron, Stewart Fenton and Liz Wright all made invaluable comments on the various drafts, and I am very grateful to them for spotting my numerous typographical errors. Stuart Antony also came up with the cover design and helped during the publishing process.

GA

May, 2019

Other Books by Gordon Anthony

All titles are available in e-book format. Titles marked with an asterisk are also available in paperback.

In the Shadow of the Wall*
An Eye For An Eye*

Home Fires*
Hunting Icarus*

The Calgacus Series:
      World's End*
      The Centurions*
      Queen of Victory*
      Druids' Gold*
      Blood Ties*
      The High King*
      The Ghost War*
      Last Of The Free*

The Constantine Investigates Series:
      The Man in the Ironic Mask
      The Lady of Shall Not
      Gawain and the Green Nightshirt
      A Tale of One City
      49 Shades of Tartan

A Walk in the Dark (Charity booklet)

ABOUT THE AUTHOR

Born in Watford, Hertfordshire, in 1957, Gordon's family moved to Broughty Ferry in the early 1960s. Gordon attended Grove Academy, leaving in 1974 to work for Bank of Scotland. After a long but undistinguished career, he retired on medical grounds in 2008 without having received any huge bankers' bonuses.

Registered blind, Gordon had more time on his hands after retiring so, with the aid of special computer software, he returned to his hobby of writing and had his debut novel, "In the Shadow of the Wall" published in 2010. Gordon's books are now being read by a world-wide audience. As well as his historical adventure stories, he has ventured into crime fiction with some spoof murder mysteries in the "Constantine Investigates" series. He is also kept busy with speaking engagements, visiting libraries, schools and community groups to talk about his books.

In addition to his novels, Gordon devotes some of his time to raising funds for the RNIB. As well as visiting schools and social clubs to talk about his sight loss, he has self-published a charity booklet titled, "A Walk in the Dark", a humorous account of his experiences since losing his eyesight. The booklet is available free from Gordon's website www.gordonanthony.net. All Gordon asks is that readers make a donation to RNIB. This booklet can also be purchased from the Amazon Kindle Store. Gordon will donate all author royalties to RNIB.

Now completely blind, Gordon continues to write stories and, in his spare time, attempts to play the guitar and keyboard with varying degrees of success.

Gordon is married to Alaine. They have three children and one grandchild. The family lives in Livingston, West Lothian.

You can contact Gordon via his website or by sending an email to ga.author@sky.com

CANCELLED

44352469R00190

Printed in Poland
by Amazon Fulfillment
Poland Sp. z o.o., Wrocław